Professional Lies

By Marj Charlier

SUNACUMEN
Press

Palm Springs, CA

Cover design: Marj Charlier
Cover photo: underflux/iStock.com

ISBN-13: 978-0-9860952-1-4

OTHER BOOKS BY THE AUTHOR:

Putt for Show (2013)
Drive for Dough (2014)
Hacienda: A South American Romance (2014)

MARJ CHARLIER

'Don't be afraid to be the one who loves the most.'

-- Anne Gaston

Chapter One

Sidney watched her feet as she carefully climbed the three low steps onto the stage. The black patent Christian Louboutins hurt her feet and made her a little unsteady, but she had to admit: they looked magnificent.

She stepped up to the podium to polite applause from her board members and the reporters who occupied a few of the two dozen white folding chairs set up to face her. She smoothed the skirt of her demure light-gray wool suit and unfolded her script.

Sidney had attended enough charitable events as a spectator to know the protocol: Smile. Stay on message. Be brief and be humble. Give credit to everyone but yourself. Own the stage, but insist that the donors and the beneficiaries are the rightful stars of the show.

She glanced up, ready to begin, and stopped.

Sitting front and center, not twenty feet away, was the last person she wanted to see. Matt. Her husband. And he was frowning.

Sidney knew what he was thinking: She was going to mess up. She would go off script, talk too much, flirt too much. She wouldn't assume the appropriate, retiring demeanor.

They had argued about it in the car all the way from

their home in Bellevue, across the lake, and into this ballroom in a downtown Seattle hotel.

"This isn't about you, Sidney," Matt had said. "You have a habit of hogging the show, and the show here is Tee for the Tour, not you. It's the charity, not the executive director, you're promoting."

"But there wouldn't be a T-Squared"—her shorthand for the charity—"if it weren't for me. People will be donating because of my celebrity. Without it, we'd never get any publicity."

"I'm not saying you shouldn't be on stage," he said. "I'm just suggesting that you not overdo it. Stick to your prepared remarks, answer a couple of questions, and get off."

She knew he meant more than that. He would watch to see if she tossed her hair, if she winked at a guy who caught her eye, if she laughed too loudly.

"Just who do you think the press is there to see?" she countered. "You? You and your buddy Greg? The press doesn't even know that you guys are on my board. They couldn't care less."

"Okay!" Matt said, nearly shouting. He reached for her hand as he slowed down for a stoplight. "I get it. I just don't want to feel like my wife is—." He stopped.

"Like your wife is what?" she demanded.

"Is acting like a slut," he said under his breath. He said it like he knew he would regret saying that word if she heard it, but she heard it. And it hurt.

"I will try to be the demure, humble Microsoft executive's wife you want me to be," she hissed. "But, I would appreciate it if you didn't insult me like that again. Don't call me a slut."

"No one else heard," he said, as if that mattered.

"I did. And I don't deserve it."

Now on stage, looking out over Matt's head at the small turnout, Sidney breathed in deeply. More spectators than this used to hang around to watch her practice putting. It would be hard to get too full of herself in front of this "crowd."

"Hello and thank you all for coming." Over the microphone, her voice was transformed into deep, resonant tones that filled the room. She paused again and smiled. She loved that sound. It reminded her of the press conferences after her wins on the LPGA Tour.

She folded up her unread script and looked up over the podium, avoiding Matt's glare, and making eye contact with each of the six reporters in the audience. "I'm going to throw this script away," she said, engaging them in a rebellious conspiracy. After only one sentence, she had lost interest in being brief and humble. She had lost interest in her husband's opinions.

She told the story the way she wanted to: the long-winded way. She did smile—a lot—as she was supposed to. But she also frowned, waved her arms, laughed, jabbed her finger in the air, and shook her head. She tossed her hair.

It was more fun that she expected. She could get a kick out of running this charity if it meant she was going to be on stage, the center of attention, the golden girl again.

She talked longer than she should have. But still, the reporters in the audience were patient. Her celebrity status as the only local woman who had won on the LPGA Tour in recent history helped. Five of the journalists were sports writers, and most likely also golfers. They were probably hoping their rapt attention would win them a golf round with her sometime. She just might make that happen.

When she opened the floor to questions, she got predictable softballs.

"Why did you decide to start Tee to the Tour instead of working with the First Tee?"

"T-Squared is taking young women with promise beyond what the First Tee is set up to do," she answered. "It's not just about life skills and basic golf skills, which are the laudable work of the First Tee. We're helping these young talented women start successful professional careers in golf."

She knew these answers like the back of her hand. Over the past six months, she and her board members had honed the mission, the strategy, the messaging, the budgets—everything needed to start a premier nonprofit. Now that they were publicly launching the charity, the answers were rote. Anyone in her organization could have recited them.

But, no one else had her cachet. Especially not Matt.

"Well, that was fun," Matt said sarcastically as he pulled his big Mercedes out of the parking garage following the celebratory dinner Sidney hosted for her board members. Sidney knew that Matt never meant "fun" as a compliment. From him, it was a synonym for "vacuous" or "frivolous."

The tally at Bin 74 had come to more than two thousand dollars for eight people. Even though she paid for it out of her own, dwindling savings, Sidney knew that if word of her lavish spending got out it could cast a negative pall on their nascent non-profit. If there was one thing donors didn't like, it was overhead.

Apparently Matt didn't like it either. But was he pissed at having spent the evening out with people he didn't find interesting or was he concerned about the frivolous use of two thousand dollars?

"What do you mean?" Sidney asked. "You didn't enjoy yourself, I know. But why the sarcasm?"

Matt didn't answer. Driving down Sixth Avenue in Seattle any time of day wasn't a piece of cake, but he certainly had the capacity to talk and drive at the same time. Sidney turned and took in his set jaw and furled brow. She could read that look. He was thinking about what to say, and his answer was going to be absolutely, precisely accurate.

He was like that. He would never have acted impulsively like she had on the podium that afternoon or in ordering that expensive wine at dinner. He followed rules. He practiced restraint. He was as fine-tuned as a Stradivarius at the start of a performance.

When they first met, Sidney was attracted to Matt's exactitude, his fastidiousness. He crossed his t's and dotted his i's with excruciating care. He was calm, collected, and rational. All of the time.

She had needed that. She'd let a lot of things in her life go to hell after her professional golf career had come to a sudden halt with her injury. Not only had she gained weight and lost muscle tone, she was also spending her savings at a furious clip, and filling her suddenly empty days with shopping and her nights with clubbing. She grew less and less discriminating about whom she slept with—as long as they treated her like a celebrity they were lucky to be around, she would tolerate them.

Sidney had won only five tournaments in six years on the LPGA, but she had finished in the top twenty-five dozens of times. Her name was consistently on the leaderboard, and her tall frame and graceful posture seemed to pull the TV cameras in her direction. No wonder her fans overestimated how many times she'd actually come out on top.

Then suddenly, it all ended. A run-of-the-mill car accident—one that wouldn't have made the evening news if she hadn't been in it—shattered her left shoulder. After a year of surgical tweaks and rehab, the doctors gave up on the mess of crushed bone and ligaments, and replaced the entire joint. It took more than six months before she could hold a club again. In the meantime, she lost the smooth, languid swing that had made her so successful.

Sidney still could have tried. She would lose the weight

easily enough once she could work out in the gym and walk the golf course again. Even if she had to rebuild her swing from the ground up to compete with the amazing long hitters coming into the league from Asia, she was optimistic. She hired one of the best coaches in the country and got back to work.

Then she met Matt and changed her mind.

ജ

Sidney met Matt at a celebrity signing at an afternoon Mariners' game. She was the least famous among the foursome signing glossy photos at the table, upstaged by a former Major League Baseball pitcher, a former Women's National Basketball Association forward, and a former National Hockey League goalie. Matt had been in charge of setting up the event as a fundraiser for the Girls and Boys Clubs of King County. She arrived early, and they had plenty of time to chat before the other retired athletes and the fans showed up.

Matt was wearing a golf shirt with a Seattle golf club logo, and they mostly talked about local golf courses and local golf stars, like Freddy Couples and Ryan Moore. Matt let it slip that he'd tried to get Freddy to sign autographs before he settled for her as the golf celebrity for the day, but Freddy was playing a Champions Tour tournament that week.

"I suppose I shouldn't let my nose get out of joint because Freddy was your first choice and not me," Sidney teased him.

"Oh, gosh, no!" he said, clearly worried that he'd insulted her. Interpersonal skills, she could tell, weren't necessarily his strongest suit. He worked at Microsoft as a software engineer, and while he was gregarious enough to volunteer for community work, he preferred the back-of-the-scenes data-crunching kind of work, not the kind that required a lot of elbow-rubbing.

"Just teasing!" Sidney assured him. "Are you crazy? You could make a bundle if you had Freddy here. The line for autographs would stretch into center field."

Instead of leaving the athletes to work the crowd alone, Matt kicked his nerdy introversion to the curb and stuck around until the autograph seekers thinned out, about the seventh inning. Sidney caught him watching her several times, and she encouraged the attention by awarding him her best celebrity smile. Together they packed up the charity brochures and left-over photos while the other athletes disappeared into the crowd. Matt straightened out the dollar bills they'd collected, and arranged them in order of denomination before putting the tidy stack into a canvas bank bag.

"I'd better get this over to the bank right away," he said. He looked at his watch. "I'd love to offer to buy you a drink, but the bank closes in fifteen minutes."

"Another time, then," she said, although she wasn't sure she would accept if he did call. He didn't seem her type. Yes, he played golf, but she was usually attracted to guys who were less careful and neat, more spontaneous. If he wanted to spend time with her, he should have stuffed those dollar bills away quickly and waited to drop the bag off at the bank the next day.

He was handsome, although in a way that she hadn't necessarily been attracted to before then. He wasn't much taller than her five-foot-nine, and his hairline had receded far enough that he simply shaved his head. He was a good ten years older than she was—maybe a dozen—she estimated, and his body was taut and slim in a way that indicated frequent gym visits, not caloric deprivation.

But, he had a settled, conservative vibe, so unlike the juvenile and reckless twenty- and thirty-somethings she'd dated over the past decade. He had two grown children and an ex-wife who had remarried. He was successful, too. About ten thousand 'Softies reported up through layers of managers to him, and he was in charge of one of the company's most iconic products. She left the ballpark wondering if she would see him again.

He called a week later to invite her to play a charity trivia game with him and two friends at a bar near the Microsoft campus.

"I thought you could bring some sports knowledge to the team," he said. "We aren't very good at those questions."

Sidney laughed. "Neither am I. All I know is golf."

"Fine," he said. "But will you do it anyway? I'll pay you back with dinner sometime."

Sidney paused before answering. Did he keep a tally of IOUs with all the women he dated?

"I doubt if my contributions will deserve payback," she said. "But, yes, I'll play."

After trivia night, they met again to play a round of golf, and then another round of golf. He was a good golfer, but he didn't play nearly well enough to challenge her dominance on the course. Then, they went to dinner. And, finally, they slept together.

It had been years since Sidney had accepted so many dates prior to sleeping with a man. She had been racking up mostly one-night stands and refusing second dates for years, as no one had interested her enough for her to endure another night in his company. She really enjoyed the sex; the men not so much.

Sex with Matt wasn't always great, and while she wasn't close to being in love with him when he asked, she accepted his marriage proposal immediately. He delivered it on one knee at an Italian restaurant on the suburban Eastside, across Lake Washington from Seattle, bending to a tradition set down by a hundred years of movie scripts. His words were carefully chosen, not for their romantic quality, but for their precision in describing their respective situations and the quality of their relationship.

He made everything seem so rational; she couldn't make sense of saying "no." And if she wasn't going to be able to play on the Tour, then she wanted to try settling down and living a more normal life.

꿴

Driving home from the press conference and dinner, Matt was visibly upset.

"I can't believe you ignored everything we talked about," he grumbled as they got past the downtown traffic and headed across the lake for the suburbs.

"I just went with what felt natural," she said. "I have to be myself, Matt. I can't turn into the quiet, mousy suburban wife you seem to want me to be."

Matt grimaced. They both remembered how he had criticized her behavior at a Microsoft picnic that summer by suggesting it would help his career if she spent more time with the other wives and less time talking about golf with the men.

Matt took his eyes off the road and frowned at her. "It's not about suburbia," he said. "I'm concerned that you're going to find the actual running of the organization tedious and not as glamorous as your days on the Tour."

Sidney said nothing. She wondered if he was right. He had an uncanny knack for deconstructing her faults.

Having formally launched the charity with the day's press conference, Sidney now anticipated the boring details: writing fundraising letters, setting up accounting systems, and finishing the 501c3 application. The next day, she had to write a letter introducing T-Squared to high-school golf coaches and another letter to teaching pros at urban driving ranges. She would rather host events like the press conference she'd just held. Or play golf with prospective donors.

"I think this is going to require you to grow up in some ways," Matt continued. "It won't be just the fun and games you've been used to up to now."

"What?" Now Sidney was pissed. "Grow up?"

"Yes, I mean it. Grow up."

Sidney steamed. They had been married eighteen months, and for the past twelve, she knew it was a mistake. He hadn't seemed like a control freak when they were dating. But then, at that point, she was glad to go along with his ideas, his plans, his rules because he was paying all of the bills. But once they were married, she had expected he would back off a bit and they'd form more of a partnership. They hadn't.

"I don't know what you mean by 'grow up,'" she said through clenched teeth. "I have managed on my own for years. I moved out of my parents' house at eighteen, paid my own way through college with scholarships, and have been quite successful, I would argue."

"Yes," Matt said. "I understand. But playing golf for a living isn't the real world. It's a play world for the few, extremely talented people who can avoid the real world by playing at a very high level."

"And that wasn't me?"

"Oh, don't get me wrong. It was you, but it isn't any more."

"I'm sorry, Matt, but I don't get where you're going with this." Sidney shifted in her seat to face him without having to turn her head. She wanted him to see the anger in her eyes.

"Well, first of all, the money that comes into T-Squared isn't yours to spend on things like those bottles of wine tonight," he said. "And this position won't be all about being on stage and flashing your pretty smile."

Sidney thought back to her half-hour at the podium that afternoon. Yes, she'd flouted all of his rules, but the crowd seemed to love it. Maybe that was the problem—was he jealous?

"And don't think it's because I was jealous," he cautioned, reading her mind. He turned and looked at her with a sweet smile that contradicted every word that had come out of his mouth since they got in the car. It communicated everything she needed to know: he was jealous.

"Do you really think I'm so frivolous that all I want to do is play games and charm people from the stage?" she asked him. "Or did I just piss you off by not clinging to your side today?"

"Nooo," he said, stretching the word out pedantically. "I did, however, see you reverting to your flirty act—the one I used to watch on TV when you played on the Tour. It's not my favorite rendition of Sidney Stapleton."

Sidney's eyes burned, and she turned away as she tried to blink back angry tears. How did she let him get so much control over her emotions? She pretended to stare out her window at the streets of Bellevue.

Matt drove up the driveway and into the garage of the sprawling suburban rambler where he'd lived for the past fifteen years. He bought it with his first big stock-option payout from Microsoft back when the stock was splitting and doubling and splitting again, and his kids were in high school. It stood as proof that he was a grown-up, smart and settled—all the things he apparently thought she wasn't.

Matt held the door into the house open for her, and she passed through, refusing to look at him.

Sidney walked straight to their master suite at the far end of the house. She threw her purse and briefcase on the desk in the small office off the bedroom and started undressing on her way into her bathroom. She was grateful for their

17

separate closets and bathrooms—she could wash her face and eliminate any trace of her tears before Matt would even know she had shed them.

She pulled off the rest of her clothes, brushed her teeth, and threw a long, silk nightgown over her head. She brushed the surviving hair spray out of her long hair, took a deep breath, and opened the door. She headed straight for the bed.

Matt caught her from behind, wrapping his arms around her waist and kissing her neck. She tried to shake him loose, but he held tight and breathed deeply in her ear.

"You are still the most beautiful woman in the world," he whispered, "and I don't like sharing you like that." She knew what he meant: sharing her as she stood on the stage and charmed her audience that afternoon. She was right; he was jealous.

His hands moved up to her breasts and he held them gently, as his thumbs massaged her nipples through the silk. He pushed against her, swaying slightly. She could feel his chest hairs against her back, and he stroked her neck and shoulders with his lips. She didn't want her body to react the way it did, but her nipples hardened, and she felt a familiar warm wetness collect between her legs. She turned and pulled his face to hers with both hands. She kissed him hard, first with her lips, and then she pushed his mouth open and swept the inside with her tongue.

Matt lifted her easily off the floor and tossed her back on their bed. He quickly pulled off his unbuttoned shirt and shed his pants and boxers in one smooth move. He was inside of her immediately, and Sidney clung to his back, pulling him in deeper and deeper until their bodies erupted in unison and collapsed in a single sweaty heap.

Matt fell asleep instantly with his back toward her. Sidney waited for her heart rate to drop, and then pulled her legs out from under him, went to the bathroom, and turned out the lights. She pushed and prodded on his limp body until she had enough room to slide under the covers.

She lay staring at the dark ceiling. Why was it that the only good sex they had was the angry kind? Unless Matt was pissed off, he never worked up the necessary fire for a good, steamy screw. Was that any way to build a future as a couple?

In eighteen months, they had lost the brief intimacy they enjoyed before marriage. Now, they disagreed too much; they spent too much time apart; he acted like he didn't even like her anymore. The financial security of his huge salary was nice, but it wasn't worth it, Sidney thought, sighing loudly.

She glanced over at Matt. He slept, undisturbed.

What she really wanted was to run her charity and support herself without his help. It was up to her alone to build the expertise and talents that would replace the golf skills she'd depended on up to now. If she was to become the kind of successful businesswoman she wanted to see in the mirror, she couldn't do it as someone's trophy wife.

"Sorry, Matt," she whispered over Matt's snores. "I've got to get out of here."

Chapter Two

Matt was the one who had convinced her that starting a non-profit made more sense than returning to the Tour or getting a corporate job. He'd created actuarial tables to calculate how much she was likely to earn playing golf at her age—just over thirty.

Professional women golfers didn't come close to making the kind of money the men did—in either sponsorships or winnings. Her two sponsorships—one with Nike and one with Footjoy—had ended abruptly after her injury took her off the Tour, and with the youth craze among women's golf fans, she was unlikely to win either of them back.

Once Matt had disabused her of the idea of rejoining the Tour, he went on to discourage her from taking a regular job.

"You won't be happy sitting in an office all day and slogging through three-hour meetings like I do," he said, as if taking a boring desk job were her only alternative. Rather, he encouraged her to use her residual celebrity to start a charity, like so many retired athletes had before her. "Then you'll be your own boss."

Sidney had never run a business, a non-profit, or even a committee before, but Matt had. He also knew plenty of people who would be glad to serve on her board as advisors.

Given her professional career, golf seemed like the

obvious subject matter for her charity, but connecting golf with some segment of the population that was disadvantaged or underserved wasn't easy.

The First Tee already helped young girls and boys learn life skills through golf, and Sidney recognized the value of the camaraderie kids could get from that program. She remembered her own loneliness and isolation when she was playing as the only girl on the high school golf team back in junior high and high school.

But Sidney also realized there were things the First Tee couldn't do: it couldn't turn golf into a career for them. Coaches and greens fees were expensive but a girl had to have them to make the leap from excelling on her school team to playing on the Tour. If she could provide a few young women with some emotional and financial support, maybe some little girl somewhere who otherwise had no chance would actually make it onto the Tour.

Matt ratified the idea by kick-starting T-Squared with a ten-thousand dollar donation. To Sidney, it seemed like a blessing to have his financial support. At least it did at first.

For the first two weeks of her new tenure as executive director of T-Squared, Sidney kept busy.

The furniture for the modest rented office at the edge of downtown Bellevue was delivered, and she decorated the walls with golf photos she bought online. Matt came in one evening and mounted a large-screen TV in the corner of the office and plugged it into the satellite feed. As soon as the DIRECTV service started, she left the Golf Channel on mute, turning on the sound whenever she grew bored with the work in front of her.

Sidney took potential donors to lunch, met for drinks with the head of the Washington State Golf Association, and

21

hosted a breakfast meeting to bring her consultants up to speed on the organization's strategy. She wrote her letters and sent them off to the marketing expert, Janie, for a final polish and printing.

But after the basic set-up was done, the pace slowed. Until some significant donations started coming in, she was at a standstill. Still, Sidney headed to the office early every morning, not so much to keep up with her workload as to escape her new neighborhood.

Before she met Matt, Sidney lived in a funky loft in Georgetown, south of downtown Seattle. Everyone around her there was either young and busy, or homeless. But now her neighbors were stay-at-home suburban mothers who called themselves "mommies," and whose incessant parade of baby strollers and baby joggers clogged the sidewalks and turned the neighborhood Starbucks into a noisy, hyperkinetic day-care facility.

Sidney couldn't wait for checks to start arriving so that she could start the real work of T-Squared and get out of the neighborhood.

Sidney's next door neighbor Carrie was one of the few over-fifty residents in the blocks that surrounded Matt's house, and the only friend Sidney had made in eighteen months. Carrie had yet to be blessed with "grandbabies"— the most stomach-turning word of the new millennium, as far as Sidney was concerned—and her kids were beyond daycare, school performances, first jobs, or anything else to brag or complain about. Instead, Carrie liked to talk about books and travel and movies.

Sidney had read a nearly endless stream of novels when she was immobilized by her surgery, and books drew the two women together. When it was Carrie's turn to host her neighborhood book club, she had invited Sidney to the weekday meeting.

Sidney followed the instructions on a note taped to the front door, and walked into Carrie's classic bungalow without ringing the doorbell. She shed her slicker and laid it on the pile of coats on a bench in the entryway, and stepped into an immaculate living room. Ten young women sat around on Stickley couches, chairs, and footstools, in front of a stone-lined fireplace, sipping tea and coffee. Engaged in a furious round of gossip about a recent neighborhood affair, none of them looked up to register her arrival. They were all in their twenties or thirties—coifed, made-up, and dressed like no one she'd ever seen in her old neighborhood.

Sidney looked around for Carrie, who was nowhere in sight. She took an empty seat in the middle of one of the big Mission-style couches. As their chatter split into smaller conversations, the young woman sitting next to her turned and acknowledged her presence.

"You're Sidney, right? How are Angie and Lyle?" she asked, referring to Matt's grown children from his first marriage. They lived near his ex-wife, Lorraine, on the East Coast, far away in both location and mindset, and they talked to Matt only on his birthday and Christmas.

"I believe they're fine," Sidney answered. "I've not seen them since our wedding, though."

The young woman frowned disapprovingly and got up to refill her coffee.

She has no idea who I am other than Matt's wife, Sidney realized. She sat quietly for the next few minutes and listened to the chatter, unfamiliar with the subjects of their gossip or the recent neighborhood events that had shocked—shocked!—them.

Bored, Sidney got up and found Carrie in the kitchen, preparing plates of fruit and cookies with Marty, a brash twenty-something who introduced herself to Sidney as the "exhausted mother of four angel-devils all under the age of six."

"What were you doing before you met Matt?" Marty asked as they carried the plates into the living room and arranged them on a side table.

"I played on the LPGA Tour for the past five years, until I was injured," Sidney said, pointing to her shoulder. "Major surgery."

"That's golf, right?" Marty said. "Did you win a lot of tournaments?"

"Yes, five," said Sidney proudly, happy to finally have an audience, if only an audience of one.

"Oh, that's not very many," Marty said, knitting her eyebrows with disappointment. "How many has Tiger won? Oh, and hey, how are Angie and Lyle? Does Matt ever hear from Lorraine?"

The not-so-subtle message was coming through loud and clear: These women were far more interested in Matt's ex-wife and his children than in her. She was an interloper, a "non-mommy" who had nothing in common with them.

The book of the month was *Gone Girl*, which had been voted onto the club's monthly list after it was made into a film and the women could go to the movie instead of actually reading the novel. Sidney had read it early on, and she thumbed through it the night before to refresh her memory.

She'd never been to a book club meeting before, but she'd read the "book club discussion guides" that popped up at the end of several books she'd read on her Kindle. Sidney didn't see herself as an intellectual, but following the examples in the guide, she planned her contributions to the discussion: questions about the motives of the characters, the political correctness of Nick's and Amy's reactions to their failing marriage, and slightly more abstruse questions about the difference between private and public lives.

Listening to the discussion get started, veer off into

neighborhood gossip, and then finally return to the book, Sidney took her time before saying anything. A series of "wasn't it gross when…" comments entertained everyone for a while and, finally, they ran out of scenes to discuss.

"Do you guys agree with the criticism that the book painted a misogynistic notion of women as manipulative, a modern equivalent of *vagina dentata*?" Sidney finally ventured.

Twenty eyes in the room turned to her and stared, horrified. She might as well have stood up and hit a ball through Carrie's living room window with a five wood; it wouldn't have been any less popular.

Silence.

Finally Marty spoke up. "Vagina what?"

"You know, the myth that women use intercourse as a way to emasculate and manipulate men."

"I have no idea, and I don't even know what that has to do with the book," Marty said.

"Me either," said two or three other women in unison, giggling.

"That's just too weird to comment on," added another.

More silence. Sidney squirmed and tried to think of a way to extricate herself from the awkward moment.

"Time for wine?" Carrie jumped up, coming to her rescue. Sidney flashed a grateful smile and fled to the kitchen to help her open bottles.

"What did I do in there?" Sidney whispered once the kitchen door swung closed behind them.

"You broke the first rule of this book group: never take anything beyond the superficial," Carrie said, sympathetically. "I should have warned you. These meetings are more about wine and getting away from the kids for a couple of hours."

"I'm so sorry. I didn't have any idea."

"No worries. It's not like you insulted their children or anything."

Sidney helped carry the wine glasses, a cheese plate, and

grapes into the living room, and excused herself, telling the group that she had to leave early.

"Matt isn't feeling well," she said, making up an excuse she thought the women would appreciate.

"That's funny," Marty said. "I saw him jogging earlier today."

"Yeah, well." Sidney gave up and fled for the front door. "I'll see you all around. Thanks for inviting me."

&

As soon as she got home from the book club, Sidney poured herself a glass of wine, took her phone out to the back patio, and called Karla, her best friend.

"I have become the neighborhood pariah!" Sidney blurted out instead of reciprocating Karla's "hello."

An LPGA player like Sidney had been, Karla had the week off. She would be heading to Atlanta at the beginning of the next week, Florida the week after that, and Singapore three weeks later. Grateful for the break and the chance to stay home in Phoenix for a while, she was doing nothing but hanging around with her roommates.

"What did you do to deserve that?" Karla asked. "Wait. Hold on a second. I'm going outside so these busy-bodies in here don't hear everything I'm saying."

Sidney heard laughter in the background. Karla shared her ranch house in Phoenix with two other Tour players. Neither of them spent enough time in one place to justify buying their own homes. Since Karla's winnings on the tour over the past ten years had been substantial enough to buy a house but not substantial enough to guarantee lifetime income, she was happy to rent them rooms.

Karla and Sidney had been best friends—on the Tour and off—for the past decade, partly due to their age. They were—at more than thirty—the oldsters in the LPGA, along with a couple of incredible, unnaturally tenured veterans like Juli Inkster. Without Sidney's looks or poise, Karla had never garnered the attention that Sidney had, nor had she finished in the top twenty-five in as many tournaments, but she continued to make enough money in both tournament winnings and sponsorships to hang on.

"So what did you do that could be considered inappropriate in suburban America?" Karla said once she had walked outside.

"Oh, probably many things. I'm not cut out for this lifestyle!"

"Is it worse than living on airplanes? Eating dinner at midnight after arriving at the next tournament? Dealing with sexist sports writers sticking cameras and microphones in your face?"

"Wow, you sound a little bitter." Karla sounded as unhappy as Sidney was.

"Yeah, maybe it's just the youthful energy around here," she said. "They make me tired. But no biggie. We'll be out of here for most of the next month, so I won't have to watch them bounce off the walls. What's up, chica?"

Sidney paused. Her sedentary, middle-American, suburban life suddenly seemed too pedestrian to complain about. How could Karla begin to identify with something so mundane?

"You might not believe this, but I'd trade your crazy travel for my days in the office, watching the clock, waiting for donations to drip in. You know, I wouldn't mind it if I could get out and actually work with the girls," she continued. "Then, I'd feel like I was helping someone. But until I get some money coming in, I can't do that."

Karla said nothing, letting her continue.

"And now I'm living in a neighborhood, surrounded by the world's most successful and narcissistic group of breeding females, and my nights with the world's most strait-laced, emotionally abusive techie who probably never loved me in the first place," Sidney said.

She knew there was no way to convince anyone that a life that looked from the outside so comfortable, so worry-free, even noble, could be miserable.

"You mean married life in the suburbs isn't the bliss we all think it must be?" Karla had a soft spot for sarcasm.

"Oh, you have no idea," Sidney said. She dropped her voice to a near-whisper. "If it weren't for sex, I'd have nothing to live for."

"At least you have that." Karla laughed. "Do you know the last time I got laid? I think it was 2001 when I was a sophomore in college."

Sidney held the phone to her ear and tried to think of how to explain her frustrations. She didn't know where to start. All she could manage was a big sigh.

"So what happened today?" Karla asked. "Something particularly awful?"

"It isn't going to sound like it from a distance, but I went to my first book club meeting, and it was horrible."

"Horrible how?"

"I tried to bring up a question about misogyny and *vagina dentata* and they all looked at me like I had just suggested skinning their children."

"What was the book? *Fifty Shades of Grey?*"

"No, it was *Gone Girl.*"

"No kidding? Hasn't everyone already read that?"

"Well I get a feeling that these women don't read anything until it's been made into a movie."

"Ah! Kind of like Cliff's Notes for grown-ups."

"Right."

"Well, maybe it would be better if you went to a weekend book club," Karla said. "Maybe there'd be more professional women there."

"I think I'll be avoiding book clubs altogether for a

while," Sidney said.

"Hey, are you coming to Taylor's bachelorette party in Vegas?" Karla changed the subject. "I have just enough time to run in for the weekend before we head off for Singapore. You're going to be there aren't you?"

"Of course," Sidney said. "I'll be in on Friday afternoon and leave on Sunday. I wouldn't miss it. It will be a nice break from the tedium."

"Great," said Karla. "But, hey, I have to run. I've got a session with my coach this afternoon. I'd better go get warmed up."

Sidney turned off her phone and held it in her lap. She wasn't significantly buoyed by talking with Karla anymore. They'd grown too far apart in the two years she'd been away from the tour. Maybe if they got together in Vegas, they would be able to re-establish some kind of empathetic connection.

She slumped in the wicker chair and stared at the blackberry bushes that were taking over the hedge at the back of Matt's immaculately trimmed lawn. It wasn't hard to get a crew to do a decent mowing job around there, but getting someone to tackle the blackberry infestation regularly enough was far more difficult. She should call someone.

She shook her head and gulped the last of the wine in her glass.

"Oh, what the hell," she said out loud to herself. "What the fuck do I care about Matt's blackberry bushes? Or any bushes. I've got my own work to do: I have got to figure out how to get out of here."

Chapter Three

Sidney had never liked Las Vegas much.

She wasn't a gambler. She saw no sense in throwing good money into a machine that paid back less than it took in. Just looking at the lavish, over-the-top buildings that housed the casinos told her who was winning at that game.

Fall, however, had come prematurely to Seattle, which meant the rains had started earlier than usual, and after four weeks of steady drips, drizzles, and downpours, Sidney was ready for some sun. For the first time in her life, she looked forward to going to the sin city.

Taylor's bachelorette party headquarters was the Bellagio, with its iconic fountain, Dale Chihuly sculpture, and Cirque du Soleil productions. Sidney cringed at the room rate—two hundred seventy dollars a night, the "special" rate Taylor's wedding planner had secured for the group. She had called it "a veritable bargain," which it might have been if not for the resort fee, taxes, and the charges everyone racked up in the restaurants and bars over the weekend.

Sidney met Karla for noon-hour bloody Marys at the bar in Todd's on Sunday to say farewell before they caught their flights home. She was fuming over her tally for three nights at the hotel: $1,498.34.

"It's outrageous." Karla agreed, gulping her drink rapidly. She was apparently in a hurry. "Mine was more than that."

"Matt's going to have a fit," Sidney said, finishing her first bloody and raising her finger to signal for another. Matt was paying her travel bills until T-Squared started drawing in enough donations. "I'm dreading going back to Seattle."

"I wish I had your problem!" said Karla. "I get back to Phoenix this morning and get back on a plane for Asia tonight."

Sidney ignored her friend's lament. With so many other women at the bachelorette party, she hadn't had the chance to talk with her friend much since they got to Las Vegas.

"I wanted to get your advice," she said. "My fundraising has started out so slow, I don't know how much longer I can sit around and wait for things to get going. Or hang around that neighborhood."

"I could use a few sedentary days," Karla countered. They were talking past each other more than sharing a conversation. "I'm so tired of traveling. Do you know how long it takes to get to Hong Kong?"

"Yes. I was on the Tour once too," Sidney replied. She didn't mean to sound so defensive, but after a weekend of listening to the other women chat about recent tournaments, mishaps on the road, and pranks played against each other in the locker rooms on the Tour, she was feeling like she'd lost all of the glamour and excitement in her life.

"Of course you were, honey," Karla said, patting her arm. "I think you've just forgotten how exhausting it was."

Sidney jerked her arm away. "Since when do you call me honey?" she demanded, nearly shouting. "Honey is what you call old pitiful women."

"Shhh!" Karla hissed. "You're causing a scene."

Sidney looked around. Karla was right. At least one person was watching them: a forty-something man at the

31

other end of the bar was chuckling at her outburst. Sidney caught his eye, and he waved apologetically and looked away.

"Okay, I'm sorry." She turned back to Karla. "I'm a little touchy about being condescended to lately. Matt does it all of the time."

"He does?" Karla asked. She seemed surprised, and Sidney realized how little she'd shared with her about her marital grievances.

"Yes, that's a subject for another time. But now, I wondered if you think any of your sponsors might be interested in sponsoring T-Squared."

"Gosh, I doubt it," Karla said. Her quick answer said it all: players were particularly possessive of their sponsors, and wary of any other player or opportunity that might wrench money in another direction. "But I'll keep my ears open for you."

"Thanks, I'd—"

"But, hey! I've got to run!"

Karla jumped off her stool, downed the last of her drink, and rummaged through her huge shoulder bag for her billfold. She pulled out a couple of twenty-dollar bills and stuck them under her empty cocktail glass.

"This should cover my tab and some of yours. I've got to catch a cab."

"Right," Sidney said, standing for a good-bye peck on the cheek. "I can't believe I'm saying this, but I envy you your rush!"

"You shouldn't!" Karla swept her bag onto her shoulder and pulled her luggage claim check out of her pocket. She moved with the practiced, professional grace of a seasoned traveler.

"But I—"

"Bye-bye!" Karla waved and disappeared into the lobby.

Sidney sat back down and covered her face with her hands, elbows on the bar. She couldn't be pissed at Karla for being so abrupt. She knew what it was like on the tour, trying to hold onto sponsors, trying to keep up with the younger girls, trying to preserve energy for the real work: winning tournaments.

Sidney, however, had four more hours before her flight back to Seattle, and nothing to do with them. Should she drink the rest of the morning, or check her bag in with the bellhop and walk around for a while?

She had thought a weekend in the sun and a couple of days around her old Tour-mates would cheer her up, but they seemed to have done the opposite. Her old friends had talked past her all weekend, and she had little to contribute. No one wanted to hear about living in the suburbs, or about her "good old days" on the Tour. They were still having theirs.

"Hey, it's not all that bad is it?"

Sidney looked up to see the man who had been at the end of the bar, now standing next to her.

"Mind if I join you?" he asked.

Generally, Sidney found meeting men in bars repulsive. But her new bar-mate was handsome and impeccably dressed, and his smile was infectious. And the way she was feeling right then, it couldn't get any worse, she rationalized.

"Why not."

"I'll pretend like that was a ringing endorsement." The man laughed and sat down on the stool Karla had vacated while the bartender took away her empty cocktail glass.

"Sorry, I'm either a little hung-over or a lot depressed." Sidney smiled wryly. "I'm usually a little more cheerful than this."

"Peter," he introduced himself, holding out his hand.

"Sidney."

"Yes, I know," he said.

Sidney sat up and blinked her surprise.

"How?"

"I follow the LPGA, Sidney Stapleton," he said. "And a lot of other women's sports."

"Oh." Sidney nodded and took a sip of her fresh Bloody Mary to distract herself from his nice smile. "But I've been off the Tour for nearly two years."

"Yes, I know that too," he said. He leaned a little closer, and bent his head down sympathetically. "I heard about your injury. Are you able to swing a club yet?"

"Yes, but my professional career is over."

"That's too bad. You were great." He clinked his glass against hers.

"Thanks. You're too kind." She clinked back.

"I overheard your lament to your friend," Peter said. "Your life's not as interesting as it used to be, I gather."

Sidney smiled and nodded. "True. But I have nothing to complain about, really. I think it's just the weather in Seattle that gets to me." She didn't want to talk about her real frustrations with a stranger. "I know we've got another six or seven months of rain coming, but I'm already tired of it."

"So what are you doing with yourself these days?" Peter motioned for the bartender to retrieve his drink from the other end of the bar.

"Actually, I'm pretty excited about what I'm doing." Sidney perked up. It was an opportunity to tell someone about her new charity—a chance to practice her spiel.

"I've started a new non-profit called Tee to the Tour," she started. "T-Squared for short."

Peter listened intently as she described the strategy and her hopes for the young girls she would recruit into the program. She put on her stage-face and quickly warmed to her subject. Talking about T-Squared was a lot more fun than sitting around and waiting for checks to come in, she realized.

"So what do you think?" she asked him as she wrapped up her delivery.

"I think you are a great spokesperson," he said, nodding approvingly. "I don't know what I think about the chance of helping poor girls make it onto the Tour, but I think you could convince Eskimos to buy ice cubes."

Sidney laughed. "Christ, I haven't heard that cliché in years!"

"Yeah," Peter agreed. "I guess I need some new ones."

"Well, by nature, clichés are never new."

Peter nodded slowly—a self-deprecating nod. "You got me there. So what are you so down about, dear Sidney? It sounds like you're pretty excited about this new gig."

Sidney thought for a moment. How much sense did it make to share her problems with him? None whatsoever. However rude Matt was to her these days, it wouldn't help to complain about him to complete strangers. And whatever doubts she had about her ability to manage T-Squared, a potential donor was the last person she wanted to share them with. It made more sense to keep up the happy façade and hope that she'd won over a convert to her cause.

"Why are you asking all of the questions, and I'm giving all the answers?" she asked instead. She pointed at his empty glass. "If I buy you a drink, will you tell me who you are?"

"I will anyway," he said. He waved down the bartender again. "Scott! Could you make my new friend and me another bloody Mary so we can continue to get to know each other? And put it on my tab."

"Sure thing, Mr. Bennett," the bartender answered, picking up their empty glasses and busying himself with fresh fixings.

"Peter Bennett it is then," Sidney said.

Peter smiled at her, and she considered how striking he was. His dark brown eyes matched his hair perfectly. His shaggy eyebrows were studded with a few gray strands, and on close inspection, she realized they were subtly sprinkled throughout his hair as well.

As she studied his face, he held her gaze. His self-confidence was attractive, too. He was one of those people, she thought, who walked the face of the earth never questioning his right to take up his fair share of space. He must not have had parents like hers—ones who withheld their love unless it was earned. His parents' affections must have been the unconditional kind.

"You seem very self-assured," she said. "What do you do, Mr. Bennett?"

"Peter," he said. "Please. Only my bookie calls me Mr. Bennett."

Sidney laughed. "And bartenders." She had forgotten how much she loved flirting. Had she lost the freedom to toss around glib small talk with strangers when she got married? She was good at it and she missed it.

"Okay, Peter. What is it you do to warrant that fancy suit and a room at the Bellagio?"

"Ah, yes. Actually, I have a suite, not a room. But, that's beside the point."

"I'll have to take your word for it."

"I am a retired insurance man, and now I dabble a little in sports management," he said.

"Ah, sports management. That's why you follow women's sports," she said, accepting her fresh drink from Scott. But insurance? An attractive insurance agent? It seemed like an oxymoron. Enough alcohol had accumulated in her bloodstream that she had lost any conversational inhibition that might have prevented her from saying what came next. "Insurance, though? Not very sexy. Do insurance salesmen make a lot of money?"

"Yes, but agencies make even more," he said, laughing at her frankness. "You'd be very surprised."

"So you had your own agency?"

"Yes, and I had several very good women who worked for me. I paid them outrageously, and they never left me. We

36

all did very well for ourselves."

"Nice story," Sidney said. "But tell me about your sports management business."

"It's just something I took up on the side. I was too young to retire but was too bored to want to be an insurance agent anymore. Now I recruit talent for an agency here in Vegas."

"Oh," Sidney said. Suddenly, her melancholy returned. "I used to be talent—"

"You still are," Peter said. He reached out and put his hand on her shoulder. It sent a shock down her spine, but she fought against showing it. "Now tell me why you're so sad."

"I have nothing to complain about," she said, but her resistance broke down. Peter was so sympathetic. Why not share a little?

"It's just that we're not getting anywhere with our donor solicitation," she said, limiting her complaint to the least personal of her woes. "I think it's hard for people to see how we're doing anything different from the First Tee. Even if they do, they probably think the First Tee is more worthy."

"I see your point." He nodded. "But if donors could hear you give the pitch you just gave me a minute ago, I think they'd get it."

"Well, thanks," she said. "But I don't have the forum. I had one press conference and now it's yesterday's news. Until I start to bring in some money, I'm never going to get out of the office and get a chance to work with the girls."

"I think I could help you with that," Peter said.

Sidney looked up at him. If his words weren't convincing, his eyes certainly were.

"How about if I arrange a dinner meeting down here in Las Vegas? I'll contribute the venue, the dinner, and extend the invitations. I'll invite a few of my wealthy friends, and you can come down and give your pitch."

Sidney was surprised. It was such a lavish offer. Did he have any idea what a boon that would be for her little struggling charity? "Why would you do that for me?" she asked. "We've just met."

"I watched you for years on the LPGA," he said. "I feel like I know you. Maybe you could say I've always had a little long-distance crush on you. I certainly know how well you present yourself. And sports marketing is my business now."

Sidney knew she still had fans out in the world, but she wasn't sure that her residual fame was strong enough to have elicited such instant enthusiasm for her charity. Peter was certainly improving her day.

"What's your cut?"

"None. I'd do this pro bono."

"Really? Okay, let me talk to my board of directors about this," she said. "I like the idea, but I want to make sure they're okay with it. And my attorney." She agreed to call him later in the week.

"It's a tentative deal then?" he asked, holding out his hand for a shake. Sidney placed her hand in his, and he closed his fingers gently around it. She looked down at their interlocked hands, and her attraction went from a platonic acknowledgement of his good looks to something much stronger. She pulled her hand away, surprised by the sensation.

"Sorry," he said, taking the blame for her reaction. "That was probably inappropriate. I know you are married, but already I wish you weren't. Here, let's toast our partnership."

A half-hour later, Peter left, on his way to a meeting with his sports-management group.

"On Sunday?" Sidney asked.

"Oh, yes," Peter said. "This is Vegas. The town that really never sleeps."

He kissed her on the cheek and pulled her in for a brotherly hug. It started that way, anyway. But the embrace ended as something else, something vaguely powerful. Sidney was still thinking about it as she boarded the plane to return to Seattle and Matt.

≈

On the flight home she struggled with a question: how could she find an insurance salesman so attractive? In her experience, guys who became insurance salesmen after college were English or history majors and mommy's boys who couldn't master engineering, architecture, or any of the hard sciences that attracted more driven men. It was sexist and stereotyping, and blatantly unfair, but she always thought that "insurance sales" was the fallback position for guys who had no idea what they wanted to do with their degrees. They certainly weren't the kind of men she had always been attracted to.

She shook off the silly infatuation and focused on his offer. Was it too good to be true? Even if she had no idea how much his dinner would raise for T-Squared, she knew that meeting a bunch of wealthy potential donors was a step in the right direction. She couldn't wait to tell Matt about it as soon as she got home.

"You met him where?" Rather than being happy for her, Matt was only interested in the fact that she had spent her morning in the bar. She shouldn't have been surprised, she realized. To him, it was another disappointing example of her immaturity.

"At Todd's," Sidney said as casually as she could, given her memory of the warm way she and Peter had parted. "I was having breakfast with Karla."

"Karla was there too?"

"Yes." It was the truth, Sidney rationalized. Karla had been there, just not during the conversation with Peter.

"Why do you think the guy is for real? What do you

really know about him?"

Sidney relayed everything she knew about Peter—except his good looks—emphasizing his "boring" profession as an insurance agent, and embellishing the story in places where her information was a little thin. She knew she was treading on dangerous ground, both with Matt and in trusting Peter. What if Peter turned out to be a flake?

Matt finally agreed to the dinner plans, although not enthusiastically. It seemed that he really wanted her to sit in an office, out of sight, where he could control what she did. Sidney was starting to realize that starting a non-profit with his money gave Matt the idea that he could control things from the start. She really wasn't going to be her own boss, as he had suggested back at the beginning. And with him looking over her shoulder all of the time, how was she going to develop the judgment and management skills she needed? She could only do that if she were allowed to make her own decisions and her own mistakes.

After getting his grudging okay, she took the question to her other board members the next week. Besides Matt, who had joined her board for the obvious reason, her panel included another former LPGA star who lived in Portland, a teaching pro from Overlake Country Club, and Greg, a co-worker of Matt's who served on another non-profit board with him.

The response was unanimously positive. And perhaps because it hadn't occurred to them to ask how she had met Peter, her discussions with them never touched on how she knew him or why she trusted him.

She had her answers by Tuesday evening, but she waited until Thursday to call Peter on the cell number he'd given her. She wanted to give herself some time to put some emotional distance between them.

"The best news I've had all week," Peter responded to her news. "And I've had a good week."

They set the date for the dinner two weeks later. His friends would have to fly in to Las Vegas from around the country, he explained, so they needed some time to make arrangements.

By the time it was all set, and she was prepared to fly out for the event, Sidney had calmed down. Two weeks of sex with Matt—however boring it was—had been enough to take her mind off her titillating parting with Peter. She didn't want to dwell on it. She was going to Vegas to jump-start her fundraising. That was all.

Chapter Four

Peter picked her up at the airport in a stretch limo.

"This is a bit over the top for a non-profit director, don't you think?" she asked, a little embarrassed at the attention she received from Peter and his chauffeur at the airport. She had dressed for travel: blue jeans and running shoes, not especially appropriate attire for a limousine.

Not surprisingly, the travelers at the curb-side limo stop paid no attention to them; she was no movie star. They saw limos arrive and depart all of the time—more likely picking up guests for a bachelorette party than a celebrity worth turning one's head for.

Peter got into the back with her and reached into a built-in cooler in the center of the spacious passenger compartment.

"Champagne?" he asked. Without waiting for an answer, he popped the cork with his thumb, expertly catching it in midair as it bounced off the ceiling. He retrieved two chilled flutes from the cooler and filled them, handing one to Sidney in a single, fluid motion.

"You are awfully good at that!" Sidney laughed. "Practice much?"

"Not as often as I'd like. But let's have a toast to tonight's success."

Sidney took a sip and studied her host. The champagne was dry and cool, a perfect antidote to the stressful, bumpy flight into Las Vegas from Seattle. And Peter was at least as attractive as she remembered. He was dressed nicely in gray slacks and a quarter-zip sweater that looked like cashmere. She fought the urge to reach over and touch it.

"Hmmmm," she said, settling back into her seat instead. "I could get used to this nonprofit work."

Peter laughed and relaxed back into the commodious leather seat across from her. "Given what you're probably getting paid, it shouldn't be all work and no play," he said.

"I'm not getting paid at all. And, so far, it's pretty much all clerical work and not much fun," she said. "But we've been over that before."

Sidney took another sip of the bubbly liquid. "Who is coming tonight? Can you give me a preview?"

"Sure, but I'll skip the details," Peter said. "It's ten businessmen I know through the sports-management business. They will all be very interested to hear your presentation."

Sidney leaned forward and opened her briefcase. "I brought some brochures we just had printed and a special letter of introduction that I wrote for tonight," she said, handing one of each over to Peter. "Tell me what you think."

Peter sat his glass down in the deep cup holder next to his seat and glanced at the two pieces.

"These look fine, Sidney," he said. He handed the papers back. "But, I think you should know that your performance tonight is as important—no, it's more important—than your business plan. These men will be watching you as much as they will be listening to what you say."

"What do you mean?" Sidney asked, returning the papers to her briefcase. His message couldn't have been more different from the one Matt had delivered before her press conference in Seattle. "Are you telling me that it's not about the organization; it's all about me?"

Peter smiled and looked down at the champagne glass in his hand. He paused for a moment.

"Let me say this, Sidney," he said, looking up and locking eyes with her. "It's as much about you as it is about the organization."

"Well." Sidney looked out the window at the casinos rising on the Strip in the distance.

She would be happy to be the center of attention again, if only for one brief dinner, and she thought she understood what Peter was telling her. Back when she was on the Tour, she had to meet now and then with representatives of her corporate sponsors, and they frequently told her something similar. Her sponsorships didn't depend so much on how far up the leaderboard she climbed as on how willing she was to schmooze with the corporate clients in the hospitality tents after her rounds. Yes, they needed her to play well, but second, third, fourth—somewhere close—was as good as winning.

"I guess I shouldn't be surprised," she said. "It's kind of like betting on the jockey instead of the horse."

"Yes," Peter agreed. "Remember, it's the jockey that has the brains."

"Then, maybe I could use some advice for tonight," she said.

"Good," Peter said. "That's the right attitude. Let me make it simple. Keep it short, hit on the highest, most emotional triggers, and let the mundane details of running Tee to the Tour alone. You're not excited about them, so don't expect anyone else to be either."

"Right," Sidney said. "But you seemed to like the way I described the organization the day we met at the Bellagio."

"Yes," he said. "And if you remember, you were trying to tell me why you were excited about it, not how you were running it. You were more interested in psyching yourself up to go back to Seattle than you were in giving me a legal description of your charity."

Sidney sipped her champagne and let that sink in. What were the things that made her excited about T-Squared? It certainly wasn't the fundraising letters or the accounting spreadsheets. It was the idea—helping young women like the Sidney of twenty years ago find that yellow brick road to Oz. It was a chance to share in their victories. She should tell the potential donors that they could be part of making a young girl's dreams come true, especially those dreams that seemed so unattainable, so impossible.

Of course, she had other goals for herself: developing the marketable abilities that would give her a professional life after golf. But that part of the story wouldn't work with donors. She had to make them believe she already had those skills.

"Okay," she said. "I think I get it. Any other advice?"

"Wear something flattering, not something you would wear to a meeting," he said.

Sidney raised an eyebrow and looked at Peter suspiciously.

"Well," he added, "this is Vegas, not New York, you know. You're not selling corporate bonds to pension funds. These men are egotistical, successful entrepreneurs and, yes, gamblers. Here in Vegas, they expect a little glamour to come along with their philanthropy."

Sidney thought about what she had planned to wear to the evening's dinner. Her black suit was slim and classy, and she could dress it up or dress it down. She had packed a plain white crew neck sweater to wear under the jacket. Maybe she would visit the shops in the Bellagio when they arrived and pick up something a little softer and, well, revealing. It wouldn't hurt, she told herself. A little more skin for a lot more dollars? It seemed like a reasonable bargain.

Luckily, she thought, she had brought her highest-heeled Christian Louboutins. The red soles never failed to impress men, even those like her husband who weren't especially interested in footwear.

Much later, Sidney thought back to that conversation in the limo and realized the implications of Peter's advice. But that day, she was just worried about trying to do the right thing to bring home some contributions and become successful again.

೭

Peter had made their reservation for cocktails at eight and dinner at nine. It seemed late for a business meeting, but then, this was Las Vegas.

The late dinner gave Sidney time to enjoy a long nap and a long bath, set her hair in big curlers, and take more care than usual on her makeup. Peter had reserved and paid for her suite, and it provided a quiet, luxurious setting for primping. It was also excessive and extravagant, but then, it made her feel special in a way she hadn't felt since she won her last LPGA tournament.

Just before cocktail time, she got dressed, brushed out her big curls, and checked out the result in the full-length bedroom mirror. The light blue, silky-soft rayon blouse she had picked out at Capri in the Bellagio lobby was expensive and looked it. She liked the way it lay trim about her waist without being tight, and the low v-neck provided just the right peek at her cleavage. It was definitely not prudish. She fastened a long diamond pendant around her neck and added her tastefully simple diamond solitaire earrings. She slipped on her Louboutins and noted how the extra four inches made her legs look about a foot longer.

Compared with the way she dressed for her last job— professional golf—this was a new persona, she thought, as she turned from side to side, admiring the new look.

"I could get good at this," she said, nodding at her reflection.

When she walked out of the elevator into the lobby, Peter met her with something other than platonic friendship in his eyes. He strode over to her and slipped his hand under her jacket and around her waist.

"Perfect," he whispered into her ear, pulling her close. "You look absolutely perfect."

Sidney laughed nervously and gently pushed him away. Peter let go.

"Yes, you are absolutely right," he said, standing back and letting his eyes travel from her shoes, over her legs, blouse, cleavage, and hair. With a broad, approving smile, he finished with his eyes on her face. "This isn't a date, is it? As much as I don't want to, let's go meet the guys."

The private dining room was dimly lit with wall sconces and at least a dozen table candles. Each place was set with a water goblet, two wine glasses and a champagne flute, three forks, two spoons, a steak knife, a butter knife, and a gold-rimmed plate atop a bronzed charger. It was elegant beyond what Sidney had seen at even the fanciest Solheim Cup dinners.

"I could easily be upstaged by this table," she said to Peter as they walked in.

"I don't think so." He shook his head and winked.

Sidney arranged her brochures on a ledge by the door and turned toward two well-dressed men in their sixties at the other end of the room, cocktails in hand.

"What would the lady like to start with?" a voice behind her asked. She hadn't heard the waiter approach, and she jumped a little at his voice.

"Oh!" she said. "How about a Scotch and water?" She didn't really like Scotch, but the setting seemed to demand something like that.

"Would Glenfiddich be okay?"

"Yes, just fine."

"I'll have the same," Peter said. He nodded toward the two men who had stopped talking, acknowledging their arrival. "Let me start the introductions."

If Peter had appreciated her upgraded look, the two men ratified his opinion. She felt a bit like a model slinking down a runway as she walked ahead of Peter the length of the table to shake hands. The men's eyes never left her.

Had she overdone it? Maybe a little less make-up, a little plainer hairdo, a little less cleavage? Maybe that white sweater would have been more appropriate, she thought. But it was too late. And, she had to admit to herself, it felt pretty nice to be on center stage again.

The Scotch was as difficult on the tongue as she remembered it could be, but it warmed her throat, and soon, she relaxed. The room filled with another eight diners—all men, all in their fifties or sixties, and all dressed in immaculate business suits that would have been acceptable at the toniest Hollywood fetes.

As they came in, Peter introduced them, describing each man as a partner, CEO, CFO, board member, or some other such lofty title, but leaving out the names of their companies. Sidney tried to connect names and faces, but she'd never been good at that, and she finally gave up. She smiled and made conversation, constructing sentences that didn't require direct addresses.

"It must have been very difficult to have to stop playing professionally," one of the younger men said early on in the cocktail hour.

"Terrible," she said, shaking her head sadly. "I am just pleased that I found something else to fill that void, and something as satisfying as helping other young women reach for that incredible experience."

She was surprised at how easy it was to turn every conversation into a plug for her charity. She was accomplishing what Matt had recommended: making it all about T-Squared and not about herself. With so much obvious approval, it was a breeze to deflect flattery and sound selfless.

When it came time to sit down for dinner, Peter directed her to the head of the table.

"When do I make my speech?" she asked him in a whisper as he pulled out the chair for her.

"I'll signal you," he whispered back, his lips so close to her ear that they brushed her hair. Still, she could barely hear him over the rattle of chairs and place settings as the ten other men settled down. "Don't worry. I think things are going very well as it is. Just remember to keep it short and heartfelt."

He sat at the other end, at a distance that seemed like a football field away.

After two appetizers, soup, and salad—all served in tiny portions, the waiter quietly walked around the table taking entrée orders: fish or filet? How would you like that prepared? Béarnaise or beurre blanc? Red or white wine? A Bordeaux or a Cotes du Rhône? It was a lot of decisions to make, especially after two Scotches and an appetizer-glass of champagne.

After the waiter finished, Peter stood up and cleared his throat.

"While we are waiting for the next course, I'd like to ask Sidney to say a few words about Tee for the Tour, which is why we're all here tonight," he said.

Sidney thought she caught a few knowing smiles around the table. What private joke was Peter alluding to? she wondered. She would have to ask him later.

"Thank you, Peter," she said, standing. "I want to start by saying how wonderfully serendipitous it was to meet you a month ago, and how much my board members and I appreciate this opportunity to introduce Tee for the Tour to a totally new and, I might say, auspicious audience."

She kept it short, partly because Peter had told her to, but also because she wasn't as sober as she liked to be when trying to put sentences together. She smiled a lot, talked about how wonderful it had been to be on the Tour, and how she hoped every little girl with talent and ambition had the same opportunity to live that dream. She thanked them for coming and sat down.

Peter stood up immediately.

"Sidney is too polite to ask, but gentlemen, I hope you are seriously considering making a contribution to T-Squared in the next few months. If you have any questions about how to do that, I hope you will contact me or the agency," he said, and then he nodded at Sidney. "Thank you, Sidney. Now, I'd like to make a toast."

The men all grabbed their wine glasses and hoisted them above their heads.

"To a new partner, Sidney," Peter said. "I hope we can all become wonderful friends."

Sidney raised her glass as well, and after clinking it against her neighbors', she took a healthy swallow. What did Peter mean? Partner? Why did he suggest they contact him instead of her? What did the agency have to do with it?

Ah, phooey! she told herself. She could ask Peter all that later. Sit back and enjoy. How many times do you get to have a meal like this with so many admiring, attractive men at one time?

The men moseyed out of the dining room slowly after dinner. Each one stopped to thank her and shake her hand. A few leaned forward to give her a peck on the cheek.

Sidney was exhausted, and as soon as she and Peter were left alone in the room, she plopped down in the nearest chair and let out a big sigh. She looked up. Peter was standing against one of the walls, smiling at her with his arms crossed, holding a wineglass in one hand. The dim light accentuated his dark eyes.

"So how did I do?" she asked. "I'm too tired to have any idea."

"Wonderful. You were exquisite," he said. He pushed himself off the wall and walked over to sit next to her. He put his wineglass down and reached for her hands.

"You need sleep," he said. "I want you to go upstairs right now. I have sent a bottle of champagne to your room. Drink it if you want, or save it for breakfast, but take a nice long bath, get some sleep."

"Will I see you tomorrow before I leave?"

Peter didn't answer right away. He looked down at her slim fingers in his hands and massaged them with his thumbs.

"Sidney," he said. "I want to ask you a favor."

"God, I hope it's not something I have to do right now!" she laughed. "I can barely hold my head up."

"No, no." He looked up and smiled. "No."

He paused, holding her eyes. "I know we have just met. You don't know me very well. Yet. But, would you consider staying another night here before returning to Seattle?"

Sidney frowned and started to shake her head.

"Wait!" Peter stopped her. "This is what I'm offering: if you stay and have dinner with me tomorrow night, I'll donate twenty thousand dollars to your charity. And, I'll give you all day tomorrow to relax and recover, do anything you like. How does that sound?"

Sidney hesitated. Just what did he expect from her? Just dinner? Something else?

She looked away and tried to think through the alcohol. Peter was incredibly charming and sophisticated in a way that Matt never was and never would be. And nice to her. Not to mention handsome. Wouldn't it be interesting to spend at least dinner with him alone? And if it was something else after that, would that be so terrible?

She shook her head, trying to think straight. What was she telling herself? That if she ended up having an affair with someone—sleeping with someone other than her husband of nineteen months—that it wouldn't be terrible? Of course it would! It would be horrible.

And, yet ...

"Can I sleep on it and call you in the morning?" she asked, buying some time. "I'm too tired and, frankly, too drunk to make that kind of a decision right now."

"Yes, of course," Peter said, standing up and pulling her to her feet. "I would call that prudent. Now, go upstairs and relax. I'll take care of the check, and I'll wait for your call in the morning."

"Thank you," Sidney said, leaning forward to kiss him on the cheek.

He caught her halfway to his face, and pulled her lips to his. His kiss was soft. And brief.

Way too brief.

Chapter Five

Sidney woke up the next morning with less of a hangover than she expected. She had taken another bath the night before, as Peter had suggested, but instead of drinking the champagne he had sent to her room, she drank two bottles of water and sat up watching an old movie. It was well after midnight before she went to bed, and by then, she was fairly sober.

The message light was blinking on her phone, and she picked it up to listen. She expected it to be Peter, but it was the concierge, letting her know that she had a free pass to the driving range at the Wynn that day, courtesy of an anonymous admirer.

But I don't have any clubs, she thought, just as the concierge went on to assure her than she could use any of the clubs in the pro shop that she would like to demo if she hadn't brought her own.

She put down the receiver and considered the offer. It was probably Peter who had arranged it. But if that were the case, wouldn't he have called her himself? Perhaps it was one of the other men at the dinner the night before. If that was true, would he be there waiting for her? That was creepy. It felt a bit like having a stalker, even if he was an impeccably dressed executive in his fifties or sixties.

She decided against it. She put on her running shoes and blue jeans, and pulled back the blinds and peered outside. It looked pleasant: sunny and still. Even if it were cool, it would be refreshing to get out of her room and take a quick walk up and down the Strip. And it would be nice to get outside in something other than the constant rain she'd been enduring in Seattle.

But first, she had to decide what to tell Peter. It was already nine o'clock, and he would want to know if she had decided to stay.

She sat down on the bed and picked up the phone. Should she call Matt first and see what he thought? Or would that just be acquiescing to the reality that he controlled her? She knew what he would say. He wasn't terribly keen on the trip in the first place. He wasn't going to encourage her to stay another night in Las Vegas at the invitation of a retired insurance salesman cum sports-management recruiter.

No, she had to decide this on her own. It was time to get back to calling the shots in her life if she was going to figure out how to go forward without Matt. So, did she want to go back to Seattle in a few hours, or stay and see what Peter had in mind?

She picked up the phone again and asked the operator to connect her.

"What did you decide?" Peter asked once she got through. "Are we having dinner?"

"Okay, I know it's silly, but I really don't want to go back to Seattle today. The sun is shining here!"

"And, I hope you will also say that you decided you couldn't pass up another fabulous dinner with your new number one fan."

"Yes, that's true, too," she said. "But, just so you know: I have nothing to wear but what I wore last night."

"Not a problem!" he said, enthusiastically. "I've already called Betty in the Armani shop in the Via Bellagio, and she's going to help you pick out something appropriate. Think of it as my thanks for your wonderful performance last night."

"Oh, I can't accept that. I only told you to warn you that I'll be wearing the same clothes tonight. You have already been too generous."

"Nonsense!" he said. "I'll see you tonight at Todd's about seven, okay? We'll have a drink there and then go to dinner."

"Okay," Sidney said, surprised that she'd allowed herself to be talked into accepting not just dinner, but what was likely to be a very expensive gift of clothing. "Why are you doing—"

"Great," Peter interrupted. "Later." And then, the dial tone.

Sidney threw herself back on the bed and looked at the ceiling. What idiotic thing was she doing? She'd been married for nineteen months, and while she was ready to leave Matt, she wasn't sure this was the way to bring her marriage to an end.

On the other hand, she'd let Matt take over her life and her self-image. She'd become passive, the victim, emotionally vulnerable. While staying a night with Peter was unlikely to make things better at home, at least it was the first step in moving on, and it might help her figure things out.

Was her problem just her marriage, or did she miss the excitement of the Tour, the notoriety, the adoring fans? Where were all of those eyes that used to watch her every movement as she warmed up on the driving range, practiced putting, and walked eighteen holes? Was she now invisible?

Peter—and his friends—certainly didn't act like she was. They had treated her like the star she used to be, not the washed-up, injured former athlete she had become. What a relief it was. And they believed in her charity. They thought she could make it a success.

Two hours later, pink-cheeked from her brisk walk up

and down the Strip, Sidney returned to her room to find a note from Betty. She had taken the liberty of setting up a noon appointment, in case the dress she chose needed alterations. Would it be possible for her to make it by then? She included a "private" phone number.

Sidney glanced at the clock. She had just enough time to take a quick shower and grab a sandwich at the bistro in the lobby. She gulped down a bottle of water and got busy.

❧

"Peter thought you might be a size 6," Betty said, taking Sidney's arm and leading her to the back of the store by the dressing rooms. "But as tall as you are, I'm guessing you're more likely an 8. I picked out a few things and put them in here for you."

Sidney followed the petite, middle-aged saleswoman into a spacious dressing room. About a dozen different cocktail dresses hung on a portable rack. All of them looked very formal, not to mention expensive.

"I don't think I should spend this kind of money," she said, looking at the first price tag. Fifteen hundred dollars. "I work at a nonprofit, you know."

"Peter has already taken care of it," Betty said, sounding suspiciously like she'd done this for him before.

"Oh, you know Peter well?"

"Oh, no." Betty appeared to backtrack. "Mr. Bennett came in this morning and asked me to take care of you. I apologize for being so informal. Let me step out now, and let's see how you look in some of these."

Left alone in the dressing room, Sidney pulled the dresses off the rack and looked at them, one by one. They were certainly not appropriate for the office. Most of them had either plunging necklines or tiny straps over the shoulders. A few were strapless. They were all far more glamorous than anything she had ever owned. They were even more formal than her wedding dress had been.

Stripping down to her underwear, she picked a cherry-red strapless number with a full, swing-era skirt. She realized she couldn't wear a bra with it, so she pulled that off too. The dress fit perfectly, but it looked a bit like a bridesmaid's dress, except for the color.

"How is it going in there?" Betty called, and then, without warning, stepped into the dressing room. "Oh, I don't like that color on you!"

Sidney rolled her eyes. As soon as she had put it on, she knew it wasn't going to work. She didn't need Betty to tell her how pasty it made her sun-starved Seattle skin look. She turned to let the older woman help her with the zipper and stepped out of it. She tossed it on the cushioned bench in the corner.

"Let's try this one," Betty suggested, pulling out a light turquoise dress. Its soft silk draped from thin shoulder straps to a tapered waist with a tiny black patent belt, and finished with a handkerchief hem. It didn't look like much.

Sidney shrugged. Why not try it? It wouldn't work with a bra, either, so she pulled it on over her head, snapped the fake buckle on the little belt, and turned to look in the mirror.

"Ohhh," she said. It looked much better on her slim body than it had on the hanger. It accentuated her narrow waist and although it draped low in the front, it was classy, displaying only the breastbone between her breasts, not her recently acquired fleshiness.

"Yes, my dear," Betty said, looking in the mirror from behind. "I don't think you have to look any further. That was made for you."

"I think you're right." Sidney nodded. "I don't really want to spend all day trying on dresses anyway."

"Do you have some black pumps to wear tonight?"

Betty asked.

"Yes, my Christian Louboutins."

"Perfect. I'll get this ready and have it sent to your room. And now, you have an appointment at the salon."

"I do?" Sidney asked. "I don't think so. I didn't make any—"

"Peter, er, Mr. Bennett asked me to take care of that for you, too. Karina is expecting you."

᭐

Sidney had never had a salt scrub performed by someone other than herself before. At first, she was uncomfortable, lying naked on the steel bed, spray nozzles hanging overhead while Karina buffed her from neck to toe with bergamot-scented, oily salts. Her discomfort turned to pain with the rough rub, and then to an all-over tingle by the end of the treatment.

A facial, a hair wash and style, and a make-up session followed, topped off with a pedicure and a manicure. It took four hours, and by the time she left the salon, Sidney realized she had missed her flight to Seattle without calling the airline to cancel. And, not only that, but she had yet to call Matt and explain why she wasn't coming home as planned.

Back in her room, she called Matt first and was relieved to get his answering service. She explained that she had a chance to bring in a big donation by staying one more night and going to one more meeting. She kept it simple. She lied and said she missed him. She hung up.

Then, she called the airline to explain that she had missed her flight and needed to book a new one. "Someone has already taken care of it," the reservations agent said. "Your secretary, Peter." Of course.

She still had two hours before she had to meet him at Todd's. She opened the bottle of champagne Peter had sent up the night before. It was sitting in a fresh bucket of ice; she would have to remember to tip the housekeepers for taking care of it. She flopped down in the big upholstered chair in the corner of her room with a full flute of bubbly and took a deep breath.

What exactly was going on here? she asked herself. She was only a month or so into her new job and she was on the verge of blowing everything she knew to smithereens for the thrill of a dinner in Las Vegas in a dress that she shouldn't have accepted after a spa day she never expected with a charismatic, gorgeous man.

She shook her head and sank farther down into the chair. At least she was making her own decisions, however bad they were.

She woke up with a start ninety minutes later. The empty champagne flute had dropped onto the carpet, and her neck was stiff from hanging sideways off the back of the chair. She checked the clock and panicked; and then remembered that her hair was already done and her makeup had been applied by someone much better at it than she was. All she had to do was shake off her sleepiness, brush her teeth, and get dressed.

She found her turquoise dress in the closet along with a note from Betty, wishing her a pleasant evening. She slipped off her bra, pulled the soft silk over her head again, and fastened the belt. She stepped into her heels and turned to look in the mirror.

She was shocked at her reflection. She looked absolutely perfect, much prettier than she'd ever seen herself. The salt scrub had left her skin radiant, and the hair and makeup were professional. Turquoise was clearly her color, and the handkerchief hem showed just the right amount of thigh here and there. The softly draped neckline provided the right frame for her simple diamond pendant.

One more gulp of champagne, and she was out the

door.

‮ℒ‬

Of all the ways in which her parents had expected her to succeed, looking good wasn't one of them.

Neat, yes. Clean, yes. They hated funky, and they hated sloppy. They also spurned makeup, hair dye, and expensive clothes. As long as Sidney avoided those, they left her alone.

Sidney grew up both bookish and athletic. Her classmates started calling her a dyke by the time she was in the fifth grade after she started playing golf on the junior high boys' team. She was the only female and the youngest player on the squad, but also the best. And she was a straight-A student.

She had time for both golf and academics because neither hanging out with friends nor looking for romance was something her parents encouraged or condoned. It was odd, because they were so in love with each other it was sickening. They were both professors at the University of Minnesota—her father in psychology and her mother in sociology. Her mother's research was on group decision-making in high-stress environments. Her father's research focused on anxiety and risk aversion. His favorite T-shirt said "Worrying works. 99% of the things I worry about don't happen."

They finished each other's sentences, edited each other's academic journal articles, and discussed heavy, jargon-laden topics at the dinner table. They sat together talking long after each meal was finished, ignoring their daughter, who dutifully got up, washed the dishes, put away the leftovers, and headed up to her bedroom to do her homework.

Her older brother had it little better: he was their first love child. They lavished so much praise on him that he felt suffocated, but it probably helped him succeed. He had a

Ph.D. in urban planning by the time he was twenty-eight. He moved to Boston and taught at MIT. He avoided his family totally, including Sidney.

Sidney was eight years his junior and clearly an accident. The only love her parents had left for her was strictly conditional. As an elementary student, she was congratulated and given a rare hug for bringing home a good report card, but simultaneously admonished that she had "better not" slack off the next quarter. Eventually, the school started sending the report cards directly to her parents, and as long as she got As, they never commented on them at all.

Even though they never came to watch her play golf, they expected her to practice diligently and be the best golfer on the team. If she lost a match in conference play, they asked her what she did wrong. If she won, they suggested that she needed to lift her game even more because others would be gunning for her.

The role model her parents expected her to emulate was Edwin Hubble, The Big Bang cosmologist who discovered the universe was expanding and who won seven high-school track and field events in one day. She, too, could be a Rhodes Scholar and an NCAA champion, if she just worked hard enough. Their expectations may have ingrained in her the competiveness that got her to where she landed: to the LPGA Tour and the top of the leaderboard five times. But they didn't teach her much about unconditional love.

One thing they didn't worry about: how she looked. In fact they never commented on it. And Sidney didn't think of herself as attractive until she finished college and started playing on the Tour. The sexy short shorts the Tour players wore, the slim polo shirts and the colorful skorts all looked terrific on her long, slim body. She had grown into her high cheekbones, and her dark eyes had never lost their lush lashes. With sunglasses and a visor, it wasn't obvious that she rarely wore make-up, and her long pony tail whipped playfully around her slender shoulders as she swung the club. The camera loved her, and when she reached the LPGA, she was one of the fans' favorites, partly because of her easy smile, athleticism, and lack of self-consciousness.

Insecurity was unattractive; self-confidence was an aphrodisiac.

❧

"You are absolutely stunning, Sidney." Peter was waiting for her outside of Todd's. He held his hands out for hers and admired her at arm's length, his besotted endorsement surpassing his approval of the night before. "I'm so glad I don't have to share you with anyone else tonight."

Sidney laughed confidently. "Well, unless you're interested in room service, I'd suggest we get to dinner soon. I'm starving and I don't think bar peanuts make a meal."

"After you," he said, stepping aside and gesturing toward the bar.

Sitting tall on the bar stool next to Peter, Sidney glanced around. The evening crowd was thick and the diners were mostly older than the weekend tourists. They were all gorgeous and impeccably dressed, but she suddenly felt confident no one would turn more heads that night more than she did. Poise was the effect Peter had on her. She looked back at him and smiled.

"I never liked Las Vegas before," she said. "But it's growing on me. All this sunshine, all of this excess, and all of these great-looking people. It's like the opposite of Seattle."

"Not to mention great company," he interjected. "Certainly, that counts for something, too." He handed her the martini he had ordered, and raised his cocktail for a toast.

"Here's to a wonderful evening and the start of a terrific relationship," he said.

"And to your incredible generosity." She clinked her

glass against his and took the first sip. Martinis had never been her favorite either, but she vowed to start learning to drink these grown-up beverages if that's what it was going to take to be successful at this fundraising thing.

"Thank you for the dress," she suddenly remembered to add. "It is the nicest thing I have ever owned, and I'm including my wedding dress in that assessment."

"Ah, yes, and thank you for wearing it tonight." He glanced down at the front of her dress, and she followed his eyes to make sure she wasn't revealing too much as she leaned forward on the bar. It seemed okay. Only the tops of her breasts were exposed—just enough to hint at their full potential, but not enough to be inappropriate.

"Now, tell me, why is an evening with me worth twenty thousand dollars to you," she asked, pulling his eyes back to her face.

"It's not just for you," he said. "You realize I am donating it to a cause that I think has a lot of merit. The donation also makes me feel good—that's what you want to cultivate, Sidney. Grateful donors."

"Yes, but I'm not having dinner with all of them, I hope," she said, not fully believing him. "I will gain forty pounds and never be able to wear this dress again."

A three-piece jazz ensemble had finished setting up in the far corner of the bar, and Sidney jumped when the piano struck the first chord.

"Oh, Christ," she said. "I wasn't expecting that."

"Maybe we can come back in after dinner and dance a little," Peter said.

"Sure, if I can still stand," she said. "These martinis are strong!"

"Sidney," Peter said. The way he said her name forced her to look him in the eye. He had a power and charisma that she couldn't explain. Where did it come from? she wondered. His voice? His looks? His confidence? The way he made her feel like she was the only other person in the room?

"I don't know how this evening is going to work out," he said quietly, leading up to something.

He looked serious—solemn even. It scared Sidney a bit. What was so serious?

"Yes?" Puzzled, Sidney nodded for him to continue.

"I don't want to mislead you. I'm attracted to you. Incredibly so. And your body language seems to be saying that your marriage is over. Is that right?"

"We'll see," she answered. Yes, it was, she knew, but she wasn't sure she was ready to announce it.

"I want to make love to you tonight," Peter said in a near whisper, "and if at some point this evening, you decide that isn't going to happen, would you do me a favor and tell me?"

The words "make love" sent a shiver up her spine. Wasn't she expecting that, or at least suspecting it? But, Peter's calm, matter-of-fact delivery surprised her.

"So, you want to know as soon as possible so that you can walk out before wasting your time?" Sidney lowered her voice to match his.

Peter smiled and shook his head. "No, I want to keep us both on the same page. I don't want you to feel like you were tricked into something, or that you owe me something for the dress, for having dinner, for anything. Whenever you're ready to end the night, just say so."

"Well, okay," Sidney said. "But it seems so contractual, so businesslike, when you put it that way."

"Look," he said. "We're grown-ups. I don't play games anymore, unless it's Scrabble, and I don't want you to feel pressure. But neither do I want to wonder if we are going to go our separate ways at the end of the evening. I like to know how to proceed. I want to know what you're thinking."

Sidney took a sip of her martini and stared at her glass for a moment. It made sense. How many times had she disappointed some poor schmuck by walking out on him just when he thought things were getting promising?

"Sounds good," she finally responded. She put her hand on his arm. "I'll let you know if I'm leaning toward sleeping alone tonight. But right now, I think I'd like some company, too."

His grin was infectious, and it made her laugh. Having the "are we or aren't we" discussion upfront certainly should lessen the tension, she thought. Now it wasn't something she had to wonder about all evening.

"Now, speaking of lonely, I would love to hear a bit about what it was like to be on the Tour." Peter changed the subject. "Were you ever lonely out there? How do you compete with your closest buddies week in and week out, and still be friends?"

Sidney had been asked the same question by newspaper and television reporters dozens of times in her career, but her glib answer for them—"We are friends first and competitors second"—wasn't going to cut it with Peter, she could tell. It was blatantly disingenuous. She thought a minute about the truth. Exactly what had it been like with her fellow LPGA pros?

"You know, we were friends," she said. "But our lunch tickets depended on chalking up victories and sponsorships. Yes, we kept our petty disagreements behind the scenes for the sake of the Tour. But, come on! Who were we kidding? We all wanted to win."

"So it was harder to be friends?"

"There's something about competition that makes you hold back a little something. Like you're afraid that if the other girls know the whole you, the real you, they'll find a way to beat you with it in the next tournament."

"So does it get lonely out there, holding back, being careful like that?"

"Yes," Sidney said, nodding. She paused. "But I think

it's probably lonely everywhere, isn't it?"

Peter, expressionless and silent, held her eyes for a long minute.

"Yes, we probably all are." He paused. "You are refreshing, Sidney. I am around a lot of professional athletes, but I don't think I've met an athletic star with your spark for a long time. You have a depth and a grace that's hard to find."

Sidney looked down at her martini and fought a smirk. She didn't want Peter to see it. The fact was: she wasn't special. As much as she loved the limelight, she knew that. Especially now that she couldn't compete—at least not at the level she once had.

Besides, compliments were still hard for her to get used to, even after all of those years of success on the Tour. She was more comfortable with her parents' rating system: excellent was okay, anything less was not acceptable.

It was Peter's turn to put his hand on her arm.

"Sidney, don't get me wrong," he said. "I'm not trying to flatter you. It's just that most of you—that is, pros who reach your level—are so practiced at delivering the expected platitudes that it's refreshing to hear someone who can still express an opinion or have an original thought."

"Okay, I'll accept the compliment," she said. "Thank you."

"But tell me more about why you think that everybody is lonely. Is it because your marriage isn't working?"

It was more than that, Sidney thought. She took her time thinking about how to answer. She wasn't sure she wanted the evening's discussion to go down this path.

"They say we come into this world alone, and we leave alone," she said, finally. "But I think it is so much more than that. Do any of us ever really know what it's like to be another person? Do we ever really invest what it takes to get close enough to do that? Does anyone ever really love someone else unconditionally?"

"I don't know," said Peter. "My parents loved me unconditionally, but I know I haven't ever loved someone like that. But I've seen couples—people who've been together for forty, fifty years who seem like they've reached some level of understanding that takes them in that direction. Haven't you?"

"Yes," Sidney said. "My parents were like that. But because of it, they had absolutely no room for anyone else in their lives."

"Including you?" Peter asked. His eyes were soft, sympathetic.

"Actually, I'd rather not go into this," Sidney said. She didn't want the evening to turn into some kind of maudlin therapy session, working through her parents' neglect.

"Still," she said, "other than my parents, I've only seen stories about old couples who share one mind in newspapers and on TV. But maybe they put it in the news because it's rare. You know what they say: if it happens every day, it's not news."

Peter grinned. Sidney smiled at his good humor. It was pulling her out of her morose contemplation.

"But, now I have to ask…" She paused, unsure whether she wanted to know.

"What?"

"Are you married, too?"

Peter shook his head. "No. I was. For two years. Right out of college. Long ago. It was a disaster. Enough said."

Sidney grimaced. She wondered what kind of woman would have been attracted to an insurance salesman. But, then, she couldn't imagine Peter as one of the listless, drifting history-majors-cum-salesmen of her college class.

"Deal," she said. "The topic is closed. Now, isn't it about time to eat?"

"Another one of my favorite things about you," Peter

said, standing up and offering her his arm. "You aren't afraid to eat. Do you know how many women are?"

❧

Dinner was fabulous.

The food was incredible, but the company was even better. Peter seemed to have grown very fond of her in just a couple of days, and Sidney couldn't help but compare their nascent friendship with the deliberate, judgmental relationship she and Matt had settled into. Yes, she and Matt still had sex—uninspired, routine sex—but other than that, Matt was absolutely disinterested in what she was thinking or feeling, and when she told him anyway, he was dismissive and critical.

Peter, however, listened to her, and far from censuring her every thought, he encouraged her to continue. She grew happier and more confident as the night went on, and only part of that was the wine.

The jazz trio had just returned from a break when Peter led her back to the bar for a dance. The musicians were playing old jazz standards in deference to the older, Sunday night crowd.

Sidney and Peter found stools not far from where they'd had their pre-dinner cocktails, and ordered a drink. They sat close, arms and legs touching.

The first song the trio started after they had settled at the bar was an old Cole Porter ballad. Holding out his hand for her, Peter invited her to come with him to the tiny, parquet dance floor.

They danced close, but in a traditional pose: her right hand in his left, his right hand at her waist, her left hand on his right shoulder. Sidney hated the 1970s slow-dance posture, where girls hooked both hands up behind their boyfriend's necks, and then swayed back and forth with no appreciation for ballroom dancing. Peter knew what he was doing.

The musicians segued from "Night and Day" into "Mood Indigo," and Peter pulled her tighter against him. She looked up at his face, and he leaned down and kissed her softly. His lips moved to her shoulder, and then he pulled her closer, eliminating the millimeter of space that had persisted between them. Sidney felt her body melding into his. They moved together to the rhythm of the slow ballad.

The song ended, Peter threaded his fingers into the hair on the back of her head and kissed her softly again.

"I don't think we need to be here," Peter whispered in her ear.

"I think you're right," she said.

After a brief few minutes of patient administration involving the bill and the bartender, they walked to the elevators, locked in a side-to-side embrace.

~

The view from Peter's penthouse suite was spectacular.

As soon as he unlocked the door and ushered Sidney in, she walked straight to the floor-to-ceiling windows and stood, enraptured.

"Boy this town is growing on me," she said. "I never saw it from this vantage point before."

"It is like nowhere else in the world," Peter agreed. "Let me pour us drinks, and I'll join you in your admiration."

Sidney walked back into the spacious living room of the penthouse and dropped her clutch onto a table.

"Can I move in here?" she asked.

"Only if you marry Steve Wynn," Peter answered over his shoulder. "And I don't think you'd like him." He finished putting ice in glasses, and poured them each a generous Scotch.

"How do you know?" she said, returning to the window's edge.

"I've heard he's a bad golfer."

"Oh, then you're right. That would never do." Sidney accepted the cocktail glass he offered her and turned back to the window. "But how, dear Peter, are you at the game?"

"Does it matter that much?" he asked, standing a few feet away, taking in the same view of the Strip.

"It depends," she said, teasingly.

"Depends on what?"

"On what your other talents are."

"Ah," he said. "We shall see, then."

They stood for a few long minutes, taking in the bright lights of the casinos below.

"Do you know why I'm attracted to you, Sidney?" he broke the silence. He put his hand on the small of her back. It was warm against the cool silk. "It's because you're smart, talented, athletic, beautiful, and successful. And, because I think I can help you."

"So something in it for both of us?" she asked, turning from the view to his face. "Is that what you're saying?"

"Yes," he said. "We were talking about the best relationships earlier tonight. I think the best relationships are built not on time, but on mutual respect. Something tells me you have not always been rewarded with the respect you deserve."

Sidney said nothing. It was true; at least it was the truth she had begun to tell herself. Certainly Matt didn't respect her. But did she really deserve it? And how did Peter know this?

"Come, sit," Peter broke their reverie and led her to the deep couch behind them.

He sat first. Sidney sat down next to him, and he put his arm around her shoulders. She leaned her head back.

What the hell am I doing? she thought. Her body seemed to

be taking her in a direction her mind hadn't yet agreed to. This was fish-or-cut-bait time. *Am I ready for this? Is it too late to change my mind?*

Peter answered her question for her. Taking the cocktail from her hand, he set both of their glasses on the cocktail table in front of them, turned, and kissed her.

This time it wasn't soft. It was deep and insistent. She was ready for it, she decided.

He slipped her dress strap off one shoulder, and reached under the soft silk folds. He cupped her breast with his hand, and lightly pinched her nipple between his fingers.

Sidney's back arched involuntarily, and she struggled to relax into his embrace. His tongue swept through her mouth and she held onto it, not wanting him to leave. He pulled away and kissed her neck, her shoulder, and the rise of her breast. He closed his mouth over her nipple and sucked gently, his tongue caressing her while he slipped his hand up her thigh.

"Stop," she whispered.

He looked up, surprised.

She stood up, a little unsteadily, and kicked off her shoes. She unbuckled the thin belt at her waist, and raised her arms above her head.

"Help me get out of this dress."

Chapter Six

Sidney walked into her office on Tuesday morning, glad to get away from the house.

When she returned to Seattle the night before, Matt was pissy. At the airport, he waited for her curbside rather than coming into the terminal to meet her or help her with her luggage. He didn't even get out of the car to throw her bag in the trunk.

"What meeting did you have to stay for?" he asked, craning his neck out the driver's side window as he pulled out into the through lanes and headed for the airport exit.

"I had the chance to meet with an executive who is interested in making a very generous donation," she said. She had practiced the answer to his question all of the way home on the plane—at least when she wasn't daydreaming and replaying the prior evening over and over in her head.

"And so, the check is in the mail?" Matt asked, sarcastically.

"I don't know, but it was promised," she said, matter-of-factly.

"And what magic made this happen?"

"I wouldn't call it magic," she said. "I must have been quite effective in telling the story to the dinner party the night before. Can't you give me any credit, Matt?"

"How much?"

"How much credit?"

"No, how much is the donation going to be?" he asked. "I hope it's more than the cost of that plane ticket."

"I'm quite sure it will be," she said. "And my room was donated by the sports-marketing guy who set up the dinner."

Matt stared ahead at the light traffic on the airport access road. He looked angry.

"Matt," she said. "I don't understand. It was your idea that I start a nonprofit, and now you seem totally opposed to anything I can do to make it successful."

"I'm not opposed to anything," he said. "I just think that this Vegas kick you're on is not a healthy way to build your reputation."

"What are talking about?" Now, she was getting angry, too. What was he implying? "No one but you, our board members, and some potential donors know that I went to Vegas to raise some money. How can it be hurting our reputation?"

"I'm not sure I said *our* reputation," Matt said. "I was talking about yours."

"Same thing, Matt! What have I done?"

"I don't know the answer to that," he sneered. "Only you do."

Sidney blushed. She turned to look out her window, hoping the cool glass would help pull some heat off of her face. Of course, Matt's suspicions were based on nothing more than his insecurities and jealousy. But he was right to suspect her, even if he had no evidence.

They stopped on the way into Bellevue, and Matt went into their favorite Thai take-out restaurant to get dinner. *Thank God we don't have to cook together tonight*, she thought.

Matt went to bed early, and by the time Sidney checked her e-mails, had a glass of wine, and watched "Castle" on TV, he was fast asleep.

He was out of the house and at work before she got up that morning. She unpacked her suitcase, and hung up the new turquoise dress. Before she put it in the closet, she held it up to her body, and looked in the mirror. It had looked so spectacular in Las Vegas, but against her bulky bathrobe in the dim light of another rainy Seattle morning, it looked plain and innocent. On the hanger, it lost its sex appeal, which was good in a way. If Matt ever saw it, it wouldn't set off any red flags. She stuck it in the back of her dress rack.

Audrey, the accountant, was already at the spare desk in the T-Squared office when Sidney came in.

"Whew!" Sidney struggled with an umbrella, her briefcase, her purse, and a sixteen-ounce latte, tossing everything on her empty desk. "I could get used to a little better weather."

"You mean like in Vegas?" Audrey laughed.

"Yes, like in Vegas. It was gorgeous down there."

"And apparently, lucrative," Audrey said, holding up a piece of paper and waving it at Sidney.

"What's this?" Sidney said, unbuttoning her raincoat and walking over to pluck the paper out of Audrey's hand.

"A wire transfer came in this morning for twenty thousand dollars. Did you know it was coming?"

Sidney squinted at the tiny type on the copy Audrey had printed. There was no name on it, just the number of an off-shore bank account the money had been transferred from. She felt her face blush.

"So, did you know we were getting this?" Audrey asked.

Sidney handed the paper back to her accountant, quickly. She didn't want her shaking hands to betray her.

"Well, it was promised at dinner the other night," Sidney said, trying to sound matter-of-fact. "I guess I didn't know whether the gentleman would actually come through with it, though. We'll need to figure out where to send a receipt."

"Gentleman?" Audrey raised her voice. "Sounds

interesting. Tell me more!"

"There is no more to tell," Sidney said over her shoulder, busying herself with her briefcase and switching on her computer. "Just a bunch of old businessmen and a nice dinner. I should think we might see some additional donations come in over the next few weeks."

"Wow," Audrey said. "You must have hit quite a nerve!"

Oh, you have no idea, Sidney thought. *You haven't got the slightest idea.*

❧

No more donations came. Sidney waited patiently for the first couple of days, figuring it would take a little while before the other men decided how much to contribute to T-Squared and then had their accountants do the paperwork.

But days turned into weeks, and after a month, she had lost hope.

Meanwhile, time dragged in the office. By two o'clock in the afternoon every day, Sidney was sleepy, nodding off at her desk, and then shaking herself awake to check the clock again. The clerical work—transferring names to the database Matt had set up for her, paying bills, writing thank you notes to the rare donors who sent modest checks—bored her stiff.

But while she hated the clerical stuff, she loved the strategic work—it was like plotting a game strategy on the golf course: weighing her strengths and weaknesses and figuring out how to navigate the terrain given what she had to work with.

One afternoon, Janie came into her office to work on their marketing plans. Janie had come to her initially through Matt. He had used her firm to do the introductory marketing for a few niche offerings that his team spun off from his main software product. He had highly recommended her, and Sidney could see why. She was smart, sophisticated, and she knew the latest tricks in social media marketing. To Sidney, she looked like a marketing person was supposed to look: attractive in a classy, nerdy way with dark-rimmed glasses and short spiky hair.

They reviewed the tentative budgets Janie had worked up, each depending on a different level of fundraising success. With the twenty thousand dollars she had from Peter, they were able to step up from the basic maintenance budget and print some new brochures and buy another mailing list.

An hour into the meeting, they'd covered the required topics.

"Hey, let's move this meeting over to the hotel and get creative over a glass of wine," Janie suggested. Sidney was surprised; the marketing maven had always seemed strait-laced and by-the-book. A four o'clock glass of wine may not have been a crazy idea to Sidney, but it seemed like thinking out of the box, coming from Janie.

"Sure!" Sidney was glad for the excuse to get out of the office. They walked two blocks to the hotel and settled into deep, comfortable seats near the windows in the bar.

With glasses of Malbec, the women toasted their afternoon's work. They had never been close friends, but they had known each other about as long as Sidney had known Matt. Sidney didn't know much about Janie's personal life; their meetings had always taken place in Matt's office—before T-Squared had its own offices—and then in Sidney's office. But Matt had told her that Janie had been married and was divorced about ten years ago.

"How are you feeling about your venture now that you've had a month or so under your belt?" Janie asked. "Are you liking it?"

"Oh, not entirely," Sidney confided. "I'm finding much of it tedious, and the isolation pretty difficult. Except for the Solheim Cup games, I've usually been a lone achiever—golf is largely an individual sport. But I've always been surrounded by other players. I've never been this alone before."

"Well, maybe we should reconsider how much of your marketing budget is spent on one-to-one meetings versus traditional mailings and e-mail campaigns," Janie suggested. "Then, you can get out with other people more. Your twenty-thousand-dollar donation indicates you're pretty good at the face-to-face."

If you only knew, Sidney thought. She felt a little thrill remembering how impressed Peter had been with her skills as well. But that was an entirely different matter.

"Yes, I wouldn't mind being on the road more," Sidney said. "I've got a chance to go to Chicago to meet with some potential donors. But, what I really want is to get to the point where I can actually start recruiting some young women for the program. I'm not in this thing because I want to raise money; I really want to help some girls get a good start on making a career of golf."

"Why don't you start doing that?"

"Not enough money, yet. And I'm worried about spending money on plane fares—Matt doesn't seem to like it for sure."

Janie nodded, and then frowned slightly. "I have a feeling that things aren't so spectacular with your new marriage, either."

Sidney was taken aback. Janie was sure full of surprises that afternoon.

"Why would you think that?" Sidney asked.

"The newlywed glow usually lasts a little longer," Janie said. "I'm not seeing it in you. In Matt either."

"Oh, have you been working with him lately?"

"Yes, we're planning a marketing and media trip to New York in a couple of weeks. He just doesn't seem to be expressing any concern about leaving town. You don't either.

Are things okay?"

"Sure," Sidney said. "But I'm surprised you're so concerned about us."

Janie narrowed her eyes and looked like she was trying to be careful in her choice of words.

"I've known Matt for a long time," she said, "and I had the highest hopes for you two. Here's to things working out."

They clinked glasses, but Sidney had her doubts. Not only about whether things would work out, but whether Janie really wanted them to.

Peter hadn't said he would call her, and he didn't. Sidney tried to tell herself that she shouldn't have been surprised. A quick liaison in Las Vegas was exactly what she should have expected it to be: a terrific night, a great memory, and nothing more. After all, "what happens in Vegas…," as they say. And, in any case, she had his twenty thousand dollars to put toward her annual fundraising goal.

She was disappointed, though, and not just in Peter. She was disappointed in herself. First, she had become a trophy wife—not so much the old-fashioned blonde bombshell kind, but more of a sports-trophy kind. And, then she had to failed to keep from becoming the kind of a trophy wife that got boring to the guy who had acquired her. If she wanted to, would she be able to win Matt's approval back?

If even Janie could see things had gone cold between them, maybe Sidney had been right: they were past the point of no return.

It didn't help that Matt was working longer and longer hours and came home tired every night. When she questioned his heavy workload, he insisted that it was normal. The first six months of their marriage, he'd been accused of slacking a bit at work, and now, a year later, he was still trying to get his credibility back with the twelve-to fourteen-hours-a-day routine.

That would have been alienating enough, but the return to "regular" Microsoft hours did nothing for his attitude toward her. He belittled her, first chiding her work ethic, then criticizing her opinions and making fun of her lack of technology skills.

"You should do a pivot table to figure out what your best targets for fundraising are," he told her one night when she complained about the weak response to her mail solicitations. "You could analyze what regions of the country, what demographics, what income levels respond to each of your different messages."

"What's a pivot table?" she asked.

Matt sat back and smirked. "You don't know what a pivot table is?"

"I wouldn't have asked if I did," she responded defensively.

"I forget how unsophisticated you are," he said, returning his eyes to his laptop, which he had set up next to his plate on the table while they ate a late dinner.

"Unsophisticated?" Her voice rose.

"Unsophisticated?" He mimicked her high pitch without looking away from his screen. "Is stupid better?"

"Obviously not, and you know it." She tried to lower her voice, but it didn't work. "Why do you have to insult me?"

"I'm not insulting you; I'm describing you," he said, calmly.

"Stupid?" She felt like she was in junior high, defending herself against some bully's comment about her above-average height. It was so demeaning. Heat rose up her neck to her face.

Matt harrumphed, still staring at his screen and tapping

on his keyboard with his left hand.

"I may not work for Microsoft, but I did graduate from college," she said, fairly spitting her words.

"Yes, and then you played golf with your degree," he said. Finally he looked up at her red face. "Look, I'm too busy to argue with you. Let's drop it. I've got work to do tonight."

Even as he disparaged her, the night with Peter had amped up her sex drive, and she tried to rekindle things in bed with Matt. At first, she reprised the sexy nightgowns that her friends had given her before their wedding. She practically paraded around in front of Matt in them, sneaking peeks to see if he was noticing. Then, she abandoned the negligees, and started walking around the bedroom naked as he got ready for bed. It changed nothing. He still turned off the light as soon as he got into bed, waited for her to join him, and then assumed the missionary position until he came, rolled over, and fell asleep.

She lay still listening to him snore, and remembered the way Peter had touched her, the way his lips had explored parts of her body Matt had never even looked at, let alone kissed. She remembered Peter's tongue bringing her to her first orgasm that evening, and how later he entered her slowly, a little more each time he moved in, until she couldn't wait any longer and begged for more. She caught her breath at the memory and rolled over.

While she still thought about him at night, Sidney gradually quit daydreaming about Peter in the day. It helped that she had something new to work on: the fundraising event in Chicago. The father of one of her board members was on the Chicago Board of Trade and had a dense network of connections in the financial community there. He offered to host a dinner for T-Squared, and then take her around to some of the philanthropic funds in the city the next day. He was also a golfer, and part of the deal was that she had to agree to play a round of golf with him and two of his buddies while she was there.

In Chicago, the dinner meeting started early and ended early, as the men needed to get to work before the stock market opened the next day. But what really surprised her was that six of the eight men wrote checks at the end of the evening. Right on the spot. That hadn't happened in Las Vegas. Sidney wondered what the difference was. Maybe it was her board member—perhaps he had greased the skids ahead of time, and the donations had already been contemplated before she stood and gave her practiced spiel.

Sidney nodded and thanked each of the men as they handed her their folded scrip, promising receipts as soon as she got back to Seattle. She didn't open the checks until she was in her hotel room that night. Another surprise was waiting: the checks were in the low hundreds. She didn't know what she was expecting; perhaps Peter's generous donation had set her expectations unreasonably high. But for the long trip, so far she had collected less than two thousand dollars.

The trip to the philanthropic offices the next day was even more sobering. The fund managers were congenial, but disinterested. They each started their meetings the same way: outlining a set of criteria for giving that were in no way aligned with her mission. She gave her pitch anyway. She hadn't expected any of them to hand over money right away; that wasn't the way these organizations worked. But when she finished the day, she also knew they were unlikely to ever send her a donation.

The final day in town, she played golf with George and his two friends, Ray and Tom. All three men played like they had once been pretty decent golfers, but their age and their thickening girths had robbed them of the flexibility and balance needed to hit the ball as far as they had in their prime. At least their short games were still respectable and kept them from generating embarrassing triple-digit scores.

Still, the game was congenial and the private club was elegant. A few of George's fellow country-club members had shown up to meet his new best friend, the former LPGA pro, and they were gracious. A couple of them handed her hundred-dollar bills for T-Squared on their way out. No receipts needed.

ৼ

On the plane back to Seattle, Sidney rewarded herself for her long three days of work with a purchased upgrade to first class, and then settled back with her wine to think.

Why was a night with her worth twenty thousand dollars to Peter, anyway? If a more usual donation was going to be more like two hundred dollars, how could he justify the huge difference? Certainly, it wasn't just sex; if it were, twenty thousand dollars would be enough for the highest-paid escort in Vegas.

Sidney wiggled down into her big leather seat and let herself revisit last night in Las Vegas with Peter again. A few involuntary sighs escaped, and her seatmate glanced over at her, suspiciously. He didn't take his earbuds out, though, so she didn't feel compelled to try to explain.

By the time she landed in Seattle, she'd made up her mind. She had to call him. She didn't need anything from him, but she was curious: was there a reason why he wasn't trying to keep in touch with her? She thought their night together had been a huge success, if you could rate a terrific night of sex that way. She would call to get his address for the donation receipt and T-Squared's records, and see where the conversation led.

Matt was in New York, marketing, so Sidney had driven to the airport herself. She was relieved to avoid more suspicious questions about her trip from him and drove home through the rain and bumper-to-bumper traffic with nothing more on her mind than what she would say to Peter.

She got his answering machine.

"Hi, this is Sidney. I'm just calling to see if you can give us a name and address where we can send the receipt for your incredible donation," she started her practiced message. She had intended to stop there, just leaving her cell phone number, but hearing his voice on the answering machine ruined her resolve. "And, I really would like to hear from you. I need to thank you for the beautiful evening, too. And the dress, of course. Well, everything ... Hey, I'd better hang up before I say something stupid and make a fool of myself. But, please ... call. Thanks!"

As soon as she hung up, Sidney wished she could erase what she'd recorded. Why didn't she stick to her planned two sentences instead of getting all emotional? Should she call and apologize? No, she thought. That would just make it worse.

Her cellphone rang in her hand, and she almost dropped it. She fumbled with the buttons, nearly hanging up instead of answering.

"Hello!"

"Sidney! Peter here." His voice quickened her pulse. She sat down.

"Peter, I hope you didn't mind me calling," she said.

"Oh, no, of course not!" he said. "I am sorry I didn't call you first. I was in Australia for the past month, working on some deals, and I just got back two days ago. You can imagine what a mess my desk is!"

Hmmmm, they do have phone service in Australia, too, don't they? Sidney thought. It seemed like a flimsy excuse for not calling for a month.

"I'm sure you are really backed up," she said, checking her annoyance. "But, when you get a chance, we do need to get a name and address so we can acknowledge your donation."

"Uh, sure," Peter said. Now *he* sounded put off. "You know, I was hoping you were calling to talk about other things as well."

"Like what?"

"Like when we might get together again," he said. "I have been assuming you had as nice an evening as I did. At least I'd like to think you did."

"Oh." Sidney caught her breath. Getting together again wasn't a great idea, she thought, however much she wouldn't mind a reprise of their time together. But now she wondered: why was she calling? Was it just to see if they could keep in touch? "Peter ..."

He waited.

"Okay, Peter. I had a wonderful time. You were so generous. And, I don't just mean in bed. Although, I mean that too."

"I take it Matt is not there."

"No, he's on a business trip."

"Good. It was a special night for me, too. You are a very special woman, Sidney."

"But I don't know that we have a reason to get back together," she said, keeping her voice as even as she could to hide her own ambivalence. "Other than your donation, we haven't received any other checks from that meeting. It would be hard for me to make an excuse to go to Vegas again."

Peter didn't say anything. The silence stretched out uncomfortably.

"Hello? Are you still there?" she asked.

"Yes, I am," he said. "Sidney, I want to talk with you about a different kind of fundraising model that many of our agency clients use. I'd rather do this in person, but maybe if I sketch it out for you now, you'll be willing to make the trip down to talk about it in person."

"What is it?"

"This is probably going to shock you a bit, but I want you to think seriously about what I'm proposing."

"Okay."

"I recruit talent for a sports-management agency, as you know," he said.

"Right." Sidney was getting a bit impatient with his build-up.

"Well, some of our clients are former female athletes like you. And, we accept invitations for appearances on their behalf. Sometimes it's an event, sometimes it's dinner with a businessman who is looking for a sidekick for the evening. Sometimes it could be golf and dinner."

"Sounds a bit like a cross between celebrity gigs and an escort service," Sidney said, laughing.

"Yes, I guess it is. It *is* like that. But, there's more. Sometimes, the customers want other things. Such as an overnight stay, or a traveling companion. We don't expect our clients to engage in anything illegal, but we let them set their own boundaries."

Sidney shook her head. Was she hearing correctly? Peter had started talking about appearances, and now, if she understood his vague language, it was sounding more like sex for hire.

"Okay, wait a minute, Peter," she said. "I'm thinking these appearances you're talking about have just morphed into prostitution. Am I wrong?"

He didn't answer.

Sidney asked again: "Am I wrong?"

"Let me put it this way," he said. "There are times when the client and customer do agree to sleep together. But that is their choice."

"This conversation isn't being recorded, is it?" Sidney was suddenly suspicious.

"Of course not, Sidney. That would be damn dangerous

for me as well as you."

She wasn't sure he was right about that. He could be trying to trap her, but if he was, that wouldn't stand up in court anyway.

Silly! she thought. *He's not trying to get you in trouble with the law. He's a pimp; he's trying to recruit you as a prostitute.*

"Okay, but frankly, this is not something I want to consider. I love sex. You probably know that as well as anyone—"

"Yes, I could tell, and you wear it well," he said.

"—but I'm not interested in being a prostitute. Not even a twenty-thousand-dollar prostitute."

"Well, most of our customers don't pay that much," he said. "That was a special night for me, and I was happy to support your foundation. But, let me just add something for your consideration."

"What?"

"The money the customers pay would be transferred directly from their accounts to T-Squared, and my guess is your fundraising efforts could really blossom under their support. It could jump-start your charity in a big way. It is just fundraising."

Sidney sat back. She didn't want to admit it, but the idea of being wined and dined, and maybe having an occasional sleep-over didn't seem as bad as she was trying to make it sound to Peter. It actually seemed kind of exciting. It had to be better sex than she was having with Matt. If the men she had met at Peter's dinner …

Wait a minute! she thought. Suddenly that Las Vegas dinner and the lack of subsequent donations were making sense! She was auditioning that night. Not just with the businessmen at the table—was she attractive and classy enough?—but also with Peter. He couldn't recruit sexual prudes as clients, and one way to be sure would be to sleep with them himself.

"Wow, your job is really not what I thought it was!" she said sarcastically. "Now I see why you had me stay 'one more night.'"

"Sidney, there's no way I will ever be able to convince you of this, but that night in Las Vegas wasn't about this."

"Sure." She let the word land as flat as she could.

"No, really. I think you and I could be more than that. If you'd let it happen. I would like for it to happen."

"I'm sure you say that to all the girls," she said.

He laughed. "I have no way to convince you other than to show you. Please come down to Las Vegas, and let me spend some more time with you. And, if you'll consider it, I'll introduce you to the head of the agency. You can still work with us, and you can limit your engagements in any way that makes you comfortable. It's not a one-size-fits-all proposition."

Sidney sat silent. It was a lot to take in. And her reactions were confusing her. Repulsed? Yes. Intrigued? Yes. Ashamed? Yes. Excited? Yes.

She wanted to say "no." She knew she should. But, in a way, she had already taken the first step in the direction of "yes." She'd slept with Peter, thinking they had something special. Thinking she could enjoy a harmless little affair in the city that keeps secrets. She had been wrong; it wasn't a harmless night of sex. It had been an audition for prostitution. And she had apparently won the part.

Worse than that, she'd really enjoyed it.

"Can I think about this?" she finally asked, breaking the silence.

"Sure. I'd expect you to take your time," he said. "Call me when you're ready to talk."

"Okay, thanks."

"And Sidney, I want to be bluntly honest with you. I want to be with you again as soon as I can and as often as I can. I hope you will consider that, too."

Why didn't she see this coming? she thought, sitting with her phone in her lap after the call. The signs were all over: the ten "friends" of Peter's at dinner were "customers" of the agency. Now she understood why no checks had come through. Peter was a pimp; to get their donations, she'd have to sleep with his friends.

Of course Peter knew who she was that day they met in the bar at the Bellagio. He followed all kinds of former female athletes. They were his targets: new potential talent coming off the pro circuits. The twenty thousand dollars was like a signing bonus—a little premature, but there it was.

But why was he insisting that he wanted to keep seeing her? He couldn't do that with all of the recruits he landed for the agency, could he? But wait, wasn't this how pimps kept their prostitutes in line? Sex? What was next? Drugs?

Sidney shuddered and stood up. She unpacked her suitcase. She had been stupid to suggest that she would even think about this new "business model." She should call Peter back right away and say no.

But, somehow, she couldn't. Something intrigued her. That night with Peter had made her feel like the center of the universe again. Wouldn't each of those men they met in Las Vegas do the same? Would a friendly game of golf, a few drinks be so bad? And, what about sex? What if they were all as talented at it as Peter was?

And, finally, she could find a way to gather the funds for her charity and start to break her reliance on Matt and his income. Instead of fretting about fundraising, she could move forward with the fun stuff: the real work of T-Squared.

She was glad Matt wasn't home. She needed to sleep on it, and sleep on it alone.

Chapter Seven

Peter picked her up at the Las Vegas airport. He was waiting for her at baggage claim, and as soon as she came in from the concourse, he trotted toward her.

He bent down and kissed her quickly. The touch of his lips, however brief, had exactly the impact she expected. It was like an electric shock, starting between her legs and shooting up her spine.

He stood back, both hands on her shoulders, and his eyes swept down from her face, over her silk blouse, and down the length of her tight pencil skirt to her legs. She had come to expect this kind of visual review from him, but she felt bad about her footwear: loafers—her concession to comfort for the trip.

"You are a sight for sore eyes, Sidney."

"You and your old clichés," she said, laughing. "It's great to see you, too. Did you get better looking while you were in Australia, or did I just forget how handsome you are?"

"Your flowery words will not work on me, Sidney," he said, reaching for her hand and steering her to the correct baggage carousel. "I am a modest man, and I refuse to be flattered into doing things I shouldn't."

"And, what would that include?" she asked, lowering her voice and putting her lips close to his ear. "Luring a married woman to Las Vegas, sleeping with her, and then selling her into prostitution, maybe?"

Peter stepped back, his eyes wide with surprise. Then he caught her grin, and smiled.

"Yeah, none of that," he said, winking.

"Well, then I guess I made the trip for nothing."

The carousel alarm blared and luggage started inching past. Sidney pointed out her bag, and Peter grabbed it. He led the way out the door and toward a rental BMW. He clicked the key fob, and the trunk popped open.

"What, no limo this time?" she asked as he threw her bag in the trunk.

"I have champagne chilling in my room. I wanted to get there as quickly as possible and I drive faster than those chauffeurs. They get paid by the hour."

"Ah." She nodded. "Good thinking."

He opened the passenger door for her, and waited for her to slide into the seat, unabashedly looking down the front of her blouse. She had chosen it for its silky texture, but as she followed his eyes, she realized how effectively it showed off her cleavage.

He settled into the driver's seat and reached over to brush her cheek. He leaned over the console and kissed her lightly.

"Is that all I get?" She frowned and pulled his face back to hers with both hands. She kissed him for a long minute until she had to push away to catch her breath. His grin indicated approval.

"More like it," she announced.

"I'll have to agree." Peter started the car, and pulled away from the curb. "And, I have to admit something up front."

"What?"

"I didn't get you your own room this time."

"Oh." She pretended to look disappointed, but he didn't

notice. He was concentrating on maneuvering through traffic.

"Then I'll have to admit something, too," she said.

"What?"

"I'm not wearing any underwear."

Peter's head whipped around to look at her. His eyes went to her slim skirt. A wide grin spread over his face, and he laughed.

"I think we are going to have a great time this week, Sidney."

❧

As she lay naked and satiated on Peter's bed two hours later, she felt guilty. Not about having sex with Peter, but about lying to Matt about where she was going. Although her husband rarely had time for her—even on weekends—and showed no respect for her, she and her charity were still both dependent on him financially. Given his disinterest in sex these days, she doubted he would care who she was sleeping with or where, as long as she didn't spend his money getting there.

Odd, she thought. *I feel guilty about using his money, but not about sleeping with Peter?*

Actually, she had no occasion to lie to Matt about where she was going. He had extended his trip in New York without explaining why, and when she asked, he told her she wouldn't understand the complexities of launching a new product. Rather than argue or try to defend her intellect again, she let his insult slide. At least she would have a couple of uninterrupted days and nights to think about Peter's idea.

For two days, she sat in her non-profit's office, opening junk mail, looking for checks that weren't coming, watching the clock, wishing she could take a nap. It was dull, and it looked like it would stretch out that way for a very long time.

91

Finally, she decided that something had to change: either her sanity or her morality had to be sacrificed. The choice wasn't hard. She had never been a saint anyway, and she apparently was a failure at monogamy. She called Peter to tell him she would meet him in Las Vegas again. She purchased her cheap flight with cash at a travel agency office downtown and packed her turquoise dress, a swim suit, and some jeans.

She flew out before Matt had returned home from New York. She left a message on his answering machine, saying she was going on a fundraising trip. She didn't fill in any details, and he didn't call back to ask her to.

All that time she had been struggling with her ambivalence about their marriage, it was clear he wasn't. He was over it. He was over her. But why? Sidney wondered. How did his interest wane so quickly?

Now, lying awake following ninety minutes of slow sexual exploration with Peter, she decided that if she took a vote, every one of her body parts would have weighed in on the side of "you made the right decision." All of the sexual frustration she'd felt over the past month had been relieved in less than two hours with Peter. She turned over on her side to watch him sleep.

Was she just an agency recruit? He kept insisting that she was special to him. But if she was, why was he recruiting her into a life of prostitution? Why would he be willing to share her? She realized how little she knew about him. She didn't even know where he lived. How much time did he spend working for the agency? What else did he do with his time?

She wanted to ask him so many things, but she also loved being close to him like this. She didn't want to spoil the moment with a bunch of questions. She'd save them for later. For now, she just wanted to relax, soak in his beauty, and give him her undivided attention.

"What?" he asked, without opening his eyes. He

surprised her. She thought he was sleeping.

"What what?"

"Why are you staring at me?"

"What makes you think I'm staring at you? Can you see through your eyelids?"

"Your presence is electric, my dear. I can *feel* your eyes through my eyelids." Without opening his eyes he reached for her, pulling her face to his and opening her lips with his tongue.

"Mmmmm," she said, pulling away. "Is this just about sex?"

"Is it for you?" he asked, finally opening his eyes and looking at her. "I hope not. Because it's a lot more than that for me."

She smiled. She imagined he told all of his recruits that. Maybe they were all special to him, or maybe some were just a little more special than others.

"Can we go get something to eat?" she asked. "I'm starving."

"Yup," he said, turning over and rolling off the bed. "I'm hungry too. How about let's skip the fancy dinner tonight and go get a burger at Margaritaville?"

"Sounds perfect." Sidney stood up on her side of the bed and pulled a robe out of the closet. "Just let me wash up a bit."

They walked hand-in-hand down Las Vegas Avenue to the Flamingo and found a table under one of the big heaters on the outside deck at the Jimmy Buffett-themed restaurant. Sidney ordered fish and chips and a margarita; Peter asked for the Cheeseburger in Paradise and a beer.

The waiter walked away. They leaned over the table toward each other and exchanged a quick peck on the lips.

"I can't tell you how wonderful it is to be with you again, Sidney," Peter said. "I've thought of little other than you for a month."

"Oh, really?" she asked. "Why didn't you call me from Australia, then? I waited a month to hear from you."

"Yeah, I figured you were going to ask," he said, accepting his beer from the waiter. "Cheers!" He lifted his big glass toward hers.

"So, what were you going to answer?" she prodded.

"I know you're married," he said. He paused.

"And...?"

"I really wanted you to call me, not the other way around. I wanted you to let me know that you weren't having second thoughts, hadn't found your marriage rekindled by our ... how should I put it? ... very successful coupling?"

"What a prude you are, for a virtual pimp," she said, laughing. "Sex, not coupling. Excellent sex." She took a long sip of her margarita and set it down.

"No," she continued. "It did the opposite. It used to be that Matt and I could have great sex if I got him mad enough or jealous enough. It's not that I like abuse, it's just that it was the only time I saw him passionate. But now, even that doesn't work."

Peter said nothing. He gave her time to think and finish.

"And, frankly, my problem with Matt isn't just sex," she said. "He doesn't respect me. I don't feel acceptance or even an expectation that I could be successful. I don't think he expects T-Squared to succeed."

"It certainly could," Peter responded. "With you at the head. You just need a jump-start."

"Yeah, and thanks for the twenty grand," she said, lifting her glass for another toast. "Here's to friends with deep pockets."

"So how is T-Squared going?"

"Well, fundraising is still very slow. I want to get going with a number of chapters, but I can't until I get donations flowing."

"So, you are at a standstill?"

"No, actually, I'm planning to go to Oakland in a couple of weeks to start our first chapter, thanks to your money. We have a couple of instructors there who have put together a small group of girls who look like good prospects. And they have a facility that's donating the space."

"Good. But, what other fundraising have you tried?"

"Well, that's what's interesting. I went to Chicago at the invitation of the father of one of our board members. The meetings went well, but I collected less than three thousand dollars. At least I got to play some golf."

"Hey, that reminds me," he said. "Want to play the Wynn tomorrow after your meeting with our top guy Milton?"

"Peter!" she exclaimed. "Isn't that like five hundred dollars? And that's if you stay at the hotel?"

"Yeah, usually, but I have a gift of a couple of free rounds from one of our grateful customers," he said. "And I've never played there."

"Are you sure your ego can take it?"

"Sidney, I can't wait to watch you play." He laughed. "Watching your swing will be like an aphrodisiac."

"Like we need one," she smirked. He smiled and nodded his agreement.

The food came, and they dived in. They'd skipped lunch, and Sidney was ravenous. They ate in silence, except for the rumble of traffic on the street below and the ding-ding of one-armed bandits inside the casino.

Sidney wiped her mouth with her napkin and pushed her empty plate to the side. She motioned to the waiter for another margarita. He nodded and trotted off to the bar.

She sat back in her chair and worked up her nerve. She needed to ask questions. Before she left Las Vegas that week, she wanted to understand her relationship with Peter. Was she just a recruit for the agency to him? If so, why did he spend so much time with her? Did he spend this much time with all of his agency "finds"? Did he continue to sleep with them all after their initial audition?

"Okay, I hate to ruin a perfect day, but I really have to ask you something," she said, stifling a burp.

"Turquoise," Peter said. "Turquoise is my favorite color."

"Yeah, I noticed how fast you stripped it off of me last time I was here," she said. "Seemed like you didn't like it much at all."

"That's because you asked," he said. "I could've made love to you in that dress. It wasn't my idea to take it off." He leaned over the table, and she met his lips for another quick kiss.

Sidney started to imagine how their evening would proceed when they got back to the Bellagio. She'd sneak into the bathroom and change into that dress, take off her underwear, and ... but she was getting sidetracked. "No, what I wanted to ask is why, if you care as much for me as you say, why would you encourage me to work as a prostitute?"

Peter pursed his lips and looked away.

"I'd rather not recruit you," he said, staring at their reflection in the restaurant window. "But it was the only way I could help your nonprofit get going, and I know how much success means to you."

"So, when you first saw me at the bar that day, you were thinking, 'oh, her charity needs help?'"

"No," he said. "You got me there. I'll be honest. I was thinking, 'there's Sidney Stapleton. She might be interested in our sports-marketing service.'"

She wanted him to continue, but he stopped, looked past her and over her head, and dramatically waved an arm as if trying to shoo away an approaching train.

"Hey, no pictures, dude!" he yelled. "This is Vegas!"

Sidney turned around. A young man was pointing a

camera at them. From where he was standing, she thought he might just be trying to get a good photo of the Margaritaville deck, with Sidney and Peter as serendipitous, good-looking models.

"Oh, sorry!" the man said, letting the camera drop on its neck cord. "I didn't mean..."

Peter waved dismissively and turned his attention back to Sidney.

"Where were we?"

Sidney tried to remember where they had left off. Oh, yes. He had admitted that his first thought was of recruiting her.

"So, when did it become something else?" she asked. "When did simply pimping me out morph into trying to help me succeed at T-Squared?"

"Well, I'd like to claim that you had me at hello," he said. "But honestly, my motivation changed when I heard you give that ardent speech about helping girls get to the Tour. I could see a warm, passionate side to you that I hadn't expected. And I don't like the phrase 'pimping me out,' Sidney."

A shadow fell across their table, and Sidney looked up to see the young man with the camera.

"Can I ask you guys something?" he asked. "Can you tell me how to get discounted tickets to shows?"

"No, we can't," Sidney said, adamantly. "Can't you see we're having a private conversation here?"

"Hey, aren't you that LPGA player? Stacy something?" The tourist backed up and pulled his camera up to his face.

Without thinking, Sidney stood up and swatted it away.

"No!" she said. "I am not! Now please, leave us alone!"

She used to love fans, even crave them. She used to compare the size of the crowds following her with those following other second-tier golf celebrities—ones who ranked slightly under Michelle Wie, Paula Creamer and Lexi

Thompson in stature. But now, fans could be dangerous. Unless they were potential donors, they were going to be nothing but trouble.

"Geez," the tourist said. "You don't have to assault me." He backed off a few yards, quickly raised his camera, and snapped another picture of them. Then he turned and scurried off the deck and into the dark recesses of the restaurant.

"I hope he doesn't sell that somewhere," she mused out loud. She sat back down.

She struggled to focus again. Oh, yes, he had said something about her passionate speech.

"Okay, at least that *sounds* honest. And flattering."

She frowned. Somehow she wasn't finding out what she wanted to know. She really wanted to know how he felt about her, but she didn't know what she'd do with the information. As it was, she enjoyed being with him, but keeping their relationship about business seemed the only reasonable approach. Letting it morph into a romantic liaison would probably put her right back where she was with Matt: disappointed.

She drained her first margarita and started the second one that the waiter had just delivered. Peter sat back and smiled at her. Was he humored by her uncertainty, or was that a look of approval?

"You are aware, aren't you, that selling sex is illegal in most places, including Las Vegas," she said.

"Yes, and you don't have to do it," he said. "Just tell the agency that you'll accept only appearances that don't include that possibility."

"Yeah, but will I make any money?"

"Not nearly as much. You're talking the difference between a hundred dollars an hour and three to six hundred an hour."

"So you think I should do this?" she said.

98

"Just for a while," he said, grimacing.

The grimace. What did it mean? she wondered. She sighed. Getting to the bottom of Peter's feelings was like opening Pandora's Box—she probably didn't want to know.

"Once you get things going and people see your success, you can quit," he said. "Nothing attracts donors like success and headlines."

Yeah, she thought. *Let's just hope none of those headlines ends up including the letters FBI.*

৵

Sidney's pointy, black-patent stilettos added four inches to her height and killed her feet. She'd only worn them thrice: at the press conference announcing her foundation and the two nights she had spent with Peter in Las Vegas.

But, as much they hurt, they gave Sidney a huge shot of confidence. The slow-paced click-click of the heels telegraphed a sexy poise as she walked through the double glass doors into the Milton Walton Agency. The half-dozen women seated in the spacious waiting area looked up to watch her long legs transport her flawlessly across the parquet floor.

Sidney threw a quick smile around the room and looked down at the thin, pretty face of the male receptionist.

"Gregory." He introduced himself, rising and reaching across his narrow counter to shake her hand. "Welcome, Ms. Stapleton." He grinned as if he were meeting the first celebrity in his life. Of course, he wasn't; the agency represented dozens of well-known athletes. There had to be a veritable parade of them approaching his desk every day. But she appreciated his enthusiasm: maybe it would boost hers.

As badly as Sidney needed the money the Walton agency could bring by representing her, just entering that office was

99

breaching a precarious legal and ethical line. It meant that she was seriously considering the agency's risky enterprise as a solution to keeping her organization alive. If she walked out of there as a client, she would be a prostitute. Yes, a high-class, thousands-of-dollars-a-night "escort," but a prostitute all the same.

"Please," she said, "call me Sidney."

Gregory shook his head gently at her request. "Mr. Walton will be with you in just a few minutes, Ms. Stapleton. Please make yourself comfortable. Would you like a bottle of Evian while you wait?"

"You're so kind," she said. "But no. I'm good."

Sidney chose a chair in the far corner of the reception area, from where she could watch the agency's quiet, graceful activity. The room looked like it belonged in a Roche Bobois catalog. Low-slung couches and tulip-shaped chairs were arranged at pleasing intervals and angles over plush, block-dyed rugs. The bamboo parquet flooring stretched from the lobby doors past the reception desk to a glass-enclosed room furnished with oversized leather chairs and a gigantic natural-form walnut table.

Peter had told her the agency was classy and discreet. She could see the classiness, and so far it seemed very discreet. If anyone recognized her, they weren't letting on. They had all returned to their newspapers and magazines. She didn't recognize any of them, either. If they were clients, they must have played sports she didn't follow. Perhaps, likewise, none of them followed women's golf.

Fifteen minutes later, Gregory escorted her into the glass-framed meeting room.

"Mr. Walton will be right with you." He opened the blinds, revealing a spectacular view of the sandstone peaks of Red Rock Canyon.

Sidney walked around the table so she could keep her eye on the reception area, trading the mountain view for the ability to watch people come and go in the office.

Her choice was rewarded. Just as the impeccably groomed Milton Walton walked in with his hand extended to meet her, a tall African-American woman glided past the glass wall toward the exit.

"Was that Tanya? Tanya Carrell?" Sidney asked, distracted from her own business by the sight of the former WNBA player. If Tanya's height and incredible musculature didn't give her away, her famous sculptured, model-worthy face would. She walked through the office as if she owned the place, leaving an electric current in her wake, and no one pretended they didn't notice. Everyone in the waiting room gawked. As inured as they probably were to most celebrity athletes, they all knew they were in the presence of greatness.

"Yes," Milton said, turning to watch Tanya walk out the glass doors into the building's lobby. "She makes quite a statement just by walking by, doesn't she? She is our biggest asset. Our customers love her."

"She's a client?" Sidney asked, still mesmerized by the woman's passing energy.

"Yes. As I hope you will be. I'm Milton Walton."

Sidney wrenched her focus back into the room and took Milton's outstretched hand. "Sidney Stapleton."

"Thank you for taking your time to visit us," he said. "We would love to represent you. I have heard nothing but excellent things from Peter about your fine qualities. Please have a seat."

Sidney blushed at the thought of what fine qualities Peter might have detailed. She gestured at the "beautiful view" and fussed with her chair before sitting, buying time for her face to cool down. She needed to cut the best deal possible with Milton's agency, and she didn't want her attraction to Peter weakening her negotiating position.

But whatever happened, she would still have the upper hand. The agency was soliciting her as a client not the other way around. Like Tanya, she was an "asset" they wanted to market, and it was up to them to persuade her to allow it.

"We are very optimistic about the caliber of patrons we think you can bring into our fold," Milton started his pitch. "Golf fans are the most affluent segment of our market, and we believe you have the reputation—the cachet I might say—to help us attract a new group of first-class customers."

It was a lot of obfuscation, a lot of euphemism. Sidney wasn't fooled. The customers would be johns; she would be an escort. In most high-end prostitution rings, the johns were called "hobbyists," and the call-girls were "providers." But, in Milton's world, the johns were "customers" and "patrons," and she was the "client." Milton would represent her as if she were still an athlete, competing in an athletic arena, and charge the customers a finder's fee for booking "dates" with her.

Seeing Tanya had slightly shifted the balance of power, though. *So, Tanya was their "biggest asset"?* Sidney thought. *Why couldn't that be me?* The camera loved her. Hours of deferential LPGA footage proved it.

Suddenly, Sidney was motivated, but she needed to put the situation in perspective first.

"Before we get started," she said, "I just want to clarify something."

"Yes?" Milton said, shuffling through a folder of documents he had brought with him.

"I'm only doing this so that I can raise the money my charity needs to help young women advance their golf careers," she said, waiting for him to raise his eyes to meet hers.

Milton looked up and held her gaze. Finally, he smiled and shook his head.

"Sidney," he said. "There are lots of reasons why our clients hire us to represent them. I don't need to know what yours are. No one here will ever make it their business to decide what you should accomplish or why. And, when you no longer need our services, no one will even remember that we worked for you."

He pulled a document off the top of his folder and passed it across the table.

"Now let's get started."

◈

It certainly wasn't street-walking. What Milton laid out for her was prostitution, yes, but in a very different style. No johns leaving the dollars on the dresser before taking off their belts. No soliciting on foot or in a bar. Her johns would be established customers of the agency, already approved from their finances down to their bills of health. No "date" would be about sex only, and some "dates" might not involve sex at all. Milton suggested that some men would be interested only in playing golf with her. That might be the extent of their engagement.

Details of the "appearances" would be negotiated by the agency ahead of time, and she would only go on those that she agreed to, with the restrictions she had agreed to. And, she could limit her customers by age, location, profession— whatever made her comfortable. She would get a dossier on each date ahead of time, along with a photo so she could recognize him when they met. All of her dates would have already been vetted by other clients, at least until she had some experience with the agency. Eventually, if things worked out, she would be asked to do some vetting as well.

Every customer knew that violence was not tolerated, and that "no" meant "no," regardless of what he had paid. If Sidney ever felt unsafe, she was free to walk away and was expected to report the incident to the agency to protect herself and the other clients in the future. The customers were required to wear a condom if she requested it.

Payment would come to her directly from the customers by wire transfer a week before her dates, and the customers would pay the agency a fee for arranging her appearances. She would be expected to pay for her own airline tickets, but nothing else. Milton estimated that she would earn about a thousand dollars for a game of golf, around five thousand dollars for an overnight stay, and more for a multi-day engagement. He wouldn't know exactly what she could earn until bids started to come in, once her availability was communicated.

And how it would be communicated was comforting. There would be no sexy photos on a website, in fact, no advertising on a website at all. The Milton Walton Agency customers were recruited only by other customers, and news of new "talent" was spread by word of mouth and at an annual cocktail party that she would be invited to after the first of the year.

When the customers called to set up a date, they knew the code. A "Golf Appearance" with Sidney would simply be booked as a golf outing, and there would be no expectation of sex. Of course, she and the customer could do what they wanted. "Multi-day Appearance" meant an overnight stay. In those cases, sex was expected, but she always had the right to decline. Payment could be refunded after the event, to keep her options open. Checks would go directly from the customer to her—and in this case, to her charity.

"Any questions, Sidney?" Milton sat back in his chair after he'd finished going over the checklist in front of her.

"Yes," she said. "Quite a few, actually."

"Shoot."

"Will you use my real name when you set up these appearances, or can I use a pseudonym?"

"I'm sure you understand your value is not just in your great looks, but in your celebrity," he said. "We are arranging appearances for you because people want to meet or play golf with a former LPGA champion. As Peter told you, this is not an escort service. This is a sports marketing firm. Your fame, talent, and championships are among the assets we are marketing. None of them has value under a pseudonym."

"I see," she said, nodding. She folded her hands on the papers in front of her, and looked Milton in the eye.

"How about drugs?" she continued. "I don't do them, and I won't be in the room with them."

"It is another one of our policies," he said, pointing to the folder he had given her. "No drugs. You can read through all of these policies at your leisure."

"Who do I call if I have a problem?"

"What kind of a problem?"

"An attack, say. Physical abuse. Should I call the police?"

"Sidney, if you ever feel in danger, call 911 immediately. Don't worry, though, it has never happened in the history of this agency."

"But aren't you afraid that a police call will lead back to you?"

"It's not a problem. We run a big, legitimate business here, and the appearances you will be making are a perfectly legitimate part of what we do. I cannot stress enough: we are not arranging sex for payment. If you decide to engage in sexual activity, that is your choice. And," he stopped and smiled, "your safety is more important than anything else."

"Okay, how about bondage? S&M?"

"You will only engage in activities that you are comfortable with," Milton assured her. "You will sit down with one of our managers early on to define your comfort zone. That will be part of what your dates will agree to before we arrange for meetings."

"It all sounds so innocent. But what happens if it all collapses—if one of your patrons decides to call the FBI?"

Milton paused and studied his neatly manicured hands.

"Sidney, you may decide this is not going to work for you," he said, ignoring her question. "But I hope you will give us a chance. I am offering you an opportunity to benefit from your celebrity. And, if you are at all like our other clients, I believe you will find this business both rewarding and fun."

He looked up.

"Go home and think about it. Call me when you've decided."

≈

That afternoon, Sidney and Peter dressed for golf and took a shuttle over to the Wynn with their golf clubs.

Usually, the only way to play the Wynn on short notice was to stay at the hotel. Tee times were usually booked full by the resort's guests, but Peter's connections came through and their tee time was not only set, but free.

"Who is the friend who did this for you?" Sidney asked.

"He works at the Wynn," Peter said. "He's a customer of the business unit you might be signing onto, but he's also interested in becoming a sponsor for some boxing clients of the agency."

Sidney was too discreet to try to extract any more details; they didn't matter anyway. What mattered was that they were playing a magnificent rectangular green oasis carved by Tom Fazio into the middle of the gray, dry city, right off the Strip.

They didn't have time to warm up on the driving range, as Sidney's meeting with Milton had lasted a little longer than they had expected. Throwing their clubs on their backs, they walked out of the Wynn Casino Hotel, and waited for their turn on the first tee.

As they waited, Sidney watched Peter go through his warm-up stretches and swings. He wore subtle gray glenplaid shorts and a fitted light-gray polo that draped flatteringly over his trim torso. Before he even picked up a club he looked like a great golfer.

Perhaps his practice swing was all show and not indicative of his game, she thought, but it was impressive. Perfect balance, great extension, sweet fluidity, exquisite timing—she couldn't have coached anyone to a better golf swing if her life depended on it.

"Okay," she said, as he returned to the tee box to wait with her for the fairway to clear. "Where did you learn to swing like that?"

"Oh, let's not get ahead of ourselves," he said, shaking his head demurely. "I have no idea where the ball is going to go today. I haven't played for months."

"But that is no amateur swing, Peter. Tell me the truth."

"I did play a bit in college."

"A bit?"

"Okay, a lot. Until I stepped in a vacated Rain Bird hole and broke several bones in my foot and ankle, and tore up my knee. It was the middle of my senior year. It ended my NCAA career, and, in fact, ended the professional career I had planned on before it started."

"Were you a NCAA champion?"

"I did well, Sidney, and it's something I still find painful to remember," Peter said, looking away. She wondered if he might actually be fighting tears, even after all those years. "Simply put, I went from PGA shoo-in to Arizona State history major in one unfortunate step."

"And you were never able to come back?"

"I was in a cast for nearly a year, and on crutches longer than that," he said. "By the time I was able to swing a club again, I was two years out of college and no one knew who I was anymore."

"That's terrible!" Sidney said, and she meant it. "Did you sue the course over the injury?"

"No, I didn't have to. They offered me a settlement right away," he said. "I used the money to buy an insurance agency right out of college, and I got busy running it. Then I got married, and then divorced, and pretty soon it was too late."

Sidney remembered her original question about him: how could someone as interesting, charismatic, and bright as Peter end up as an insurance agent? Now she had her answer. No wonder he empathized with her about the injury that sidelined her golf career.

"And your wife?" she asked. "You met her in college?"

"She thought she was marrying a future PGA player," Peter said with a wry smile. "When it was clear that wasn't going to happen ... well, as they say, the rest is history."

"Well, let's see what you still have left of that championship form," she said, motioning for the tee.

"Oh, no," he said. "As long as we're playing the same tees, ladies first."

Sidney stepped through her set-up routine and lined up for her first tee shot. The ball flew straight and far, and ended up positioned well enough that she could easily reach the green on her second shot.

"Beautiful, Sidney," Peter said. "I feel privileged to play with a woman who can probably beat 99 percent of the golfers in the world."

He stepped up to the tee, took an easy practice swing, and then set up for his first tee shot.

Sidney watched him execute one of the prettiest swings she'd ever witnessed in her life. She couldn't think of any move outside of the bedroom that could be sexier than a powerful, controlled, precise golf swing. And Peter's was the epitome of sexy.

"Peter." Sidney stood and stared down the fairway at where his ball hand landed, at least fifty yards beyond hers, right in front of the green. "Peter, that was glorious."

Playing with a better golfer could elevate anyone's game, and playing with Peter that day was no exception. He may never have become a professional golfer, but he was better than anyone Sidney had ever played with, and that included all of her LPGA teammates. Watching him lifted her game to the best she had played in two years. They both ended up on the eighteenth hole, playing in the spray from the huge waterfall next to the green, with scores under par.

"I can't remember a better round in my entire life," Sidney said, grinning widely as they walked their bags to the clubhouse and headed for the patio and a celebratory drink. "You are amazing."

"And you, my dear," Peter said. He stopped and held out his hands for hers. He seemed suddenly shy, like he was afraid to let her know what he was thinking. "I really wish you weren't married," he finally managed to say.

"Me too," she said.

Chapter Eight

Sidney beat Matt home. He'd extended his stay in New York yet another night. It seemed he wanted to be anywhere but home with her these days.

She picked him up at the airport, and he was amazingly cheerful for just having flown across the country, into a headwind.

"Why did you have to stay so long?" she asked once they hit the freeway and headed toward Bellevue.

"We managed to get a bunch of media interviews that we didn't expect," he said.

"Get a lot of good stories? Did Janie think it went well?"

"She didn't say, and no, we got no stories. It was mostly background interviews. She says they should pay off in the long run, though."

"Well, I'm happy for you. Did you do anything fun? See any shows?"

"Nah," he said, looking out the side window. He didn't seem very forthcoming.

"Not even a nice dinner or two?" she asked.

"Sure, but why the fifth degree?" he asked petulantly.

"Not the fifth degree," she said. "I'm just trying to be part of your life. Seems like we've not been very close lately. You really don't want me to know what you're doing?" She grimaced at the irony of her question.

Matt said nothing. They drove through the dark drizzle in silence.

Sidney hated this time of year—late fall. Nothing but long, dark days and rain for the next three months. In mid-February, people would start planting primroses, and the daffodils would start popping up through the mold and moss, making everyone think spring was just around the corner. But in February, spring wasn't even close to arriving. April was wet and dreary. Yes, May could be decently warm, but June was usually miserably wet and cold again. It wasn't until the second week of July that the sun became a reliable feature in the Pacific Northwest sky.

"How did your meetings go?" he asked as they pulled off the interstate onto Bellevue Boulevard.

"Fine. Nothing set in stone yet. I'm going to go to Oakland next week," she said. "I have a better feeling about that trip."

"Hmmm."

He seemed amazingly disinterested in the progress of a nonprofit that had originally been his idea. She looked over to catch his eyes, but he was staring out the side window again. Disengaged.

Oh, well, then he wouldn't mind her absence. Maybe he wouldn't even notice.

She was going to meet with two instructors at a course southeast of Oakland. The first group of young golfers was waiting, ready to benefit from the free coaching and equipment that Peter's twenty thousand dollars and the other small donations made possible. Finally, she could start implementing her strategy and start helping young women get ready for the Tour.

But, also, she was going to go on her first date with a customer of the Milton Walton Agency.

Laurie, her manager at the agency, told her it was a trial run. If she changed her mind, there was no contractual requirement to stick with the agency. Peter had also assured her she had no obligations. And her date would know her boundaries: no S&M, no bondage. But, it was a "multi-day appearance." Sex would be expected.

She was still on the fence about signing up, but if she wanted T-Squared to be a success, it appeared to be her only option. She had no other prospects for funding, and with the money she had so far—most of it from Matt and Peter—all she could fund so far was this one startup program in California.

வ

When Sidney reached the public golf course outside of Oakland to hold her first official launch of Tee to the Tour, she was excited to get things going.

But, watching ten young girls work with the professional golf instructors who had agreed to sign up for the T-Squared, her spirits waned. For one thing, they weren't serious enough. She remembered herself at that age—eleven or twelve. She was dead serious. She didn't giggle. She didn't huddle with friends and whisper and check text messages. There were no text messages then. She focused on the task at hand: learning the golf tip, the golf lesson, the golf secret of the day.

Most of the day, the recruits looked bored. The only one who impressed her was a tall black girl named Betta. She had seemed as listless as the others during the talk Sidney gave and the lectures from the two instructors, but with a club in her hand and the freedom to swing it, she came alive. As the driving range lesson progressed, each of her swings got a tiny bit better. A little better balance, a little better extension, a little better finish. Sidney stood at the edge of the tee ground and watched her work. For a twelve-year-old, she was amazingly intense.

She reminded Sidney of herself eighteen or nineteen years ago.

This girl, Sidney thought, has it. The potential. The drive to listen, perfect, suffer, practice, hone, focus, and suffer some more—maybe for the chance to run away from her birthright, her family's legacy of poverty. Maybe she had what it took to make the Tour, and then to keep herself there. Of all of the things that Sidney had seen since she decided to start T-Squared, Betta was the most gratifying.

Of course, Sidney didn't want to discourage any of the girls. So she tried to spread her attention around during the practice. The kids were all deserving, after all. For any of them, getting even this far—to a chance to try out for a program of lessons—hadn't been easy. They'd all started out in the First Tee, and most would probably end up back there, which was fine. It would serve their needs. The program Sidney had designed with the instructors was probably too arduous for all but a couple of them.

Nine of the girls wandered out at the end of the practice session, chatting and texting at the same time. But as the other girls left, Betta hung back.

"Mrs. Stapleton?" she asked. She looked down at the club in her hands, avoiding Sidney's eyes. Sidney excused herself from her conversation with the instructors.

"Yes?"

"I wanted to thank you for doing this for us," she said. "I am not sure I can keep coming, but I really enjoyed it today."

"Well, I'm glad," Sidney said, putting her hand on the girl's shoulder and directing her to a couple of chairs in the pro-shop café. "But let's talk a minute about why you might not continue."

"It's not easy to get here," Betta said. "Mama doesn't have a car and I have to take the bus. If I miss the first one after school, I'll be too late."

"Can't you ride with the other girls?"

"They come from a different school," Betta said. "Can't you tell by the way they dress?"

Sidney hadn't noticed it before, but now that Betta had mentioned it, she tried to remember what the other girls were wearing to compare it with Betta's golf attire. The girl's polo shirt looked like it might have fit her perfectly six months ago, but her maturing body had filled out about as much as the shirt would tolerate. In another couple of months, she'd have to abandon it.

"I can talk to Ben and Randy and see if they have some ideas," Sidney said. "With your talent, I hate to see you have to drop out. Wouldn't your mom be disappointed?"

"Nah," Betta said, shaking her head emphatically. "She thinks golf is silly."

"What does she want from you?" Sidney asked. She had been imagining that Betta's mom had been like hers—focused on perfect grades and perfect performance.

"She wants me to be home to watch Lilly and Jacob. They're my little brother and sister. My friend did it today, but she won't watch them every week."

"Well, what if you could pay your friend to do it? Wouldn't it be like a baby-sitting job?"

"Yeah, maybe, but we can't afford that."

Sidney studied the young girl's face. Like any twelve-year-old, she had yet to grow into her face, but there was no reason to expect she wouldn't be attractive. She was shy, but many pre-teens were. And golf was largely an individual pursuit anyway. You didn't have to be gregarious and a team player to do well. Otherwise the teen-aged Sidney wouldn't have made it either.

"Well, there is nothing that says our program can't help cover those kinds of costs," Sidney said. "Let me talk to the guys about that. I don't want you to miss this opportunity, Betta. I believe you have some talent. I don't want it to go to waste."

Sidney stood up, pulled the girl to her, and gave her a hug. For all of Betta's problems, discomfort with hugs didn't seem to be one of them, because she didn't shy away.

ॐ

Gary was waiting in his Jaguar outside of the clubhouse when Sidney finally shook herself free of the day's activities.

She knew who he was because she'd received his dossier the night before by messenger, and he looked just like his photo. A former golf pro himself, Gary had left the PGA Tour because of an injury, as she had, but his second career was as an actor. He was temporarily in San Francisco where Bravo was filming the TV series he'd landed. She had been surprised that he was a customer of the agency. It seemed that a man as attractive and successful as Gary would never need to pay for a date.

His smile was dazzling. He reminded her of a young, low-key Seve Ballisteros. Dark hair, wiry, and quick to laugh. He was wearing the classic costume of the Silicon Valley entrepreneur he was playing on TV: an untucked oxford shirt, khaki pants, low-top Converse sneakers and no socks.

He sprang up to help her and dropped her golf bag and overnight case in the back seat of his convertible with his bags. "No room in the trunk with the top down," he explained.

Then, he zipped around the car to open the passenger door for her. She wasn't worried that anyone in the pro shop would find their rendezvous suspicious: they would assume that two former golf pros would know each other and enjoy spending time together.

"Ms. Stapleton, you are far more attractive in person than on TV," he said, closing her door and leaning over to give her a kiss on the cheek. "I am honored to meet you."

"Oh, come on!" she said, as he rounded the car and hopped into the driver's seat. "I am the one who should be honored! You're still famous! I've kind of slipped into the realm of 'Sidney who?'"

"So here we go," he said. "Are you ready for a cruise through the countryside?" He winked at her, smiled broadly, and pulled out into the street. He drove like a man who had been driving in traffic for, oh, about five hundred years—confident and calm. She loved his attitude. They'd only been together for a minute and she felt comfortable with him already.

"I hope you don't mind," he said, smoothly moving over into the HOV lane, "but I've made reservations for us out at Saddle Creek. It's about an hour away, but I didn't want to subject you to some kind of inspection and curiosity at the Olympic Club."

"Oh, you belong there?" She had to shout over the traffic noise and the wind.

"No, but I have friends who let me play there," he shouted back. "I don't belong anywhere. I am too busy to make the membership fees pencil out."

"So tell me about Saddle Creek."

"Well, it's a dramatic track. Great views and challenging. Plenty of sand, plenty of water, and nice and long. I like it, and it's got these great bungalows on the course. Very quiet, especially late in the season like this. I had to call to be sure there'd be someone who could give us our key."

"Uh, I hate to ask," Sidney said, "but I didn't have lunch. Will there be food?"

"Don't worry," he said, reaching over to tousle her hair. "They leave dinner for us in the kitchen."

"Sounds great." Sidney sat back and relaxed. She dug into the pocket of her golf shorts for a scrunchie and pulled her hair back into a loose ponytail. Between Gary's tousling and the windy ride, it was going to be impossible to brush out if she didn't get control over it.

She watched Gary as he concentrated on navigating a nasty traffic snarl through a construction zone. She had worried about her first "date" being a "multi-day appearance," but she could see no reason to object to staying overnight with this guy. He was a heck of a lot better prospect than any of the guys she'd slept with before she met Matt.

Luckily, it was still early in the afternoon, and rush hour was still an at least hour away. They sped up as the traffic thinned on the freeway out of town, and dispensed with the effort to converse. Sidney watched the suburbs whip by, and once they passed Stockton, the scenery opened up to grassy hills and oak trees.

They arrived at the old mining town of Copperopolis just as it was getting dark. The town had withered from its heyday during the Civil War to not-much-of-anything until the new golf resort and nearby town center were started in the 1990s.

Gary turned up the four-mile manicured boulevard to the resort, and they checked in at the clubhouse. A lone employee greeted them at the office in the front lobby.

"Your dinner is in the refrigerator, Mr. Sheeley," the attendant said. "You will just want to warm up the hot items in the oven. About three-hundred degrees for an hour."

"Great, thanks," Gary said, discreetly placing a large bill in the young man's hands. "We'll be fine. Thanks for sticking around." Sidney was surprised; her date seemed more considerate of the low-level employee than she would have expected him to be. Matt was usually incredibly rude to service workers.

"Thank you, Mr. Sheeley," the young man said, bowing slightly as he moved out of the way of the Jaguar. "Have a good night and enjoy your round tomorrow."

Their bungalow on the ninth hole overlooked a small

lake that separated the fairway from the green. They located the roasted chicken and side dishes in the refrigerator and placed them in the oven. A couple of bottles of wine—a Sauvignon Blanc and a Malbec—were waiting on the granite counter, and Gary lifted them both up.

"What's your druthers?" he asked.

"How about Malbec now and the white with dinner?" she asked.

"Perfect."

He stuck the white wine in the freezer to cool, and opened the Malbec with a practiced flourish. He poured them each a big glass, and motioned to the patio. "Want to check out the course?"

"Not much to see right now. It's getting pretty dark," Sidney said, but she opened the back door, and they stepped outside. She chose one of the two deck chairs, put her wine on the small patio table, and sat back. She took a deep breath.

"Nothing smells better than a golf course in the evening, just when the dew starts collecting on the grass," she said.

"Agree." Gary stood behind her and put a hand on her shoulder. "And, nothing is better than an evening with a beautiful woman and a nice glass of wine."

Sidney was surprised by the quick intimacy Gary had assumed. She forced herself to accept his overture and leaned her head back onto his hand. They watched the ground fog rise over the fairways and the swallows swoop through the air, collecting their evening bug meal. Sidney suddenly shivered, realizing how chilly the night had become without her notice.

Gary felt it. "How about some golf on TV while we wait for dinner?" Gary asked cheerfully, reaching for her hand and leading her back inside.

She kicked off her shoes, settled down into the deep couch in front of the wide screen, and pulled her legs to one side, tucking her feet under her. Gary located the Golf Channel, which was airing a European Tour tournament, and set the remote on mute.

"So, tell me how has it been, making the transition off the Tour?" he asked. "Has it been easy or rough?"

Sidney took a deep breath and composed her thoughts. "Mainly rough," she said. "I felt lost for a while, making bad financial decisions, hanging out with worthless characters. I really missed the focus and the discipline. I'd never been adrift like that before."

"And you had surgery, right?"

"Yeah. Right shoulder," she said. "Thank God it wasn't my left shoulder or I might still be on the DL."

"So how is your game now?"

"Rough. Really rough. I'm glad I don't have to make a living at it." She turned and smiled. He sat close, but not uncomfortably so. "How was it for you, leaving the Tour?"

"Brutal," he said. "I went nuts for a while. Until I fell into this acting gig, I was like a ship without a rudder. I went to clubs, I drank too much. I went to Monte Carlo and gambled. It was pretty shameful."

"What changed? How did you settle down?"

"Luckily my sports agent—you know them, Milton Walton—got a call from this TV producer who liked my looks, and I auditioned for this role on Bravo."

"I have to admit," Sidney said, "I haven't seen it. Sorry."

"Oh, I don't know how many people have," he said. "Don't apologize. But I guess it did well enough last season that we're doing another fifteen episodes. That's what is taking up my time now. It's great, but I'm not getting to play much golf these days."

"So what was your injury?"

"Knee," he said, flexing his left leg out straight. She could hear his knee joint crack. "I had the meniscus removed, and I thought that would be enough, but it has a tendency to collapse on me."

"Why not get it replaced?" Sidney asked, reaching out and putting her hand over his knee cap.

"I will eventually."

"But it doesn't sound like enough to make someone quit. Was it?"

"It was time. I hadn't won a tournament in two years, and I think I needed a handy excuse to move on. I'm just lucky I didn't drift too long."

They stopped talking and watched the French golfer Victor Dubuisson make one of his trademark escapes from the rough, putting his impossible chip shot within two feet of the hole.

"My God, he's good at that," Sidney said.

"Yeah, miraculous."

"And so damn cute!"

"I'm a guy and I have to agree," Gary said, laughing. "Not just a girl's guy. He's also a guy's guy."

They fell silent again, and Sidney felt herself nodding off. It had been a long day, starting with an early morning flight from Seattle. She didn't fight it, and the next thing she knew, she woke up alone on the couch. She straightened up to see Gary busy in the kitchen, setting plates and silverware on the breakfast bar. He'd turned off the TV, and had put on some music. It sounded vaguely like Cuban jazz, although she didn't recognize the artist.

The warmed-up roasted chicken was salty but tasty, with plenty of garlic and thyme rubbed into the crisp skin. The broccoli was a bit soft, and whipped potatoes a bit hard, but it was all edible. Sidney ate what she wanted, and when they both had pushed back from their plates, there was still plenty left over.

"I wish this didn't have to go to waste," she said, gesturing at the cooling food in front of them.

"It wasn't that much money," he said. "Don't worry.

"I met a young girl today," Sidney said. "Very talented. I can't help but think she and her brother and sister never have this much food left over."

Gary didn't answer, and Sidney wondered if he was too far removed from anything less than his luxurious life to dredge up empathy for someone like Betta. He was clearly capable of empathizing with her—trying to find a new career after professional golf, and had been kind to the employee who let them in their bungalow. But how widely could he cast his emotional net? How widely could she?

"Do you think we need to do these dishes?" she asked.

"No, I don't," he said, filling her glass with the last of the Sauvignon Blanc. "That's part of the deal here. Someone will clean up after us. I think it's time for us to listen to some music and relax."

He stood up and took her hand. He led her back to the couch, and they sat down.

Sidney settled back into her spot, held her wineglass, and willed herself to relax. *Was it only two months ago when she and Peter started with a similar pose?*

They sat quietly for a long time, listening to the music, watching it grow dark outside, and slowly finishing the rest of the wine. Sidney felt herself nodding off again.

"Hey," Gary said, reaching over and lifting her chin off her chest.

Sidney shook herself awake.

"I know this is your first date with the agency," he said. "And I can't imagine what is going on in your mind right now."

Actually, nothing was, Sidney thought. She was nearly asleep.

He continued: "But let me just say this: I've been on very few first dates in my life—and I don't mean just the ones I arranged through the agency—that were a lot less comfortable than this."

Sidney smiled. "Me, too," she said, setting her empty glass on the coffee table in front of them. "I think you really understand where I am right now, how much I miss my old life. There aren't many people I can talk to about it."

Gary reached up and gathered her long hair in one hand, and gently pushed it back over her shoulder. He leaned forward and kissed her. It was soft and brief, but effective. She reached up and slid her hand around the back of his neck. He pulled her in close and kissed her again, this time slowly, nibbling on her lips, and pushing them apart with his tongue.

Then, abruptly, he sat back.

"Now is the time for you to say yes or no," he said, looking her in the eye. "If it's no, I will be very disappointed, but rules are rules. If it's yes, I'd like to move into the bedroom right now. I really want to see what's under those golf clothes, Sidney."

Sidney expected that at this point she would think about Matt and her marriage. Instead, Peter's image was butting in on her date. She closed her eyes and imagined him sitting next to her in Gary's place, and she felt a warm, wine-enhanced thrill in her crotch. It had been so natural, so easy with Peter.

Peter hadn't played golf professionally like Sidney and Gary had, but she had felt more of a connection with him from the beginning. And he was sincerely interested in her charity; it didn't seem that Gary really cared about it.

Let it go! she chastised herself, silently. Was there one good reason to wish she were with Peter instead? It was Peter's idea that she engage in this sex trade. It was he who had set things in motion that led to her sitting here with Gary. And she was certain that Peter wasn't thinking about *her* right then.

Gary waited for her answer, and Sidney wondered just

how much of a choice she really had at that moment. If she said no to sex with Gary, she wouldn't get any more "multi-day engagements," and maybe that would be for the best. But, this was her chance to raise the money that would make a success of her venture and win her freedom from Matt. And, she told herself again, the men she'd been sleeping with over the past few years were far less worthy partners than Gary.

She stood and reached down to help him stand up. Holding one hand, she led him into the bedroom. She stopped next to the bed, turned and pulled off her polo shirt.

"Your turn," she said. "Shirt or pants first?"

Janie charged Sidney two hundred fifty dollars an hour for her marketing services. Audrey, her accountant, charged her one hundred bucks an hour, and the attorney charged a non-profit rate of two hundred dollars. Sidney had figured that if she subtracted the six hours she expected to sleep on this twenty-four-hour date, she'd be making a little more than three hundred dollars an hour for her five-thousand-dollar appearance with Gary. That was close to her attorney's for-profit rate.

Not bad.

In the short time between completing her surgery and meeting Matt, Sidney had looked into some possible jobs besides returning to the Tour—part-time local TV sports announcer, marketing rep for golf clothing lines, working as a teaching pro or club pro. None of them would have paid more than thirty-five thousand dollars a year, and after she got married, none of them seemed worth the time. Matt's huge salary provided all the income they needed.

But Milton Walton had promised her she could make at least five thousand dollars per overnight engagement, and if she did four overnighters a month, she could make close to a quarter of a million dollars a year. Or rather, her charity could. She wouldn't have to get any special training, go back to school, or get licensed. All she had to do was learn on the job, and be flexible.

Learning to go with the flow and be flexible in sex shouldn't be that hard, she thought. It couldn't be any worse than putting up with Matt's dispassionate missionary position over and over. But she didn't know what her customers would expect her to do, how they'd expect her to act. Did they want indifference or passion? Could she be indifferent at one point and passionate at another?

She sat down on the edge of the bed and watched Gary reach down and untie his shoes. He kicked them into the corner, and with one, swift move, pulled off his pants and boxers and kicked them aside. He stood in front of her, his penis growing large in the time it took him to unbutton his shirt.

"I think you're falling behind, Sidney," he said. "Or do you need help?"

She stood up and unzipped her shorts. It didn't seem that Gary needed her to do any fancy, sexy dance as she undressed; surely he hadn't performed one. She let her shorts fall, and pulled down her panties. She stepped out of them, and reached around to unhook her bra while Gary finished taking off his shirt. He watched her breasts fall loose.

"Well, this was worth the wait," he said, moving toward her with an approving smile and circling her waist with his hands. He backed her up, and she sat on the edge of the bed. He knelt down and spread her legs with strong hands. She lay back on the bed and willed herself to concentrate on purely physical sensations. She had to stop thinking about what she was doing and just enjoy the sex. This was all she had wanted from Matt, after all, some foreplay, some fun, some passion.

Gary tongue explored her between the legs only for a

minute before he climbed onto the bed and pulled her on top of him. His fingers explored her wetness, and then together, they pulled him inside. He reached up for her shoulders and she leaned forward, supporting herself on her hands as his tongue hardened her nipples. Her vagina started to throb as she rubbed against him. Briefly she worried: she could be too quick to climax. She tried to slow down, but her breathing betrayed her.

Gary closed his eyes. She rode him mindlessly, frantically. He arched his back against the bed and she felt him release inside her. She let go, her vagina pulsating on his thick, slick erection.

Ah, the thrill of the simultaneous orgasm, she thought, smiling widely and closing her eyes as they decelerated their synchronized rhythm. She was pleased that it had happened so quickly. She was exhausted. She lay down next to him, happy to accept success and sleep.

They slept briefly, and then Gary kissed her awake.

"Let's shower," he whispered.

She took a deep breath, and sat up. *This is what it means to go with the flow*, she thought, rising sleepily and following him into the bathroom and the shower.

They shampooed each other slowly, and then he reached out of the shower door, pulled a washcloth off the towel rack, and handed it to her. It was the first chance she'd had to examine and admire his muscular upper body and legs. She soaped his chest, back and buttocks roughly. Then she stroked his new erection softly, not wanting him to lose it yet. He took the washcloth, soaped it lavishly, and started with her shoulders, working methodically down to her feet.

Sidney turned around and around under her shower head to rinse off. She turned her water off and then reached to turn off the rain shower over both of their heads, but he stopped her. He eased her back against the cool tile, and knelt down between her legs.

"This time, I won't be in such a hurry, I promise," he said, looking up at her face.

But she was the impatient one. She wanted sleep so badly, she sighed audibly. She wanted to dry off and fall into bed.

Gary held her against the tile, and gradually, she did what she had told herself to do: go with it, focus on the physical pleasure of his tongue and his lips pressing and stroking. She came again, her face pointed up into the warm spray from the shower head, this time with nothing more than one of his fingers inside. She preferred his fullness to the vacuum of his absence, but she was in no position to complain.

His erection told her he wanted her again. She turned to the bedroom with damp hair and glistening skin from toweling off. He followed her, putting his arm around her waist and stopping her. She leaned forward with her hands on the messy bed they'd just left. He entered from behind, kneading her full white hips, and came quickly, without waiting for her. She didn't mind. She only craved sleep. She crawled into bed with his liquid flowing down the insides of her legs, and collapsed.

≪

They didn't get to sleep until well past midnight, but they still made their nine o'clock tee time, grabbing bananas and coffee for breakfast in the clubhouse.

Sidney agreed to play the blue tees—the tee set for low-handicap men—with Gary to simplify things. She generally played the white tees these days, one tee-box further forward for higher-handicap men and expert women. But she wasn't trying to prove anything with her score.

They threw their bags on their shoulders and took off for the first tee without another soul in sight on the course.

"Gotta love off-season golf!" she exclaimed as they put their bags down next to the tee box and started to stretch.

"In honor of your perfect performance last night, I'd like to offer you honors," Gary said, gesturing that she should take the first shot.

Sidney blushed. She wasn't the only one who had performed well, she thought.

But then she wondered: had he said that to knock her off her game? It was a bit hard to concentrate on a good shoulder turn, smooth rhythm, and a perfect finish when her heart was racing and her mind was swimming through memories of their night together.

"I'm not going to let you get to me, mister," she said, pointing her driver at him and walking up to the tee box. She set her ball on the tee, stood back and picked a target, and then stepped up quickly and took her swing.

"Christ!" Gary exclaimed as her ball flew down the fairway, picking up a slight draw before hitting the ground and rolling to a stop at least two hundred eighty yards away. "You are going to mess with my head – or should I say my groin? – if you keep swinging like that, Sidney. I don't think I've ever seen anything so incredibly sexy in my life."

He walked up to the tee box and lifted her face to his with a finger. He kissed her lightly and she felt her knees weaken. She was glad he had waited to do that until after she had hit her drive.

Golf is an incredibly sexy sport, she thought, as she watched Gary go through his pre-shot routine. The intense focus on the player's face, the graceful move to address, the smooth swing that required all of the big muscles to release their power within one explosive fraction of a second—it was kinetic and poetic at the same time.

Gary wasn't Peter, but his swing was good enough to remind her of him.

He swung gracefully and powerfully, his ball landing a

dozen yards beyond hers. He turned toward her and bowed. "I think I just blew by you!"

"Yeah, but I'm a girl!" she said, laughing. "And now, let's see your short game."

They picked up their bags and walked directly down a mowed path to the fairway side-by-side.

"Does your husband play golf, Sidney?" Gary asked. Sidney hadn't expected him to bring up Matt.

"Yes," she said, recovering from her initial surprise. "He's a decent weekend golfer. Usually in the mid-teens." His handicap was usually around fifteen, which wasn't bad for an amateur who played as little as Matt did.

"Do you miss the competition?"

"Yes, and no," she said. "I love playing my best and having a reason to do so. I don't miss the letdown of a bad performance."

"Yes," Gary said. "The yin and yang. I felt the same way. It's like manic depression. Nothing but a win feels good, and everything else feels horrible."

The early morning walk down the middle of the fairways with her bag on her back brought back some of her best memories—summer practice rounds on her high school team, early morning tee times on the Tour, and the emotionally charged tee-off with Peter on the Wynn course in Las Vegas.

This would be how she would design paradise, she thought. No one would grow old. No one would get injured. There would be no golf carts, and just a light spray of dew on the grass at daylight. There would be wild sex at night, great golf the morning after. Everyone would enjoy good wine before dinner and beautiful sunsets in the evening.

Watching Gary stick his narrow ass out over a putt on the fifteenth green, she surprised herself thinking how nice it would be to have him once more. How did she get so hungry for sex? She walked up and put her hands on his butt as he watched his ball roll on a perfect line and drop into the cup.

He straightened up, turned, and kissed her hungrily. She wondered if anyone would notice if they …

She shook off her desire and picked up her bag. She followed Gary as he headed toward the next tee, but halfway there, he put down his bag and grabbed her hand.

"Leave your clubs," he said in a harsh whisper. "I have something to show you."

He pulled her into the women's side of the restroom between the green and the tee, and locked the door. He turned her around, her back against the wall. He placed her hand on his crotch and pulled her toward him. Anticipating pleasure equal to that of the night before, she quickly pulled off her shorts and threw them on the cabinet. He dropped shorts and boxers, and reached down, lifting her up and lowering her onto him. She wrapped her legs around his buttocks. His strong hands supported her butt.

He came quickly, and smiling, let her down onto her feet.

"I'm sorry," he said, suddenly looking chagrined, lifting her chin and looking her in the eye. "I should have been able to wait for you. It's the second time I've done that."

"No, it's fine," she said. "Just help me."

She lifted her polo shirt over her head, and pulled his face to her chest. She reached down between her legs and wetted her fingers and stroked herself. Gary enthusiastically obliged, pulling down her bra and lifting a breast to his mouth. It took only a few seconds, and she came, shuddering and, once again, missing his presence inside of her.

They redressed quickly and walked back out to the cart path. Sidney was relieved to see no one on the fairway behind them. She walked the final three holes relieved of the sexual tension built up over the previous fifteen holes and in awe of their chutzpah. Gary wasn't Peter, but he sure as hell wasn't Matt either. This date had been a rousing success, in her estimation.

As he pulled the Jaguar up to the departure gates at the Oakland airport two hours later, Gary let out an audible sigh.

"That was too short, Sidney," he said. He looked over at her with regret, and then spun out of his seat to retrieve her golf bag and suitcase from the back seat. He placed them on the sidewalk next to the Alaska Airlines curbside baggage kiosk, and turned. He backed her up against the side of the car and kissed her softly. "Can we do it again?"

"I hope so, Gary," she said. "I really don't know why I'm not paying you for this incredible twenty-four hours. It doesn't seem quite fair."

He grinned. "Them's the rules."

Chapter Nine

Gary's check arrived three days later. The negotiated amount was five thousand dollars, but he had added an extra thousand. She surmised it was either for her victory in their golf match or for the extra activity in the restroom on the fifteenth green.

By the time she got back to the office, the agency had called. Was she ready to sign on as a regular client? Sidney called back and talked to Laurie. Yes, she had a wonderful time, and yes, if they had more customers like Gary, she'd be pleased to make another appearance.

"I'm very happy," Laurie said. "I'll call you in a couple of days with what I've got for you."

The difference was going to be that the checks from now on would arrive before the appearance, Laurie explained. Didn't that imply that she no longer had the right to say no? Sidney asked. Laurie assured her that was not the case. Her appearances were never booked with the promise of sex.

"That will still be your call," she said. "Every time."

Matt hadn't seemed to miss her much, Sidney realized when she got home. He was still working long hours, which he now blamed on the fact that his team was on the verge of releasing a new version of one of their niche software products. She was in bed long before he came home the next five nights, and he didn't even bother her for his usual monotonous sexual routine. Days passed without a nasty comment about her intelligence; they didn't talk enough for him to bring it up.

Sidney's first task when she settled back down to her office work was to try to solve Betta's problem. She re-read her charity's charter, and talked with her attorney. Was there a problem with paying for Betta's siblings' babysitter? No, there wasn't, he said, but he suggested she make sure any babysitter they hired was licensed and bonded in California.

Sidney remembered her own, brief babysitting career; she certainly didn't have a license or a bond. It lasted only four weeks because she hated it. The kids were little Tasmanian devils, and she couldn't establish any kind of authority over them. She decided she preferred to live without the extra money to spending miserable weekend evenings tending to brats.

She called Betta's instructors in Oakland, and they agreed to work with her mother to arrange for both transportation and babysitting to keep Betta in the program. Meanwhile, they were working on finding a location closer to her home where Betta could practice between her weekly coaching.

Problem solved! Sidney thought. But now she needed to get more programs up and running. They had enough money to open two or three more locations, and Portland, Palm Springs, and Phoenix seemed to be her next best bets. She had at least two instructors and a private course in each of those locations willing to teach and host a T-Squared chapter. But now she faced a challenge of trying to coordinate her visits to the chapters with her appearances for the agency.

Matt certainly wasn't getting in the way. He was busy at work, and had been disengaged from their relationship for so long, it no longer surprised her. It wasn't until she was packing the night before her next trip that he confronted her about leaving again.

She planned to drive down to Portland the next morning, work with the chapter most of the day, stay alone that night, play golf on her date the next day, and stay with him the next night. She was pretty excited about the trip, given how well the date with Gary in California had turned out.

"Oh, you're home," she said, looking up from the pile of clothes she was folding for the trip as Matt walked into the bedroom.

"Packing again?"

"Yes, I have a meeting with a new chapter forming in Portland," she said. "Six girls have signed up, and we have two instructors ready to get started with them."

"Really?" he said. He sounded like he didn't believe her. "Why don't you just fly down there in the morning on Horizon and fly back tomorrow night? Why do you need to stay?"

Sidney stopped. Immediately her mind jumped to the worst case: somehow he had found out about her work with the agency. But how?

"I guess I could fly," she said, slowly, trying to think her way through the conversation without slipping up. "It's just that by the time you get through security and everything, it's about as fast to drive. And you don't have to worry about delays and cancellations."

"Hmmmm," he said, sounding unconvinced. He sat down on the recliner in the corner—where Sidney once thought she'd sit reading late at night when she had insomnia. That didn't happen because Matt wouldn't let her turn the reading light on when he was trying to sleep.

Sidney kept packing, feeling her ears burn under his steady gaze. She reached into a drawer, pulled out a cotton nightgown, and dropped it in the suitcase. She wasn't going to pack her negligee in front of him: she would have to do that the next day after he left for work.

"I think there's something more going on here," he said. "Is it possible you're having an affair?"

"Why would you think that?" she asked adamantly, putting her hands on her hips.

"Well, you've been gone an awful lot lately, and you seem to have no interest in how things are going in my life."

"I thought the only thing going on in your life was work. Do you have something else to tell me?"

"Yes, but first, are you having an affair?"

"No," Sidney answered flatly. She wasn't sure if it was the truth or not. She knew you couldn't call her work with the agency "an affair," and the thing with Peter was strictly business.

She was relieved that his suspicions hadn't come anywhere near to the truth. Prostitution was much worse than having an affair; she would almost be willing to cop to an affair if it satisfied him and kept him from knowing what she was really doing all these nights out of town.

"Okay, then," he said, "can I come with you to Portland?"

"Sure," she said, calling his bluff. "Pack your bag. I'm leaving about eight in the morning." She walked into the bathroom and retrieved her traveling makeup pack. She dropped it in the suitcase and looked up. He was still watching her.

"Makeup?" he asked, suspiciously.

"Yes, I'm going to have a nice dinner with the two instructors from Lake Oswego who have volunteered to work with the students, and then dinner and golf with a potential donor," she said. "Is that all right, or do I have to start clearing these things with you ahead of time?"

Matt said nothing.

"And, you'd better start packing," she said, zipping her

case closed. "I'm leaving in ten hours. I don't want to be late."

"I don't have time to go gallivanting off to Portland in the middle of the week," he said. "And you know that. But, Sidney, I'm not impressed with your work habits. You seem to have turned this non-profit thing into a series of pleasure trips, and that's not what it's all about."

"Well, why don't you tell me what it *is* all about then, Matt," she said, leaning forward with her hands on the suitcase. "You're so smart about these things, you tell me."

"It's about helping young women succeed," he said.

"And why do you think I'm not doing that?"

"Because you seem to be enjoying yourself a little too much," he said.

"Oh, if it's a nonprofit, then I'm supposed to suffer? I am supposed to sit in the office all day, waiting for things to happen? Matt, you're making no sense!"

They stared at each other for a long minute. Matt had no answer, which was rare. Usually he responded to her with a quick, nasty put-down of some sort. Finally he got up and walked out of the room.

"By the way, my mother is dying," he said over his shoulder. "Not that I would expect you to care."

Sidney sat down hard on the bed, angry. It was hard to summon up sympathy for him. His mother had been ill for a very long time, and so it wasn't a surprise that someone had come to the conclusion she was dying. To link her illness to their argument was cheap and unfair.

But what made her angry was Matt's assertion that she should be suffering, not enjoying her job. That was just like a Microsoft guy, she thought. If they weren't all making each other miserable inside the halls of that snake pit of a company, they were out fighting dragons—the Europeans, the Commerce Department, Google, Apple—and losing more battles than they won.

Still, as she started to calm down, she had to admit how afraid she had been that he really did know what she was up to. It was eventually going to look suspicious if her trips numbered more than her chapters. She was going to have to start calling some of her trips "fundraising" instead of chapter visits. Perhaps she could go to Oakland a few more times to work with Betta and pick up some dates there. But, eventually, the board was going to start looking at her donor records and wondering how she was doing it. She could imagine one or more of them wanting to come along sometime.

And sooner rather than later, she was going to have to bring up the subject of divorce. As soon as she could see the light at the end of the financial tunnel. Maybe Matt would be relieved when she did, she surmised. Maybe it was going to be the world's most mutually acceptable separation ever.

On the way to Portland the next morning, she called Peter. She had three hours alone in the car and no one around to eavesdrop on her conversation. Once again, she left a message, and once again, he called back immediately.

"Is that how you screen your calls?" Sidney asked as she answered.

"Is that how you say hello?"

"I asked first."

Peter laughed. "How did your appearance in Oakland work out?"

"Oh, the girls were largely uninspiring, but I think I have one good prospect there," she said. "She has some serious challenges in getting to the golf course every week, but if we can work those out for her, I think she's got potential. Isn't that great? If we find one good prospect in each chapter, don't you think that is success?"

Peter didn't answer right away. "Uh, that's great to hear," he said finally. "But, I meant, how did the date with Gary go?"

"Oh," she said, embarrassed to have missed his point. He must have thought she was missing it on purpose. "Good. I think it went well. We had a great day on the golf course."

"That's what I hear," Peter said. "Great golf."

"What? Do you talk with these guys afterward?"

"No," he said. "I don't talk with all of them, that is. Gary, however, is a good friend. He was one of my first recruits to the agency."

"You mean you recruit customers and clients?"

"Well, actually, I have recruited mostly customers," he said. "Milton only asked me to bring in clients in the past couple of years."

That was new information. Sidney hadn't thought much about how the agency's customers were brought together or how they communicated with each other and with the agency. She had assumed that Peter's job was just finding and sleeping with former athletes like her. Now she wondered if he himself had once been a customer.

"Are you still there?" Peter asked as the silence stretched over her thoughts.

"Oh, yeah," she said. "Sorry. I just didn't know."

"So, I had the impression from Gary that it wasn't just good golf."

Sidney was even more embarrassed now. Of all the things she had expected might happen in taking on this new fundraising strategy, she didn't expect to have to talk about the sex on her dates with anyone.

"Oh, well, I'm glad he thought that," she said. "But could we change the subject?"

"Yes, please," Peter laughed. "I'm with you. Enough information already."

Sidney wondered if that were true. Obviously he was a little curious, or he wouldn't have brought it up. But she was glad to get to the point of her call.

"Well, I called to tell you that I have agreed to sign on. And I wanted to ask you something."

"Yes, I heard. What's your question?"

"If I get the money in advance of the date, how do I say 'no' if I don't want to have sex?"

"Those are the rules," he said. "Any customer who does not respect the rules puts the agency at risk. If sex is guaranteed, that changes the appearance from a marketing sale to prostitution. The agency can't let that happen."

"Well, do you ever have cases where the customer gets angry? Doesn't accept no?"

"I don't know," Peter said. He paused. "I don't know if we have. But I do know that the agency has never been investigated for prostitution, and none of our clients has ever been harmed on a date. Other than sports injuries, that is. An Olympic skier once fell during an appearance and broke her leg on a tree. She was apparently goaded into taking an icy run that she wasn't comfortable with. That customer is no longer with us, by the way."

"Well, okay," Sidney said. "That's helpful. I think."

"And, our customers are very carefully vetted," he said. "They can only become customers with a referral from a longtime patron. No strangers."

"Okay, good to know. Thanks."

"Sure," Peter said. "So, how are things at home?"

"Not good," she said. "Probably worse. Matt is suspecting me of having an affair."

Peter didn't respond to that.

"And he tells me how stupid I am all of the time, and now he tells me his mother is dying," she said. "I am guessing we'll be taking a trip to New York for the funeral soon."

"Gee, I'm sorry," he said. "Were you close to her?"

"Oh, no. I met her once after we engaged. She has been in a nursing home in Ridgewood for about two decades. She couldn't even make it to the wedding."

"What did you tell Matt?" he asked.

"That I'm sorry," she said. What difference did that make? she wondered.

"No, I mean about having an affair."

"I told him no."

"Did he still suspect something?"

"I think so."

"You know, some of our clients actually tell their husbands or boyfriends what they're doing," Peter said. "Have you thought about that? If you want to stay married, that is."

"Oh, God," Sidney said. "You have no idea how strait-laced Matt is. He voted for Romney, and that was hard for him, given Romney's acquiescence on gay rights."

Peter laughed. "So what else did you call about?"

"That's about it," she said. "Oh, wait a minute … Okay, so here's something I don't know. Where do you live?"

"Wisconsin. Madison, Wisconsin."

"Really?" Sidney was surprised. She expected the answer to be somewhere in Florida or Arizona or California, not the Midwest.

"Yeah, if it's good enough for Steve Stricker, it's good enough for me."

❧

Ten adolescents showed up for the first session of the Portland chapter at a beautiful golf course about fifteen miles west of Portland. She had expected six. Not only had the instructors—Sally and Patricia—recruited a good group of contenders; they'd even arranged the transportation from the city out to the course for those girls whose parents couldn't chauffeur them around. Sidney was relieved: one less thing she'd have to worry about.

She had learned from Betta's example: these young girls were going to need more than just golf lessons. They lacked things that wealthier youngsters never had to worry about, like transportation, baby sitters, parental involvement.

While the group was at least moderately talented as a whole, Sidney didn't see anyone who impressed her with the intensity she had seen in Betta. Still, she was drawn to the shiest of the group, Lydia, a young girl who hung back and didn't call attention to herself like some of the others.

Sidney's own struggles had been different: she had been lonely, but never shy or retiring. That was part of what made the eighteen months with Matt so confusing. How had she lost her verve? Her confidence? Her drive?

Oh, well, she thought. She was getting it back, and if Matt didn't care for her coming back into her own, she was fine with that. She was done with him.

Shaking off her narcissistic mental detour, Sidney stepped in to give Lydia a little one-on-one instruction. She hoped the girl would survive the rigor and eventually thrive with the program. Luckily, T-Squared didn't require the instructors to cull the field. Any girl chosen for the program could stay as long as she was willing to show up for coaching and put in the practice time.

Sidney was also drawn to the instructors. Sally and Patricia had different talents. Sally was compassionate and patient; Patricia was enthusiastic and vociferous. Working together, Sidney thought, they'd be able to bring out the best in all of the girls by giving each the kind of coaching that fit her learning style.

After the long afternoon, the three women met at Henry's Tavern in the Pearl District in downtown Portland for dinner. Sidney wasn't much of a beer drinker, but she liked the idea of a low-key burger and beer night in advance of the golf and dinner date she had accepted through the agency for the next night.

Sidney reveled in being the center of attention, as the two teaching pros flattered her and quizzed her about her days on the Tour. She remembered to mention her impressions of Lydia and ask that they keep an eye out for her. But as much fun as it was, she begged off early in the evening. Not only did she want to get a good night's rest before her golf game the next day, she also wanted to get back early and call Matt. She wanted to be sure he knew she was turning in early—and alone.

Matt didn't answer the phone, which didn't surprise Sidney. He had been working late nearly every day for months. She left a message, including a tepid, rote "I love you" sign-off.

The next day, Philip met her at the golf course to start their twenty-four hour date. She had his photo and résumé from the agency, but it wasn't until they met in the pro shop that she realized he was one of Peter's "friends" who had attended their first dinner in Las Vegas.

Like most of the men, he was silver-haired and well-tanned, but with skin that looked like it was getting professional wrinkle repair. He was athletic but not skinny, dressed in Tommy Bahama golf attire. "Dapper" was the word that came to her mind. She could find much less agreeable playing companions on any private course in the country, she thought. So far, she was optimistic about the day—and night to come.

"Yes, I was there," he answered her question about the Las Vegas event. "You looked spectacular that night. Your enthusiasm for your project was infectious."

"Well, thanks for deciding to make this donation," Sidney said, trying to swallow the sarcasm in her voice. She remembered how she had expected donations to pour in after that dinner, how disappointed she had been, and how that night was her true introduction to the agency.

Philip either didn't get her acerbity or chose to ignore it. He ushered her to his private golf cart, and they took off for a pleasant, but uneventful round. She soundly beat him from the white tees, but he seemed to enjoy the outing for golf's usual benefits: the challenge, the fresh air, the tranquility of grass and trees and water. He was a quiet man, not exactly taciturn, but not effusive as Gary nor as charismatic and talented as Peter.

As he drove their cart from green to tee, and from tee to their fairway shots, Sidney studied him. What would drive a good looking, successful man in his late fifties to resort to hiring an escort for sexual satisfaction and a round of golf? It challenged all of civilized society's notions of how men and women satisfied their basic needs. Why wasn't he getting sex and companionship from a wife? Or a girlfriend? Why was he paying for a golf partner?

Part of the answer to that question became obvious when they made plans for the evening. Rather than a rendezvous at a hotel or restaurant, he arranged for a taxi to pick her up and deliver her to his house that evening. He would take her back to her hotel after dinner, he said. Clearly he wasn't married. Or his wife was out of town. She bet the former was more likely.

She had no idea when or where they would have sex— if they did, but she didn't worry about it. She was learning to go with the flow.

"Beautiful," Philip said, greeting her at the door.

Sidney wore her Christian Louboutins, but at the last minute she had decided not to pack the turquoise dress Peter had bought her in Las Vegas. It felt like infidelity to wear it on a date with someone else. Instead, she wore a conservative but elegant dress she had bought for the rehearsal dinner before her wedding. Dark green and simple, it accentuated her waist, and with a hem falling at the knees, it showed off her muscular calves and trim ankles.

Philip's home was spectacular. It looked over the Columbia River, sitting high on a bluff west of the city. Huge picture windows provided views for those who preferred to stay inside, but Sidney and Philip took advantage of his expansive deck and pleasant fall weather to have cocktails outside, where they could enjoy the panorama without the interference of reflections off the glass.

Dinner was served by a caterer Philip said he discovered while serving as president of the local branch of his college alumni organization. The service was respectful and unobtrusive. The food was fresh, light, and flavorful. Sidney relaxed. The evening didn't conjure up any of the sensual anticipation of her date with Gary, but it was certainly civilized.

"My greatest desire was to travel and to experience as much of the world as I could through the business," Philip said, explaining how he got into the business of importing European cabinetry and appliances. "I never really cared whether I made much money or not. I grew up with little, and having a place like this was never what I expected. It just all worked out better than I could have planned."

Sidney appreciated his humility. On the Tour, she met many successful tournament sponsors who considered their fortunes evidence of their brilliance and hard work, never crediting their lucky births or any of the help they got along the way.

Sidney looked around. His modern single-story modern home was furnished with artifacts from Africa, the Near East, India, Southeast Asia, and Europe. Philip's taste, as far as she could tell, was impeccable. Of course, with no background in art, she wasn't the best judge, she admitted to herself.

"Were you ever married?" she asked toward the end of the evening. She'd had enough wine by then—fine Willamette Valley Pinot Noir—to have lost some inhibition.

"No," he said. He looked sad. Sidney studied his face. His square jaw, gray eyes, and shock of silver hair indicated his bachelorhood had nothing to do with a lack of attractiveness. He'd been successful. He had traveled widely. Obviously, it had been his choice not to marry. She wondered if she, too, should have made that choice.

"I put it off too long," he said. "I always intended to find the woman of my dreams, but I was always looking somewhere new, traveling, not focusing. Also working too much. Then, it seemed like it was too late. The women who are interested in old farts like me are only interested in finding an inheritance for their grandchildren, and rectifying all of the mistakes of their first marriage. Or marriages."

The conversation made Sidney sad. She had married, but as she thought about what made her happy, she knew it had been for the wrong reason. She'd settled for Matt's proposal because she didn't have the imagination or the energy to look for someone more suited to her. Actually, she hadn't made it a goal to look for someone at all. It was the same mistake Philip had made. He didn't make finding a lifelong companion a priority.

"I understand," she said. "I wish I had put more thought into the commitment I made."

"You are married." He said it as if he understood her point, not like he was asking a question.

"Yes. Twenty months now."

"And yet, here you are."

❧

Philip was so polite and so warm that she half expected him to change his mind about having sex that evening, and drop her off at her hotel alone.

But, then again, this was his life: a world of short-term relationships with women willing to sleep with him because he had money, he was good looking, and he was *so* nice.

They finished dinner and drove to the hotel. She was prepared for—and not unhappy about—him staying with her that night, and indeed, he parked in the hotel garage, not on the street. They walked up to the first floor, and he suggested they stop at the bar for a nightcap.

She headed to the restroom while he found seats for them at the bar.

"Sidney?"

She looked up. It was her worst nightmare. Standing between her and the women's room was Matt's best man, Kerry. His best friend.

Oh, shit! Sidney thought. She remembered that he was from Portland. He worked at one of the local mutual fund managers that invested public pension fund money in Oregon. They were early, big investors in Microsoft, and Kerry and Matt had bonded at some investment conference back fifteen or so years ago.

"Oh, Kerry!" she said, forcing a big smile. "So good to see you. What are you doing downtown at this time of night?"

"I live here!" he said, laughing at her question. "But how about you?"

Sidney scrambled for a reasonable explanation, and then realized the real one was the best.

"Fundraising dinner," she said. "Having dinner with a potential donor."

"Oh, yeah," Kerry said. "I read about your foundation. Golf-related, right?"

"What else?" she said, lifting her arms in a quizzical pose

and making a funny face. "Whoda thunk it?"

"Want to have a drink with Karen and me?" he asked. He pointed toward the window where his wife sat. She was a pretty, very young redhead. They'd been married only three months or so, if Sidney remembered right. She and Matt had missed the wedding because he had to be in Europe at the time, plotting the Microsoft's strategy against one of the European Union's antitrust actions.

"Gosh, thanks," Sidney said. She could feel her face turning red with her sudden panic at being discovered. "I would love to, but I have to get back on the road early tomorrow. I'll just have this one obligatory drink with my donor and turn in."

"Sure," Kerry said, leaning in to peck her on the cheek. "You look terrific, by the way. Haven't I seen that dress before?"

Sidney excused herself, went into the women's room, and tried to calm down. She returned to the bar and to Philip, still struggling to relax and get her heart rate down.

"Sorry," she said, nodding at the table where Kerry and his wife were enjoying a dessert and bit of newly-wed footsie. "I ran into an old friend of Matt's."

"Oh." Philip was no dummy. He got the implication immediately. "I will act accordingly."

"Thanks," she said. "This is so awkward. Maybe I should not arrange dates so close to home."

Luckily, Kerry and his wife left the bar before Sidney had finished her Black Russian.

"Are you coming upstairs?" she asked Philip. It wasn't obvious. Gary had been affectionate from the beginning of their day together. Philip had been kind and pleasant, but not demonstrative.

"Is that a yes?" Philip asked, sticking to the Milton Walton protocol.

"Definitely," Sidney said. Her heart wasn't in it, but she

was going to do her best. Philip deserved it.

Upstairs, Philip got right to business, kissing her well and then suggesting she change and meet him in bed. It was so "It Happened One Night" nice. A little staid, but nice.

Sidney had proactively hung her negligee on a hook inside the bathroom. She grabbed a hanger, slipped in, and closed the door. She brushed her teeth, hung up her dress, and slipped on the soft silk sheath. She brushed her hair and stepped back into her Louboutins.

Philip was waiting in the bed, the covers pulled up to his waist, hands locked behind his head on the pillow.

"You look nice," he said. "Please don't turn off the light."

They made love slowly and pleasantly. He held her breasts under the silk sheath, and when he was ready, she didn't mind that he had chosen the missionary position. Philip watched her face as he entered and took his time. She had no problem reaching the point where she begged him to thrust harder. He didn't seem to mind that either.

Philip left sometime after she fell asleep. He wrote a thank-you note on a piece of hotel stationery, and left it for her next to the sink in the bathroom.

"No, thank you," she said out loud when she found it the next morning. That was incredibly nice.

When she got back to the office that afternoon, Sidney called Laurie at the agency and told her she wouldn't take any more dates in Portland. None in Seattle, Spokane, or Vancouver either. They were just too close to home.

Chapter Ten

Karla had won the tournament in Singapore, to everyone's surprise. Surrounded by dozens of incredibly skilled Asians in that part of the world, who would have guessed an over-thirty Caucasian American would have a chance?

Sidney called her as soon as she figured Karla would be back in the States. They talked about the tournament and about Karla's plans for the rest of the season. Karla was slurring her words, like she'd already had a couple of celebratory cocktails by four in the afternoon.

"But, how are things there?" Karla asked when they'd exhausted the subject.

"Well, fundraising is going well. Finally," said Sidney. "And we've started up two chapters already. So, I guess it's all good."

"Well, it sounds like you're not so bored anymore, so that good," Karla said. "How about at home?"

"Not so good."

"As in bad?"

"Let's just say dull."

"Honey, even your wedding was dull," Karla said, giggling.

Sidney was surprised. Not shocked, but surprised. Karla

was better than most at being blunt, but even given the cocktail excuse, she had overachieved.

"Uh, wow, Karla. Sorry I inconvenienced you that weekend."

"Oh, no worries," she said, oblivious to Sidney's hurt. "We had a great time in downtown Seattle. I need to get back there sometime."

Off the phone, Sidney sat at her desk and tried to remember if Karla was right. Was their wedding dull?

☙

Neither she nor Matt wanted a big to-do. They decided on a simple ceremony on the grounds of a winery in Woodinville. They had dinner the night before at the Herb Farm. They called it a rehearsal dinner, but they didn't really need to rehearse anything. They just talked about the ceremony over dessert—Karla and Sidney would walk down the center of the chairs, followed by Matt and Kerry. They'd stand in front of the judge and listen to someone Matt knew sing a song—she wished she could remember which one— and then they'd say their vows and turn around and mingle. Wine would be the beverage of choice, and the winery provided the heavy hors d'oeuvres.

They invited only twenty people to witness the ceremony, including her parents and brother, four of Sidney's LPGA friends sans boyfriends, and a half-dozen Microsofties and their wives.

Her brother couldn't make it. Her parents came, constantly at each other's side. They had become even more codependent in their later years than she remembered. They clung together, seemingly uncomfortable in even small groups. How did they ever become social scientists? she wondered. Doesn't that require getting out in society?

"Your parents are so *cute!*" Karla said, sidling up to

Sidney late in the evening. "They are really in love, aren't they?"

"Not so much in love as joined at the hip," Sidney said. "You should try growing up with that. Yuck."

"Funny thing to be saying on your wedding night."

"Yeah," Sidney looked around to be sure Matt was not close. "I know I'm not as excited as I should be."

"But maybe you guys will turn out like that," Karla said, gesturing at the parents, now huddled together at the very edge of the party, sharing a plate of olives and cheese.

"Yeeuw!"

"It could be worse," said Karla. "My parents weren't speaking by the time I was in kindergarten. By the time I was in high school, they exhibited vocal, open hostility toward each other. The week I left for college, my mom split and went back to the Northeast and left dad in Arizona. I guess my expectations are pretty low when it comes to marriage."

Sidney grimaced. Her desire to get married had never been very strong, and now that she had done it, she wasn't building up much hope for all the happiness people were wishing for her that day.

"Hey, we girls are going to head into Seattle, if you don't mind," Karla said. "It's a rare weekend when we get to go out on a real town and kick up our heels. You don't mind, do you?"

Sidney got the report later: they stayed out all night, leaving the Purple Room wine bar at midnight to join a party in Wallingford at some high-school football coach's house. What a great newspaper photo spread that would have been, Sidney remembered thinking at the time. Imagine the fun the sports columnists would have with that.

∾

It didn't take long for Matt to hear from Kerry. The

news that his best man had run into Sidney at a bar in a Portland Hotel having drinks with an older, well-dressed man reached Bellevue the day she got back to Bellevue.

Audrey, Tee for the Tour's part-time accountant, was in the office that afternoon. She looked up from the spreadsheet she was creating on her computer when Sidney returned early in the afternoon.

"Hey, Sidney," she said, tossing her big red curls. "I don't get it."

"Don't get what?" If Audrey had a bookkeeping question, Sidney wasn't likely to be able to answer it. She knew nothing about accounting; that's why she paid Audrey to manage the books.

Audrey's long fingers paused over the ten-key pad on the right side of her keyboard. "Well, except for the few donors who gave you checks in Chicago, I don't have names and addresses for the other donations you've brought in. They're all made by wire transfer and they're all from offshore accounts. And none of them have contacted us for charitable donation receipts. Doesn't this seem strange?"

Sidney hadn't thought about it before, but Audrey's question was reasonable. The accountant would expect T-Squared to attract the more usual forms of donations— personal checks or checks drawn on business accounts, like the other nonprofits she worked with.

"Yes, a little strange." Sidney nodded. "But is it a problem?" She didn't want her accountant to worry. It would be no good to have her bookkeeper suspecting something nefarious.

Audrey thought for a moment, threading her fingers through her thick hair. It struck Sidney that she was a little vain about her voluptuous, colorful locks. But then, she mused, as remarkable as they were, anyone would have been proud of them.

"No, I don't think it's a problem," Audrey finally

answered. "I just think it's curious. I just wish I knew why they're coming in that way."

Sidney tried to come up with a plausible explanation as fast as she could. Obviously, she couldn't share the real reason her donors were hiding their identity: to keep the FBI from tracking their donations back to them if the agency's escort business was ever investigated. The agency recommended that approach to its customers.

"Maybe they don't ask for receipts because their donations aren't tax deductible," Sidney improvised. "If the donations come from foreign companies, they don't have the same tax benefits as domestic donations, right?"

"Yeah, maybe," Audrey said. "I'll look into it. But it still seems weird that they're all from offshore accounts. We're talking about thirty-one thousand dollars of the approximately forty-five thousand we've brought in so far. That's just weird."

"Hmmm." Sidney stalled and then changed the subject. "But, can you tell me if we're doing well enough to open another chapter? I'm thinking either Phoenix or Palm Springs."

Audrey opened a new Excel spreadsheet on her computer and started clicking away on the keypad again with a skill that impressed and humbled Sidney.

"As long as we bring in twenty thousand in donations a month, one more chapter is possible," her accountant said. "That would give you enough cash flow to pay me and an attorney and to start building up nine months of operating reserves. But that assumes that you won't start taking a salary and that our marketing expenses level off."

"Well, I don't think Matt needs me to make a salary right now," Sidney said. That was the easy part. Matt made plenty of money to support the two of them. But, Sidney wondered, how reasonable was it to expect that she could bring in twenty thousand a month in donations from her escort business? That would require at least four dates a month and a lot of travel, and even then, she'd still be dependent on Matt at home.

Sidney left Audrey to finish her bookkeeping and closed the door to the inner office. She sat at her desk and figured out the amount of travel she'd have to do to raise twenty thousand dollars a month. The only way to make it work would be to take more than one date in each location. If she went to Phoenix, she'd have to make two "appearances," to use the agency's vernacular. It was already complicated trying to coordinate one appearance and a chapter visit at the same time. Arranging two dates at each location would be that much more difficult.

But, I have to do it, Sidney thought. *I have to make this thing a success.*

⊷

That evening, Matt surprised her by coming home shortly after six o'clock.

"You're home early!" she said. "I didn't have anything planned for dinner."

Matt put his briefcase down on the kitchen counter and opened the refrigerator for a beer. He snapped the tab, and stood with one elbow resting on the granite. He watched Sidney choose a bottle of wine from the wine refrigerator and open it.

There was a time, Sidney remembered, when he would have grabbed the corkscrew from her hand and demanded to uncork the bottle for her. She didn't like it when he did that, as if she were incapable of uncorking a bottle by herself. And now, she wasn't sure she liked him not doing it. He didn't care enough to offer?

"Do you want to go out to dinner?" she asked. "How about that Mexican restaurant we used to go to downtown?

Juanita's?"

"Sure," he said. He didn't move while she pulled a wine goblet down from the cupboard and poured a generous glass. She sat down on a bar stool.

It had been a long time since they had spent more than a couple of minutes together, except when they slept side-by-side, not touching, in bed. Matt's gaze was unrelenting, as if he thought he could see through her.

What was he looking for?

They didn't know each other very well, she thought. They got along fine for the first six months of cohabitation and marriage, but even then, they talked very little. And when they did talk, it was about plans for the weekend or the evening, work, golf, or travel arrangements.

To say they had drifted apart since then was an overstatement. They'd never really been together. Sidney knew Matt's political views were fairly conservative, but she had no idea where they came from, what basic philosophy they rested on. If he believed in God—she didn't know. He never asked her if she did either.

What kind of strange relationship had they forged? she wondered, returning his gaze. It certainly wasn't her parents' cloying, mind-melding intimacy. Perhaps that explained things: her marriage was her rebellion against her parents' devotedness. But he had asked her to marry him. Did he know it would end up like this?

Now Sidney wondered if, when she left him, she would want to try again. Would a relationship with anyone else be any different, or was she just not cut out for monogamy?

"I'm going to go check my e-mail, and then let's go," Matt said, finally looking away, grabbing his briefcase, and heading for his den.

Sidney picked up her cell phone and clicked on the text icon. The last text she had received was three days ago from Peter. Her heart jumped a little reading it again.

"Have good time in Portland," he had texted. *"But not too good Im getting jealous!"*

She smiled. Perhaps that was an answer to the question she had tried to unravel in Las Vegas a month before. If Peter was hard to read, it wasn't because he was as inaccessible as Matt, she thought. It was because their relationship demanded distance. They had jobs to do, and neither of those jobs could accommodate exclusivity or overt affection.

❧

"You'll be gone how long next time?" Matt asked after they sat down and reviewed the menus. The hostess at Juanita's had ushered them to a booth, and Sidney was glad for the privacy.

"A week," she said, sipping the beer they'd picked up at the bar while they waited to be seated. "I'm going to Phoenix and Palm Springs right after Christmas. We can only afford one new chapter, and I need to meet with the instructors before we decide."

"How much have you raised so far?"

"A little over thirty grand," she said.

Matt looked a little surprised. But he nodded, and Sidney took that as his version of high praise.

"How much did you get from that guy in Portland?"

"What guy in Portland?" It was Sidney's turn to be surprised.

"Oh, didn't I tell you?" he said. "Kerry called me today. He said he saw you at a bar downtown with an older man."

"Oh, yeah." Sidney tried to recover her composure. "He is one of the donors I met at that dinner down in Las Vegas. Remember?"

"No, I don't remember," he answered. "I wasn't there. Remember?"

155

"No, I mean don't you remember that dinner I went down to Vegas for?"

"Yes, I do. I just really don't know what happened there. Was he the guy who you stayed to meet with the next day?"

His questioning was starting to irritate her, in part because his voice betrayed him. He wasn't just curious, he was suspicious and critical. And, besides, she didn't want to divulge any more "who is who" details.

"No, but he did give us some money," she said.

"How much?"

"I don't remember," she lied.

"You're not having your affair with him?"

"What affair?" She frowned and felt her heart start to pound.

"The one I asked you about last week."

"I'm not having an affair, Matt," she answered testily. "You are a little too old to play these jealousy games, aren't you?"

"What do you mean, too old? Is there an age limit on fidelity?"

"I am not having an affair!" she repeated, too loudly. She looked up to see their waitress standing over them.

"Should I come back?" the young woman asked, looking like she wanted to be somewhere else—anywhere else.

"No, no," Matt said. "We're just having a little marital spat. I'll have the carnitas, please. Flour tortillas."

They finished ordering, and Sidney sat back, leaning against the tall wooden divider of the booth.

"Look, Matt," she said. "I have to travel, and I have to meet with older men with money. I have to play golf with them. That's where the donations are coming from. What else can I do?"

"Isn't Janie helping you with fundraising?" he asked. "Can't you use social media? Direct mail?"

"We are doing all of that," she said. "But so far, we've

brought in less than five hundred dollars that way. It seems that personal appeals work much better."

"Especially if you don't know anything about data analysis," he added for her. He smirked, and shifted to sit sideways in his seat, his back against the wall. He looked around the bar. Sidney had no clue what he was thinking, and she wasn't sure she wanted to know. They sat silently, watching customers come and go, and waitresses pass with armloads of rice and beans, pork, beef, and chicken in various forms of Mexican entrées.

"How is work going?" she asked. "Did your release go okay?"

"Hmmm, what?" Matt had apparently been deep in thought. "Oh, yeah, it was fine. I'm now trying to figure out how I can squeeze through the rest of the year on the budget I have left."

"Well, it's only a little more than a month," she said. "Christmas is just five weeks away."

"No, our fiscal year ends in June," he said, condescendingly. "I thought you knew that. I have seven more months to go, and I've spent too much on this last release and all of those products we spun out this fall."

"Oh." Here was another problem, Sidney thought. His business bored the hell out of her. Maybe it was just because she understood so little about it, or maybe it was the dry, unemotional nature of creating and distributing software. How could anyone get passionate about creating spreadsheet tools for financial managers?

"I have something to ask you." He interrupted her thoughts.

"What?"

"Do you mind if I go back to New Jersey for Christmas? I think this will be the last Christmas I will have with my mom."

"Do you want me to come along?"

"No. It won't be any fun. Why don't you go spend the holidays with your parents? You know, go ice skating, sledding. All of the things you did as a kid."

"How do you know what I did as a kid?" she asked, irritated. "I've never ice skated in my life, and I'm sure as hell not going to go sledding after the pain I went through with this shoulder injury."

"Well, then, just spend some time with your folks."

Sidney considered his suggestion. Given the questions she'd had lately about her relationships with him and Peter, it might make some sense to take her adult perspective and watch her parents for a few days. What was it in their relationship that she had been rebelling against? Just being left out?

Their food arrived, and Sidney sat up. She was hungry. She had driven back from Portland straight to the office and had skipped lunch.

"I'll call them and see if they'll have me," she said.

"Why wouldn't they?" Matt asked.

"They're very focused on each other," Sidney answered. She blew on a spoonful of black beans to cool it off, and then burned her tongue with it anyway. If she were ever to have to design a new insulation for homes, she would consider beans, she thought. They sure held heat for a long time.

Sidney called her parents on Thanksgiving, and asked if she could come for Christmas.

"What about Matt?" her mother asked, not answering her question.

"His mother is dying, and he wants to spend the holidays with her," Sidney said. "I understand, and it's fine with me. So can I come to see you?"

"Well, let me ask your father." Sidney heard the squeak of a hand covering the mouthpiece on her mother's end of the line, and a muffled conversation she didn't even try to parse. Most mothers would have answered "yes!" enthusiastically to a grown daughter's request to come home for the holidays without having to check with her husband. But, her mother wasn't like most.

"Okay," her mother came back on the line. "We think that would be nice. How long will you stay?"

Not how long *can* you stay, but how long *will* you stay. The qualitative difference wasn't lost on Sidney.

"Oh, just a couple of days," Sidney said.

"Okay, fine. Just let us know when you're coming in. Your dad will come to get you."

Oh, my, thought Sidney, sarcastically. The two of them were willing to be separated for the hour or two it would take him to retrieve her at the airport? This was going to be a special day!

She and Matt went to a steakhouse for Thanksgiving dinner, the second time they'd spent an evening meal together in less than two weeks—some kind of record. Sidney wondered if this sudden attention—however frigidly it was delivered—was the result of some kind of guilt trip of his. He didn't really seem to relish her company. They had little to say to each other, and Sidney spent most of the meal thinking about her travel plans and her next few dates.

She called Karla in Phoenix after dinner to wish her a happy Thanksgiving, and ask if she could stay with her a night or two early in January.

"Will it be one or two?" Karla asked.

"You're sounding like my mother," Sidney said.

"What do you mean?"

"Never mind. I don't know yet," Sidney said. "I'm still working on my itinerary. Does it make much difference?"

"Oh, no!" Karla wasn't like her mother. She actually sounded enthusiastic about a visit. "Stay as long as you want. I'll love the company."

Sidney spent the next two days watching shoppers at the big Bellevue mall from the vantage point of a latte stand, and wishing she had someone other than Matt to shop for. She couldn't get her parents a gift; they had expressly prohibited it from the time she was old enough to ask them what they wanted.

Sunday, Matt surprised her by taking a whole day off and spending most of it with her. They played a wet, but surprisingly warm round of golf at Willows near the Microsoft campus. They walked with their bags on their shoulders, without talking, and Sidney couldn't help comparing it with the perfect day she'd had with Gary in California just a month before. It wasn't nearly as much fun, and there was no chance of having a quick dalliance in the bathroom. Even if they'd been so inclined, there were too many golfers on the course.

Sidney outplayed him considerably. She'd been playing a great deal more golf lately than he had, and so that wasn't unexpected. What she didn't expect was his complete silence in response to her impressive drives, birdies, and long putts. He used to at least give her credit for playing golf well. Now her talent seemed only to corroborate his impression of them as a couple: he was the brains, she was the brawn.

Monday, she called Laurie to arrange dates in Phoenix and Palm Springs for the first week of the new year. She was going to need to double up in at least one of the cities if she was going to keep up the fundraising momentum she'd set for herself and keep from arousing more suspicion on Matt's part. She was probably not going to have any dates over Christmas.

Chapter Eleven

Back when she was on the Tour, the couple of weeks before Christmas constituted her major vacation break of the year. Sidney and Karla usually went to Hawaii or to the tip of Baja for some stress-free sun and beach time, limiting their golf practice to a couple of resort-course rounds a week. Sometimes another player or two went along. Getting out of the darkness of Seattle was as much an incentive as finding warmth. The sky over Puget Sound didn't turn light until after eight in the morning, and the sun usually gave up on their corner of the world before four in the afternoon—as if you could tell, given the persistent, heavy cloud cover.

Nothing needed Sidney's attention at the office, and Matt was back to his 14-hour-day work routine. He apologized unconvincingly, off-handedly, saying he had to work extra to catch up before taking off for Christmas.

Suddenly, a trip to Minnesota didn't seem like such a bad idea, even if it would be as dark and much colder there. Maybe the sight of a little snow at Christmas would cheer her up.

The night before she left, she was already in bed when

Matt got home, but he woke her up by dropping his shoes on the floor and shuffling around the bedroom.

"When are you leaving for the East Coast?" she asked.

"The day after you," he said. "How long are you staying in Minnesota?"

Sidney had no reason to rush back before New Year's, so she planned to stay a week. She was thinking that maybe she would try to sneak off and see Peter in Wisconsin after she tired of her parents' quiet neglect.

Matt let himself in under the covers and turned his back to her. It seemed curious, she reflected, that he used to need sex every single night, but recently, he seemed to have forgotten it was even a possibility. Given his limited talent or concern for her satisfaction, she decided she wasn't missing anything.

Matt left for work the next morning after saying goodbye with no more than a peck on the cheek. He said he had slipped a "little something" in her bag for Christmas. She'd find it when she got to Minneapolis. Sidney thanked him and watched from the living room window as he backed out of the driveway.

Suddenly she felt alone and empty. She wished that watching Matt drive away meant that she was going to miss him. But she didn't believe it would, and that made her feel lonelier than ever. Even her parents' inattention and emotionless expectations seemed warm and fuzzy compared with her life with Matt. How had it gone so wrong so fast?

They were just wrong for each other, she concluded, sipping her coffee and staring at the light drizzle out the window. She knew what he was like when he proposed. She knew the day they got married. Why hadn't she been smart enough, brave enough, committed enough to say no?

An hour later, Sidney had pulled her car out of the garage and was putting her suitcase in the trunk when Carrie surprised her by popping her head around the corner.

"Hey!" she said. "Boy, you have been gone a lot. Leaving again?"

"Yes," Sidney said, straightening up and reaching over for a quick hug from her neighbor. "I'm heading back to Minnesota to see my parents."

"Is Matt going with you?" Carrie's face screwed up with puzzlement.

"Uh, no," Sidney answered, slamming the trunk door shut. "He's going back to the East Coast to see his mother. She's probably having her last Christmas, although I'm not sure she's aware that it is Christmas."

"Why aren't you going with him, then?" Carrie asked. They stepped into the garage to continue their conversation out of the steady drizzle.

"Well, he thought it might be better if he went alone," she said. "He actually suggested I go see my parents. The idea hadn't occurred to me. We're not really close these days, you know."

"Yeah, I had that impression," Carrie said. "But are you sure that Matt is actually going home too?"

"I think so," Sidney said, taken by surprise by the question. "Why would you suspect otherwise?"

"I don't know. You've been gone a lot lately, and I just wonder if he hasn't found some other, well …" Carrie paused and scratched her head as if she were trying to figure out if she should continue. "How can I put it? I think he's found some other companionship."

Sidney was dumbstruck. She took a minute to process the implication of Carrie's words.

"Do you have reason to suspect that?" Sidney's voice shook.

"I don't know, Sidney," Carrie said. They locked eyes and Carrie seemed to decide she'd gone too far. Or at least she had brought up her suspicions at the wrong time. "I'm probably just imagining things. Let's talk when you get back."

"What are you talking about?" Sidney asked.

"It just seems when you're gone, he's never home," she said. "I suppose he's just working a lot. But you'd think he'd come home at some point."

"Yes, you would," Sidney agreed. "You mean he's out all night long?"

"Look," Carrie said, looking like she was regretting what she'd already said. "I don't know. Maybe he comes home really late and leaves again before I wake up. I could be wrong."

"Hey, don't worry," Sidney said. "I will see if I can figure it out. It's not like I couldn't tell that something was going on. But, I need some time to think about this."

"Well, don't worry, girl," her neighbor said, putting on a tough grin. "I've got your back. If I figure out what's going on with Matt while you're gone, I'll let you know."

The two women hugged quickly, and Sidney went back into the house for her purse and coat. She was both shaken and encouraged by Carrie's suspicions. While Matt had been suspecting her of having an affair, she had never considered the possibility that he was, too. And yet, wouldn't that explain all his late nights at the office, his recent demeanor? Wouldn't it be good news? Wouldn't it make it easier for her to leave him?

She gathered her things, turned off the light, and left through the garage door. As she pulled out of the driveway, it occurred to her that she was lucky that her fundraising activities didn't take place next door to Carrie.

&

Sidney's parents lived in a neighborhood just northeast of the University of Minnesota campus in an old four-square Craftsman house surrounded by bungalows and other four-squares that had been turned into apartments for student housing. They had bought it in the early sixties for ten thousand dollars, and it was the house Sidney grew up in. It had been run down by neglect and low property values when Ingrid and Torvé had bought it, but over time, spending a little each year, they had it restored to its 1930s perfection.

They were among the last professors in the neighborhood. Most of their colleagues had fled the influx of students, noise, and drunkenness to nicer neighborhoods farther from campus. But Sidney's father didn't like to drive. He preferred to ride his bicycle to campus, even in the winter, and even though his wife drove alone to the same social sciences building every day. Moving farther out would have destroyed not only his exercise routine, but also his image of himself: as the tweeded, bearded old professor, clinging to tradition and parsimony, even though he was ten or even twenty years too young to legitimately inhabit that skin.

Torvé was waiting for her as she exited the secure gates and entered the main concourse at the Minneapolis airport. They hugged superficially. Walking toward baggage claim, they passed through the new mall-like corridors, flanked by trendy stores and Midwestern stalwarts. When Sidney had left for college in Seattle, none of these shopping and dining options existed. People went to the airport to fly somewhere. But, with airlines recommending arrival two hours ahead of flights, and with frequent delays and lengthy layovers, travelers had apparently started to consider shopping and dining at the airport as necessities.

While they waited for her luggage, Sidney brought her father up to date on her charity work. They didn't talk often, and while he was curious about her project, it didn't surprise her that he didn't show any enthusiasm for it.

"And how is Matt?" he asked. She was somewhat surprised that he remembered her husband's name.

"Fine," she said. "He's going to see his mother in New

Jersey. He thinks it's going to be her last holiday."

"And you didn't go with him?" Her father still seemed to find it hard to fathom that other couples weren't joined at the hip like he and her mother were, in spite of the plethora of proof around them.

"No, dad," she said. "To be honest, it hasn't been that great lately. We seem to be living different lives and passing in the night."

"Hmmm," he mumbled. "Maybe you should have better evaluated the risks before you jumped into this."

She chuckled to herself. Was it possible for him to consider any social or psychological situation without putting it into the context of his area of research—risk aversion? He had focused on it for so long, he undoubtedly saw the world mainly through that spectrum.

"Yeah, you are right," she said, not willing to contradict him.

He smiled at her answer. She wondered if he would rather have her world fit his theories than see her happy.

They drove off the highway and onto snow-packed side streets. It seemed so much like home, Sidney thought, even though she'd been away from the bitter cold, snow, and ice of winter for the past thirteen years. Seattle was as far north as Minneapolis, and as dark, but its winters were milder, if wetter. And, much of the time she was on the Tour, she spent entire winters in warm places like the desert or south of the equator.

She pulled her suitcase out of the trunk of her father's Subaru while he held the door from the garage to kitchen open for her. Her mother rose from her easy chair, pulling off her reading glasses and dropping her paperback on the floor as she clumsily strode forward to greet her only daughter.

"Thank you for coming to see us," she said, almost formally. She gave her daughter the same superficial hug that

Torvé had offered at the arrival gates. Then, she walked back to retrieve her paperback from the floor. Sidney caught a glance at the cover. It was a cheap mass-market romance. Her mother had always had a weakness for them, and between those slutty stories and her joined-at-the-hip relationship with her husband, they provided all of the emotional sustenance she needed.

Sidney dragged her roller suitcase up the stairs to her bedroom in the northwest corner of the house. It was the coldest room, facing the brutal winds of winter with minimal insulation. She was glad to see her bed still had a stash of thermal blankets folded at the foot. When she lived at home, they were her lifesavers. She remembered how she would get into bed shivering, but in just ten minutes, her body heat accumulated, trapped by the fluffy wool knits.

She heard her parents' quiet conversation in the living room below. Maybe if she hadn't been so repulsed by their inimitable fidelity, she would have figured out how to love someone that way. Maybe she would have developed a taste for monogamy instead of a love for the stage, for the adoration of one instead of the accolades of many. Maybe she'd be home with a husband—cuddling, warm, and happy—instead of shivering alone in this frigid house, trying to stay out of her parents' and Matt's way.

It was funny, she thought, as she threw her suitcase on the bed and zipped it open. Most people worried that they would repeat the mistakes of their parents. She had assiduously avoided the very thing that defined her parents: their ferocious dedication to each other. And look where it got her? Into a marriage without love—and now even without sex. Into a job that was as much about prostitution as it was about charity.

Her parents had kept her bedroom intact; even her old prom dresses and high school golf uniforms still hung in the closet. Very rarely was overnight company welcomed into this house, lest they disturb the singular, reciprocal focus of her parents on each other.

She walked across the hall and opened the door to her brother's bedroom. In spite of the fact he'd been gone for nearly twenty years, it too lay undisturbed. His sci-fi books cantilevered against each other in the makeshift bookcase. Eric Asimov, Arthur Clark, Robert Heinlein. She'd read them too, long after he had left home, always returning them to his bookcase, conceding they were only on loan. Obviously, he never would have missed them, she realized sadly. He hadn't been back here in two decades.

His high school band uniform hung in the closet along with a few dated shirts and pants, but nothing hung there that would have hinted of what or who he would become when he grew up. Clearly, most people didn't indicate a career preference through their high school wardrobes, she acknowledged. Neither would her closet reveal her future as a prostitute, she hoped.

Consumed with nostalgia and regret, she returned to her own bedroom and unpacked her suitcase. She hung up the dress she had brought for Christmas Eve services at the Lutheran church down the block, and the sweaters, jeans, and boots that would suffice for the rest of the time. She found the "little something" that Matt had hidden in her bag. It was a tennis bracelet: expensive but devoid of personal or romantic significance. He'd included no card, not even a "From" and "To" tag.

Then she lay down on her bed and pulled a blanket up over her legs and torso to her chin. She expected her mother to call her down to dinner soon, but she needed a moment to push back the creeping chill from her room and the cold memories of her childhood. Despite her expectations, she had still hoped she could find some evidence that it was actually a warm, inviting, loving place. It was disheartening to acknowledge the reality that it wasn't.

Outside, the neighborhood was quiet. Most of the students had disappeared for the holidays, either going home to their rural and suburban Minnesota homes, or taking off for Colorado to ski for the holidays, as the upper-middle-class kids had done in her college years. In spite of her mental and physical chill, her mind and body succumbed to the pacifying memory of the known—that room, that neighborhood, the smell of pot roast in the oven, and the muffled commiserating downstairs—and she quickly fell into a deep sleep.

She was awakened by her father and joined her parents at the round Early American dining table that had been her father's gift to her mother on their twenty-fifth wedding anniversary. Her mother had never been an adventurous cook, but she did the basics well. Sidney used to think that if she brought truffle oil home as a present for her parents, it would still be there when she cleaned out their house after their demise.

For the first time she could remember, her parents made an effort to converse with her, and about her life. And, here she was with little she wanted to share. Her new life as a high-end escort and her failing marriage were not exactly topics she wanted to explore with them. Instead, she talked about politics in Seattle, about Karla's success on the tour, about the book club disaster.

"So explain to me what your charity is doing," her mother broke the uncomfortable silence that ensued after Sidney ran out of safe things to talk about.

"We're setting up programs around the country—well, right now, just in the West—that provide top instructors to young women who want to make it on the Tour."

"Why don't their parents pay for that?" her mother asked, pragmatic as ever.

"We are targeting inner-city girls, ones whose parents can't afford greens fees and driving-range balls, let alone instructors."

"But don't the high schools have those things?"

"Some do, some don't. The poorer schools never do. And high school-level instruction isn't going to get anyone on the Tour."

"You got there," her father interjected, "and we never paid for special instructors."

"Well, that was then," Sidney explained. "Now, I'd be competing with a horde of Asian women who have had professional training from age five on, and where the entire culture is focused on golf."

"Entire culture?" her mother asked.

Sidney knew she shouldn't have used any words that brought up any concepts that touched on social science. She was going to be shot out of the water by her parents' insistence that she be more scholarly, more precise when using such terms.

"Okay, bad use of 'culture,'" she said, trying to skip over the issue. "I mean, those countries are maniacally focused on turning out the world's best female golfers."

"But what I don't understand, dear, is why people would donate to this charity," her mother continued. "Why don't you work to eradicate world hunger or the spread of Ebola or something? A bigger problem?"

"Well, there are lots of charities addressing those problems," Sidney said defensively. "This is a unique issue that no one else is focused on." She thought about Betta's family problems in Oakland and Lydia's shyness. "We're giving some young girls a future they'd never have a chance for otherwise."

"Well, I guess as soon as there are no little girls in the world who are starving or dying of malaria, I would consider donating to someone's possible professional career in golf," her mother concluded thoughtfully. She followed the comment with a snicker.

So much for the cozy confines of home, Sidney thought.

✍

By the time Sidney rose the next day, her Midwestern parents had been at their desks, silently working on their scholarly projects for a couple of hours. She called out to them cheerfully and left the house to find the nearest Starbucks. Her cellphone directed her to walk a mile and a half south across the river into downtown.

She met no one on the residential sidewalks until she reached the Mississippi. It was well below freezing, which rarely kept Minnesotans indoors. But the students were gone, and on the day before Christmas, the streets were abandoned. As she crossed the arched footbridge, she noted how many new condo complexes had gone up in recent years between the river and downtown. She nodded silent greetings to office workers shuffling out of them on their way to the office, clad in bulky down coats and Sorel boots, looking as excited about working on Christmas Eve day as she would have been. The resignation on their faces bespoke one thing: "I'm going to get out of there by noon."

Sidney ordered her latte in the Starbucks on the ground floor of a glass bank tower, and sat at a tiny corner table to wait for the barista to work her way through the six orders lined up on the counter before hers. She checked her messages. She had turned off the phone the night before in deference to her parents, who anachronistically held onto the belief that no one should ever call after dinner unless there was a death in the family.

She was surprised to find a missed call from her Milton Walton manager. Who would be looking for an escort this week? she wondered. Next week, New Year's Eve, sure. She might expect that. But the day before Christmas seemed a bit strange. She returned the call, but Laurie's voice mail

171

message indicated she was out until the day after Christmas.

It must not have been an emergency, Sidney thought, smiling at the idea that needing an escort could be considered an emergency. Certainly not up to the equivalent of her parents' "death in the family."

Sidney spent the entire morning wandering around the streets, looking in a few shops, noticing what had changed in the dozen years since she'd been home. New high-rise apartment buildings had brought a plethora of new, young residents downtown in recent years, and as the day progressed toward noon, they tumbled down onto the street and filled up pricey new cafes and coffee shops, as focused on tiny screens in front of them as young people were anywhere in the country.

When she returned to the house a few hours later, her parents were gone. They left a note for her: lunch was whatever she could find in the refrigerator, and they were out at a small Christmas lunch with some colleagues. Sidney was glad she hadn't been asked to go along. If her parents made her feel undereducated, an entire lunch table of psychologists and sociologists would probably make her feel like an idiot.

Christmas Eve services at her parents' Lutheran church were more casual than she remembered them as a child. As atheists, her parents attended out of a sense of social responsibility, more an act of community support than a religious gesture.

Sidney had always gone along for the singing. She loved Christmas carols, even though the day after Christmas she knew she would cringe at the sound of one of them on the radio. When Christmas was over, she wanted it to go away. Even lingering Christmas decorations irritated her.

Sitting in the pew next to her mother, Sidney looked around for high-school classmates. Only a dozen years or so had passed since she graduated; she expected to recognize someone, even if she couldn't remember all their names. She had been confirmed in this church when she was twelve, along with thirty other members of her high-school class. Surely she wasn't the only one who had returned home for Christmas this year.

Her search was futile, and she stopped trying. But, after the service. shuffling out of the nave toward the front door and the cold night air, her parents stopped to talk with a couple she recognized. Blake's folks. How could she forget them? What she remembered most was how clueless they were when she and Blake were making out—and one very memorable prom night doing more than that—in their basement. His parents slept soundly upstairs, assured that their perfect son, destined for Harvard Business School, would never do anything to disappoint them.

"Blake will be back tomorrow," his mother announced to Sidney. "He took his wife down to Madison to stay with her parents for a few days. She's pregnant, you know. It's a boy!"

Her bubbly joy was lost on both Sidney and her parents, but they congratulated her.

"Maybe I'll have Blake call you," the prospective grandmother suggested. "You can catch up on old times."

Old times would include that prom night, senior year, when she lost her virginity to Blake, Sidney thought. Golf-team soul mates, they had kissed and fondled for a good year. They started going out as juniors, and team trips around the Minneapolis suburbs and his parents' naïveté gave them plenty of opportunities to fumble around the edges of sex, but never enough time or privacy to bring their young fascination with each other's bodies to its logical conclusion.

After the prom, they had changed clothes and joined their classmates at an all-night party, chaperoned at someone's parents' house. Sidney and Blake left quietly after an hour or so, fortified with sufficient amounts of cheap wine and beer to experiment with "going all the way." Blake parked his old Dodge Dart a block away from his house, and they snuck into his basement, with the plan to have oral sex—an alternative to the scary prospect of losing her virginity and risking pregnancy. She had promised to give him a blow job, and he said he would try cunnilingus, although just saying the word made him giggle nervously.

Not wasting any time, he sat on the old vinyl couch in the family room, and she settled down on her knees between his legs. He unzipped his pants and pulled his briefs down enough to free his floppy penis. She looked up at his determined eyes, frightened.

"I have no idea what to do," she whispered. "What if I hurt you?"

His face softened, and he pulled her up onto his lap and kissed her. At first, they explored each other's lips and tongues familiarly, but then with a purpose they'd never had before. Without talking about readjusting their plans, he lay back on the slippery plastic, and she straddled him.

Sidney remembered how much it hurt, but also how kind Blake had been afterward. She was fairly sure his orgasm hadn't met his expectations either, formed as they were by private masturbations to Playboy pages that overpromised the breast size of the average North American woman. Together, they cleaned the blood off the shiny vinyl, and then held each other and listened to their favorite, ancient Cheap Trick albums until they had calmed down enough to sneak back out of the house and rejoin the chaperoned overnight party.

Christmas was bright and cold. True to tradition, Sidney's parents made a brunch of scrambled eggs with chipped beef. She was surprised and pleased to find they had added mimosas to their Christmas menu in recent years.

They toasted the day and settled down to open her presents.

She received two "fascinating"—according to her father—nonfiction tomes written by her parents' colleagues, and she spent the rest of the day, lazily thumbing through them, refilling her mimosas until the champagne ran out. She made some eggnog with a bottle of bourbon she suspected had been in the pantry since before she left for college, and switched to a novel she had started on her Kindle on the flight to Minnesota.

They had leftover pot roast for dinner, and cordially bid each other a merry Christmas and good-night, and Christmas was over.

Sidney had no idea why she was so tired, but she slept until after nine the next morning, awakened by the ding of her cell phone. She reached over to answer it, and knocked it off the night stand. By the time she retrieved it from under the bed, the ringtone had stopped and she saw that she'd missed another call from Laurie.

"I'm so sorry," Sidney said once she got Laurie back on the line. "I have reverted to my teenage clumsiness. I'm back in Minneapolis for Christmas."

"So I hear," Laurie laughed. "One of our customers called and wanted to know if you're available tonight."

"Someone knew I was in Minnesota?"

"Yes, actually, he called two days ago, but I couldn't get ahold of you. Apparently he knew you a long time ago, and his parents told him you were coming to town."

Sidney knew. It would be Blake. The idea of seeing him again made her smile.

"Sure, I'll see him," she told Laurie. "But it's odd he didn't just try to call me. He could have gotten my number from my parents."

"Hey, don't knock it, girl," Laurie said. "This way it's worth real money. Maybe this is how he lets you know that he doesn't just want to have coffee with you."

Right! Sidney thought. A call to her parents' house would be appropriate if he wanted to catch a movie or have dinner while his wife was out of town. A call through the agency meant he wanted to reprise their youthful fumbling. Except it likely wouldn't be fumbling anymore, and they certainly weren't young.

She was to meet Blake mid-afternoon at an indoor driving range in Edina. She'd receive his dossier—totally unnecessary in this case—by e-mail.

Sidney accepted the date with mixed feelings. She didn't know Blake's wife; he and Sherry had met at Harvard, so Sidney had no facial image to disturb her as the date progressed. But was it fair to charge Blake her usual fee when she probably would have accepted the meeting for what it should be: a sweet reunion—with benefits—of old friends?

Chapter Twelve

When Sidney pulled into the parking lot of the driving range, Blake was waiting, leaning up against his SUV and chatting on a cellphone.

Thirteen years had passed since they had seen each other, but there was no mistaking who he was. He was handsome—not a surprise, she noted, getting out of her parents' car and clicking the lock button on the key fob. He had been a pretty boy and a "cute" teenager, in the vernacular of teenagers.

Walking carefully across the ice and packed snow between the cars, she waved. He ended his phone conversation and opened his arms to greet her. His hug was warm, and he held her for a long minute.

"You look absolutely terrific, Sidney," he said, finally pushing away and holding her shoulders at arms' length.

"And you, Blake," she responded. "You've become a very handsome man. Why did I ever let you go?"

He laughed. Gloved hand in gloved hand, they entered the big dome, letting out a warm blast of air. Inside, Blake handed her a shoe box.

"I didn't figure you had any golf shoes with you," he said. "I asked your mom to spy on you and get your size."

Sidney shook her head. The brand-new Footjoys were

the top of the line.

"Blake!" she said. "These must have cost more than two hundred dollars!"

"Well, merry Christmas, then," he said. He leaned over and kissed her on the cheek. "I would think that you would only play in the best."

"Well, thanks," she said. "But I don't have my clubs with me either. Could you buy me a new set of Pings?"

"Don't push your luck, lady." Blake laughed. "We're both playing with rentals today."

Most of the forty-six bays were occupied, but they found a couple of mats at the far end of the range on the lower level. Sidney stretched for a few minutes. She hadn't swung a club in about three weeks, and since her fundraising success depended on her ability to play golf with her dates, she wanted to ensure she didn't injure herself swinging with cold muscles.

She touched her toes and did some lunges behind Blake, watching him execute some short-iron shots.

"Nice tempo," she said. "You haven't lost it, have you?"

"Thanks," he said. "I don't play much anymore, but I have never stopped loving this game. It's how we grew up, Sidney."

"Or in my case, how I'm growing up," she joked. "If it weren't for golf, I wouldn't have much of anything going for me."

"Other than your stellar looks," he said.

As she set up for a few warm-up chip shots, Sidney thought about that. Being with Blake suddenly put her in a long-term frame of mind. They'd known each other for twenty years, ever since junior high school. Looking ahead another twenty years, what would she have going for her? Looks fade. Even golf games fade. She hoped she wouldn't still be working as an escort, even if her proficiency with sex didn't fade.

Working through the rental clubs from short irons to the driver, Sidney let her mind go blank. Golf was even better than sex that way: she could forget every worry, every problem, every duty and responsibility, and just focus on her set-up, her backswing, her weight shift, her downswing, her follow-through.

After a while, she sensed she was attracting a few admirers besides Blake. They stood respectfully behind her and whispered as she transitioned from warming up to full swings. No one else in the facility was hitting balls as well as she was, she guessed.

Eventually, the crowd dispersed, and Blake put his clubs in his bag and waited behind her.

"Ready to go?" she asked.

"Only when you are," he said, sitting back as if he could watch her swing all day. "Have you ever noticed how incredibly sexy a good golf swing can be?"

Sidney set up and swung with the driver. The ball sailed out and hit the fabric at the other end of the range. She turned and slipped the club into the bag.

"Actually, I was playing with a guy in California a few weeks ago, and I was thinking the same thing," she said, remembering her date with Greg. She didn't mention how she felt about Peter's swing; it was too powerful to share. She picked up her bag.

"Are you trying to make me jealous?" Blake laughed.

"No, but I could see why you might be," she said, winking at him, and then turned serious. "You know, Blake, this is just a bit awkward for me."

"Yeah, I guess it is for me too," he said. "Let's go get a hot toddy and talk."

જ

In her parents' car, Sidney followed Blake's BMW to a

bar closer to downtown Minneapolis.

He was still easy to be with, she acknowledged, in spite of the fact he had become a very successful investment banker at his own Minneapolis financial concern. Yes, they had been an item back in high school, but even then, she didn't remember their relationship as romantic. He always seemed more interested in her for her willingness to "mess around" and for her abilities—grades, golf—than for her personality, than who she *was*.

But what did that mean? she wondered. What is a person other than what they do? Is it their history? Their values? Their opinions? How much of those do you have, let alone share, as a teenager? If they'd stayed together past adolescence, could they have built something more substantial together?

She hadn't ever considered it. She got a scholarship to play golf at the University of Washington. He went to Harvard to study economics. It wasn't a difficult parting. It wasn't emotional. It was full of hope.

The bar Blake chose was new but on the inside, it looked ancient. It had an old medieval-castle ambiance with a huge fireplace that took up the entire wall across from the entrance, and a dark bar and dark tables made from rough-hewn wood. Not surprisingly, the room was nearly empty the day after Christmas. Most people were still celebrating the holidays, and in-laws weren't sick enough of each other yet to need an escape to a tavern.

Settling into a deep red leather chair at a table, Sidney let her eyes adjust to the dim light and waited for Blake to return with drinks from the bar. She relished the homey Midwest feeling she was getting from huddling indoors on a short winter day with snow blanketing the cold, quiet world outside.

"When did you become a Milton Walton customer?" she asked him as he set her red wine down and took the seat next to her with a big mug of beer.

"A year ago," he said. "And, I heard that you joined as a client about two months ago. Is that right?"

"Yup," she said. "Were you surprised?"

Blake considered her question for a couple of minutes, sipping his beer and wiping the foam off his lip.

"You know, I was surprised," he said. "I remember you as a woman of many talents and many brains, and I wondered why you chose this path."

"Money," Sidney said. "Not money to live on. Matt has made plenty of that and I don't need a salary. But I need money for my charity, and until we build momentum from some successes getting girls on the Tour, it's hard to pull in the donations."

Blake sat quietly. He was clearly happy to see her, but he seemed sad about the circumstances.

She didn't like to think that she was a disappointment to Blake. They hadn't seen each other in thirteen years, but somehow, his approval meant more to her than her parents' or Karla's. More than Matt's.

"Why did you call the agency to see me instead of just calling my mom's house?" she asked.

"I didn't want to take advantage of you," he said. "I'm a customer; you're a client. I didn't want to circumvent the rules."

"Okay," Sidney said. "Let me be honest. I don't have any skills beyond golf. I wish I did. I wish I had some business expertise. Finance. Accounting. Something! But, after eight years on the Tour and no real work experience, I have nothing to offer. This was the only way I knew to be successful again."

"You mean, by selling sex?"

It hurt to hear him say that.

"No, by running a successful charity," she said. "I said the escort business was just a way to jump-start the fundraising."

"Does Matt know?"

Sidney shook her head.

"Does your wife know you are a customer?" she asked.

Blake explained that his wife was eight months pregnant, and he had not had sex with her since then. The night they had conceived, he'd waited nearly a year for her to relent to sleeping with him. He didn't tell her about his Milton Walton membership, but he believed she was relieved that he gave up asking for sex.

"Why?" Sidney was shocked. She could see no reason why any sane woman—heterosexual woman, that is— wouldn't be perfectly happy to be in bed with him.

"I don't know," he said. "Sally comes from a Calvinist family in Boston. I think she's got religious issues that started way back in her childhood. I wish I'd known, but I thought she was just a stickler about premarital sex. I didn't know she didn't like it in general. But don't get me wrong, I'm happy to be starting a family."

"Where is she today?"

"I took her down to Madison to visit her parents for the week," he said. "It will be the last time she'll travel for a while until after the baby comes."

Their frank talk about sex brought her back to prom night, the plastic couch, the mess they made; how he'd asked her for a blow job, and instead they ended up "doing it." Wasn't the old vernacular funny? "Doing it." "Going all the way." Kids these days probably just said "fuck."

"So how is it for you, having sex with all of these strangers?" Blake asked, interrupting her reverie.

"Weird," Sidney said, nodding. "Generally not creepy though. Most of the time, it's actually fun. Turns out I really like sex, which obviously helps. And really, it's not a whole lot different from my sex life before I got married. You know, lots of one-night stands. I guess the difference is I get paid for it now. And by and large, Milton Walton customers are a little higher class than your average Seattle barfly."

"Why do you work with the agency instead of just going out on your own?" he asked.

Sidney chuckled. It would be just like him to analyze the business model rather than the morality of her career choice.

"I feel safer this way," she said. "The customers are all approved by Milton first, and then they're vetted by more experienced clients before I ever see them. And, given the prices we charge—both my take and Milton's fee—we're assured a certain kind of client."

"Well, you know what?" Blake said. He leaned in over the table, his face close to hers. "All of this talk of sex is making me awfully horny. Are you willing to give it a try for old times' sake?"

Sidney smiled. To relay her answer, she tipped her wine glass up and drained the liquid down her throat.

"Let's go see what trouble we can get ourselves into," she said. "Should I drive myself?"

Sidney followed Blake downtown, through quiet streets, and he let her follow him into the garage of one of the new high-rise condos she'd admired a couple of days before. They rode up the elevator together and entered a surprisingly modern space with high ceilings, polished concrete floors, huge floor-to-ceiling windows, mid-century furnishings, and stainless steel cabinets and appliances.

"Wow!" Sidney exclaimed. "You guys live here?"

"No," Blake shook his head sadly. It was obvious that he wished he did. "My wife is a suburban girl. We're living in Edina. This is my corporate apartment; I put up clients here. I reserved it for myself this week to get away from the 'burbs while Sherry is in Madison. I don't have any clients in town over the holidays."

Blake opened a sleek pewter cabinet in the living room section of the open floor plan and turned on the music. "I hope you don't mind jazz," he said. "Remember I used to play trumpet in high school? I always wanted to be the next Miles Davis."

"I do remember," Sidney said, taking a seat at the breakfast bar. "I once had a plastic turkey with a solar-powered neck that nodded in five-fourths time."

Blake laughed. "At first I thought that was the worst nonsequitur of all time, but that's pretty funny. 'Take Five.'"

He opened a cupboard and reached up for a cocktail glass. "Drink?" he asked. "What's your poison of choice?"

"Wine, actually, if you have any," she said. "Just not Merlot or Chardonnay."

"The two most popular wines in America," he said, replacing the cocktail glass and pulling down two wine goblets. "It would be just like you to be the iconoclast even in your wine choices."

"Or maybe I'm just difficult," she said. "Iconoclast sounds far too interesting."

Blake opened a bottle of wine. "Tell me what this is," he challenged, handing a glass across the counter. He turned the label away from her so she couldn't cheat.

She smelled and tasted the wine. "I'm guessing Syrah, but it might be a Rhône blend," she said. "I'm not that good at this."

"Yes, it is a Rhône blend," he said, smiling approvingly. "Not bad for a girl from Minnesota."

"I've been living in Washington for the past thirteen years," she said. "Almost fourteen. You should be pleased to know that I have learned something in that time."

"Come over here." Blake walked into the spacious living room and wiggled a finger, beckoning Sidney to join him. He put his glass down and reached for her shoulders. He kissed her softly, and pulled her close. They held each other for a long minute, and Sidney felt a wave of nostalgia sweep over her. Blake pushed away, and she wiped her eyes.

"I know we parted without regrets way back when," he said, as they sat down on the couch, facing a panoramic view of snowy downtown Minneapolis. "But I'm starting to wonder why."

Sidney said nothing. She didn't want to trigger any more tears by talking about a time that was all about hopes and possibilities, and not about regrets or failure or limits.

"Hey, I'm sorry," Blake said, putting his hand on hers. "I know we're too far down our separate paths to try to make anything more of this than what it is."

He pulled her close again, and she laid her head against his shoulder.

"I don't want your money," she said softly. "I want to sleep with you … No, that's not exactly right. I want to make love with you. But I don't want your money."

"I already sent it."

"I'll send it back."

"Whatever makes you happy, Sidney, but trust me. I won't miss it. Keep it and help some young girl become the next Sidney Stapleton. Help someone win five tournaments and grow up to be a beautiful, capable woman."

Sidney immediately thought of Betta. She looked up at his face and smiled.

"Hey, I don't want to rush things," she said, "but I think I still owe you a blow job."

Blake laughed and sat up straight. "Yes you do!"

Sidney put her glass on the coffee table, pushed it away from the couch, and sat down on her knees between his legs. She unbuckled his belt and unzipped his pants. He had already started to stiffen, and she freed his erection from his boxers.

Did she remember this? she wondered. Was he this big back thirteen years ago on prom night? She started to put him in her mouth when he reached down and lifted her up by her arms.

"No," he said. "I want to do this the right way. Just like we did before, except better. And this couch isn't plastic. Let's go to bed."

❧

They made love slowly, quietly, conventionally. It was the sweetest sex Sidney could remember. Afterward, she turned her back to him, and they spooned. He fell asleep immediately, and she fell asleep more slowly, shedding silent tears over feelings that she had no words for.

She slept for an hour or so, and then slipped out of bed and got dressed. She wrote a thank you note and placed it on the bed beside him. She kissed him on the forehead. He looked so calm, so innocent. She was sorry that his wife didn't appreciate him—at least the part of him she had just shared.

"I think you will make a good father," she whispered, smoothing his long bangs back over his head. "Goodbye, Blake."

Driving back to her parents' house on the dark, icy streets, Sidney wondered where she should go next. Heading back to Seattle made little sense to her. Yes, her home was there. Yes, her charity was there. But it all seemed like make-work, not like her life's work. And together, her sad marriage and her charity had drawn her into this life of prostitution, a life that had clearly disappointed Blake, even if it had brought them back together for an afternoon.

Maybe, she thought as she pulled into the driveway, it was time to call Peter and see if he was doing anything in Wisconsin. He was the only person she could imagine wanting to be around. She turned off the car and reached for her cell phone.

He didn't answer. She left a message and went inside to give her parents the Reader's Digest version of her reunion with Blake—the condensed, sex-free version.

ॐ

Peter called her back the next morning, and she answered the phone while still in bed. He sounded like he was next door, but he told her he was in Paris, "the city of lights."

"This is the best place in the world to celebrate Christmas," he professed. "I walk the streets, look in the shops, eat fine food, take in the lights, watch lovers stroll arm-in-arm, slipping on the snow."

"Do you always do this?" she asked.

"Yes, at least for the past ten years. I would love you to come along next time, Sidney."

"Wouldn't that spoil it for you?"

"Quite the opposite," he said.

Sidney wasn't sure if he was expecting an answer to his invitation. It was so unexpected and next Christmas was so far off. She decided to change the subject.

"Is the weather nice there?" she asked. "It's colder than bejeezus here."

"I heard you had a date there in Minneapolis. Not bad, considering how quiet the holidays usually are for the agency."

"Wow! Word gets around fast in your world!" Sidney exclaimed. "It turned out to be an old high school friend."

"Did you know that before he showed up?"

"Of course," she laughed. "Remember I get a dossier beforehand."

"Oh, right. So how was it seeing an old flame?"

"Actually, it made me nostalgic and a little sad."

"Why sad?"

"I realized how much potential I once had, and now I'm sleeping with men for a living. That's sad."

Peter didn't respond. The line went silent for a few seconds, and Sidney wondered if they'd lost their connection.

"Sidney," he finally said. "I know this is a long distance call, and it's probably not the best way to break this to you, but I have something I have to say. It can't wait any longer."

"What?" Sidney was puzzled.

"It used to be that being in Paris at Christmas didn't make me lonely. In fact, it was the opposite. But now, this year, all I can do is think of you. I thought being here—my little tradition—would help me shake it off, but Sidney, I am in love with you."

She sat up in bed.

What is he saying? Is he crazy?

Images of the last time she saw him flashed through her mind. It was in Vegas. They had played golf, went bowling, ate dinners and lunches together, and made love at least a dozen times. It was the best week of her life, even surpassing the weeks when she won tournaments back on the Tour.

He had been attentive and loving, but she never thought that meant he actually *loved* her. And even as their affection had built over the week, she was certain it was episodic. She couldn't assume it would last. And then she signed up with the agency, and they'd done nothing but talk on the phone since then.

Sidney felt a huge lump in her throat. She should have been thrilled; instead she was afraid and confused. She was certain that she didn't love him. Or did she? Was she worried that whatever she did feel for him, it would dissipate the second she accepted his affection? She had said "yes" to Matt, and that was the beginning of the end of their chance at love.

After an awkward pause, she decided to say nothing. It seemed to be the wisest choice, given her ambivalence. She pretended she hadn't heard what he said.

"Hey, so when will I see you again?" she said cheerfully.

Silence. Peter seemed at a loss for what to say. No doubt he had expected her to reciprocate instead of ignoring his "I love you."

"The agency party the middle of January," he answered finally, flatly.

"Oh, yeah."

"You are coming down to Vegas for it, aren't you?"

"Yes, I have a date already set for that week as well," she said. "A former professional golfer like your friend Greg."

"Great," he said. He didn't sound like he thought it was.

"Hey, I'd better go," he said, suddenly in a hurry. "It's starting to get dark here already, and I need to get moving if I'm going to get to dinner. Take care, Sidney, and I'll see you in three weeks."

He hung up quickly, and Sidney put the phone on the bed table. She lay back in her childhood bed and tried to understand what had just happened. He was wonderful—the most attractive, sexy, sweet, lovable man she'd ever met. With a great golf swing. But did she love him? And, if she did, why didn't she know it?

Chapter Thirteen

Sidney stayed two more days in Minneapolis with nothing to do but walk the quiet, snowy streets and think about her life. She reached no conclusions, and in the end, she realized the only place she could go was back to Seattle, her charity, and Matt.

Driving home from the airport, Sidney took a call from Janie, her marketing and PR guru.

"Hey, we have finally gotten a call from that nonprofit reporter who attended your original press conference," she said. "She wants to know how you're doing. If the numbers are impressive enough, we might get a nice story out of this."

Sidney did the quick math in her head. With Matt's original ten-thousand-dollar contribution, Peter's twenty thousand, and all of the contributions from her dates, she'd reached more than sixty-five thousand. The small mail-in contributions and the money she collected in Chicago brought her fundraising total to almost seventy thousand dollars in the first four months.

Not bad, she thought to herself. If she could bring in triple that in her first year, she could easily support five or six chapters. If she managed to nurture a Tour player out of half of them, three women might someday owe their Tour careers—however short or long—at least in part to her efforts.

She settled into a routine of going to the office mid-morning, taking care of whatever small amount of business needed to get done, and then she called her instructors in Oakland and Portland to chat about how the girls in their programs were getting along.

Blake had sent five thousand dollars for their date in Minneapolis, and when she called his office to find out how to return it, his administrative assistant talked her out of it.

"Blake told me to tell you that he wants to contribute to your charity," she said. "Just because you were old friends, he said, doesn't change things." It was clear that she didn't know the whole story. Sidney hoped no one back in Minnesota did.

A few days later, she and Janie met with the reporter at a Starbucks on First Avenue in Seattle. She was young—not surprising, Sidney reflected. There wasn't enough money in the newspaper business anymore to pay decent salaries. Only young and idealistic kids and old and stymied geezers with nowhere else to go were willing to work that hard for so little pay.

Sidney didn't expect Annie to be impressed with her fundraising numbers. After all, she covered the local nonprofit hospitals and the Bill and Melinda Gates Foundation with their millions of dollars in endowments and huge annual contributions.

But she was wrong. At least Annie made her feel like her success was notable.

"How have you managed, starting from scratch, to find so many donors?" Annie asked in the interview.

"Our success is largely built on individual donations by successful businessmen—pretty much all of whom play golf on the weekends," Sidney told her. She wanted to keep as close to the truth as she could without hinting at her illegal activity.

"How do you meet them?" Annie wanted to know.

"Networking," Sidney said. "Many of these successful guys know each other, and after I meet with one, I usually get introduced to a couple of others."

"So do you call them, or send them direct mail? Or is it social media?"

"Well, I hate to tell you, but there's no magic to it. Social media certainly isn't the answer for my audience. It's mainly shoe leather and a lot of travel," Sidney said. "It takes one-on-one appeals. If I couldn't cover my own travel expenses, I don't know that we would be as successful."

She saw Janie frown. Her PR guru wanted her to assign some of her success to the Facebook page and Twitter accounts she'd set up for T-Squared. It just wasn't true. Sidney hoped Janie would never know the real key to her fundraising prowess, but she wasn't interested in helping her score new PR clients by crediting trendy social-media gimmicks that hadn't done a thing.

In the car heading back to Bellevue after the interview, Janie sat stiff and mute. At first, Sidney decided to ignore her mood. She was paying the woman good money, and it wasn't Sidney's fault that most of her funds had nothing to do with Janie's efforts.

"Tell me how your fundraising trips go," Janie asked, finally relenting to Sidney's indifference. "What makes them work?"

"I play golf and have dinner," Sidney said. "These guys are suckers for playing with quote-unquote celebrities. How do you think all of those PGA players' foundations are so successful?"

"Yes, but you're no PGA player," Janie sneered.

"Well, thanks for reminding me," Sidney said. What was Janie worried about? Whatever the reason for it, T-Squared's success was Janie's success. "But my donors get to play one-on-one with me instead of attending some pro-am tournament where they get two minutes with Phil Mickelson."

"Well, you're lucky that Matt is supporting all your travel," Janie said, contempt dripping from her words. "Without his money, you wouldn't be able to do it that way."

"I agree, and I said that," Sidney said, straining to not react to Janie's attitude. "But it's clear that we wouldn't be anywhere if we were depending on contributions from our social media or direct mail campaigns."

"Maybe they would work better if you focused on them," Janie countered, her voice rising. "Maybe if you wrote a weekly blog. Or tweet something about your sessions with the girls. Things like that."

Janie was being ridiculous, Sidney thought. Just a few weeks ago, Janie had encouraged her to increase her "one-on-one" marketing efforts. Why was she dissing her for her success now? So far Janie's "professional" marketing efforts had raised about two thousand dollars, while Sidney had brought in about thirty times as much through her not-so-conventional efforts. Sure, if Janie had come up with the Facebook-centric bucket challenge before ALS had, maybe they would have made some progress. But throwing a bucket of ice over somebody's head to help find the cure for a lethal disease was a heck of a lot more appealing than doing it to help some kid become a pro golfer.

Still, Sidney didn't want to raise any suspicions about her fundraising technique. It was better to agree with Janie than belabor the discussion.

But, how had their relationship soured so fast? Sidney wondered. Hadn't only a month or so passed since they had drinks together in the hotel bar in Bellevue?

The next day, Janie called her at the office.

"I'm sorry, Sidney," she said, "but I am going to have to resign your account."

"Why?" Sidney knew things hadn't gone well between

them the day before, but this abrupt resignation was still a shock.

"I don't think you value my advice," Janie said. "You aren't even trying to follow it. I suggest some fairly well-tested concepts, and you ignore them."

Sidney paused. She had nothing to say. What she really thought was *your advice is worthless*, but it seemed a bit harsh, and perhaps premature. Maybe if she tried ...

"I understand," Sidney said. "I hope that we can work together again in the future. Maybe you'd be willing to work on special projects or events for us?"

"I don't know," Janie demurred.

Sidney might have been imagining things, but it sounded like something other than a disagreement about social media was at the bottom of Janie's desertion. "Is there something else you're not telling me?" she asked.

"What do you mean?" Suddenly Janie sounded defensive. Sidney couldn't figure it out. What was really going on? Surely, Janie had no inkling of her escort business, did she?

"I don't know," Sidney said, trying to smooth things over. "It just seems like your decision was kind of sudden."

"Yeah, well, I think I've run into a conflict of interest," Janie said.

"What? Another charity? Can't you work with more than one charity?"

"No, it's not that," Janie said. Now she sounded exasperated. "It's just a decision I had to make. I have to run, though, Sidney. I'll send you my final invoice this afternoon. I've discounted it to make up for my sudden departure."

And, that was that, Sidney thought as she put down the phone. It seemed odd, and in a way, a bit scary. She didn't know if she could keep up the travel and energy needed to raise money through her escort business, and someday, she'd want to give it up and return to more traditional marketing.

Who would she turn to then?

❧

Karla's rambler in an older neighborhood of Scottsdale was close to the Phoenician, where Sidney sat down with two prospective T-Squared instructors at an outdoor café overlooking one of the resort's three nine-hole courses. Sitting in the sun, sipping iced tea, and listening to them describe how they would work with young talent, she couldn't help but let her mind wander.

Wouldn't it be nice to live somewhere like this where it is warm in January? she wondered.

"Sidney?" Kevin, the instructor with the blonde hair, nudged her out of her reverie.

"Oh, sorry," she said. "I'm not used to this much sun in January. I must have drifted off."

"So when will you decide which chapter you open next?"

"Later this month," she said. "I'm hoping to have another influx of donations this month, and then we'll be set."

"Who are your donors?" Brad, the other instructor chimed in.

"Hmmm," she started, tentatively. How to describe them?

"Generally, older, wealthy golfers with professional careers."

"You mean retired golf pros?"

"No, I mean careers in the professions. Like lawyers, doctors, and such."

"Why don't they contribute to the First Tee instead?" Kevin asked.

"Um, I'm not sure," she said, thinking that she should probably have an explanation.

One of the keys to good fundraising was the differentiation of the appeal. Donors could pick and choose any charity they wanted; her task was to find that emotional trigger that pulled them her way. But, so far, her differentiation was in her fundraising technique. Sex with her was not so much an emotional trigger as it was an ego boost and entertainment for the donor.

"I suppose that the donors like the idea of investing—at least emotionally—in a possible future LPGA star." Sidney finally answered.

"Sure," Kevin said. "It's like the Tour guys who get hometown investors to help start their golf careers. Like Zach Johnson."

"I'm playing with one of my potential donors here tomorrow," Sidney said. "Maybe you can ask him why he prefers T-Squared to the First Tee."

She might kill two birds with one stone with the suggestion. If she ran into one of the instructors the next day while she was on her golf date, she wanted to make sure they saw it as an innocent fundraising meeting. And, by listening in to her date's response, she might gain some intelligence that would help her fashion social media and mail solicitations in the future.

She stayed with Karla that night. They grilled a steak and had dinner on the patio by Karla's pool, listening to the heavy holiday shopping traffic on nearby Scottsdale Road. Karla begged her to stay another night or two, but Sidney told her she had to rush off to Palm Springs and then on to Oakland to work with Betta and her instructors.

In truth, she wasn't rushing off to Palm Springs. She was staying two more nights—one at the Phoenician, and one at the Princess Resort in north Scottsdale, each night with a different golf partner.

"You know, I have a funny feeling," Karla said as they settled down on the patio after cleaning up their dinner mess.

"About what?"

"I just feel like something is going on that you're not telling me about," Karla said, tilting her head as if trying to figure out what it was.

"Why do you think that?"

"Well, on the one hand, you say running the charity is kind of boring, but on the other hand, you have this nervous energy, like you're excited about something. I know it's not Matt either. Are you having an affair?"

"Ha, that's kind of funny," Sidney said, trying to sound more calm than she felt. "Matt asked me the same thing."

"So? ...."

"No, not an affair," Sidney said. "It's just business."

"So there's another guy?"

"Not really."

"Not really?"

"Well, okay, we've slept together a couple of times, and pardon my French, but it was fucking wonderful."

"Then why isn't it an affair?"

"It's just business," Sidney repeated, worried she was telling too much. "I mean to say, he helped me bring in some donations, and I guess for him, it was just part of the transaction."

"Oh my!" Karla said. "Did you promise him sex for helping?"

"No. It just happened."

Sidney sat back and tried to hide the smile that formed at remembering her times with Peter.

"So, is it going to keep happening?"

"I don't know," said Sidney. "He wants it to, but I don't know if I'm in it for any kind of duration."

"Well, most affairs aren't about duration," Karla said.

But now she was curious. She leaned forward with her glass of wine and prodded.

"Tell me more," she said. "What's he like? What's his business? Where does he live?"

Sidney gave her what sounded like safe details: he lives in Wisconsin, plays incredible golf, was an insurance agent, does some work with a sports-marketing agency in Vegas, and travels all the time.

"I met him after you left Vegas after Kim's bachelorette party," she added. "I've only seen him twice since then."

"I'm sorry, my dear, but I'm thinking three times sounds like an affair."

"Well, that first day when we met, we just talked," Sidney countered. She hated the thrill she was feeling, finally sharing the story with someone—even if it was only half of the story. Or one-quarter of the story. She couldn't help divulging a little more salacious detail. "It's the best sex I've ever had, though. I couldn't stand it if Matt touched me now."

"He doesn't? Sounds like you guys are doomed."

"You mean Matt and me?"

"Yeah. I mean how do you undo that?"

Sidney shuddered. She knew Karla was right. She and Matt were doomed. Even if she and Peter never saw each other again, it would be impossible to resign herself to a love life with only Matt in it.

Chapter Fourteen

Rich's photo and bio in the pre-appearance package surprised her. From his picture, she couldn't remember him being at the dinner party Peter had thrown for her in Las Vegas, but Laurie assured her he had been there. But the bio was the real shocker.

"A former FBI agent?" she yelled into the phone at Laurie. "Are you fucking crazy?"

"Sidney, calm down," her manager said. "He's been with us now for ten years. We have a wonderful relationship with him, or we wouldn't keep him as a customer."

"Was he investigating prostitution for the FBI?"

"Of course not," she said. "Financial stuff. You know, bankers? I know him quite well, and I think you'll like him a lot."

He was certainly a looker, she thought, studying his photo.

When she met him the next day outside the Phoenician's pro shop, she immediately forgave him for being a former FBI guy. His photo had been seriously out of date, but he was still handsome. Once she saw him in person, she remembered meeting him at the Las Vegas dinner, one of the two men who were already there when she and Peter arrived. She made a mental note to mention to Laurie that it might be time to update Rich's file picture.

His handshake and his smile were warm. His attractiveness wasn't just in his face, his dark gray eyes and his silver hair, but in his calm power. It was sensuous, and it revealed itself instantly, although she couldn't put her finger on how. If he was investigating her, she thought, she might have trouble not confessing to anything he wanted her to admit.

By the time she got to the Phoenician pro shop, he'd already paid for their round and had loaded his clubs on a golf cart.

"I'm sorry we can't walk the course," he apologized, reaching for her bag and securing it on the back of the cart. "They don't allow walking on the weekends here. Too many old farts like me."

"That's not how I'd describe you." Sidney laughed. His self-deprecation was unnecessary.

The round went quickly. The two nine-hole courses they played were "resort" courses—not too hard for the tourists and snowbirds who flocked to the valley. Sidney played from the blue tees with Rich in order to find some challenge in the easy tracks.

They stopped for a quick lunch on the same patio where she had met the instructors the day before, but she saw neither of them. Soaking up the sun again, she asked Rich about life in Phoenix. Would she like the town? Could she handle the summers?

"You're from Seattle, right?" he asked.

"Yes."

"I think this would be a hard adjustment," he said. "No trees, no hills, no mountains." He pointed to the Camelback Mountain, just nominally a "mountain," and shrugged. "They call that a mountain, but it's no Mount Rainier."

She laughed. He was a fun guy. She started to wish she could play both days—and nights—with him.

"And the politics," he said. "It's a bit conservative here

even for me, and I'm old law enforcement."

"Then, why are you here?"

"This was my last assignment with the bureau," he said. "My kids are here. They both went to college here, and they settled in the area. Although as big as Phoenix has gotten, I think it would be faster sometimes to fly somewhere to see them than to drive out to where they live."

"And your wife?"

"She died from ovarian cancer fifteen years ago. That's part of why I couldn't leave my kids. They were both teenagers at the time. We got past the worst of the trauma together. I miss her, *we* miss her, but I would miss them even more."

Dinner that night was casual, sitting around the generous bar in the resort hotel. They talked alternately about his investigations—*sans* real names, of course—and her tournaments. His stories were chosen for their humor, not their financial intrigue, which she appreciated. Financial shenanigans were front-page material, but they usually lacked pathos or sympathetic characters. It was hard to feel bad for the rich folks who got hoodwinked by greedy money managers. Yes, the mortgage crisis had left a lot of people struggling, and she could read those stories. But the rest … well, meh, as Karla would say.

"I have to ask you something," Sidney finally dared to bring up her big question. A bottle and a half of wine helped loosen her tongue.

"If you have an FBI pension, wouldn't getting caught paying for an escort jeopardize it?"

"Probably, yes," he said. "Although not always. But, this operation Milton has put together is truly bullet-proof."

"How so?"

"Offshore money, no marketing of sex, no sexy photos, and no payments – or in your case, donations – go through the agency, only marketing fees. They have set it up right."

"Okay, but how about me? What are my risks?"

Rich studied her face, and then surprised her by leaning forward and kissing her forehead.

"I worry a bit for you," he admitted. "Most of the clients are probably booking their payments in sole proprietorships. Self-employed in marketing. But your income may be under more scrutiny because it's going into a 501c3. You might consider giving up the nonprofit designation and just doing this as a personal mission."

Sidney thought about that for a minute, and decided it was something she should ask Peter about later. "But, if I get caught, doesn't that endanger you?"

"Not likely," he said. "I'm pretty well covered."

His analysis sobered Sidney up considerably. So far, things with the agency had gone swimmingly. She liked Gary, she liked Philip, and she liked Rich. She liked Rich a lot. The only glitch in the operation so far had been running into Kerry in Portland. Otherwise, she had felt fairly bullet-proof herself.

Oh, but wait … how about that photographer in Las Vegas? She'd never been able to totally shake her suspicions about that guy. Was he just a tourist? Or was she fooled by the unprofessional appearance of his camera?

"Hey, don't look so glum," Rich said. "I think your risks are low. Very low. Just not as low as mine. Now, wait here. Give me your claim check, and I'll retrieve your bag for you at the bell desk and be right back."

When he got back, he was toting not only her bag, but a small gift bag, with crepe paper sticking out of the top.

"You might want to look at that a little discreetly," he whispered in her ear.

Sidney stuck her hand in the bag, and felt something silky. She peered into the crepe paper at a peach slip of lace and silk. The sight of it sent a familiar electric shock from that spot between her legs up her spine. She was starting to appreciate the excitement of these dates. Sex was fun.

In fact, sex with Rich was more than fun. It was a blast. Somehow, she kept that peach negligee on all night, even though they sampled every position that either of them knew. What variety, she thought, halfway through the night. And what stamina Rich had for a guy in his mid-fifties. After each orgasm—either his or hers or both of theirs—they teased each other about their clumsy moves and execution.

Finally, at about two o'clock, Sidney fell away from their last orgasmic embrace, collapsing on the bed, panting, and declaring a truce.

"You win!" she said.

"I didn't know we were competing," Rich said, his lungs working hard as well. He leaned over her and kissed her, grinning like he'd just won.

"Maybe we weren't, but I have a golf round tomorrow. You have to give me some rest."

"Okay, but maybe we can try again in the morning. A kind of goodbye present?"

She fell asleep before she could come up with an excuse or an answer.

She met her next date, Larry, at noon the next day in one of the dining rooms at the Fairmont Scottsdale Princess.

"Thanks for meeting me," he said, which seemed a bit odd to Sidney.

"Yes, of course," she said. "Are we going to have lunch first, or head out to the course for a quick nine?"

"Lunch, then golf," he said. "But, unfortunately, I have to leave after golf. I have been called to a board meeting that is a bit of an emergency. So no staying the night and no golf tomorrow."

Sidney couldn't help letting a frown show on her face.

This was going to make it hard for her to reach her goal of twenty thousand dollars in donations for the month.

"Oh, don't look so sad." Larry lifted her chin with a finger. "I know I look like the best catch this side of the Rio Grande, but honestly, you're probably lucky."

He leaned forward and whispered in her ear. "I'm a horrible lover."

Sidney couldn't help but smile. "Well, I doubt that," she said.

"And I am not going to ask for a refund of my donation. You did get it, didn't you?"

"Yes, thank you," she said. "That's very generous of you."

"Well, getting to play a round of golf with Sidney Stapleton is worth every penny. And, I think you'll like your room." He handed her a key card. "It's already paid for. And help yourself to the mini-bar."

They had salads and then quickly ran through the pro shop, got their receipt for the starter at the first tee and took off.

Larry was nice. But he was no Rich or Greg. He didn't have Rich's good looks or sense of humor, and his swing wasn't sensuous like Greg's. She had been lucky. If one of her dates was truncated, she was glad it was this one. Anyway, she could use the sleep.

Taking off the next morning on the second leg of her trip reminded Sidney of the weariness she used to feel from time to time on the Tour. It made sense to try to combine a couple or three dates in one trip, as she could fit in more fundraising in a shorter period of time and raise less suspicion back at home. But, hopping through two towns and three hotels in four days was exhausting.

Back on the Tour, she'd flown farther away—as far as Thailand and Japan several times—but she always stayed for at least a few days, and usually for a week. Maybe if she took a series of appearances in a big city like New York or Chicago from the agency sometime, she could garner a few donations while staying in one place, and it wouldn't be as tiring.

Flying into Palm Springs was always thrilling to Sidney. She'd been in the Coachella Valley many times, most of them to play in the Kraft-Nabisco Tournament in April. She always felt that the stay was too short, that she would have liked to hang out at Bighorn with Michelle Wie for a few days and enjoy the endless sunshine.

Circling down between the mountains into the tiny Palm Springs airport, she sighed at the sight of neat communities of red tile roofs on modest stucco houses, their backyards dotted with azure pools and neat cactus gardens. It would be lovely to retire here, she thought. Even better than Phoenix. At least Palm Springs had mountains. And many fewer six- and eight-lane highways.

Even renting a car in Palm Springs was easy. The cars were parked no more than a hundred yards from the rental counter, and getting out of the airport didn't even require showing a rental contract. You just had to be able to follow the exit signs, and, *voila!*, you were on your way.

Sidney's best hope for a Palm Springs chapter of T-Squared was at Tahquitz Resort, a fairly mundane and dated public course at the edge of the city, right next to the poor sister of the valley cities, Cathedral City, and a noisy water park. If she was going to benefit girls whose families couldn't afford high-priced coaching, she needed to base the chapter at the west end of the valley, away from the pricey, Republican enclaves down-valley in Palm Desert, Indian Wells, and La Quinta.

The best thing about Tahquitz was its large practice area:

a wide driving range and a couple of putting greens, including one that allowed chipping and pitching as well. The girls needed more time on the practice greens and driving range than on the course when they were working with the coaches. Further, greens fees were much lower than they were at most of the valley's fancy public courses, where a round could easily top one hundred and seventy-five dollars at high season.

The agency had arranged for Sidney to stay in Palm Springs at the Parker—it used to be the Parker Meridian, but it had been purchased and remodeled in a strange retro-1960s style in 2007 by new investors. With its pricey rooms and eccentric décor, it was a magnet for trend-setters and hipsters. Sidney didn't care for it much.

She dropped her suitcase off at the bell desk, checked in, and without going to the room, headed for the golf course.

Tahquitz was certainly no Phoenician. The club house featured daily breakfast buffets of cold scrambled eggs and cold sausage patties, and a round of golf for locals with breakfast and lunch could be had for under seventy-five dollars most days—even in season.

As a consequence, the two courses were usually overbooked, and a round could stretch to six hours on the weekend. But, as a charity, T-Squared couldn't be picky. If the course and the city's managers were willing to host a T-Squared chapter and give the girls a chance at some decent coaching and practice, who was she to look down her nose at the amenities?

Sidney grabbed a soda water at the bar, and met Jake outside the clubhouse on a concrete patio with cheap metal tables and chairs. The pro brought the names of eight girls whom he had worked with in junior high and high school programs in the Palm Springs and Cathedral City school districts. All of them, he maintained, had potential. All of them needed help. Their parents were all service workers in town, and most of them had Hispanic surnames.

"You have tapped into exactly the population I want to help," Sidney told him. "Now tell me something about what you think it will take to make each of these girls succeed."

They talked for an hour and a half, and although the ambiance was far less pleasing than that of the Phoenician, Sidney left the meeting believing that a chapter in Palm Springs made more sense than one in Phoenix.

She had a couple of hours between her meeting and her scheduled date with Russ, a retired journalist and avid golfer. She preferred to start the day playing golf with a customer, and then spending the night with him. It gave her the chance to evaluate her partner before deciding whether she would or wouldn't spend the night with him.

Her tight schedule meant that things would be turned around this time. But, it had worked out okay with Greg, she thought. So, she was optimistic.

Russ met her at the bar next to the registration desk at the hotel, and they took their drinks out to one of the pool decks on the sprawling hotel property. In his mid-fifties, he reminded her of other journalists she had met: bearded, a little careless in his dress, casual in his attitude. Given the low salaries of most newspaper reporters, she wondered how he came upon the kind of money that allowed him to pay for a five-thousand-dollar escort and a night at this pricey joint.

He told her before she had a chance to ask.

"I wrote two very successful golf novels," he said, as they relaxed by the pool. "Maybe you've read them?"

He named two novels she had indeed tried to read; male fantasy novels with golf prowess serving as an aphrodisiac that got big-busted, long-legged women into bed with losers who did little but play rounds with their loser buddies and gossip about the women they wanted to screw. They were funny in places, but generally disgusting in their treatment of women as nothing but breasts, asses, and legs. She'd never managed to finish either of them.

"Yes," she said, diplomatically. "I am sure I read them, but it was some time ago. Did they sell well?"

"Yes, very," he said. "I'm working on a sequel to the second one. It's going to be set in Europe though. What do you think?"

"Gosh, I guess that's not much to go on," she said. "I'll have to wait and see when it comes out. When will you be done?"

"I've only started," he said. "It seems that whenever the weather is nice out, I have trouble sitting my ass down at the desk and getting anything done."

"Ah," she said. "And it's nice here pretty much, what, eight months of the year?"

"Yup. And I travel much of the other four," he said.

"Hmm. Nice life if you can get it."

He seems awfully full of himself, Sidney thought. And he proved her right. Over the next three hours, he talked incessantly about his own golf game, his writing style, his many admirers—mostly women, he maintained—in the valley, and the mansion he was building. She couldn't believe he used the word "mansion."

He never asked her about her golf career, which had been a favorite topic of her other dates. He never asked her about T-Squared. He just talked and talked about himself.

Sidney couldn't help but imagine that Karla would think poorly of her for sitting and listening to this guy, let alone having sex with him. Would Karla lower her standards to the extent that she would be willing to put up with this? Sidney wondered. She hoped not; she wanted better for her friend. Then why was she willing to? Just because her golf career was over?

Whatever his faults, though, Russ chose a perfect restaurant for dinner. He retrieved his bright red Camaro convertible from the valet and drove only a mile or so back toward downtown Palm Springs to a little neighborhood restaurant called Europa.

The second she stepped through the passageway into the courtyard between the little Villa Royale Inn and the restaurant, Sidney wished she were there with Peter. To get to the restaurant, they passed through an interior plaza with low olive trees and wrought-iron tables next to a tranquil pool. Tiny lights in the trees and candles on the tables lighted the way to the arched doors of a cozy bar. The host led them past a couple of intimate, baroque, low-ceilinged dining rooms, and out onto a rough-tiled back patio. A fireplace at one end of the tiny, brick-enclosed space crackled. The full moon above peeked through the leaves of huge hibiscus bushes surrounding the brick wall, spreading quivering shadows over the tables.

"Beautiful," Sidney whispered, nodding approvingly at Russ.

He smiled a crooked grin. He was clearly pleased with himself.

"Welcome to Sonja Henie's home," he said, pulling out her chair. "She lived here in the 1940s. Her groundskeeper lived here in this restaurant."

"Wow," said Sidney. "Wasn't she a Nazi sympathizer?"

"Yes," he said. "Or it's rumored. But what a beautiful home, huh?"

More than rumored, Sidney thought. She had written an essay in a college English class about famous female athletes who had tainted their reputations by hanging out with unsavory characters, and Sonja Henie's friendship with Hitler was one of her most egregious cases in point.

But, she had to admit, someone had taken this little hacienda of Henie's and turned it into a spectacular oasis.

209

Some lemons were made into lemonade.

Russ ordered a bottle of wine and a steak. Sidney ordered a Caesar salad and osso bucco, and ate about a third of it, turning down the waiter's suggestions for dessert.

Russ described the plot of his new novel in great detail. Sidney stifled yawns and tried to find something attractive to latch onto that would make the coming night-time activities bearable. He wasn't unattractive, and the manly facial hair and khaki jacket might have held some masculine allure if he'd only shut up, she thought.

As he talked and she nibbled at her dinner, Sidney tried to steer the conversation away from his sexist, misogynist novels and toward golf—an avocation they apparently had in common.

"Tell me about your golf game," she said. "When did you take up the sport?"

He was no less besotted by his golf game than he was of his writing career. He explained his early rejection of the sport his father loved, his re-discovery of it in his thirties, and his mastery of it now in middle age.

"Not very many people get to my level of proficiency at this age," he said, as if that proficiency was an accepted fact, not as-of-yet hypothetical.

"Well, how good are you?" she asked, a little sick of his braggadocio.

"I play to a two. Sometimes a three," he said, indicating he nearly parred the courses he played, which would place him in the top 1 percent of amateur golfers, something that Sidney had trouble believing.

"Well, I guess we will see tomorrow," she said. "Where are we playing?"

"Mission Hills," he said. "It's a private course down on Dinah Shore in Rancho Mirage. I have a friend there who is on the board. He owed me a few favors."

Obviously he had little appreciation for the LPGA or

her career, Sidney realized. Mission Hills was where they played the Kraft-Nabisco, and she was very familiar with the club and its location. And, she could have gotten them a tee-time anytime she wanted with a simple call. Why was he such a schmuck?

Sidney smiled as she finished her glass of wine. She would have no trouble taking this guy to the cleaners if he wanted to put some money on their game the next day. She considered levying a little wager, and padding her "appearance" fees with it. She decided to wait and see how the rest of the evening went first.

They returned to the Parker and the lobby bar a little before midnight for a nightcap, and then Sidney led Russ to her room. This was going to be the first "grin and bear it" session of her nascent career as an escort, she thought. She decided to ask him to use a condom and to use the entire episode as a learning experience. He was unlikely to be the last unsavory date she would have at the behest of the Milton Walton agency.

Sidney unlocked the door to her room, and to her surprise, Russ passed through in front of her with his small overnight case, letting her hold the door for him. She considered herself a feminist, but still, she was surprised at his lack of chivalry.

"Nice," he said, looking around. "Can we raid the mini-bar?"

"I guess," she said, forcing a laugh. "It's on your tab."

He opened the mini-bar refrigerator and grabbed a tiny bottle of Scotch. "Do you have any ice?"

She pointed to the bucket on the sofa table. Housekeeping apparently filled them as a matter of course. Russ poured his Scotch in a cocktail glass, grabbed a few ice cubes bare-handed, and went to the bathroom to add some water.

Sidney shrugged her shoulders and shook her head.

Don't worry about me, she thought. *I'll get my own.* She reached into the refrigerator and pulled out a bottle of chardonnay. It wasn't her favorite, but it was handy and didn't require a corkscrew. She had a feeling she was going to need all the alcohol she could ingest to get through the night.

Russ turned on the TV and sat down on the couch with the remote. He flipped through a few channels as she watched him. He seemed oblivious to her presence. Is he paying for a night with me, or for a night in a nice hotel room with a big TV? she wondered.

She finished the little bottle of wine, pulled off her jacket, and rummaged through her suitcase for the negligee she had packed for the evening. She pulled the door closed to the bathroom and changed, covering her silk nightie with a terry-cloth robe from the closet, slipping a condom in its pocket.

When she returned to the bedroom, Russ had removed his jacket and his pants, and sat on the couch watching the Big Bang Theory re-runs. On the coffee table were two pairs of handcuffs.

Sidney forced another laugh. "What are these?" she asked.

"Toys," he said, looking up with a grin.

"Uh, didn't the agency tell you about my personal restrictions?" she asked. No bondage was one of the limits she had laid down.

"Oh, they're not for you," he said, getting up and unbuttoning his shirt. "They're for me."

Oh Christ, Sidney thought.

"You want me to tie you up?" she asked, raising one eyebrow and lifting one set of the cuffs with an index finger.

"Yup," he said. "Whatever you might think of me, I'm really a feminist."

"What? Feminists believe in male bondage?" she asked, incredulously.

"Whatever," he said, pulling his shirt off and flicking off the TV. His chest was covered with wiry hair that matched his beard, and it was nicely muscled. For all of his bad habits, he apparently kept himself in good shape. He lay down on the bed and put his hands up above his head. "Let's get going, Sidney. I want to see how mean you can be."

Sidney gulped. *This might be disgusting,* she thought, *but at least I'll be in control.* She untied her bathrobe and let it drop to her feet. An approving smile crossed Russ's lips. At least he found something about her that he could appreciate as much as he appreciated himself, she thought.

She picked up a set of the handcuffs, and examined them. She'd never seen a pair up close before, let alone used them. But it seemed pretty obvious. They were open, and she figured all she had to do was put them around his wrists and push them closed. But what was she going to do with two sets? She decided to just start with one.

"I suppose you have the key for these," she said, approaching the bed.

"Maybe," he said, teasingly. He dropped his arms as she reached him, and pulled her chest down to his face. He pulled her slip down with his teeth and nuzzled his bearded chin between her breasts.

Sidney was surprised at her reaction. She expected to be repulsed at his touch, but instead she shuddered with anticipation. She grabbed one of his wrists and snapped the cuffs in place. She grabbed the other wrist and made the connection. He lifted his cuffed hands above his head and grinned again.

"What are you going to do with the other pair?" he asked her.

"Your feet?" she asked.

He looked disappointed. "Really?" he asked. "That's it?"

Sidney retrieved the second set of cuffs, but instead of hooking them around his ankles, she connected one side to the pair on his wrists and connected the other to a rail on the head board.

"How's that?" she asked.

"Oooh, nice," he said. "It's a start." His boxer shorts were bulging as he swelled.

Sidney climbed on to the bed, and straddled his thighs. She didn't understand it, but she was definitely turned on. She flipped her slip off her head, and watched him stare at her breasts.

"If you're really nice, I'll let you lick them," she said, surprising herself.

"Oh, I'll be very nice, thank you," he said. "Please hurry up and do what you are going to do to me."

Sidney hooked a finger under each side of his boxer shorts and pulled them down. He was swollen and throbbing. She tore open the condom envelope and rolled the rubber down before lifting her hips and letting him inside her slowly. He watched himself disappear inside her, and his eyes drifted up to the ceiling.

"Oh god," he said. "Slap me. Slap me hard."

Sidney stopped moving. He felt big and wonderful inside of her, but she didn't want to slap him. She just wanted him to push up as she pushed down, matching her rhythm with his thrusts.

"Please Sidney, make me hurt!" he begged, his eyes pleading. "Make me hurt!"

His sudden desire softened her resolve, and she slapped him lightly on the side of the face. He looked disappointed, and she could feel his erection softening inside her. That was definitely not what she wanted to happen.

She slapped him harder, and a smile started to grow across his face. She slapped him harder again, and he cried out, his erection stiffening again.

"More!" he yelled. Sidney didn't know what to do. She'd never played any games like this before. She grabbed him by the hair on the top of his head and pulled his face to a breast.

"Shut up and do something!" she demanded, not letting go of the big shock of hair in her fist.

He obliged and began moving his hips up and down. Sidney couldn't help herself. She countered his thrusts with her own against his hard pelvic bones. She came quickly, and she felt him release inside of her a moment later. He moaned, and she let go of his hair

"So, you really like getting slapped?" she whispered hoarsely.

He watched her lift herself off as his erection withered. He smiled sheepishly.

"That was okay, Sidney. That was just fine. But, next time, you are going to have to hit harder."

That night with Russ was the only the second time any of her dates had been satisfied with just one screw, and she was fine with it. She was tired from her travels, and given Russ's predilections, she was glad he hadn't asked for any more adventurous activities.

The next morning, she got up before he stirred, and took a shower. She dressed in her golf clothes before leaving the bathroom. He was still sleeping as she packed her bag. Finally, she walked over and kissed him on the forehead.

"Time to get up," she said. "We have a tee time to make."

Russ hurried around, acting a little sheepish and a lot less arrogant than he had been the evening before, perhaps because he had shown her too much of himself in bed. He quickly dressed in madras shorts and a bright green polo, and packed his small overnight case. They left the key in the room, and headed immediately for the valet to retrieve their cars. They were at the golf course by nine o'clock for their nine-thirty tee time.

"Sidney Stapleton?" The man at the counter in the Mission Hills pro shop recognized her as they entered.

"Yes," she said. She couldn't remember the pro's name, but she didn't want him to know it. "Hello! How are you? Good to see you again."

"So how is your shoulder? Are you fully recovered? Are you going back on the Tour?"

"No," she laughed. "But thanks for asking. I've moved on, and I'm running a small charity for young girls who want to make a career on the Tour."

"Great," the pro said, turning to Russ with a raised eyebrow. "And is this your husband?"

"No, just a friend."

Russ stuck out his hand and introduced himself. "I'm Russ Blanton, the author?" he said, expecting the pro to recognize his authorial significance. He didn't. "We have a nine-thirty tee time."

"Oh you don't even need a tee time if you show up with Sidney Stapleton," the pro said, making the point that Sidney was too polite to make at dinner the night before.

As she had expected, she outplayed Russ spectacularly. She quit keeping score by the fifth hole to spare him the embarrassment, but she figured she probably beat him by at least a dozen strokes. He was a good sport about it, although he shouted gleefully the few times he outdrove her, and they parted as friends when he headed back into town.

Chapter Fifteen

No airline flies directly from Palm Springs to Oakland, so Sidney decided to drive up the next day, which gave her a pleasantly unrushed evening in the desert and plenty of time to think on the seven-hour drive north.

Thursday night's Village Fest in downtown Palm Springs was billed as a weekly festival of "arts, crafts, food, and entertainment," but from what Sidney could see, the main draw was people watching. The "art" was marginal, the musical acts largely canned and unforgivable, and the food reminded her of the offerings at the state fair when she was a teenager.

She walked up the middle of Palm Canyon Drive, glancing at the booths and into the tents set up along the eight-block fair, dodging dogs and their leashed owners, kids in strollers, and couples locked together, hip-to-hip, paying more attention to each other than where they were going. On the way back to her car, she turned into the sidewalk patio of the Alicante, grabbing an empty bistro table with a clear view of the crowd. The wine list comprised a decent number of inexpensive blends, and she sipped her way through three of them along with appetizers of olives and an artichoke dip.

That date with Russ could have turned out much worse,

she thought. The evening before hadn't been a disaster in retrospect, but it didn't change her mind about the whole kinky sex, bondage thing. His little S&M routine was pretty tame compared with what it could have been. But the next time, he would probably need a bit more stimulus, and she wasn't interested. She'd had the last date she'd ever accept with Russ.

Should she call Laurie at the agency and tell her about the handcuffs? Or was she being too much of a prude, not seeing them for what they were: a little harmless toy for an overgrown boy? She decided to let it go; Russ had been vetted by others and had been a Milton Walton customer for a few years, so the other clients must have found his behavior unremarkable.

The night was warmer than usual for early January, and Sidney slouched in her chair and watched the crowd mill past, focusing on nothing but the soft evening air and the taste of the wine on her tongue. She was just thinking how nice it was to be alone with her thoughts when the Tahquitz golf pro stopped directly in front of her.

"Hey!" he said.

She looked up to see Jake holding his hands out as if to ask, "Are you who I think you are?"

"Oh, hi Jake," Sidney said, not too enthusiastically, trying to pull out of her reverie. "Yeah, well, what are you doing here?"

"I just walked a couple of customers up to the Hyatt and was heading back to my car," he said. "I thought you were leaving town yesterday."

"Actually, I had a meeting at Mission Hills earlier today," she said, waving her hand to indicate it was nothing interesting. She hoped he wouldn't ask any more questions about it.

"Mind if I join you for a quick one?" he asked.

She did mind, but it seemed both rude and inadvisable

218

to turn him away, so she gestured toward the empty chair across the table. He wasn't hard to look at anyway, with his pleasant boy-next-door freckled face, long legs, and lean torso. He was definitely an improvement on Russ.

"So where are you off to now?" he asked, while they waited for the server to notice he had joined her.

"Oakland," Sidney said. "I have a very promising young recruit up there, and I'd like to check in on her and see what I can do to help."

"It sounds like you've found something you really have a passion for," Jake said. "You're lucky. Most of us just go through the day, wondering when that great life we once imagined is going to get started."

"You mean you don't like being a golf pro?"

"Oh, I do," he said. "I guess. It's just like, well, that couple I just dropped off? They're never going to be any good, and I wonder what the hell I'm doing trying to teach people to golf who really shouldn't be. It is tedious and hopeless."

Sidney laughed. "Yes, but I guess if talent were a gating factor, only about 5 percent of the people who play golf today would be doing it. And then imagine how few golf courses there'd be to play."

"But what you're doing, now that has value," Jake said. It sounded like he really meant it. "We see so many kids come through those school programs, poor kids who will never hold a golf club again in their lives, but golf could be a real opportunity for them."

"You mean like football or basketball is for boys?"

"Yeah," Jake said. "I think it could be their way out of this sucky service economy down here. Do you know much about the demographics of this town?"

The waitress stopped by and took Jake's beer order, and Sidney let him lecture her for a few minutes about the population of the different schools and housing

219

developments in the valley. He seemed articulate and surprisingly liberal for a golf pro. Most pros she knew were as Republican as their adult clientele, and as unconcerned about the inequities of their communities as Matt would have been.

Jake's enthusiasm for her program was just the tonic she needed, and she found herself smiling and enjoying his company. At one point she even let herself imagine what it would be like to go home with him. Would it be like her first agency date with Gary? That wouldn't be such a bad way to end her trip to Palm Springs.

What the hell has happened to me? she wondered as soon as the thought crossed her mind. It had to be Peter's fault, she thought. It was the effect of experiencing such good sex and wishing she could have it more often. She shook off the thought and re-focused on what Jake was saying.

A half-hour later, she cut off their conversation.

"I need to get back to the hotel," she said. "I planned on leaving by about six tomorrow so I can get to Oakland in time to work with the girls."

"Sure," he said, standing up with her. "And drive carefully. I want to see you back here again soon."

She wasn't sure if she was relieved or disappointed when he stuck out his hand for a shake instead of leaning in for a hug or a kiss.

Betta seemed shy and nervous when Sidney arrived at the golf course outside of Oakland the next afternoon. The ten young girls had already started their lesson with the pro, Ben, and when she got there, she realized that he had kept her appearance a secret from them. He wanted it to be a surprise.

Walking up from the clubhouse to the driving range, she

looked for Betta and immediately recognized the smooth, almost-grown-up swing of her star recruit. The other girls were trying in varying degrees to follow Ben's instructions, but none of them had Betta's balance, extension, or rhythm.

Ben saw her coming and held up his hand to stop her. He held a finger to his lips, and then clapped his hands to get the girls' attention.

"Young ladies," he announced. "Look who's come to practice with us today!" He pointed down the hill and signaled for Sidney to join them.

All ten girls waved enthusiastically, but Betta's smile was tentative. While the others immediately raked another ball forward on their mats and resumed hitting, Betta stood frozen. Sidney wondered if her approval mattered too much to Betta. Couldn't she swing with her benefactor watching?

Sidney looked away and watched the other girls practice. Ben stopped them to give a tip, and then signaled for them to start again. Then, he started at one end of the line of girls, and Sidney started at the other, giving each youngster a little individual attention. By the time it was Betta's turn, her star recruit had resumed swinging, but she stopped again when Sidney approached.

"You're doing fine, Betta," Sidney assured her. "Don't stop."

"But I'm probably doing lots of things wrong," Betta said, averting her eyes.

"Hey, what happened to that confident girl I met a couple of months ago?" Sidney teased her. "Forget that I'm standing here or that anyone is watching. Or better yet, use me as an excuse to really, really focus. Imagine that you love—I mean *really love*—the gallery."

"What do you mean?" Betta asked, nearly in a whisper. "I hate it when people watch me."

"Ah, but it is so beautiful to see you swing," Sidney said, putting her hand on Betta's shoulder.

She thought about herself at Betta's age. She had been too tall, too thin, too athletic, and too brainy, and she believed that all of the other kids in school knew it. But she also knew that she had the best swing, the most golf talent in the entire school. That's what she wanted them to see. It was all she wanted them to see.

"You would be surprised how truly impressive a good golf swing can look," Sidney continued. "Imagine you are a ballerina showing off your grace and balance." Sidney knew better than to say "grace and beauty"—she remembered how *not* beautiful she felt at that age.

"I'd rather watch you," Betta said.

"See! That's what I mean," Sidney said. "Watching a good golf swing is a wonderful thing, isn't it? And you, my girl, have one."

"Okay, but stop me if I'm doing something wrong," Betta said, pulling a golf ball into position on the mat with her club head.

She took her stance, but then hesitated. It took her about ten seconds before she could move, and the swing showed how tense she was. The ball flew farther with her seven iron than any of the other girls' did, but the execution wasn't up to her potential.

"I don't know what to think about!" Betta turned to Sidney, exasperated.

"Okay, then think of only one thing," Sidney said. "Think about finishing pretty. Think about ending up balanced on your left foot with your club over your left shoulder and your belly button pointing at the target."

"You mean like this?" Betta asked, taking a finish pose that would have made Paula Creamer proud.

"Exactly!" Sidney said. "All I want you to think about now is getting there at the end of your swing. Don't think about anything else."

Betta tried it. Her finish pose was good, even if the ball

flight wasn't.

"See how good that feels?" Sidney said. "How perfectly balanced and in control?"

"Yeah," Betta said. She smiled big for the first time that afternoon. "Let me try it again."

"Beautiful!" Sidney complimented her when she reached her finish pose. "You are getting it!"

Betta laughed. "This is fun! Now I know what to think about!" She hit another dozen shots, each one improving as she nailed her finish. The other girls had stopped to watch.

"How does she do that?" one of the other girls asked Sidney between shots. "She looks like a pro."

Betta pretended not to hear, but from the look in her eyes, Sidney could tell the comment fueled her commitment to perfection. Finally, she stopped to rest, and the other girls broke out in appreciative applause.

"Thanks," Betta said, dropping her eyes self-consciously. But Sidney caught her smile—a smile that said she'd just discovered the thrill of the gallery. The thrill that got Sidney onto the Tour and where she was today.

∼

"What you did with Betta today was like magic," Ben said, as he and Sidney sat at the clubhouse bar and ordered beers after the girls left. "How did you get her to relax like that?"

"I just remembered what it was like to be her age," Sidney said, "what it felt like to have people watch me."

"Scary?" Ben looked confused.

"Yes, but then empowering," Sidney said. "The key was to turn something scary into something that gives you power. A great swing is not only powerful, it's sexy. And a twelve-year-old girl may be terribly confused—and wrong—about what sexy looks like, but believe me, she knows what it feels like. All of those eyes on you. You on the stage, performing the one thing you do better than anyone else around you. That's what sexy feels like to a young woman."

"From what I can see, they seem to believe that sexy is tiny skirts and see-through blouses," Ben said, disapprovingly.

"That's what they think because that's what the media tell them," Sidney countered. "But once they feel the power that comes from showing their strength, from perfecting something, they never forget it. They learn what a truly sexy woman is made of."

"Wow! The voice of experience, I'm guessing!" Ben said, accepting his beer from the bartender with a laugh. "Well, I'll toast to that! I'd love for every one of those girls to figure that out. I really hate what I see going on with these young girls, the way they parade around in front of boys when they are too young to even know what boys are!"

"You sound like you're a father," Sidney said. She took a long swig from her beer. "Are you?"

"Yup." Ben nodded. "I have a ten-year-old daughter, and I cringe at what I see every day when I let her off at school. And you? Any kids?"

"Nah," Sidney said. "I have avoided it so far. I'm not exactly the mothering type."

"Well, you're one heck of a teacher. Have you ever thought about becoming a teaching pro?"

"Never interested me."

"Why, not glamorous enough?"

His question struck Sidney wrong. It sounded like something Matt would have said, but she looked Ben in the eyes and saw none of Matt's condescension.

"You're probably right," Sidney said. No use denying it. "It seems I need a bigger stage."

"And T-Squared gives you that?"

Sidney thought for a minute. Certainly, if she counted all

of the men she'd been having sex with lately, plus the rare occasions when she got to stand on a real stage, he was probably right. T-Squared was giving her that. Maybe it was a lot like the power she felt when people watched her swing, just like Betta had learned that day. But did she still really need all of those eyes on her? Wasn't she confident enough now? Hadn't she outgrown that?

❧

In the six months since T-Squared was launched, Sidney had called only one board meeting, and that was in the first month of operation, long before she started bringing in serious donations.

Now, she had plenty to bring her board members up to speed on. Of course, she wouldn't tell them *everything*, but she was hoping that her early fundraising success would impress them, and she wanted to talk about Betta and Lydia as great examples of what she thought they could accomplish.

What she didn't expect was Greg's subterfuge. Her board chair wasn't simply unsupportive; he seemed intent on calling into question everything she was trying to label as success.

It didn't help that Greg had arranged to host the meeting in one of the buildings on the sprawling Microsoft campus, giving him and Matt home-field advantage. She would have suggested a more neutral setting, but when the meeting was set, Sidney had no idea how much Matt's growing antipathy toward her had infected Greg.

"And how exactly do you get these donors to shell out so much?" he asked early in the meeting after Sidney had just started explaining her one-on-one fundraising success.

"They are making these donations for the opportunity to play golf with a former LPGA pro," she explained.

"You are telling us that all you have to do is play golf

with these guys, and they shell out money?" Greg asked. He overdid the body language, nearly falling backwards out of his chair as he threw up his arms in disbelief.

"Why would you find that hard to believe?" she answered.

"I certainly wouldn't pay that," he said, laughing. "But my question is more about whether that is a long-term revenue strategy. And, I have to ask, is there any money left from those donations after you pay your travel expenses?"

Immediately, Sidney knew that Matt had planted that question with his friend. She looked over at her husband, but he sat expressionless, his stone face honed perhaps through his years of negotiations with antitrust regulators for Microsoft.

Why did he dislike her so? Where had all of this animosity come from? Sidney wondered. But it wasn't the time to try to figure out the failure of her marriage.

"My travel expenses aren't coming out of our organization's budgets," she said. "Yet."

"And eventually, you think they will?"

"I have prepared a five-year budget for discussion later that shows at what point I can quit relying on our own savings to fund operating expenses," she said, pointing from herself to Matt and back to indicate she meant their household money.

"You mean Matt's money," Greg said. Sidney saw Matt nodding out of the corner of her eye, but she refused to look at him.

"It is a community property state," Sidney said. "And I think this conversation has gone onto a distracting, personal, and unproductive tangent. Do you mind if I go back to a discussion of our operations? I have some good news to tell you."

"She's right," interjected Angela, the LPGA pro from Oregon. "If you have some problems with how Matt and

Sidney spend their money, I believe it has nothing to do with our business here."

"Thank you Angela," Sidney said. Angela's interruption broke some of the tension in the room, and Sidney took a deep breath before continuing.

"The point is that we have raised somewhere north of seventy thousand dollars in the first six months, and that has allowed us to start two chapters. One in Portland and one in Oakland."

"Two?" asked Greg, again sounding perturbed rather than curious.

"Yes, and I am investigating the possibility of starting another one soon in Palm Springs."

"And how do we know that these chapters are going to produce a professional golfer? How do we know that they won't just give some lower-class girls false hopes?"

Sidney pushed her eyebrows together as she listened to him. Was this also a question Matt had suggested, or had Greg come up with this one on his own?

"There are no guarantees," Sidney answered, her voice starting to rise. "I don't understand your question. Wasn't this the mission we agreed to last year?"

Now she was getting angry. "The First Tee doesn't guarantee every kid they work with is going to become a model citizen either," she added.

"So how many girls in your two programs do you think have a reasonable chance of going pro?" Angela asked.

"Two so far," Sidney said. She took advantage of the opportunity to segue into a discussion of Betta's talents and progress and Lydia's promise.

Again, Greg interrupted. "So at the end of our first year, you think you'll have one young woman—maybe two—to showcase for your efforts?"

"I hope so," Sidney said. She knew where he was going—it seemed like a lot of money to help only two girls realize their golf potential. But he knew that before he signed onto the board, didn't he?

"From the start, we knew that funding a dozen chapters would yield only a half-dozen to a dozen prospective professionals."

She had heard enough. Greg's intent to sabotage her meeting and undermine the other board members' confidence had to stop.

It was tempting to accuse him and Matt right then of colluding to demoralize her and call her leadership and judgment into question. But there was no way to prove it. And, it would give Matt a victory of sorts—the meeting would be reduced to ad hominem discussions, instead of the kind of productive dialogue she had hoped to have that day.

So she plowed ahead.

"This may be a good time to review the budget plans that I have drawn up," she said. "Then we'll know how much we think it will cost to nurture these young players."

"I agree," said Tom, the teaching pro from Overlake Country Club. "And, before we continue, I'd like to commend Sidney on the progress she's made so far. Some organizations would have barely managed to complete their 501c3 applications in this amount of time. Sidney, you have my respect for an incredible effort to get this program up and running so quickly. I don't know what's going on here."

He looked at Greg and then at Matt. "But I have a feeling that you guys have another agenda the rest of us don't have. I'd appreciate it if you would lay it on the table."

Sidney smiled at Tom and nodded.

"No, I think we're just trying to be sure we're making wise choices and building a solid foundation," Greg said. Matt said nothing, but he folded his arms across his chest in a classic defensive posture.

"Great, then, let's continue." Tom nodded at Sidney.

Sidney was relieved. Now it appeared she had two

members of the board on her side, and given the fact that she too was a board member, their combined three votes would be enough to overcome any attempts by Matt and his accomplice Greg to sabotage her management at this meeting, at least.

The rest of the session flowed more pleasantly once Greg realized he wasn't getting the results he and Matt had apparently wanted. At the end, Sidney invited the board members to join her for lunch, but everyone had too much on their schedule to spend any more time with her that day.

"Great meeting," Angela whispered to her on her way out of the meeting room.

"Good job," echoed Tom as he slid out the door. "Hang in there."

"Thanks," Sidney said. "I appreciate that."

She turned to Matt, who had been sitting the farthest from the door.

"Could you wait just a minute, honey?" she asked him. She doubted calling him "honey" would fool him. Could he really believe that she wasn't angry? That she hadn't seen through Greg's attempts to ruin her meeting and know where they came from?

Sidney closed the door behind Greg, and scowled at her husband.

"Would you mind telling me what that was all about?"

"What?" Matt feigned innocence. "What are you talking about?"

"How much of Greg's attitude can I attribute to you?"

"I don't know what you're implying."

"I'm not implying anything," she said, crossing her arms and standing between her husband and the door. "I am calling it out straight. It's clear that you two were in on this together. What the hell has happened to you? Why are you working against me all of the sudden? What did I do to make you hate me like this?"

"I don't hate you," Matt said, dropping his poker face and feigning hurt. "Why would you say that?"

Sidney stood her ground. She looked him straight in the eye and waited for him to give her an honest answer.

"I think you're paranoid," he said after a long uncomfortable pause. "Perhaps you're not management material."

"Precisely the point you tried to make today," Sidney said, nodding. "I get that. What I don't get is what happened to us. What I don't get is why you've come to hate me so much."

"I don't hate you." He scowled, his face indicating how little truth there was in his words. "Again, an example of your paranoia."

A knock at the door behind her made Sidney jump. A young woman opened the door slightly and peeked around.

"We have this room at noon," she said. "Are you guys about done?"

"I think that pretty much sums up exactly what we are," Sidney said, not taking her eyes off Matt's face. "I believe we are very much done here."

Matt avoided having to answer for his collusion with Greg by not coming home until well after midnight and leaving again before sunrise the next five days. Without knowing how to get him to come clean, short of finding some way to bind and torture him into confession, Sidney decided to let it go. She had all of the support on the board she needed in Angela and Tom, and as long as she still had access to Matt's bank account to bankroll her fundraising trips, she thought it better to let it slide. At least until she could make a go of it on her own.

A week after the board meeting, Sidney left for Tucson.

Betta was competing in a national girls' amateur tournament, and her instructors asked if she could come down to watch and chaperone.

The word "chaperone" made her frown. The idea that she, as a prostitute, was suited for the job of chaperoning young women was ludicrous. She just hoped that paradox never came to light.

Her enthusiasm for the escort business was waning quickly. She didn't feel guilty about having sex for money as much as she felt remorse for having found no better way to proceed with her life. She had to find another way to raise money soon.

Maybe a little more publicity would help. Maybe if Betta was successful, it would garner some attention and some donations. But if she tried to get media attention that way, would it be using the young girl? Sidney wondered. What if Betta's story turned out to have some negative story lines that the media decided to focus on instead of her success? Would that be fair to Betta?

Despite her ambivalence about how she was making her money, Sidney called Laurie to see if she could arrange a date in Tucson while she was there.

"Hey, this is a great coincidence," Laurie said. "Tanya is going to be there, too. She apparently has a niece who is playing in the tournament. Maybe I can arrange a double date. Our customers rarely get that opportunity."

"You know I won't do threesomes," Sidney reminded her. She grimaced at the thought of sex with another woman, regardless of whether a man was present.

"Oh, no, that's not what I'm suggesting," Laurie said, laughing. "No, you'll just have dinner together and then you'll each decide how to spend the rest of the evening together with your separate dates. No worries, Sidney."

❧

In the tournament, Betta played admirably for a girl who had only taken up the sport seriously in the past year, and had worked with her new professional instructors for only four months. She didn't get close to the leaderboard, but she posted respectable scores. When Sidney drove her to the airport to return to Oakland, Betta maturely summed up her performance as "a growing experience."

"I'm very impressed with you," Sidney told her as she waited in the security line to see Betta off. "Your attitude is wonderful, and you comported yourself like the pro you will someday be."

"What does 'comported' mean?" Betta asked, at once both pleased with the praise and shy about accepting it.

"It means you handled yourself well," Sidney said. "You behaved like a pro. Now, get back to Oakland and don't let up. You could be great someday, young lady."

Sidney returned to the resort hotel with just enough time to shower and dress for dinner with Tanya and their dates.

As she toweled off and dried her hair, she realized she was nervous. Tanya's success on the basketball court and her popularity with fans and the media were far more impressive than Sidney's. And given Tanya's exceptional height and elegance, even tall and graceful Sidney was likely to pale in comparison.

It was the first time since she joined the agency that Sidney worried more about how she looked than about how her date would behave. What was the right approach? she wondered as she looked in the mirror. A lot of makeup and a big, curly hairdo might make her look more glamorous, but it could also make it look like she was trying too hard to compete with Tanya. For a blast of self-confidence, was it time to reprise the turquoise dress?

Sidney decided she needed all of the self-assurance she could pull together, and spent the next hour perfecting a large, wavy up-do, and refining her makeup. She pulled on the turquoise dress and slipped on her black pumps. She looked in the mirror, smiled, and thought of Peter.

He was the one who got her into this business, for good and for bad. But when she thought of him, it wasn't his culpability that rose to the top of her mind. It was the way he made her feel: comfortable, special, and successful. It was a bit like the feeling she got from being around Blake, except without the "I knew you when" baggage and the Midwestern guilt.

She looked herself in the eye in the mirror and shook her head. *This isn't the time to sink back into that contemplative swamp!* she told herself. *You've got a date to please.*

Sidney twirled in front of the mirror and watched the handkerchief hem swirl around her knees. She had nothing to fear from Tanya, she decided. She was going to hold her own. Her date wasn't going to wish he was dating Tanya instead.

Her resolve nearly evaporated as she approached the hostess desk at the restaurant. Tanya was already there, waiting, looking strikingly beautiful in a satiny rose-colored dress. Her thick hair was also piled high on her head, and her tasteful diamond earrings hung just low enough below the ear lobes to scatter a bit of light around as she moved.

She saw Sidney approach, and flashed her famous, enormous smile. She reached out, and bending down slightly, looked Sidney in the eye.

"I am such a fan of yours!" she exclaimed, holding both of Sidney's hands. "I am so happy to finally meet you. We are going to have a fabulous time tonight!"

"Oh, no!" Sidney said, trying to laugh as engagingly as she could. "You are *my* heroine! I wish you were still playing so I could still watch you!"

"Girls, girls!" Sidney heard someone scold them from behind. She turned and faced two men, one of whom she recognized as her date for the evening. They were both shorter than either Sidney or Tanya, and considerably older. "We are your dates tonight, not each other!" her date said, reaching for her hand and then pulling her close for a cheek kiss.

"I'm John, and this is Bill," he said, as the other man swung an arm around his shoulders. Looking chagrined, John peeled Bill's arm off and winked at Sidney. "We've known each other since high school."

"Well, we've known each other for years, even though we just met," Tanya retorted, pointing from herself to Sidney and back. It sounded a bit like one-upmanship, but her smile deflated the punch. "So, let's go party, folks!"

At the table, the conversation lagged as the foursome studied the menu and passed around the wine list. Tanya tossed her menu down first. It seemed every move she made was big, even though she did them with exquisite grace.

"I'm having the lamb chops," she announced, as if everyone at the table was waiting to hear her verdict. Actually, Sidney was glad to hear it. She worried that Tanya might out-class her by announcing she had turned vegan after reaching some lofty, enviable spiritual realm that Sidney couldn't begin to understand, let alone achieve.

"Great," said Bill, slightly slurring his words. "I'll have the same. If we're going to swap saliva tonight, we might as well taste the same."

Eeewww, Sidney thought. What a gross thing to say right before dinner! Had he been drinking? She glanced at Tanya and saw a similar sentiment cross her face. Their eyes met briefly in dismay.

Sidney put down her menu, refraining from announcing her dinner choice, and John did the same. Maybe she was going to be the lucky one tonight, Sidney thought. Her date appeared a bit more restrained and a lot more sober than Bill.

The men had retired from careers in real estate, and for

a few minutes, they shared their impressions of the state of the market in Tucson, a topic that held little interest for Sidney. Tanya looked equally disinterested, and Sidney wished they had sat beside each other rather than boy-girl-boy-girl around the table. Perhaps they could commiserate about life after retiring from the limelight. Or life as a high-end escort.

It wasn't long, though, before John turned to Sidney. "How is the golf game holding up now that you're no longer on the Tour?" he asked, pleasantly.

"Not badly, considering I'm only playing a couple of times a month now," she said. "I can still squeak out a single-digit handicap, but I'm not sure how long that will last."

"Do you play golf?" Bill asked Tanya.

"Never took it up," Tanya said.

"What do you do, then, to stay in shape? Do you play pick-up games at the Y?" Bill laughed at his own little joke, although no one else did. Tanya forced a weak smile, but it was far from the brilliant beam she had made famous.

"I do play on a nonprofessional league with some folks at a fitness club I belong to in Chicago," she answered tensely. "What do you do to *try* to stay in shape?" Her emphasis on the word "try" wasn't lost on Sidney, although Bill didn't seem to notice.

"I jog every morning," Bill said. It was the first time Sidney had heard someone say "jog" instead of "run" in about a decade. Bill was clearly communicating his age as well as his lack of refinement.

"I'll bet you do," Tanya said under her breath, turning away from Bill so that only Sidney and John could hear her, but not Bill.

The waiter appeared with the champagne that John had ordered to go with their appetizers, relieving some of the tension that was building at the table. John suggested a "toast to a lovely evening in beautiful Tucson," and they clinked their glasses.

It was expensive champagne and Sidney sipped appreciatively. Bill, however, drained the glass in one quick move and burped. He waved at a passing waiter and asked for a Scotch and water.

"I'll tell your waiter," the young man said.

"Why don't you just get it for me yourself?" Bill asked belligerently. The waiter ignored him and walked away.

"Hey!" Bill called after him. "Don't walk away from me!"

The waiter stopped, turned around, and returned to the table.

"Sir," he said quietly, bending down to direct his comments to Bill, "there is no reason to be rude. Your waiter will bring your drink right away."

"Rude?" Bill retorted at a near shout. "Who is the customer here?"

"Bill," John intervened, raising his palm to stop his friend. "Let it go. You'll get your drink in a minute. Let's not ruin the girls' evening."

Bill frowned at his friend and turned to Tanya. "Am I ruining your evening? Already?"

Sidney held her breath. She wondered how Tanya would respond, glad that the more experienced of the two of them was Bill's date. She could learn something about managing difficult clients, but she still felt bad for both Tanya and John.

The waiter disappeared. Tanya turned toward Bill and placed a long-fingered hand on his wrist.

"Bill," she said. "Let's just start over. Now tell us a bit about your exercise routine."

Brilliant, thought Sidney. Tanya had returned to a topic that Bill himself had introduced. She let him get comfortable again so he would settle down. She hoped the waiter would put plenty of water in that Scotch.

Bill's voice returned to a normal, fancy-restaurant volume as he told Tanya the details of his morning work-out. Sidney took the opportunity to turn to John.

"The champagne is wonderful," she said. "Tell me about your golf game."

"I'm a solid fifteen," he said. "I used to be a low-single-digit player myself. But, too much work and too much travel—and a little too much steak and eggs—have taken a toll." He rubbed his stomach and laughed. "I hope to get more time on the links after I retire later this year."

"It definitely is time consuming," Sidney agreed. She finished her champagne, and John reached for the bottle to pour her another. Given Bill's disagreeable proximity, she decided not to refuse. "I don't even find enough time to play now, and I'm hardly working too hard."

Bill had stopped talking, and Sidney glanced at him. His eyes were half-closed, and he was listing forward, as if he were ready to fall asleep.

"I apologize," John said, nearly whispering to both Sidney and Tanya. "I think he was intimidated a bit at meeting you, and he overmedicated himself with Scotch."

"Yeah, well, it's not the best date of my life," Tanya whispered. Her smile told John she was not blaming him. "Perhaps you can convince him to wait for me upstairs, and I'll join him later. Maybe he'll be asleep when I get there."

"I heard that!" Bill shouted, suddenly jerking himself fully awake. "I paid for this date! You know I can tell folks what you do for a living."

Diners around them turned and stared. The maître d' appeared out of nowhere, and put his hand on Bill's shoulder and squeezed it.

"Sir," he said. "I'm going to have to ask you to lower your voice to a more appropriate level or leave the dining room."

Bill threw his hands up to knock the man's hand off, but

237

the grip was too strong. He flailed and knocked his champagne glass to the floor. It shattered under Sidney's feet, and she jumped back, nearly tipping her chair over.

John stood up and walked around the table.

"Bill," he said. "I'll escort the girls to our party later. Why don't you go upstairs and relax for a few minutes. Tanya will be happy to join you later."

Sidney didn't expect Bill to follow John's advice. He sat, fuming. Finally, he stumbled to his feet, and with the maître d' walking behind him, left the restaurant.

"I am so sorry," John said, stopping behind Tanya's chair and putting his hands on her shoulders. "I didn't know he was drinking so much this afternoon, or I would have warned you."

"Well, this is a first for me," she said, attempting a weak laugh. "What do you think we should do?"

"Let's eat and enjoy ourselves," John suggested, taking his chair. "I don't think Bill is going to feel much of anything for a while. Let's let him sleep this off."

"But, his threat," Sidney said. "What are the chances he'll out us all?"

"Not a chance in hell," John said, calmly. "Even he knows the consequences of that."

Sidney wanted to feel relieved at John's assurance. She sat back as the waiter brought their salads and ground some fresh pepper over them.

"Do you ever worry?" she asked Tanya as the waiter picked up his tray and left them alone. "I mean, there have to be many folks in this room who know who you are. After what Bill said ....?"

"Not really," Tanya said with amazing cool, cutting her salad into small pieces. "I've been making appearances for five years, and in that time, I've only had a couple of dates that worried me. Usually, it was more about their need to impress me with their physicality. This is the first time I've been nearly outed in a restaurant by a drunk customer. I don't think anyone will think much about it."

"Well, I am very sorry," John said. "I hope we can still enjoy our date." He looked at Sidney expectantly.

Sidney wondered how she could just forget what happened and, not only eat, but also take him upstairs later and have sex with him. But, what else were they going to do? Bill was out of sight as far as she and John were concerned. And Tanya didn't seem overly concerned, as absorbed by her salad as she was.

If she was going to stick with this high-end escort thing, Sidney needed to develop some thicker skin.

John turned out to be a charming date, regaling Sidney and Tanya with stupid real-estate buyer stories, his humor more than making up for Bill's crude behavior. After what turned into a long, leisurely dinner, they accompanied Tanya up to her suite to ensure she'd have no problems with Bill, who turned out to be fast asleep and snoring loudly in his own room.

Up in her suite afterward, Sidney shared another bottle of wine with John, followed by some unexceptional but passable sex, and fell asleep.

When she woke up the next morning, John was gone. He left her a note: "I think we made the best lemonade we could out of sour lemons last night. Thank you for sticking with me."

On the flight to Vegas the next day, Sidney considered the risks she was taking with the Milton Walton solution to her fundraising issues. So far she'd dodged all the bullets: Russ's S&M proclivities, running into Kerry in Portland, Bill's drunkenness the night before.

But how many more close calls would she have before

something, someone slipped up enough to cause harm to either her person or her reputation?

Chapter Sixteen

Sidney wanted to be fashionably late, so she walked into the Milton Walton Agency party in Las Vegas thirty minutes after it had started.

The elegant Monet Ballroom at the Bellagio was already crowded with traditional sports-marketing clients: active football, basketball, and baseball players and their significant-others; representatives of sponsors like Nike, Adidas, and myriad car companies; and team owners. She also expected a few escort clients and customers to show up. The annual party was one way the agency recruited new ones.

Sidney was pleased that access to the gala was strictly limited to invitees. She had been afraid the place would be crawling with sports writers and their photographers. The last thing she wanted was for Matt to see a photo in the sports pages of her partying in Vegas.

She stood in a corner by the entrance and looked around, smiling at her own hubris. With all of the real sports celebrities here, there was no chance that a photographer would have wasted his time with her anyway, or that any newspaper, magazine, or website would have chosen a picture of her over any others.

The gathering was about 80 percent male, she estimated, but the women made up for their low numbers with their ostentatious jewelry. Sidney reached up unconsciously to touch the simple diamond solitaire she had chosen to wear with the simple, sparkly jersey shift she bought for the occasion. Like her necklace, she thought the dress was classy in its understatement.

"You, Sidney Stapleton, are the very personification of class," someone whispered in her ear from close behind, as if ratifying her opinion. Sidney twirled on her heels and nearly knocked Milton Walton over with her elbow. He grinned broadly and spread his arms for a hug.

"Thanks for coming," he said. "You've had a very successful first few months with us."

"Thank you," she said. "I'm surprised you know. You can't keep track of everyone."

"You'd be surprised," said Milton. "I have a pretty good idea of how all of my clients are doing. I trust that it's been working out well for you too?"

"Yes, of course," she said. "It has really jump-started our fundraising efforts."

She was surprised at how nervous she was around the head of the agency. He was charming, but so were lots of people she met and worked with over the past decade.

"Hey, let me buy you a drink," Milton said, gesturing at her empty hands.

"Oh, did I need to bring cash?" Sidney asked. "I never even—"

"No, my dear," he said, smiling at her misunderstanding. "I'm buying all of the drinks tonight. I was just making sure I got credit for this one."

Offering her his arm, Milton wove them through the crowd, deflecting attempts by at least a dozen people to get him to stop and talk.

"I don't want to keep you from your important clients," she protested. "I am only—"

"You are only the most attractive woman I've seen all night," he interrupted her, leaning in to whisper in her ear.

"Please. I'm honored to walk across the room with you."

Sidney knew outrageous flattery when she heard it, but she smiled in spite of herself. People turned to watch them weave their way up to one of the many bars set up around the periphery of the ballroom. It was nice to be treated like a star again.

After retrieving a large glass of viognier for her, Milton led her to a small group of men, introduced her, and begged her forgiveness for having to abandon her for "a while." The men, all representatives of sports-clothing companies, welcomed her into their circle warmly and resumed bitching about offshore manufacturing investigations by consumer groups.

Sidney stood with them and listened politely for a few minutes, and then excused herself. Tanya had said she planned to attend the party, and Sidney headed across the room to look for her. As she gracefully slipped around elbows and gesturing arms, she also kept an eye out for Peter.

She had come to the gathering with no expectations that he would have time for her, but she still hoped to see him. Of course, all of his recruits were there, she tried to warn herself. And, the annual party was one way the agency recruited new ones. Why would he have time for her? Especially after their phone conversation over Christmas?

She found Tanya in the center of the room, surrounded by some very tall men Sidney assumed were basketball players. She welcomed Sidney with a big hug and introduced her to her giant friends as a fellow former athlete—a former LPGA star—not as a "fellow escort."

Sidney noted Tanya's discretion. Most of the clients at the party were active sports stars, not retired players. And few of them, she realized, were aware of the business segment that she and Tanya were most actively engaged in. It was a side business for Milton, not his bread and butter.

Sidney stayed and listened to the group discuss the coming NBA playoffs for a few minutes, but her neck started to ache from looking up at their faces. She excused herself again and worked her way to the back of the room. The doors to the patio were open, and several gaggles of men were gathered outside, smoking beneath huge patio heaters.

Sidney was jealous of their obvious camaraderie. From the banter and jokes they tossed around, it was clear they were friends, or at least that they had something in common. She could search all night and not find someone who wanted to talk about her LPGA career, or her charity, or probably even the incessant rain in Seattle.

She stepped outside and surveyed the groups. She was about to go back inside when she recognized Philip, her date from Portland, standing in a circle on the far edge of the patio with another half-dozen men. She sidled around to get a better look and recognized Gary from Oakland, and Rich and Larry from Phoenix as well. And, then, she saw Peter. He was gesturing with his cocktail in one hand, telling a story to the group. Clearly it was a good one. Whenever he paused, the men laughed in unison. They encouraged him to continue.

Sidney froze. These were all men she had "dated." Were they talking about her? Were Peter's engaging stories about her? Were they comparing notes on her various appearances?

Suddenly she imagined that most of the partiers knew her as one of only two things: a nobody or a prostitute. By and large, to them she wasn't a famous athlete, and she wasn't a former champion of the LPGA Tour. She was only a whore.

All her ambivalence about her fundraising suddenly seemed silly. She shouldn't have been debating her choice; she should have rejected it a long time ago!

She turned and slipped back inside the ballroom just as Peter caught her eye. She hurried. Humiliated, she wanted to slide through the crowd and disappear into the night.

He caught her as she set her empty glass down on a tray by the door.

"Sidney!" he said. "Why are running away? Didn't you want to say hello?"

She turned to face him with tears welling up in her eyes. He held her by the arm, and she stared at his beautiful face.

"Sidney, you look exquisite!" he exclaimed loudly enough that people around them turned and looked. Peter leaned in closely and brushed her face with his hand.

"Please tell me you bought this dress for me," he whispered in her ear.

Sidney felt her tears build and her chest tighten. She swallowed hard and took a deep breath.

"I guess I bought it for you and for all of your friends back there on the patio, Peter," she said. Her tone was sarcastic, not grateful.

His face fell.

"I mean, really, Peter," she said in a harsh whisper. "What am I? Who am I? When I stood there and saw the group of you talking, I realized what I've become!"

"What do you mean?" He looked puzzled and hurt.

She leaned in and whispered in his ear. "I'm a whore, Peter. That's what I am. I used to be a golfer, a wife, a daughter. Now I'm just a whore. A lousy whore for you and your friends."

She pulled away from his arm, and walked through the ballroom door and down the hallway.

"Sidney?" he called after her. "Sidney, wait!"

She stopped and turned. He caught up and put his arms around her waist. He pulled her close and she didn't have the fortitude to resist.

"I understand," he said quietly. "I get it. Can we talk about it? Can I come with you?"

Sidney pushed away, but he kept his hands on her waist.

"Don't you have to go back with your customers?" she asked more sarcastically than she wanted to. "Maybe drum up some more business for your clients?"

"I don't need anything more than I need to be here for you," he said. "I am sorry. I truly am. Let's go upstairs and talk."

Sidney looked away as the tears started to run down her cheeks. His eyes were too soft, his face too pretty. She couldn't think straight. What did she want from him? She was the one who had thrown away an "I love you" without acknowledging it, not him. How could she expect him to leave the agency's biggest marketing night of the year to hold her hand?

She closed her eyes and imagined literally reaching inside herself for strength. She had made the decision to be an escort herself. She did it to prove that she didn't need Matt, that she could make it on her own. And now, she was taking it out on the one man who loved her?

"No." She turned toward him. "I'm a big girl. I'll be fine. I'm just going to go upstairs and get a good night's sleep. You know, I have a golf match and a date tomorrow. I am tired, and I really need some beauty sleep."

"Well, I disagree with that last statement entirely," he said, a smile creeping across his mouth. "I'll let you go. But, can I come up later?"

She took a deep, shaky breath, and wiped the tears off her face.

"Yes," she said. "I would like that. I would like that very much."

In her room, Sidney took off her dress and heels and washed her face. She brushed out her hair and put on a nice silk slip and the bathrobe that the hotel had hung in the closet. If Peter did show up, she wanted to look her best. If he didn't, she'd have to face reality. She was a prostitute.

He'd told her he loved her and she blew it off. Now she

was acting like a temperamental adolescent. Maybe Matt had been right. Maybe it was time to grow up. Time to go home and figure out how to make a real living.

Sidney opened a bottle of wine and sat down to think. She wished she had a book to read. How long had it been since she'd opened a book? How long had it been since she tried to learn something new, expanded her universe, traveled to a new place? She flicked on the TV and watched the evening news. She watched Jimmy Kimmel, and surprised herself by laughing out loud. She recorked the wine bottle, and lay down on top of the covers, leaving a nightlight on. Just in case.

The light knock on her door slowly drew her out of a deep sleep. Drowsily, she tried to remember where she was. Then she jumped.

Peter!

Sidney slid off the bed and peered through the security hole in the door. He was making a face for her benefit. She wondered how long he had held that expression for the sake of a chuckle.

She opened the door, and he slipped in, wrapping his arms around her. His kiss was urgent and hungry, and she broke it off to lead him to the bed. She dropped the bathrobe, pulled the covers back, and crawled onto the cool side of the bed. She turned to see Peter nearly naked, pulling off his socks.

He slipped under the covers next to her, and for the next few hours, she was the center of his universe again. Their bodies molded together, moved together, celebrated together. She fell asleep again, her lips nestled into the crook of his neck, his arms folded around her.

They woke together before the sun came up, made love

again, and then lay still for a long time, wrapped together by their arms and a tangle of sheets.

"I'm sorry about last night," she said at last, breaking the silence. "I don't know why I got so upset."

Peter stroked her hair back from her face and kissed her forehead. "I'm sorry, too," he said. "I'm sorry I got you into this escort business. But, if I hadn't, I would not have had last night and this morning."

"I want to ask you something," she said. "When I saw you talking with those customers last night, I realized that you might all see me the same—as I said, as a whore. I just want to know if that's true. Were you guys talking about me? About us 'clients?'"

Peter didn't answer for a long minute. He looked hurt, vulnerable, and Sidney realized that what she was asking him—to divulge his private conversations—wasn't reasonable. She had no right to question his feelings toward her. He'd told her he loved her, and she changed the subject.

"I don't know where this is going, Sidney," he said finally, staring at the ceiling. "I know you depend on these donations to fund your charity. I don't like it. I know I got you into it, but I can't deny that I don't like it."

"Meaning?"

"It means I want you to quit."

"But then what?" Sidney couldn't let someone else decide her future again, like she had Matt. And, besides, while the truth stung last night, things were turning out well. Her charity was working, the funds were coming.

"I know," Peter said. "That's the problem. Then what? You're married. You have a life. You don't need me."

"I want to fund the charity differently, too. I just don't know how," Sidney said, deliberately ignoring his point.

He turned his sad face away and turned to get up.

"I think I'd better get ready." Sidney turned quickly and got out of the other side of the bed. "I have a golf game in a couple of hours, remember?"

"Yes," he said, frowning. "And then you will have sex with another customer."

"But all of the time I'm with him, I'll be thinking of you."

"That helps a little bit, Sidney. It helps a little bit."

Sidney met her date at the Cascata Golf Club course a half-hour southeast of Vegas. As usual, she had a dossier on him so she recognized him from a distance. Daniel—not Dan—was an auto dealer from Chicago with a big head of sandy hair, freckles, and a bodybuilder's physique. He was a golfer who had made it no further than the Cactus League, a farm team for the farm team for the PGA. Despite its lowly status, the league comprised many excellent players. They had just never been able to break through to the big Tour for one reason or another—mental or physical.

Sidney looked forward to a fun golf match, but after her night and morning with Peter, she wasn't sure about how she would respond to sex afterward. She'd have to play this by ear, one date at a time. Perhaps she'd figure out how to separate sex with her customers and sex—however infrequent—with Peter into different parts of her brain. Was it possible? Or, in order to maintain her sanity, would she have to give up the idea of running a charity and funding it with lucrative one-night stands?

Daniel was a fine gentleman, a Kansan by birth and a Chicagoan by choice. He showed his humility and kindness by suggesting they play from the gold tees instead of the blues or blacks where only idiot-amateurs dared tread. The course wound through red rock outcroppings with great desert views that harbored hundreds of nasty traps.

"Thanks," Sidney said. "I've heard this course is a real

bear. I don't really need to get beat up on today."

"Did you go to the party last night?"

"Yes, but only briefly," she said. "Were you there?"

"Yes, but only briefly." He laughed. "Only from about eight until three!"

"Yikes!" Sidney said. "I'd better go easy on you today."

Daniel didn't need to worry; Sidney didn't play her best round of the year. Not only was the course challenging and the air chilly, but she was distracted. Several times, Daniel had to repeat himself, as Sidney had spaced out and missed what he was saying.

They finished with less than respectable scores, given their backgrounds as pros, and wandered around the large pro shop afterwards, commenting on the over-priced merchandise.

"I used to pick up a polo shirt from every course I played," said Daniel, shaking his head. "Do you know how many polos I now own?"

Sidney chuckled. "I used to collect golf balls," she said. "That was bad enough. I have buckets full. Do you need any?"

They decided to head back to the Bellagio rather than get a drink before driving the thirty minutes back. Sidney parked in the casino's garage, and met Daniel in Todd's—the same bar where she'd met Peter.

"You seem distant," Daniel said. "Something on your mind?"

Sidney smiled and apologized. "I'm just remembering this is the place I first heard about Milton Walton," she said. "Peter Bennett recruited me right here."

"And we're all better off for it," Daniel said. "I really enjoyed the round today, although I can't remember when I've played worse."

Sidney stared at her drink on the bar in front of her and tried to shake off her thoughts of Peter. Finally, she gave up and turned to face Daniel. "Do you know Peter very well?"

"No," he said. "He did recruit me to the customer base, but he's kind of dropped out of the social circle lately."

"What do you mean, social circle?" she asked.

"It's just a group of guys—well, a big group—that keep in touch, mainly by phone. Peter used to be pretty active, but in the past few months, he seems to be less involved. It was good to see him last night. Same sense of humor, but I get the feeling that he's not as dedicated to recruiting as he once was."

Sidney considered that. So, Peter was telling her the truth when he said he was losing his enthusiasm for the business.

"Have you dated any of his other client recruits?"

"Sure," Daniel said. "Plenty. Guys like me have trouble settling down in the conventional ways. Even on the mini-tour, you get used to moving around, meeting different women all of the time. And now, I travel for work. Still no chance to create a long-term relationship. The Walton clients turn out to be my friends and confidants, if only for a night or two."

"I guess I've never thought much about this business from the customer side," Sidney said. "All of the guys I've dated so far have all been golfers, and I figured they just liked playing golf with a woman who didn't slow them down."

"You are the first professional golfer on the roster," he said. "What a relief for a lot of us. It's not a lot of fun to play tennis with an ex-pro, you know. It's a real ego buster."

"You know," Sidney said, leaning an elbow on the bar and studying his face. "You're a really nice guy. I think it's sad that you can't find someone to settle down with and quit this run-around."

"Well, how about you?" Daniel said. "I can't think it's any easier for you. You're married, right? What about that?"

"It's a dead marriage," Sidney said. "I thought when I

started this client thing I was just doing it to raise money for my charity. But now I'm starting to wonder if I didn't do it because my relationship with Matt is so dissatisfying."

"That's sad," Daniel said. "But, hey, at least we can have a little fun for a day or so. And we don't have to use the Internet to make it happen."

"Right," she agreed. "Match dot-com sounds like a nightmare."

"How about we get some dinner?" Daniel asked, reaching for her hand and giving it a brotherly squeeze. "We'll figure out where to go from there once our stomachs aren't growling. Okay?"

With the aid of wine and a nearly coma-inducing meal, Sidney managed to enjoy the evening, including the quick and quiet sex they shared at the end. Daniel was funny and sensitive, and although she had to close her eyes and imagine she was with Peter in order to reach a mild orgasm, she was able to get through the date and make her customer happy.

Maybe she could still make a go of this fundraising solution, she thought on the plane home. But it was getting harder, not easier, she thought. The first couple of dates had been satisfying— even exciting. But now, it just seemed like work.

Confusing her even more was how she was treating Peter. First she'd refused to acknowledge his love, and then, when he suggested she quit the agency, she brushed it off, as if she had no other option.

How much do I feel for Peter? she wondered, forcing herself to focus on the question she'd been avoiding. She wasn't sure she could tell. She had never been in love, really—not with Blake in high school, not with any man she dated in college, not even with Matt. None of them had ever made her hands sweat the way Peter did. None of them made her head swim when she saw them. None of them had the ability to excite her in bed the way he did. None of them made her feel so happy and comfortable as they held each other after making love.

The situation wasn't yet untenable, she thought. She could probably keep up the agency work until she figured out another fundraising strategy, and he could probably live with her ambiguity a little longer. He wouldn't be happy about it, but it wouldn't kill him, would it?

But was that what she really wanted?

She got home late in the afternoon the day after her date with Daniel. Matt wasn't home from work yet, so she called Karla. She wasn't willing to share her agency business with her best friend yet, but she wanted to talk about Peter with someone who might be able to empathize, or even better, give her some advice.

"So are you in love with him?" her friend asked, reasonably.

"I don't know," said Sidney.

"What do you mean you don't know? Everyone knows when they've fallen in love."

"Not true," Sidney said. "I feel a crazy attraction, almost a dizziness around him. I love his face, his smile, his hands on my body. I could go on, but you get the picture. But is it infatuation or am I falling in love?"

"Probably love," Karla said flatly. "You're too old and have too much sexual experience to fall for an infatuation."

Whew, if only she knew how much sexual experience I've had lately! Sidney thought. But Karla's point resonated. She was having great sex and mediocre sex with lots of men, but none of them were doing to her blood pressure what Peter was. It certainly wasn't just sex that she wanted from him.

"Why are you fighting it? What do you want from him?" Karla asked, as if reading her mind from a thousand miles away.

"I have no idea," she said without thinking ahead, and the words started pouring out. "I want to know someone out there cares about me more than they care about anyone else in the world. I've never had that. I've started to crave it. I thought I would get that from Matt, but it's not even close. But now I'm afraid to ask for it again. Do you know what I'm saying, Karla?"

"Oh, yes, my dear," her friend said sympathetically. "I get it. It's what we all want. I've never found someone like that. I guess I envy you in a way."

"But where do I go from here?" Sidney asked, nearly crying. "I'm married, I'm virtually unemployed, I'm conflicted. I'm not sure whether I'd be happy with Peter or what kind of commitment he wants from me. I sure as hell don't know what I want."

"Well," Karla said, "I don't really understand your relationship with this Peter, but it sounds a bit like you're more interested than he is."

"I thought so too," said Sidney. "I was afraid of that at first. But he said he loves me and that he wants our relationship to be free of its business entanglements."

"What the hell do you mean by that?" Karla sounded shocked. "What business?"

Sidney realized she'd probably said more than she should have, and she tried to backtrack.

"Oh, he works with that sports management agency that might do some marketing for me," Sidney said.

"What? Did I know about this?"

"Yeah, we talked about it in Phoenix, remember? But it's nothing. Anyway, we met through business. Peter feels that makes things too complicated."

Karla didn't respond for a few seconds and Sidney started to feel guilty—both about lying and about whining like a sick teenager.

"I wish I knew what to say to help," Karla said, finally. "Maybe someday I can meet this handsome affair of yours."

∾

If conversations with Karla had become difficult, they weren't nearly as strained as talking with Matt.

He came home late, well after nine. They stood in the kitchen and looked at each other like strangers.

"Do you want to order a pizza or something," Sidney asked. "I didn't fix anything because I didn't know when you'd be home."

"Nah, we ordered delivery at work," he said. "I'm just going to go watch some TV."

"Okay, but how are things at work? How is your mother?"

"Work's fine. Mom's not good. I'll probably be heading to a funeral before the end of the month."

"Oh, I'm sorry," Sidney said. She stepped forward to give him a hug, but he slipped past her and headed for the TV room.

The next day he called her at work from his office. His mother had died. He was planning to head out to the funeral in a couple of days.

"Do you want me to come with you?" she asked.

"You don't have to," he said flatly. "I'm not sure you should."

"Well, I would like to," she said, not sure why she was volunteering. Perhaps she didn't want his family to know their marriage had failed until they formally called it quits.

"Okay," Matt said. "I'll have my assistant get us tickets."

He didn't sound particularly sad about his mother's death nor particularly concerned whether Sidney was coming along or not. Did this man have any emotions at all? Sidney wondered.

"I'll fix dinner tonight," she said. "What time are you going to be home?"

"No, don't bother," he said. "I'll be working really late. If I'm going to take a couple of days off, I'd better see if I can get ahead on some things. Don't wait up for me."

Chapter Seventeen

Two days later, Sidney and Matt flew to Newark on Alaska Airlines. His assistant had put them in first class, which Sidney figured must have cost a pretty penny, given how late she had made the reservation. It felt strange sitting in the big, comfy leather seat, sipping wine, and thumbing through a magazine on the way to a funeral. The only funerals she'd ever attended had been in Minneapolis—for her grandparents and for a high-school friend who had died in a motorcycle accident. It would never have occurred to her that people would travel to one by plane, and certainly not in such comfortable decadence.

They had talked little the two days since his mother died. Once the plane had leveled off and the flight attendants had served a first round of drinks, Sidney pulled the earbuds out of her ears and reached over for Matt's hand.

"How are you doing with this, Matt?" she asked. "It must be hard, but I can't tell what you're thinking."

"I'm fine," he said, shaking off her hand without looking at her. "I have expected this for a long time. It's not like it was a surprise."

"Well, surprise or not, it's one of those things that one can never be ready for," she said quietly.

"Oh, really?" he said. "And how would you know? I

think you told me your parents were fine and healthy."

Sidney said nothing. She studied his face as he flipped through the in-flight magazine.

"What are you listening to?" he said, still not looking up.

"Some playlist I got from iTunes."

Matt snickered and rolled his eyes. For some reason, he hated iTunes, iMacs, iPhones, iPads—the whole Apple universe. He mumbled something about the "safety of a walled garden," and continued to turn pages.

"Why?" she asked. "Why do you make fun of me?"

"Because you are such an amateur at everything. I'm surprised you don't still use AOL. Why do you let Apple decide what you listen to?"

The question made no sense, but then, Sidney knew that Matt's animosity toward Apple had little to do with the company's services themselves, and everything to do with the endless Microsoft-Apple battles that had taken place over the years.

"I supposed I could let Zune choose for me," she said with a smirk and turned to her Kindle. Out of the corner of her eye she could see Matt's hard, mean stare. Microsoft's iTunes competitor Zune had been such a failure—such a quick failure—it seemed impossible that anyone who worked at Microsoft could make fun of iTunes without knowing they risked ridicule in doing so. But Matt was a little short on self-awareness, and his blind loyalty to his company made it impossible for him to rationally debate any Microsoft venture.

Other than learning more and more about his maniacal love for anything Bill Gates ever did, Sidney realized that she didn't know Matt any better now than she did two years ago. Even at the beginning, when they were still enjoying each other's company and spending every evening at home cooking together, reading, watching TV, they didn't talk much.

Rather than growing closer together, as she had expected, they had not just grown apart, they no longer even liked each other. He spent less and less time at home. She spent more and more time with other men.

She turned to look out the window. The plane passed over the northern Cascades, snow glistening off the top of the peaks. She thought about how little she knew of anything beyond the suburban borders of Seattle. She had never been over the pass to the eastern side of the state—not to visit the hundreds of Columbia Valley wineries, not to play the beautiful golf courses around Walla Walla or Cle Elum. Between her marriage and now her efforts to raise money for her charity, she had no space in her life for exploring, for living, for loving.

She shouldn't feel sorry for herself, she thought. She had plenty of money, a huge home, plenty to eat. She could play golf, travel. She could buy clothes, jewelry, purses, shoes. She was lucky, privileged.

Just think of Betta, she told herself. *All of that talent and so few resources to help her realize it.* Sidney thought of what she was dealing with every day: a single mother who had no time for her and struggled to put food on the table; brothers and sisters who didn't know their father.

In her drive to be successful, the center of attention, had she lost sight of what might really give her joy? Play? Discovery? Love?

Sidney stuck the earbuds back into her ears and settled down to enjoy the playlist of ballads she'd collected on her iPod. She downed her wine and closed her eyes.

She woke up with a jolt when the plane touched down at Newark and skidded to the end of the runway. It took her a minute to remember what flight she was on, where she was going.

She looked over to see that Matt was shaking himself awake, too. She sat up, turned off her iPod, and stuffed it in her purse. She pulled out her cell phone and turned it on to check phone messages and e-mails. The only message was from Laurie. She decided to ignore it. She would put off setting new dates until she got back to Seattle.

They rented a car and drove an hour north of Newark, directly to the funeral home, and pulled into the snowy parking lot. The funeral service was scheduled for the next day, and the visitation for family and close friends had started a half-hour before they arrived.

Sidney was surprised how little had changed in the time between her grandparents' funerals in the mid-1990s and Matt's mother's funeral. Her body was on display along one wall of the visitation room, embalmed and resting in its coffin. His brother, sister, and five of their cousins were sitting on folding chairs, chatting and laughing as if there weren't a body in the room, while the funeral director hovered by the door to greet people as they came in. Soft liturgical organ music played over speakers on the ceiling, barely discernible above the chatter, and across the room from the coffin, a buffet table offered up cookies, coffee, hot water, and tea bags.

"Hey, sweetie!" his sister Lynnette cooed, standing up and running to greet Matt. She put her arms around his neck and he leaned down to accept her hug. Sidney noticed his face soften with her embrace.

Ted, his brother, rose and strode over to slap his brother on the back. "Good to see you, bro," he said. "Long time."

Matt glanced at Sidney. She tried to hold his eyes. Long time? she wondered. Weren't the brothers just together at Christmas?

"Not that long!" Matt said, a little too enthusiastically. He put his arm around his brother's shoulders and led him toward the refreshments and out of Sidney's earshot.

Lynnette grabbed one of Sidney's hands in hers and pulled it to her breast.

"Thank you so much for coming," she said, tipping her head demurely. "I know it means a lot to Matt to have you here. Please, come and join us."

She led Sidney to the folding chairs and introduced her to the cousins. Sidney didn't even try to remember their names as Lynnette announced them, and she imagined they had little interest in remembering hers. As Lynnette reached the man at end of the small semicircle, Sidney saw him tip some liquid from a flask into his coffee and offer it to the cousin next to him.

She escaped Lynnette's grasp and sidled up next to the cousin who had what she hoped was whiskey. "I could use some of that," she whispered.

"Sure," said the one with the flask. "It's whiskey. Grab a cup of coffee and leave some room." He winked at her.

It's going to be a long two days, she thought. *I might as well anesthetize myself.*

"You're the professional golfer, right?" one of the female cousins asked as she sat down with her cup of coffee and accepted a splash of bourbon.

"Well, I was," she said. "I'm retired now."

"Can you teach me?" the cousin pleaded. "My husband disappears every Saturday and Sunday morning to play, and he says I can't come along because I suck."

"Wow!" Sidney said. "That's horrible. Has he ever offered to help you learn?"

"Hell no!" the cousin looked around at the others and laughed. "Actually, he doesn't care if I suck; he's just trying to get away from me!" The cousins all laughed uproariously as if it were the funniest thing they'd ever heard. It seemed a bit inappropriate for a visitation, but what did Sidney know?

"What do you do now?" asked the cousin with the whiskey.

"I'm running a nonprofit that helps young girls get into professional golf," Sidney said, ducking down in her chair a

261

bit to keep from looking too full of herself.

"Great!" said the cousin with the disappearing husband. "Maybe you can help me!"

"You're not a young girl!" one of the cousins pointed out the obvious. He slurred a bit as if he'd accepted quite a few splashes from the whiskey flask. "Young woman would be stretch. Hell, woman would be a stretch!"

Sidney sat back and listened to them laugh at that. As crude as this conversation seemed, she thought she would probably enjoy hanging out with Matt's cousins more than she would hanging out with him. At least they had a sense of humor.

She glanced over and caught Matt's eye. He was standing by himself in the corner, frowning and shaking his head. "No," he mouthed from across the room.

Sidney excused herself from the circle of cousins, and walked over to her husband.

"What is your problem?" she asked in a whisper.

"You don't need to be drinking and carrying on with that crew," he hissed. "They're not exactly the side of the family I'm most proud of."

Sidney stepped back and put a hand on her hip. "What side of the family *are* you most proud of?" she asked, dropping the whisper. "The side that has just you? Or would you go so far as to include your brother?"

Matt's face went from displeased to angry. "We are leaving here, now," he said, grabbing the coffee cup from her hand and sniffing it before setting it on the side table by the coffee pot. "I won't have you embarrassing me in front of my brother."

"I don't see your brother," she said casually, looking around. "Perhaps you kicked him out for bad behavior too?"

Matt grabbed her elbow and pulled her toward the door, but Sidney slipped out of his grip and walked back to the circle of cousins.

"Hey, I'm sorry but old sourpuss thinks we should go," she said. "I guess I'll see you at the funeral tomorrow?"

"I'm not surprised," said the cousin with the whiskey. "Matt never has been any fun. See you tomorrow." He lifted his Styrofoam cup as a wave.

✌

Instead of staying in a Marriott Courtyard or other reasonably priced hotel in Paramus or Ridgewood, Matt headed across the bridge into Manhattan, and down the West Side to the Mandarin Oriental at the southwest corner of the Central Park. It not only seemed like a hassle to get there, but also quite extravagant. Matt explained that he could take some meetings and get some business done while they were there if they stayed in Midtown.

Heaven forbid he should just focus on the death of his mother! Sidney thought as they drove over the bridge and into the city. She knew his mother had been mentally absent with dementia for a long time, but it still seemed odd that this final separation wasn't more emotionally weighty for him. Maybe that helped explain his distance from Sidney as well, she surmised. He wasn't really a bad guy, just more judgmental, introverted, humorless, and impervious than she had expected two years ago when she accepted his marriage proposal.

They checked in at the front desk, Matt handling the registration while simultaneously talking with his office back in Redmond on his cell phone.

"I can take care of this," she offered when his phone rang, but he brushed her aside, and she stepped back and stayed out of his way.

The suite was huge and ostentatious, with dining and sitting areas, a large wood desk with a printer, a powder room, a bathroom with a jetted tub and relaxation chair, and an entrance hall that alone was as big as some hotel rooms that she'd stayed in on the Tour.

"My God, who's paying for this?" she exclaimed as she walked up to the floor-to-ceiling windows to take in the one-hundred-eighty-degree view of Central Park and the north end of Midtown.

"Microsoft," he said, nonchalantly. "We have a special rate here." He threw his overnight case on one of the luggage racks in the big bedroom and closed the door to the ensuite bathroom after himself.

Special rate? Sidney wondered. It would have to be incredibly special before most people could justify staying there on business—like 90-percent-off special.

She heard Matt's muffled voice. He was on the phone again. In the bathroom, on the phone. Precious, she thought. My all-work, no-play husband had no time for grief or family, and now couldn't even stay off the phone long enough to go to the bathroom.

She wandered around the room, touching the finely polished, immaculate surfaces of the furniture and window frames. She found the bar, stuck discreetly behind a buffet in the dining area. She opened the door and selected a Scotch. It had never been her drink of choice before, but ever since that night with Peter …

"Hey, those are charged to the room." She hadn't heard Matt walk up behind her. But here he was, chiding her over a one-ounce bottle of Scotch.

"Oh, I suppose it will show up on the bill, huh?" she said. "What is it going to cost? Ten bucks? On top of a thirty-five-hundred-dollar hotel room, do you think Microsoft is going to care?"

"It's a matter of policy," he said. "No booze on the company ticket unless it's part of a business meeting or dinner."

"Okay, fine!" Sidney said, putting the little Scotch bottle

back in the cabinet and throwing up her hands. "So can we go somewhere and get a drink and then maybe dinner?"

"Sorry," he said, shaking his head and walking into the bedroom. He opened his suitcase and pulled out a tweed sports jacket. "I have a meeting this evening. Why don't you enjoy a nice dinner here in the hotel. I'll call and arrange for them to put it on my personal credit card. Where would you like to eat?"

"No, no, never mind," she said. It was crazy. Here they were, three thousand miles from home, and he didn't have time to have dinner with her? And of course he'd pay for it. She had no money. "I'll take care of myself. I have your credit card."

"Are you going to stay in the hotel?" he asked. It seemed like an odd question. She'd been in New York at least two dozen times. She felt safe in Midtown, knew her way around, and saw no reason she shouldn't go out and find one of her favorite Italian joints.

But to assure him, she said yes. She would stay in the hotel. She'd probably be in bed before he got back from his meeting.

He pulled on his jacket, reached over to kiss her on the forehead, and walked out the door without his briefcase or portfolio. Sidney shook her head and sat down on a big divan that faced the windows. What a waste of money! What a waste of a great room! If Peter were there, they could go out on the town, come back and raid the Scotch stash, and make love on any number of different pieces of furniture.

She had just started to nod off on the couch when her phone rang. It was Laurie at the agency with a special request from Milton. Did she have a minute to talk to him?

"Sure," she said, sitting up. She had no idea what the head of the agency would want from her.

"Sidney!" Milton shouted into the phone happily after Laurie connected them. "Where are you?"

"In New York," she said. "In an incredible hotel room at the Mandarin Oriental. You wouldn't believe this place."

"Ah, I would," he laughed. "I've been there many times. Did you get the Central Park suite?"

"I believe so," she said. "I'm looking out at the park right now."

"Oh, you are living right, young lady! But, hey, I have a favor to ask of you. You have been getting such rave reviews, I'd like to ask you to take an appearance with a new customer. As you know, we prefer to introduce our customers to experienced clients who can give us good feedback on whether we have a keeper. I usually wouldn't ask a client to vet a customer after being with us only a few months, but I think you would do just fine."

"Sure," Sidney said. She was flattered. "When and where?"

"Well, when will you be back from New York?"

Sidney hung up the phone with the details set. She would travel to St. Louis on Wednesday of the next week and meet Allen. It would not only be her first first-timer, it would also be her first date outside the Western U.S. And the agency would pay her an extra two thousand dollars in an "appearance fee" for taking on the challenge.

Sidney picked up her winter coat, pulled on the rubber-soled boots she had brought for walking on ice and snow, and set out to find one of her favorite Italian restaurants. She wandered down 59th to 6th Avenue and strolled south at a leisurely pace, enjoying the vibe of the city. The noise, the crowded sidewalks, the shops, the purse hawkers—they were all part of what made the city the country's number one tourist attraction. Most people may never want to live there, but everyone she knew loved to visit.

She turned into a familiar café and asked for a table near the front window so she could watch people walk by. It was still early in the evening, and it wasn't hard to get a window seat. Sidney settled back into the comfortable dining chair and vowed to make dinner last at least two hours. She certainly had no reason to hurry back to the hotel.

A bottle of Italian Pinot Grigio, a superb Caesar salad, a fine pasta puttanesca, and a de rigueur tiramisu later, she sipped on a rich cup of decaf with a shot of Baileys. Next to her dinner with Peter four months ago, it was one of the finest dining experiences she'd had in recent years.

Finally, she reached her two-hour minimum, and stood up to leave.

"Would the lady like me to call a cab?" the waiter asked, helping her put on her coat.

"No, I love to walk in New York," she said. "Besides, it's a very short walk back to the Mandarin."

"Nice place to stay, miss," he said, bowing slightly and holding the door open for her.

The temperature had dropped significantly while she was enjoying her meal, and Sidney pulled her stocking cap out of her pocket and yanked it far down over her ears. She pulled her scarf up over the bottom of her face and, hugging her coat tight around her body, took off for the hotel.

She had just turned the corner onto 59th when she noticed a man and woman walking in front of her, scurrying along the sidewalk in the same direction. The man, underdressed for the weather, had his arm around the waist of a woman in a warm parka. His tweed jacket looked familiar.

Wait! she realized. It's not just the jacket that's familiar! That's Matt!

What the hell is he doing? A business meeting, my ass! She felt her heart rate quicken, but she held back, watching them from behind.

She couldn't see the woman's face, obscured as it was by the hood of her parka. But Matt was turning to look at the woman every few steps, as if he couldn't get enough. They stopped at the light at Columbus Circle, and she turned to kiss him. Sidney held back in the middle of the block.

That's why he wanted me to stay in the hotel tonight! Sidney thought. He didn't want to risk running into her on the street.

The woman stepped back and Matt held her by the shoulders, smiling at something she said. She turned and looked back down the sidewalk toward Sidney, gesturing like she needed to get on her way.

Janie! It was Janie! Sidney realized. "No, it couldn't be!" she said out loud, catching the attention of a stranger scurrying past her. So that was what Janie was referring to as her "conflict of interest"?

"No shit, it's a conflict!" Sidney couldn't help herself. Some things just had to be said out loud.

Sidney had a split second to make a decision. She could confront Janie as she walked back toward her, or she could turn and hide her face behind her scarf. Quickly, she opted for obscurity. Before she confronted anyone about what she had seen, she had to have time to think.

Sidney ducked into a bar on the first level of the shopping center connected to the Mandarin and ordered a nine-ounce glass of Syrah. An expensive one.

Was it an affair? It sure didn't look like a first kiss. Of course it was an affair.

Discovering it wrapped up so many mysteries at once. Matt's incredible workload. His disinterest in their marriage. Janie dropping her as a client. Her neighbor Carrie's concern for her well-being and "Matt's other interests." Matt's brother saying it had been a "long time" since they'd seen each other.

So, Matt hadn't gone to New Jersey for Christmas. Then

where had he gone? Or, most likely, where had he and Janie gone?

The bartender set the wine down and waved in her face to break her reverie.

"Anything to eat, miss?" he asked.

Why were people insisting on calling her miss? Sidney shook her head dismissively.

She really didn't care where they spent Christmas, but given Matt's position and his virtual marriage to his job, why would he risk having an affair with a vendor? Wasn't that one of those things executives lost their jobs over?

And why Janie? What did she have that Sidney didn't? Was she more interested in his business? Was she more interesting in bed? Did she tell him how important he was? How powerful he was? Or was it just the excitement of being involved in something risqué?

Sidney tipped her empty glass, searching for its last drop, and realized she was gulping her wine.

"Well, who the fuck cares," she said under her breath. "Waiter!" she called out and pointed at her empty glass. He retrieved the bottle from the back bar and hurried over to refill her glass.

"You must have been thirsty!" he said, smiling.

"Nope, just drowning some angst," she said, lifting her glass in a one-sided toast. She was relieved when the bartender walked away without asking her to elaborate.

Sidney tried to discipline her thoughts. She needed to figure out what she was going to do, not just sit there and ask "why" questions. Certainly, there was no room for pious outrage. After all, she was working as a prostitute. She wasn't just sleeping with another person, she was sleeping with many other people and for money. How could she be sanctimonious about this and not laugh at herself? What were her options?

In a way, Matt had done her a favor. It was now easier

for her to walk away from their horrible marriage without having to come up with excuses or reasons. And while she didn't want to use his affair as a bargaining chip in any divorce settlement, she probably wouldn't have to. He would probably offer her far more than she wanted if she would just walk away and not make a stink. All she needed was a place to live; an interesting place to live. Maybe back in Georgetown, maybe South Lake Union. That, and her freedom.

She finished her second glass of wine, laid down a fifty-dollar bill, and slid off her bar stool. She was a little unsteady from the alcohol and glad she had on her funky boots instead of high heels. All that wine should help her get to sleep, though, she thought. That wouldn't be a bad thing.

She woke up at two in the morning with her heart pounding. At some point, Matt had returned to their room and slipped into bed. Where he had been between the time she saw him with Janie and one o'clock? She didn't know. And she didn't care. But now, the alcohol in the wine had turned to sugar, and her heart was excitedly pumping it through her body.

She knew she wouldn't get to sleep again for at least a couple of hours. She slid out of bed and pulled on one of the hotel bathrobes. She closed the bedroom door and sat on the couch, staring at the darkened park and the city's light halo hanging above the trees.

She wanted to call Peter. She wanted his advice. But now wasn't the time. Not only was it one o'clock in the morning in Wisconsin, but she needed to figure out her own next moves first. And she didn't want to conflate the two issues: her affections for Peter, and her desire to get out of her marriage.

Should she confront Matt right away? Or should she do some investigating first, see what she could learn about his affair? All she had now were questions, and the night before

Matt's mother's funeral, alone in the greatest city in the world, seemed like an impossible setting for answering any of them.

Eventually, Sidney nodded off to sleep, and that's where Matt woke her the next morning.

"I've got to go to breakfast with some guys," he said, pulling on the winter coat he had apparently forgotten to take with him the night before. "I'll be back by noon, and we'll head back over the river to the funeral."

"Some guys, my ass," Sidney said out loud after he left. She knew who he was having breakfast with, and she didn't care. She sat up and let her head list to one side. It felt like it was full of the wine she'd consumed the night before. Slowly, she stood up and went to the bar cabinet. She twisted open a big bottle of water—probably it cost ten dollars, she chuckled—and downed it. She grabbed another bottle and headed for the bathroom. Locating her toiletry bag, she tipped out four Advil into the palm of her hand and chased them down with the second bottle of water. There was no better cure for a hangover than a lot of water and a lot of ibuprophen.

Sidney stood and looked in the mirror. She looked bad. She looked tired. She looked worried. She was glad she was going to a funeral rather than on a date that day. Nobody was expected to look good at a funeral. Perhaps she could even gin up some tears for Matt's mother, and then everyone would give her a break for looking like hell.

Chapter Eighteen

Figuring out how to respond to Matt's affair wasn't as easy as it would have been if she hadn't been whoring herself for the past six months, Sidney knew.

If she blew the whistle on him by letting his boss at Microsoft know about his affair with a vendor, it would definitely hurt his career and his earning power. But, wouldn't that be cutting her nose off to spite her face? She didn't want his money; she just wanted the money she was rejecting to be substantial.

If she confronted him immediately and privately, then they would be able to make a decision about their marriage right away. Did she want that? Or did she want to delay the confrontation until she had a chance to decide what she wanted from Peter?

Procrastination won. As far as Sidney was concerned, her knowledge about Matt's affair was like money in the bank. As long as she left it there, she could choose how to use it. As soon as she cashed that check, her options would be limited.

They attended the funeral, paying little attention to each other, and then boarded the five o'clock flight back to Seattle from Newark. Anyone seeing them sitting side by side in first class would have thought they were complete strangers, as little as they interacted.

Saturday morning, Sidney got up late and moseyed around the house until Matt left. He didn't say where he was going, and she didn't ask. She waited until he had pulled out of the driveway, and then she walked over to Carrie's house and rang the doorbell.

"Sidney!" Carrie exclaimed when she saw her neighbor at the door. "Come in! How did things go in New Jersey?"

"Fine," said Sidney. "I've never seen someone affected as little by a parent's death as Matt. It wasn't difficult for him at all."

"Well, that's good, I guess," Carrie said, stepping aside to let Sidney into the entryway. "In a way. Would you like some coffee?"

"Actually, I'd love some," Sidney said, "if I'm not keeping you from things."

"Not at all," Carrie laughed. "What do you think I have to do? Nada! I'm retired and bored. I love your company!"

Her neighbor led Sidney into the kitchen and pulled a couple of mugs out of the cupboard.

"Regular or decaf?" Carrie asked, pointing at the stash of K-cups stored under her Keurig machine.

"Oh, the fully leaded, please," Sidney said. "This will be my first cup of the day."

"Bold or medium roast?"

"You're making this really hard on someone who hasn't had any coffee yet," Sidney said.

Carrie laughed. "I'll just pick something for you."

Sidney sat down at the breakfast bar and watched Carrie move around her kitchen. She demonstrated an efficiency of motion that indicated she had lived in her home for a long time, or that she had a natural grace and a sense of space worthy of a ballet dancer. Or both.

"Cream or sugar?"

"Cream," Sidney said. "Just a little to cut the acid."

Carrie pulled a milk carton out of the refrigerator and retrieved a mug from the Keurig machine and placed both in front of Sidney. She made a second cup for herself and sat down across the high bar.

"So good to see you Sidney," she said, holding her coffee cup up for a toast. "You haven't been home a lot lately."

"And, I'm leaving again on Tuesday," Sidney said, sighing at the anticipation of making another trip to the airport.

"Where is Matt today?"

"I have no idea," Sidney said, taking a sip of her coffee. "He left without saying anything."

"Sidney, are things okay between you?"

Sidney took another sip, and set her cup down. She stared at the hot liquid for a moment.

"You remember when you asked me if Matt was coming to Minneapolis with me for Christmas?"

"Yes."

"Well, you said something back then about not being sure what Matt was up to."

"I think I was just worried because he's never home when you're gone."

"And you said something about wondering if he had some other 'companionship,' is the way you put it."

"Yeah, but I don't know. Maybe he just stays at the office," Carrie said, splashing more milk into her coffee. "I don't want to cause problems, Sidney."

"I know," Sidney said. She reached across the counter and put a reassuring hand on her friend's wrist. "But now I think you were right. I saw him with another woman in New York."

"I thought you went to New Jersey." Carrie was confused.

"Yes, but we stayed in the city, and I saw him on the

street, kissing another woman."

"Are you sure?"

"Yes, and it was someone I know."

"Oh, God. That must feel horrible."

"Well, yes and no," Sidney said. "Things haven't really been going that well between us."

"So what is it?"

"Just a bad match, I'm thinking," Sidney said. "Actually, I think when he married me, he knew I had no income and he thought I would be some kind of milquetoast wife, easily controlled. He suggested the charity startup, and I think he thought he would be my major funder, and he'd keep control over me that way. But, it turned out, my other fundraising has been pretty successful. I think he hates that. Now, we don't even have sex, let alone talk. And we haven't even been married two years yet."

"Well, I didn't want to say much," Carrie said, "but ..." She paused, like she was unsure about whether to continue or not.

"It's okay," Sidney said. "You can't hurt my feelings. What did you see?"

"Well, I told you he wasn't home much, right?"

"Right."

"Well, when he was home, he often had company."

"Early forties, a little nerdy, glasses, but attractive?"

"Sounds right."

"Yeah, that's her," Sidney said. "She's a marketing consultant. She did work for both of us, but she quit working for me a couple of weeks ago. Said she had a conflict of interest."

"I'll say," said Carrie. "That's a nice way to put it."

"Yeah," Sidney said. "Now I have to figure out what to do about it."

"Well, sue the bastard!" Unlike Sidney, Carrie didn't harbor any ambivalence.

Sidney laughed. "That's too easy, Carrie," she said. "I have to figure out what's the best way to move forward. I guess I need an attorney."

"Well, if you need a witness…"

"That's wonderful," Sidney said. "I'll let you know."

Back home later, Sidney busied herself with housework. She didn't particularly like cleaning house, but she didn't despise it either. It was mindless work that allowed her plenty of time to think.

She was dusting the master bedroom furniture when the phone rang. She expected it would be Matt, giving her some lame excuse why he couldn't make it home in time for dinner.

"What?" she said, answering her cell phone without looking at the caller ID.

"Is Matt there?" the voice on the other end asked.

Sidney looked at the caller ID. It was Peter. He rarely called.

"Oh, God, Peter, I didn't know it was you."

"Are you alone?"

"Yes," Sidney said, her heart suddenly pounding in her chest. "We can talk. I have something I wanted to tell you, anyway."

"Good," Peter said. Then he paused and Sidney waited.

"Well …" she finally prompted. "Why did you call?"

"Sidney, I have quit working for the agency," he said.

"What?" she shook her head and sat down on the bed. "Why?"

"I need to talk to you," he said, "but I don't want to do this over the phone. I want to come to see you."

"What do you want to talk about?"

"Us."

"Us?" Sidney was confused. "Is there an 'us?'"

"Well, I'd like there to be," he said. "That's why I quit. I realized that what I have done to you, what I have gotten you into … well, I told you before. I don't want you to stay with the agency anymore either."

Sidney said nothing. She wanted to quit too, but she needed to find another way to fund her charity first. They'd been over this before, and they'd gotten nowhere.

"Maybe we can find another way," he said, as if reading her mind across the phone line.

"We?" Sidney asked. Suddenly she felt frustrated and angry. For some reason, she started to push back. "Why do you say 'we?' You don't run my charity."

"Really, I want to talk with you in person, Sidney," he said. "I don't think we can figure this out on the phone."

"I don't know what we're trying to figure out here, Peter," she said. "You quit, you want me to quit, but I can't quit. Not yet. Not until I find other ways to support T-Squared."

"When we were in Vegas, you sounded like you didn't like who you'd become," he said. "I thought you were unhappy, and I felt responsible."

"I see," Sidney said. "But you aren't responsible for my life. And feeling guilty doesn't solve my problem. I still need to find a way—"

"We're talking in circles," Peter interrupted. "Please, let me see you."

"Peter, you can see me anytime you want," she said. "Ever since I met you, I've wanted to see you anytime I could. Can you come to Seattle?"

"But what about Matt?"

"Peter, that's what I wanted to tell you. Matt is having an affair. I found out in New York. I need to talk with someone about what to do, and you're the only one I know who will understand how really awkward this is. How can I complain about an affair when I've been out having sex for money?"

"Sidney, do you love him?"

"No, Peter, no," she said, shaking her head as if he could see it through the phone. "I guess I never have, but I'm not sure that's the operative issue here."

"Do you want to stay with him?"

"No," she said. "But, I have no money of my own. I can't even afford to fly for agency assignments without Matt's support."

"Can I come to see you? We can talk this through. Maybe tomorrow?"

"Wow," she said, surprised at his urgency. "No, you can't. I'm going to St. Louis on Tuesday for an appearance."

"Do you have to go?"

"Peter," she said. "You know the rules. I accepted the date, I have to go."

"When will you be back?"

"Thursday afternoon."

"Okay, I'll meet you wherever you get back. Or somewhere else. I really need to see you."

After they hung up, Sidney lay back on the bed and stared at the ceiling. For months, ever since they met, he had been loving and passionate when they were together, but he had tolerated long stretches without her. She had no idea why he needed to see her so badly now.

But worse, she had no idea why she was pushing him away. Perhaps, she thought, she had become so intent on regaining her independence that she'd lumped all men together and labeled them "Do Not Touch"—Peter along with Matt. It wasn't fair to Peter.

What was it going to take for her to accept his love? Hitting some kind of bottom in her life? And how does a woman get to the point that she *wants* that to happen?

Sidney would have preferred to meet Allen in a public

place—like a shopping mall—where she could observe him from a distance before walking up and introducing herself.

But Allen insisted on picking her up at her St. Louis hotel. Didn't he know what a cliché that was: picking up an escort in a hotel? But, then, he was new to this kind of exchange, or at least new to the Milton Walton Agency.

She dressed the part of a businesswoman in a classic light gray suit and low two-inch heels, hoping to camouflage the true nature of their meeting from the other hotel guests. To soften the look for Allen's sake, she added the blue silk blouse she had bought for her first dinner with Peter's friends in Las Vegas.

Sidney waited as far from the entrance as possible, shielded by a huge potted fern. She saw him walk into the hotel and stand in the center of the big terrazzo star under the grand chandelier in the middle of the lobby. He rocked back and forth on his tasseled loafers, his dark gray trench coat pulled back at the sides and his hands in his pants pockets like a bad guy in a 1950s film noir.

He reminded her of how men in their fifties and sixties looked when she was growing up: thinning hair slicked back, tight Windsor knot high on his neck, the wrinkled eyes of a smoker. He had a long, straight nose and a high forehead, and looked chunkier than any of the customers she had dated on the West Coast. Sidney thought she could have passed a hundred men like him on the street every day and never noticed one of them.

He looked around, making eye contact with women as they walked by as if he was anticipating each one to be Sidney. Apparently, he had no idea what she looked like, even though there were hundreds of photos of her on the Internet and in LPGA archives.

He rocked back and forth, and turned completely around three or four times before she felt guilty for prolonging his wait and abandoned her hideout.

"Mr. Johnson?" she said, approaching and reaching out for a formal handshake. If they acted like this was a business meeting, they could get out of the hotel without people winking at them.

"Are you Sidney?" He pulled his hands out of his pockets and played with his tie, backing away from her outstretched hand like it was a handgun.

"Yeeeeees," she said, stretching out the syllable and tilting her head quizzically. "Is there a problem?"

"Oh, no," he said, finally putting a flabby, sweating palm in hers. He didn't shake, but left his hand there for her to grab and move up and down. He smiled feebly, showing a set of cheap dentures that looked too small for his mouth. "But, you are really tall."

Not a great way to ingratiate yourself, Allen, she thought.

"And, I believe you are a little late," he said, glancing at his watch.

"Then, let's go," she said, trying to sound cheerful. Breaking in the newbies, she was starting to realize, might be harder than she had imagined.

They walked out the revolving door, and he led her to a Lincoln Town Car in the *porte cochere.* He opened the passenger door for her, and as she slid into the seat, she saw a uniformed bellman run toward the car.

"Thanks for nothing, bub!" Allen chastised the young man, and elbowed him out of the way to open his own door and slide behind the wheel. He treated people the way Matt did, Sidney thought.

"I expected you to be dressed a little different," he said, settling into his seat and starting the car.

"Really?" Sidney forced a little laugh, but she wasn't feeling humored. First, he didn't like her height. Now her clothing. "What did you expect?"

"Something a little dressier, I guess," he said, his lips forming "dressier" but his face communicating "sexier." He glanced over at her and frowned. Back when she bought her blouse in Las Vegas, she had worried that it revealed too much cleavage, but apparently, it wasn't revealing enough for Allen.

They drove through a light rain in silence. The car smelled like stale smoke. Sidney cracked her window a bit to let in some fresh air.

"Don't do that!" Allen ordered. He pushed the window buttons on his side, first reclosing her window and then locking the controls.

Shocked, Sidney looked over at him. What was his problem? He stared straight ahead, squinting as if the light rain was making it hard to see the road. She'd been with him for less than ten minutes and she already had a sinking feeling that this would be the most uncomfortable date of her life—even worse than all of those awful, groping encounters of her mostly miserable college romances.

"Tell me a little about yourself." She attempted some conversation to loosen the tension. "What is it you do for a living?" Sidney knew the answer to that—it was part of the pre-date e-mail package she received before heading out to St. Louis, but it was usually easy to get guys to talk about themselves. It was usually their favorite subject.

"I'm a businessman," he said. "A very successful businessman. And I think that's all you really need to know." He looked at her knowingly. "I'd guess the less you know, the better, don't you think?"

Not only was he mean, he was stupid, Sidney thought. He should have known that she had his dossier, or had he forgotten that part of his agreement with the agency? She shut her mouth and turned to watch the mostly empty streets and sidewalks whip by in the rain.

They pulled up to a restaurant with big, colonial columns and a large, semicircular portico. A valet rushed out to take the car, and they walked up the steps and inside to an unattended hostess stand.

Allen stuck his hands back in his pants pockets, and started rocking back and forth on his heels again. Sidney watched the servers move among the diners, listening to the soft muffle of voices and the clink of dishes and glasses in the open dining room. A minute later, no host or hostess had come forward to greet them.

"This is rude!" Allen blurted out loudly to a passing waiter. "Hello! We have a reservation!"

Sidney blinked hard. He had to be the most disagreeable human being she'd ever met—even if she included Tanya's date Bill. At least Bill had the excuse of being drunk. How did guys like Allen ever become successful in business?

She glanced at her watch. It was going to be a long night.

ॐ

"How did you get introduced to the agency?" Sidney asked, once they were seated, had ordered, and were served their first cocktails.

"I don't know if I can tell you that," Allen said. "Is it appropriate to talk about connections with the agency?"

"Well, I'm not exactly going to run to the FBI," Sidney joked.

Allen stared at her as if he were evaluating one of the used cars he was asked to sell on his lot.

"How do I know if I can trust you?"

"Allen!" she said, leaning forward. "We're in this together. What is your issue?"

"Well, I'm usually fairly discreet in my business dealings," he said, sitting back and tucking in his chin. "I need to maintain a certain distance."

This guy was really full of himself for a used car dealer, she thought. She covered her mouth quickly to hide an involuntary smirk.

"Well, you don't have to worry about that with me," she said. "I'm not going to sue you for selling me a lemon. And, I'm not sure how we can proceed this evening if you maintain your—quote, unquote—distance."

Allen said nothing. He stared at her, looking at once both intimidated by her directness and unrelenting in his need to be in control.

"I'm not sure I like you, Sidney," he said. "I chose you because of your golf, but I wasn't looking for someone so butch."

"Butch?" Sidney asked. "What do you mean?"

"Well, you don't seem very feminine."

"You've got to be kidding," she said. "With this hair and these boobs"—she waved at her chest—"I'm not woman enough for you?"

"You show up for a date in flats and a boring suit, and you expect me to like it?"

Sidney considered arguing that two-inch heels were hardly flats, but why bother? This guy wasn't worth it.

"Can't we talk about something other than my looks?" she asked, perturbed. "Is there something we can discuss that you don't think is too secret to reveal?"

"I expected a prostitute to be more humble," he said, ignoring her question and waving his cocktail glass in her face for emphasis.

"I can't believe you just said that," she whispered loudly, leaning across the table toward him.

"Well, why not?"

"Because ..." she realized she didn't have an answer. Was she just a prostitute? Was there any difference between a common streetwalker and what she was doing right then and there? How had she lost that distinction?

"Look, sweetie," Allen said, leaning in as well. "I know what I'm getting when I buy a Chevy or a Ford, and this is no different. I knew what you were when I hired you. What is your problem? Are you having second thoughts about what you have for sale?"

Sidney sat back and took the napkin out of her lap. She folded it in half and then in half again. She placed it carefully on the table in front of her. She paused. Was she ready to do this?

Yes. She pushed her chair back from the table and stood up.

"I'm sorry, Allen, but your audition is over," she said, leaning over to whisper in his ear. "You are not accepted as a customer of the Milton Walton Agency." She started to walk away.

"What?!" he shouted, standing up and knocking his chair over backwards. The diners at the tables around them turned to stare. "You're too good for me? A common whore? You're too good for me?"

Sidney turned back. She walked up to him until his nose was about six inches in front of her chest, and looked down.

"And you, Allen, are a sick excuse for a human being. You don't deserve a common whore, let alone a professional like me."

She turned on her heels and strolled out of the dining room with at least twenty pairs of eyes following her.

She stopped by the hostess desk to ask for a cab, and stepped outside to wait in the light drizzle. She shivered, not so much from the chilly rain as from disgust. She expected a belligerent Allen to come out and berate her for leaving, and she was relieved when the cab arrived before he did. She jumped in and directed the driver to her hotel.

Once in her hotel room, she called the front desk and requested that all calls to her room be sent directly to voice mail. Then she called Laurie at the agency and left a message, and Alaska Airlines and rescheduled her return to Seattle.

She plugged her cell phone into the compact stereo and

chose a playlist of ballads, poured a deep, hot bath, and climbed in with a half-bottle of Malbec she found in the minibar. Slipping down into the soapy water until it just covered her shoulders, she sipped the wine and evaluated her life.

It was such a long journey, it seemed, from her earliest childhood memories until today. How many mistakes! How many forks in the road! How many times she had made the wrong choice! Why did people only get one chance? she wondered. How was anyone expected to do everything right the first time?

It was definitely time to get things back on the right track. She just had to figure out what that was.

Chapter Nineteen

Sidney didn't sleep in very often, but she let herself drift in and out of consciousness longer than usual the next morning. Her flight wasn't leaving until mid-afternoon, and there was no one in St. Louis she wanted to get up to see. Certainly not that disgusting Allen Johnson.

She was startled out of a light snooze by the hotel phone. She'd asked for her calls to be held. How did someone get through? She glanced at the alarm clock on the nightstand—nine o'clock—and reached for the receiver.

"I'm sorry to disturb you, Miss Stapleton. I know you asked us to hold your calls, but I have the St. Louis Police Department on the line," the hotel operator said. "Could you hold a minute while I transfer it?"

Sidney's heart thumped hard. *What the hell?*

"Ms. Stapleton?" Sidney was surprised to hear a woman's voice. Why did she assume a policeman would be a man? "Detective Ann Riley here, St. Louis Police Department. I wonder if you could come down to the station?"

"Why?" Sidney asked, sitting up straight in bed and combing the hair out of her face with her fingers. "What's going on?"

"We have had a complaint filed against you, and we

need to talk with you."

"A complaint about what?" Sidney was hoping detective Riley would say "disturbing the peace." Or maybe murder. Perhaps Allen Johnson had disappeared, and she was the last person known to have seen him. The last answer she wanted was "prostitution."

But the detective didn't answer at all. "I would rather do this in person," she said. "Can you get down here or should I send a squad car?"

Sidney pulled her legs out from under the covers and stood up. "No, no, don't send a car," she said, panicking. She certainly didn't want anyone to see her getting into a police car in front of the hotel. "I'll catch a cab. Where is the station?"

She wrote the address down and promised she'd be at the station within the hour.

"Perhaps it's obvious, Ms. Stapleton," the detective said, "but we really don't want you to leave the city until we've had a chance to talk with you."

"Christ, am I some kind of flight risk?" Sidney asked. "Am I in that much trouble?"

"I'd rather talk down here at the station," the detective repeated. "Just come on down as soon as you can."

Sidney hung up and sat down on the bed. She knew who would have filed the complaint, but why, if he was so worried about discretion and anonymity, would Allen have risked calling the police? The man must be nuts, she thought.

"I thought he was difficult, but I didn't know he was crazy," she mumbled.

She tried to figure out who she should call. Two people, she decided: Laurie at the agency and Peter. She'd left a message with Laurie the night before, but it was only eight o'clock in the morning in Las Vegas. She probably wasn't at work yet.

She unplugged her cellphone from the stereo and looked

for Peter's number. Her hands were shaking. She dropped the phone and picked it up just as Peter answered.

"Sidney! What a surprise so early in the morning," he said cheerfully. "What's up?"

"Peter, I'm in trouble," she said, her voice trembling. "I don't know what to do."

"What are you talking about? What's wrong?"

Her voice shaky, she tried to explain the situation to him calmly, but her words came out in big, jerky gulps.

"Sidney, don't worry." Peter tried to calm her down. "He isn't going to implicate himself any more than necessary."

"But, he already filed a complaint!"

"My guess is that's as far as it will go," Peter said. "He just wanted to harass you. He'll never testify and expose himself, and without his testimony, the complaint goes nowhere. And you don't know what the complaint is about."

"But what am I going to tell the police? What if he says he was solicited by me?"

"Tell them the truth: you had a dinner date with plans to play golf today. If he assumed that there was a promise of sex, well, that was his mistake. You and I know that there is no promise. And, even if he's new to the agency, he had to know it too."

"And I don't mention the agency, right?"

"Sidney, tell them what you have to, but generally, giving less information is better than pouring your guts out. The most important thing is to protect yourself. I'll get on a plane and be there as soon as possible. Where are you staying?"

"Really?" Sidney was surprised. "I don't expect you to do that. I just needed your advice."

"No problem, Sidney," he said. "I got you into this mess, it's the least I can do. And, I want to see you anyway."

Sidney hung up and sat down to try to stop shaking. Knowing that Peter was on his way helped. It was ironic, though, that it was the man who got her into this quandary and not her husband that she had called for help, she thought.

She looked at the clock. She had another half hour before Laurie would be at work in the agency. She would have to head for the police station before she talked to her, she realized. But she'd follow Peter's advice: say as little as possible.

After a quick shower, Sidney called for a cab. On the way to the police station, she called Alaska Airlines and rebooked her flight again for the next day. She was glad she had MVP Gold status with the airline; otherwise all of these changes would be expensive.

At the police station, she was escorted back to a small interrogation room that looked just like the ones she'd seen on "Law and Order" and "Castle" on TV. She sat, hands folded on the Formica-topped table, and waited, staring into the one-way mirror in front of her.

"Ms. Stapleton," said a thirty-something woman who finally entered the room with a notepad. She was short and a bit stout, but attractive in a professional sort of way, her hair tied back in a long ponytail like Sidney had worn on the Tour. "I'm Ann Riley. We spoke on the phone."

"Yes. What is this about?"

"You don't know?"

Sidney shook her head slowly, holding eye contact with the young detective.

"Well, do you know a gentleman by the name of Allen Johnson?" Detective Riley sat down across the table.

"Yes, but I wouldn't call him a gentleman."

There was a good chance that detective Riley agreed, thought Sidney, as she watched her fight to keep a smile from spreading across her face.

"Why is that?" the detective asked.

"He was very rude to me last night at dinner, and I left

him at the table."

"Well, he says you propositioned him as a prostitute and he rejected you. That's why you left in a huff, isn't it? As you probably know, prostitution is not legal in Missouri."

"I have no reason to know that," Sidney said. "And, I did not solicit anything from that man last night. We had a date for dinner, and we were supposed to play golf today."

"And how did that come about?"

"We apparently have a mutual acquaintance who introduced us," Sidney said.

"Who is that?"

"He wouldn't tell me." Sidney was relieved that so far, she didn't have to lie to answer the detective's questions. Allen's "discretion" was helping her more than she could have imagined.

"So you do this often?" the detective asked. "Fly halfway across the country to have dinner and play golf?"

"Yes," Sidney said. "It's marketing. People are willing to pay to play golf with me."

"Are you famous or something?"

"I'm surprised you don't know that," Sidney said. "Didn't you look me up on the Internet before I came in?"

Ann Riley looked embarrassed. She pursed her lips and flipped open her notebook. "Why don't you tell me what I would have learned about you if I had found time to do that this morning," she said.

"I played golf on the LPGA for years, and won five championships," Sidney said. "I had to quit when I was injured in an automobile accident, and now I make money for my charity by showing up at events and playing golf with people who are willing to pay to play with a former professional golfer."

"Your charity?"

"Yes," Sidney sat back in the hard chair and smiled. This interrogation wasn't going as badly as she had feared. "Do you want me to tell you about it?"

"No, I don't think so," the detective said. "But you are saying your date had nothing to do with sex?"

Sidney considered the question for a minute. How could she answer the question in such a way that she was denying Allen's allegations, while also looking forthcoming and honest?

"Let me be honest with you," she said, leaning back over the table toward the detective. "I am no angel. I have slept with men other than my husband. If one of them was this mysterious friend of Allen's who connected us, then I think Allen got the wrong impression. I play golf with men for money."

"Are you going to be staying in town for a while?" the detective asked, closing her notebook. She had written nothing down, which Sidney took as a good sign. "I may have more questions for you."

"I'm leaving tomorrow," Sidney said. "Mid-afternoon."

"Well, I'll call you at your hotel if I need something more before then," the detective said, standing. She held out her hand, businesslike, for a shake. Sidney stood and accepted the gesture.

"I'm not sure this matter will go any further than this conversation." The detective opened the door for her. "But, I'll let you know. Please stay in town until I get in touch with you."

"Do I have to?" Sidney asked. "Am I under arrest?"

"No," the policewoman answered. "I can't make you stay, but I hope you will. It will be easier for both of us if you wait to hear from me."

Sidney took a deep breath and let it out slowly as the detective opened the door and ushered her out. The interview had gone as well as she could expect, and she felt confident that she would get out of St. Louis without having her reputation sullied.

Unfortunately, she was too optimistic.

᷍

As she pushed open the door to leave the police station, a thin man with a camera and a baseball cap stepped in front of her, snapping photos rapid-fire. Surprised, she slipped off the step at the door, and fought to keep her balance. When she looked up again, the photographer had moved over to let another man step around him. The second man shoved a tape recorder at her. Was he a reporter?

"Ms. Stapleton!" the man shouted excitedly and unnecessarily loudly, given that he was right in her face. "Have you been arrested for prostitution?"

"What?" Sidney fell back a step, trying to create some distance between herself and the rude interrogator. He was short, balding and thick in the waist, and his jeans barely hung onto his hips, well below his belly. "Who are you?"

"Niles Tenaka, St. Louis Weekly," the man spat out. "We understand you have been called in for questioning for solicitation. Have you been arrested? Are the allegations true?"

"Who the hell told you that?" she demanded, trying to get around the reporter and his photographer, who continued to snap photos. It was going to be difficult to hail a cab with these two in her way, but she couldn't get around them.

"A source told us you had propositioned him last night and that you would be here for questioning," the reporter said. "Now is it true?"

"Who is your source?" Sidney realized there was no escape. She would have to stand her ground and wait for the reporter to run out of questions.

"I can't disclose that," the reporter said. "But tell us what you are doing here."

"I'll bet you don't even know who your source is," she said. "I'll bet he didn't tell you. And yet you were willing to waste your time to come down here and harass me. What newspaper did you say you work for?"

"The St. Louis Weekly," he said, digging a dog-eared business card out of his jeans pocket. "So why are you down at the police station? Was it about prostitution?"

"I don't think I have to answer that," Sidney said. "Now if you don't get out of my way, I will have to go right back in there"—she pointed to the police station behind her—"and ask them to charge you with harassment."

"Ma'am," the reporter sneered. "People threaten that all the time. We're just doing our job. Are you going to answer our questions or not? Are you a prostitute?"

"Definitely not," she said. She did a quick calculation: if she stepped forward, they would have to step back, wouldn't they? She was taller than both men, although the reporter weighed significantly more than she did.

She tried it, but neither man gave her an inch. She was standing within a foot of the reporter's notebook and protruding belly.

"I wouldn't suggest you touch me," the reporter smiled and gestured toward the photographer. "He'll catch it on film."

"Film?" she said, sneering back at him. She turned to the cameraman. "What? You haven't advanced to digital yet there at the weekly?"

"It's a figure of speech," the reporter retorted. "But that's not the issue here. The question is why you were here for questioning."

"The issue is that you're in my way," Sidney said, angrily, looking down at the reporter's face. Her voice was starting to shake. "Now, move!"

"Are you looking for a fight, lady?" The reporter dropped his notebook to his side and puffed out his chest.

"No, but you are," she yelled in his face. She felt the anger rise to her shoulders. Her fists tightened and she took a half-step back.

Without thinking, she replicated the same sequence of moves she had perfected on the golf course. She stepped forward with her left foot, turned her hips toward her target, and landed a solid underhand punch in the reporter's soft belly with her right hand.

Niles doubled over, holding his stomach and coughing. He fell to the ground. She looked down at him and then at her hand. It was still balled up in a fist. She expected it to hurt, but the reporter's fat had cushioned her blow. It hadn't hurt any more than it would have if she'd socked a pillow.

Sidney stepped around his prone body, but the photographer jumped in front of her, continuing to snap pictures. "Do you want me to flatten you too?" she shouted. "Get out of my way."

Before she could step back and repeat the punch she'd delivered to Niles, the door behind them swung open with a bang, and Sidney turned to see two burly police officers step out.

"What's going on here?" one of them demanded.

"She assaulted me, officer!" Niles croaked out loudly, still lying on his side and holding his stomach.

"I can't imagine why," the other officer said, a grin spreading across his face. He stepped toward Sidney and put his hand on her elbow. "You probably had better come back inside until we get this figured out."

"He wouldn't get out of my way!" Sidney exclaimed in protest.

"Yes, he has a habit of doing that," the policeman said, leading her inside and directing her to a bench across from the front counter in the waiting area. "But, if he presses charges against you, it's going to be your ass that's in trouble. Now sit here, and I'll be right back."

Sidney sat down and looked out the window. The other officer was squatting down to talk with Niles, who still hadn't gotten up. He was overacting a bit, she thought, smiling crookedly.

The asshole deserved it. And, that was a pretty good punch. Maybe if the prostitution thing didn't work out, she could turn to boxing. Talk about your high-class occupational options!

The photographer stepped through the door into the lobby. He walked toward her but had only snapped a couple of shots before another policeman shot out from behind the counter and stood in his way.

"Get out of here!" he yelled at the photographer.

"I have a right—" The cameraman started to argue, but the policeman cut him off.

"So call your fucking lawyer!" the officer shouted. "You don't have a right to harass people. Get out!"

The photographer smirked, raised his camera to his face and snapped a picture of the red face of the officer before turning on his heel and running out the door.

"Hey Sidney," he called out over his shoulder. "Be sure to buy a copy of this week's paper. We'll try to pick a flattering photo to use with the story."

Outside, Sidney watched Niles sit up, and then with the help of the policeman, stand up. The policeman pulled a notebook out of his pocket and was scribbling while Niles shouted at him. Sidney couldn't make out his words through the thick glass and brick walls of the building, but she didn't need to. It was clear what was happening.

"Oh, Sidney, what the hell?"

Sidney looked around. Detective Riley stood in the door to the back of the station where they had held their discussion just ten minutes before.

Sidney shook her head sadly and shrugged her shoulders.

The detective motioned for her to come back with her, and held the door open. This time, she led her to a chair by her desk and sat down across from her.

"Is that how a trapped animal feels?" Sidney asked, sitting down. "Is that why the hunted lunge at the hunter?"

"Pretty poetic, Sidney," the detective smiled. "But I doubt that will be the quote they use in the paper when it comes out next week. Why did you do it?"

"I don't know. I couldn't get around him."

"You could have come back inside for help."

"Could you have made him leave?"

"No, it's public property, but we could have made him give you clearance."

"Look, I wasn't thinking," Sidney said. "I just wanted to get in a cab and get to the airport and get home. This has been a nightmare."

"Yes, but now I'm afraid your trip will be postponed even more," the detective said. "You know, the sad thing is that I had decided to not pursue Mr. Johnson's complaint. This could have blown over with nothing but a photo and some unsubstantiated innuendo in the Weekly. Now, I'm afraid, you'll probably be charged with assault, and you've just made yourself into the celebrity of the week."

Sidney shook her head and looked down at her feet. "I've never hit anybody in my life," she said. "I don't know what got into me."

"Tell me what happened," the detective said, opening her notepad.

◈

Two hours later, Sidney got in a cab in front of the station, and her cell phone rang.

Her caller ID showed the call was coming from the agency in Las Vegas. "Laurie," she answered. "I'll call you as soon as I get to the hotel. Maybe ten minutes. Will you be there?"

She hung up and two seconds later, the phone rang again.

"I'm at the airport," Peter said. "My flight gets in there at 2:30. I'll come directly to the hotel. How did it go with the police?"

"You aren't going to believe this," she blurted out. "I was just arrested and charged with assault. I was accosted at the door to the station by a photographer and a reporter. I ended up punching the reporter in the gut."

Silence. Peter was apparently too shocked to respond.

"But," she continued over his silence, "they let me go pending my arraignment tomorrow, and I'm headed back to the hotel."

"God, I'm sorry," Peter said, finally. "Hang in there, and stay low. Probably stay in your room. Call room service and raid the mini-bar. Watch re-runs on TV. I'll be there as soon as I can."

"Well, I can't leave town until I see the judge tomorrow, at least," she said. "So I'm not going anywhere."

"Did you really punch the guy?"

"Oh, yeah." Sidney smiled, remembering how Niles buckled over and fell down. "You should have seen it. It was epic. He crumbled like a dry biscuit."

The cab let her out at the hotel and Sidney went straight up to her room. She grabbed a half-bottle of Pinot Grigio from the mini-bar refrigerator, sat down on the loveseat, and called Laurie back. She told her the whole story, starting with the horrific evening with Allen Johnson and ending with her release from the police station.

"Oh my God," Laurie said when she finished. "You really punched him?"

"Yeah, but I thought you'd be more interested in the prostitution allegation," Sidney said. Why was everyone focusing on the punch? Didn't they think she had it in her?

"Hey, I'm no lawyer, but my guess is that Allen Johnson wasn't going to provide the police with any more information to go on. The matter would have disappeared, and we'd just let Allen know that he wasn't accepted as a customer."

"But wouldn't he have tried to expose you to get revenge?"

"Not if he didn't want the world to know he tried to hire a professional golfer to sleep with him," she said.

"So has this happened often?"

"No, but we always knew it could," Laurie said. "We've had close calls before, but I think this is the first time someone actually called the police."

"Well, what now?"

"Mr. Walton will want you to come to Las Vegas to sit down with him," Laurie said. "We'll pay for your flight this time. When will you get out of St. Louis?"

They scheduled a meeting for late the next day, assuming she was able to leave Missouri.

Sitting back with her wine, Sidney tried to reassure herself that she'd be back home in a couple of days and that word of Allen's allegations and her assault charge would never reach Seattle. She finished the wine without coming to any conclusions, and ordered a sandwich through room service. She was glad she was in a nice hotel. *Imagine sitting this out in a Super 8!*

Peter was due to arrive just after she gave up on her soup and sandwich. She had lost her appetite even before the lunch had been delivered on a large tray, draped with a starched white cloth.

Sidney had left instructions with the front desk to give Peter a key to her room, but sitting around waiting was driving her nuts. She went down to the lobby and waited by the big fern where she'd watched Allen arrive the night

298

before. Peter walked into the hotel, crossed the big terrazzo star on the floor, and headed for the registration desk.

The receptionist smiled brightly and handed him the keycard, and he turned to the elevator. Sidney snuck up behind and slipped through the elevator doors after him.

He turned, startled to see her. But he didn't hesitate. He wrapped her in his long arms and they rode the elevator in silence to her floor. He swiped his card through the lock and kicked the door closed after them. Sidney leaned into him, and suddenly, tears ran down her face onto his sweater. He pulled her to his side and walked her to the love seat.

He held her face with both hands and kissed her tears.

"Hey," he said. "This is all my fault, you know. I started you down this path."

"No," she said. "I am a grown-up. I made these decisions on my own. I can face who I am and what I've become. I'm sure I'm not the first prostitute in the world to slug some guy."

"I'd like you to quit using that word, Sidney," he said softly. "That's not what you are."

"Peter!" she exclaimed, pulling back from his embrace. "That *is* what I am. Let's quit fooling ourselves. That's what I've been ever since the first time I slept with you."

"You didn't sleep with me for money," he said. "I asked you to stay with me in Vegas because you were the most attractive, intelligent, interesting woman I had ever met."

"But you sleep with all of your recruits," she answered, pushing his hands away from her face. "And you paid me twenty thousand dollars. Isn't that the regular signing bonus?"

Sidney stood up and stomped across the room. She leaned against the dresser and looked disdainfully at Peter. She hated the way she was acting. Here she was, berating the one person she wanted by her side at that moment. The only person she wanted at her side. What had happened to her?

She had become an angry, self-loathing woman. She'd taken the stage, she'd performed for the crowd, and she reveled in the adoration of all of the men she'd had sex with in the past few months. But that was no longer what she wanted. Suddenly she realized she wanted a different kind of life— one, she shuddered to think, that was more like her parents'.

"I've never slept with a recruit other than you," Peter finally responded, slowly and quietly. "I didn't know you thought it was routine. Sidney, I've been in love with you since that very first night."

"What?" Sidney squinted at him, and shook her head. "Then why did you let me sleep with all of those other men?"

"That's why I wanted to come to Seattle this week. I needed to tell you in person," he said. "I have never hated myself so much as I have the past few months for getting you into this racket instead of just coming out and telling you how I felt from the beginning. And now, I need you to tell me if I'm wrong. I think you love me. Do you?"

He stood up and walked over to her. He put his hands on her shoulders and kissed her on the forehead.

"You have every reason to hate me," he said, looking her in the eye. "I don't blame you."

She held his eyes and tried to accept what he was saying. Was he telling her the truth?

Peter sensed her doubt. "You have to believe me," he said. "I need you. I know you are married, but I can't help but believe you love me too. And I hope that eventually you will forgive me."

"Oh, Peter," she whispered, the tears suddenly started flowing down her cheeks again. Her eyes searched his face for an unfamiliar wrinkle or blemish. There wasn't one. She'd studied it so many times as he lay sleeping next to her that she knew every inch of it. So many times, and yet not often enough.

She breathed in jerkily, fighting off sobs. "Why couldn't I tell you? Why did I have to be totally defeated and needy before I could admit it, even to myself?"

He held her and waited.

"Yes, I love you, Peter," she whispered, her face in his chest. "I love you so much."

He pulled back and looked in her eyes. His grin was wide and spontaneous. "I knew it!" he said. "But thank you. Thank you for that."

He pulled her toward him and kissed her again.

"Hey," he said. "Sit. You seem a little shaky."

Sidney didn't argue. She sat down beside him on the bed with her feet dangling over the side, and leaned against his shoulder. Slowly, the tears stopped, and her breathing returned to normal. They sat quietly, leaning against each other. Finally calm, she reached over, put her hand on his crotch, and felt him respond.

"Maybe we should get a room," he whispered in her ear.

Sidney laughed, wiping the last drying tears off her face. "I think we've got one," she said, unbuttoning her shirt. "How about we get our money's worth out of it?"

Having sex with someone she had just professed her love to was a first for Sidney. But, then, this was the first time she'd ever told a man she loved him and meant it. And, in fact, it was the first time she'd been in love, she thought, spooning and cooling down with Peter afterwards.

How much more powerful it was! She shuddered at the memory of their explosive, mutual climax. She hoped the walls were soundproof, or that the next-door neighbors had not checked in yet.

Why had it taken her so long to accept her own feelings? Did she think that a successful life and a love life were

301

mutually exclusive? That she had to choose one over the other?

An hour later, Sidney was awakened by the hotel phone. It was Laurie. The agency had called St. Louis and arranged for an attorney to represent her, saving her from having to accept a public defender. He was coming to meet them.

Brian joined them in the hotel café that afternoon, and they talked through the facts of the case and possible tacks to take with the judge the next day. Clean-cut and baby-faced, Brian was nice, but all business. He didn't allude to any knowledge of the real reason she was in the city, but instead, took the "golf date" story at face value. She appreciated his discretion. He also didn't ask why Peter was there, or what his relationship was with her. Perhaps Milton had already filled him in.

As Sidney and Peter waited in the bar with a bottle of wine, Brian called the city's prosecutor, and came back with good news.

"They're going to ask for probation," he said. "Apparently, Mr. Tenaka is not anyone's favorite reporter in this town. I thought for a minute the prosecutor was going to ask why you didn't shoot him instead."

"Yeah, he is quite the creep," she said. "So what does probation mean?"

"You'll have to check in with a probation officer once a week, and there may be some other restrictions on your activities," Brian said. "But you can go back to Bellevue. You can probably go back to your marketing work as well. I doubt there will be any travel restrictions."

❧

The next morning, Brian escorted Sidney into the courtroom. "You are lucky," he said. "Not only does the prosecutor dislike your victim, you pulled a judge who has had his own run-ins with Mr. Tenaka."

"I'm guessing that his lawyer will ask for a change in judges, then, right?" Sidney asked.

"Maybe, but the prosecutor doesn't care for Mr. Tenaka any more than the rest of us do," he whispered back. "She is the one who would have to ask for a change in venue. In any case, the judge would deny it. Niles could try to appeal that decision. But this isn't going to go that far."

"I hope you're right," she said. As she sat down on the gallery bench, she spied Niles across the aisle from them. He looked smug, letting out a little huff as he met her eye. Sidney looked away.

She turned to make sure Peter was following them into the courtroom. He sat two rows behind them and winked at her. She winked back and then turned to watch and listen to the judge work through the docket ahead of them.

"The people versus Nola Barnes!" the bailiff called out. Across the aisle from her, Sidney saw Nola rise with her attorney and step through the half-door between the gallery and the judge's bench. Her clothes—a cheap, pink polyester suit and a pair of pumps with the leather peeling off the heels—looked as tired and haggard as her thin, long face.

"Charge is prostitution," the judge read the citation in front of him. He spent a minute skimming the police report.

What were the chances? Sidney wondered. What were the odds she'd face her own sins right there in the courtroom like that? She wasn't being arraigned for prostitution that day, but she could have been. She was no better than that wretched woman standing in front of her. She turned and caught Peter's eye, and grimaced. *This is what I've become!* She turned back to the court scene in front of her.

"How do you plead, Miss Barnes?" the judge asked as he finished reading and looked up.

"Not guilty," the woman said, barely audibly.

"Bail?" the judge asked, looking at the prosecutor, a

middle-aged woman dressed in a classic, tailored suit and comfortable ballet flats—probably much better suited for a day standing in court than Nola's heels, Sidney thought.

"Ms. Barnes isn't a flight risk, your honor," the prosecutor said. "The people aren't requesting bail."

"Okay, we'll see you back here …," the judge said. He paused, looking at a calendar in front of him. "How about next Thursday at ten a.m.?" he asked, looking at Nola's attorney.

"Fine." The man nodded, and with his hand on Nola's back, directed her out the swinging door and out of the courtroom.

One more arraignment preceded Sidney's—a charge of petty theft at a liquor store. The old defendant shuffled through the swinging gate with an attorney who looked just about as aged as he was. The two mumbled through the proceeding and left within two minutes.

"The people versus Sidney Stapleton!" the bailiff called.

"What's the charge?" the judge asked, watching Sidney and her attorney walk through the gate, and smiled.

"Assault, your honor," the prosecutor said. "Ms. Stapleton assaulted a reporter, Niles Tenaka, in front of the police station yesterday morning. Ms. Stapleton was arrested and cited at the scene."

Sidney saw a smile cross the judge's face. He chuckled quietly and shook his head.

"I would like to say that we could use a few more citizens like you willing to stand up to what has become an epidemic of media thuggery in our city," the judge said, nodding at Sidney. "But, unfortunately for you, assault is not tolerated in our civilized society."

"Of course," he continued, looking over her head to glare at Niles, who was sitting right behind her, "one could argue that society isn't very civilized with the likes of Mr. Tenaka on the streets, but we cannot try the victim here. You are charged with assault, Ms. Stapleton. How do you plead?"

"Guilty, your honor," she said.

"And what is the prosecution asking?" the judge asked.

"Probation, your honor," the woman said, glancing over at Sidney. "Ms. Stapleton has no criminal record and probably could have argued self-defense in this case. She has cooperated with police, and the prosecution is grateful that she is not demanding a trial that would take up the court's time with this matter."

"Hey!" From behind her, Sidney heard Niles shout out. "This woman assaulted me, and you're letting her go with nothing?"

"Sit down and shut up, Niles," the judge said.

"This is bullshit!" Niles yelled.

"Officer!" the judge called to the policeman by the back door. "Escort Mr. Tenaka out of the courtroom, please. Niles, if you don't leave now—peacefully!—I will charge you with disorderly conduct and contempt!"

"She's a fucking whore and a bully, and I'm the one kicked out of the courtroom?" Niles yelled, shuffling out of his row and down the aisle, the policeman's hand gripping his arm. The courtroom doors banged open and shut, and Sidney turned back to the judge. She let out her breath; she hadn't even realized she was holding it.

"Ms. Stapleton," the judge looked down. "I apologize for the unruly behavior of our so-called media in this city. Now, because you are a resident of the state of Washington, we will be contacting your local district attorney to be sure that you meet the requirements of your probation. Do you understand?"

"Yes, your honor," she said, nodding at the bench. "Thank you."

"Okay, next case!" He banged his gavel on the bench.

Outside of the courtroom, Sidney thanked Brian, and he gave her a warm hug.

"How much do I owe you?" she asked.

"Your uncle Milton paid the bill," he said. "He seems to think you're the cat's pajamas. I think I can see why. Take care of yourself, Sidney. My guess is I'll never see you in St. Louis again."

"Right." She laughed. "Thanks again and take care."

She watched him walk away and felt Peter's arms circling her waist from behind.

"Congratulations, lover," he whispered through her hair. "I think you've become a super-hero here in St. Louis. At least in this courthouse."

Sidney leaned back into his embrace. "I'm just glad it's over. I'm lucky that I slugged a guy who had plenty of enemies in high places. It could have been so much worse."

She turned around and reached for his hands.

"I'm going to tell Milton I'm quitting," she said. "I should have done it after the agency party when you did. I realized today that as much as I was getting paid for my dates, I am no different than poor Nola back there in the ugly suit."

"Oh, you're a lot different!" Peter laughed.

"Yes, but my crimes have been the same." She smiled, remembering an old joke about a prostitute soliciting a john. "You know the biggest difference between her and me is price. And she probably has to do this to put food on the table. I don't."

"I don't know about that, but I like your decision to quit," Peter said. "I don't want to share you with anyone else anymore. We'll find another way to fund T-Squared."

Sidney looked away. She hadn't thought about her charity much over the past couple of days. She needed to see how much damage this assault charge—and the photo in the Weekly—were going to hurt her reputation, and therefore, her ability to run T-Squared. Maybe she'd have to quit that too.

But now, she had things to celebrate—getting off with only probation, quitting the agency, and being in love. And most of all: finally accepting that someone else could love her.

"Let's go drink lunch, take advantage of that nice room for the rest of the day, and then, leave this town forever," she said, dropping one of Peter's hands and leading him out of the courthouse with the other.

Chapter Twenty

Sidney and Peter said goodbye with a long hug in front of the Alaska Airlines baggage valet. She watched him walk away while she waited to check her golf clubs. He turned to look back at her three times before ducking into United's entrance to the terminal.

She had a lot to accomplish in the next couple of weeks before she could see him again. She needed to navigate through the negative publicity that was likely to arise from her assault conviction and the photo that the St. Louis Weekly was undoubtedly going to publish. She had to make the first moves toward the inevitable divorce with Matt and figure out how to fund her charity going forward, if it was going forward.

She needed to call Karla and tell her what had happened in St. Louis so she wouldn't find out about her assault charge through the media and the LPGA gossip network. She had to check in with the probation officer the county attorney would assign to her.

She even had to find a place to live, but until she and Matt worked through the financial decisions of their separation, she had no money to rent an apartment.

"I'm so angry for letting myself become so financially dependent on him," she had told Peter on the way to the airport. "Now, I'm in a bind. I have no paying job, I have no savings left. And it's my own fault."

"I can help—" Peter started to offer, but she cut him off.

"Replacing one dependency with another isn't going to solve my problem," she said. "I have to either get a salary for running T-Squared or quit it and find a real job."

"But in the short run," Peter said, "I can lend you some money."

"Well, I'm certainly going to get some kind of support from the divorce settlement," she said. "Matt *is* a Microsoft millionaire. But I don't want to make that my long-term financial strategy. The sooner I'm free of him, the better off I'll be."

"The better off we'll be," Peter added. "Would you consider moving to Wisconsin?"

"Sheesh! It's cold there!" Sidney laughed. "I don't know if I can do that."

"Well, think about it. We could always spend the winters in the desert."

Sidney leaned over in the backseat of the cab and kissed him on the cheek. "You are making some rather rash assumptions, old man," she teased. "I tell you I love you and now you think I should move to the tundra?"

"Didn't you grow up in Minneapolis?" He laughed.

"Yes, and therefore I know about that of which I speak!"

As her plane landed in Las Vegas, Sidney decided to call Karla right away. She pulled her golf bag off the baggage carousel and lugged it to the taxi stand. On the way to the Milton Walton Agency, she called her friend.

Karla was often at a golf tournament on Fridays, but it was an off weekend for the LPGA, and she was relaxing at her Phoenix home by the pool.

"Sidney!" she said, answering the phone. "I was just

thinking about you. How is that sexy affair going?"

"Funny you should ask," Sidney said. "We're getting closer to moving beyond the affair state of things. But I have some other things to tell you about first."

Sidney started with the assault charge and guilty plea, which she knew would be the piece of news most likely to reach Karla first. But, that story led to the obvious question: what was she doing at the police station in the first place?

As she stammered around, trying to figure out how to answer the question, Sidney made a decision.

"Karla," she said. "I'm in Las Vegas to meet with that sports-management agency I told you about. Then, I'm going to come to Phoenix and see you. I have a little bit of 'fessing up to do."

"What are you talking about?"

"No, I want to do this in person," Sidney said. "While I still have access to Matt's credit card, I will fly over. Can I stay for the weekend?"

"Well, sure," said Karla, suspiciously. "But now you really have me wondering."

"Oh, my dear friend." Sidney chuckled. "It will be worth the wait, trust me. It will be worth it."

Sidney hung up, called Expedia and booked a flight that afternoon from Las Vegas to Phoenix. Then she called Matt and left a message. She wouldn't be home until Monday. She didn't explain.

It was only the second time she'd ever visited the Milton Walton offices. The first time was back when she was considering signing on with the agency. It had only been five months, but it seemed like it was years ago, Sidney realized.

As she walked through the glass doors and crossed the parquet to the front desk, Gregory looked up. As soon as she saw her, he jumped out from behind his reception desk and reached out for a hug.

His smile was so genuine, Sidney couldn't deny him. She leaned down for his embrace and reciprocated.

"It is sooooo wonderful to see you, Ms. Stapleton!" he said. "Let me see if Mr. Walton is finished with his last meeting."

Gregory ran back around to his chair and strapped his telephone headset back over his ears.

Ten minutes later, Sidney sat on the couch in Milton Walton's private office, sipping a freshly made latte delivered by an obsequious older man whom Milton introduced as "my butler."

"That must have been quite the horrific experience," Milton said, his eyes communicating sympathy for what happened in St. Louis. "I'm more sorry than I can ever tell you. We've never had a potential customer turn into such a disaster like that. What can I do to make it up to you?"

"How did Allen get introduced to you?" she asked.

"I'm guessing by 'you,' you mean the agency," Milton said, cautiously. "I never met the man, I assure you."

"Oh, no," Sidney said. "I meant the agency. Who introduced him to the agency?"

"I don't think I can tell you that," Milton said. "Our customer network is protected by some pretty stringent policies on anonymity, and I know you can understand that. But, I assure you the customer who brought Allen in has lost his privilege to recommend new customers."

"I would hope so. He obviously has very poor instincts."

"I would agree. Now tell me what the outcome of the assault charge was."

Sidney explained her probation to the extent that she understood it. She would find out more when she returned to Seattle.

"It could have been so much worse," Sidney concluded. "If Niles Tenaka hadn't been public enemy number one, I would not have gotten off so easily. And, if Allen hadn't been so untrustworthy, I could have ended up with a prostitution charge."

"It seems we were all lucky," Milton agreed. "I'm sure Allen Johnson is going to disappear into the night before he risks his used-car dealership by implicating himself as a john."

"You mean 'customer,'" Sidney countered with a chuckle. "Remember, they're customers."

"Yes, but the press wouldn't call him that."

"No, you're right. So, do you think he'll try to get revenge on the agency?"

"No, I don't," Milton said, thoughtfully. "But I don't know. We'll see what happens in the next couple of weeks."

Milton reached over and grasped Sidney's free hand. "I can't tell you how much I appreciate your calm, professional manner," he said. "Are you always this unflappable?"

"Uh, no," Sidney said, setting her empty coffee cup on the end table next to the couch. "But, I need to tell you what you can do for me. You asked, and I will tell you."

"Okay," Milton said. "Shoot."

"I want to be released from the agency."

Milton dropped her hand, stood up, and walked to the window that looked out at the Red Rock Canyon peaks in the distance. He stood with his hands clasped behind his back for a few minutes. Sidney was sure he would agree; he couldn't risk having her as a client anymore anyway. The Weekly story was still likely to suggest she was engaged in prostitution, and Milton wouldn't want that news to eventually lead reporters to him.

He turned and confirmed her expectations.

"I understand," he said, nodding. "I don't like it, but I understand. You have become one of our most successful clients in just a few months, and I hate to lose you. But, I can't ask you to stay after what happened in St. Louis."

"Thank you," Sidney said, standing up. She didn't know what good it would do her to pretend like he was doing her a favor, but she figured it wouldn't hurt if she left with his gratitude, however unarticulated. "It has been an experience, that's for sure. And in a way, it helped me figure out some things about myself."

"How are you going to fund your charity from now on?" he asked.

"I don't know yet," she said. "I may not have a charity to worry about, depending on what the Weekly publishes."

"Let me help," Milton said. "I'll send you a check."

"But wouldn't that betray you?"

"It won't be traceable."

"Of course not," Sidney said. She shouldn't have doubted him. She turned to leave.

"If you ever change your mind, Sidney, you're always welcome to come back to us," Milton said, crossing the room and opening his arms for a hug.

"I don't see that happening," she said, accepting a brief squeeze. "But thanks all the same."

She was halfway out the door when Milton stopped her.

"Hey," he said. "I'm really pleased about you and Peter. Good luck. He's a great guy."

Sidney turned back. "How did you know?"

"He's not been the same since he met you," Milton said. "I've never seen a man so quickly smitten quite like that."

Funny, Sidney thought, leaving the office. *Why did it take me so long to see it?*

❧

Karla was having her best year ever on the Tour, which was amazing, considering she was now one of the oldest players on the LPGA. She'd won two tournaments, and had risen to the fifteenth best golfer in the world on the Rolex Rankings.

Sidney waited for her friend curbside at the Phoenix airport, nervous about how Karla was going to react to her story. She didn't want her confessions to trump Karla's great season, but not knowing if the St. Louis Weekly would print allegations of prostitution against her, she decided she had better tell her friend everything. And, then, she'd have to decide if that was the best tactic with Matt as well.

If it hadn't been for that car accident, could she still be on the Tour? Sidney wondered as she waited to see Karla's Pathfinder. How much simpler things would be, if she were. On the other hand, without everything that had happened to her since she left the Tour, she never would have met Peter.

Sidney didn't believe, as she often heard other people profess, that "things happen for a reason." There were reasons *why* things happened, but she didn't believe in a teleological universe. Growing up the daughter of two social scientists, she knew the difference between the belief in determinism and belief in fate.

To Sidney, the accident didn't happen *so that* she could meet Peter. But without the accident, she probably never would have. And, maybe she never would have had a chance to fall in love. Who knew?

Karla whipped her Pathfinder in close to the curb and jumped out to hug Sidney. Karla was her fourth hugger of the day, Sidney thought, chuckling quietly.

"My friend, you are skinny as a rail!" Karla exclaimed. "Let's get you home and feed you!"

"I don't know why," Sidney said. "I think I eat all of the time. Maybe it's stress."

Karla helped Sidney throw her golf bag in the back of her SUV, and they jumped up into their seats.

"I thought stress was supposed to make you gain

weight," Karla said, throwing the transmission in gear. "But who knows? Now what's been going on that made it so urgent for you to come and see me?"

"Let's wait until we get to the house," Sidney said. "I don't want you driving off the road when I tell you."

"That good?"

"Oh, yeah." Sidney nodded. "At least that good."

As they relaxed by Karla's pool with margaritas in hand thirty minutes later, Sidney congratulated Karla on her great year on the Tour. She let Karla tell her two championship stories, starting with the first tee through all fifty-four holes of each win. Only passionate golfers could understand—or even follow—that kind of play-by-play, but even for them, it could be tedious. Sidney, however, was glad for the temporary distraction.

"Do you think there's any chance I could get back in?" Sidney asked as Karla wrapped up her soliloquy.

"Sure, there's always a chance," Karla said. "I'm still playing at your age. But, as I told you last fall, it's a whole different game out there now. If you're not driving two-sixty or two-seventy, on *average*, you're not going to compete. And these young girls are getting stronger and longer every day. And, they're good putters, too. I'm guessing I've got only a year or two left of serious competitiveness."

"Really?" Sidney stared at the reflection of the palm trees in the calm water of the pool and let Karla's skepticism sink in. Her friend was probably right. If she'd never left, perhaps she could compete, but it would be hard to work her way back into championship form.

"But why do you ask?" Karla interrupted her thoughts. "Aren't you doing well with your charity?"

"I don't know if there's going to be a charity anymore." Sidney sighed. "Let me start at the beginning."

"Holy shit." Karla's summation wasn't unexpected. It had taken Sidney an hour to take her friend through the events of the past five months, and as she told it, she realized what an incredibly salacious tale it had turned out to be. Even with its happy ending of Peter and falling in love, the story was more "holy shit" than "good for you."

"I thought my life was exhausting," Karla said. "I had no idea. All that travel; all those men!"

"Actually, there were only nine, not counting Allen, whom I didn't sleep with or play golf with," Sidney said, although she realized that the number didn't do much to bring the tale down to normal proportions. "I didn't even finish dinner with him."

"So what's going to happen with you and Matt? And you and Peter?"

"I have to figure out the Matt side first," Sidney said. "I think Peter and I can go forward together somehow, but it certainly it can't happen until Matt and I are through."

"How much of this does Matt know?"

"None, as far as I can tell. But when I get back, we'll see how much damage the St. Louis Weekly has done."

"Well, now I can see why you were asking about coming back on the Tour," her friend said, getting up to retrieve a bottle of wine from the outdoor bar refrigerator. "It is definitely easier to manage than what you've been through."

"Do you think I could make it back?"

"No, I'm not saying that," Karla said, shaking her head sadly. "I just meant that... Well, I just meant that I had no idea."

"The frustrating thing is getting to this point in your life and realizing you have so little to fall back on, so few skills," Sidney said. She walked over to the pool, kicked off her flip-flops, and stepped into the shallow end. She sat down and swung her legs in and out of the water.

She laughed. "You know what, Karla?"

"No, I'm not even going to try to guess what's next."

"Oh, no, I've given you the whole story. I just realized this is the first time I've put my toes in water outside a bathtub in a year."

"And your point is?"

"It's been crazy," Sidney said. "No time for a lazy day by a pool. Here I've been spectacularly unsuccessful, and yet so busy at it!"

"I guess it depends on your definition of success," Karla said, popping the cork out with corkscrew. She pulled two chilled glasses out of the pool-side refrigerator and delivered a cold Sauvignon Blanc to Sidney. "You were a very good, productive client at the agency from the sound of it. And, your charity was off to a pretty good start."

"Yes, but all for naught," Sidney said. "Without my agency customers, there's no way I can maintain the level of donations I would need to keep the chapters funded."

"Right." Karla sat at the edge of the pool and dipped her feet in the water beside Sidney. "Maybe you can teach golf lessons."

The next morning, the phone woke Sidney from a deep sleep. She couldn't remember where she was, but reached out and managed to open the screen.

"Yeah," she croaked, her voice not yet awake.

"Sidney, this is Matt." He didn't sound happy. "Where are you?"

Sidney sat up straight and looked around.

"I'm at Karla's place in Phoenix."

"What are you doing there?"

"I needed someone to talk with and I was already down this way, so I shot over."

"What do you mean, 'down that way?'"

"I was in Las Vegas—" Sidney stopped. Whoa! She hadn't told Matt anything about going to Las Vegas. What was already going to be a tough conversation just got harder.

"Vegas!" Matt shouted into the phone. "So were you seeing this guy? This guy I see in this photo of you in this sleazy supermarket tabloid?"

"What are you talking about?"

"*Sidney Stapleton, former LPGA professional golfer, and a man identified by sources as a part-time sports agent in Las Vegas share an intimate moment at Margaritaville on the Strip.*" Matt was apparently reading something.

So that pain-in-the-ass cameraman in Vegas five months ago wasn't just a tourist, she thought. It had taken him a long time to find a buyer for that photo, but clearly selling it had been his intent all along.

"I'm quoting from the caption under the picture," Matt said, not waiting for her reaction. "You two are kissing. Who the hell is he?"

"Matt, this is no time to talk about this," Sidney said slowly, trying to counter her speeding pulse. "I'll be home in a few hours." She was going to have to cut her weekend with Karla short.

"I would say it's high time you get your ass home, little lady," Matt said harshly. "I think you have a lot to explain here. Why the hell were you in Vegas again? Visiting your 'sports agent?'" He said the last two words like he was mimicking a lie.

Sidney paused and considered: what good would it do to say anything more at that point? None.

"I'll be home this afternoon. Goodbye, Matt."

Sidney wrapped her bathrobe around her body and tied the belt, pulled on the slippers Karla had lent her, and padded out to the kitchen. Karla was already up, reading the sports section of the Arizona Daily Republic.

"Hey, I've got to get to Seattle," she said. "Is there coffee?"

"What happened?" Karla jumped up and retrieved a K-cup from the cupboard and stuck it in the Keurig machine.

"Apparently some supermarket tabloid got ahold of a picture of Peter and me at a café in Las Vegas," she said. "Christ, that picture was taken five months ago. I'd nearly forgotten all about it."

"Your life is way too exciting," Karla said, laughing. "I don't know how this is going to end up, but I think it has made-for-TV potential!"

Sidney tried to laugh with her, but the sick feeling in the bottom of her stomach wouldn't allow it.

Sidney got home in the middle of the afternoon on Saturday. For once, Matt's car was in the garage. She hadn't seen him on a weekend day for two months, although she had no idea where he was spending all of his time. It couldn't all be with Janie, could it?

Lugging her clubs into the garage, Sidney looked up to see Matt standing in the door to the mudroom, arms folded, glaring at her. He didn't offer to help put the clubs up on the shelf where she kept them, or to retrieve her overnight bag from the car.

He stepped aside to let her walk into the house. She lifted the roller board over the transom and pulled it immediately into her closet in the back of their bedroom. She took off her coat and hung it up and pulled off her wet sneakers.

"I might as well get this over with," she mumbled to herself, taking a deep breath and walking back to the kitchen. Matt was standing and staring at a tabloid newspaper spread out on the counter in front of him.

On the flight home, she had considered her myriad options, among them: feigning surprise and disbelief at the photo, pleading that it was a momentary peck that meant nothing, describing Peter in platonic terms as her agent, or coming clean with the truth about her relationship with him. All of those options didn't even touch on the big issues: Matt's affair, her arrest for assault, and her five months as a high-end escort.

Without waiting for him to ask questions, she started in.

"Yes, that is Peter, my sports agent in Las Vegas," she said, opening the refrigerator and pulling out a bottle of cranberry juice. She busied herself preparing an iced cranberry and soda and continued.

"I am fond of Peter, and that photo was taken back in October when I was signing on as a client of the agency. We were celebrating our new deal." Could he possibly believe that a quick peck on the lips was a reasonable gesture between client and agent?

"Sports agent? Signing on with the agency? What the hell are you talking about?" Matt was furious. "You didn't tell me anything about that!"

"Well, I haven't been bringing in all of those donations by flashing my pretty smile," Sidney said, trying to be as condescending to him as he had been—time and again—to her. "The agency has been arranging those golf dates I've been going on."

"How much do you pay them?"

"Nothing. The golfers pay the agency, not me."

"So, you kiss all of the agents who arrange dates for you?" Matt seemed at a loss, trying to put the pieces together. "What does that have to do with this photo? With this particular agent? There is more to you and him than that, isn't there?" he said, his tone more accusatory than curious.

Sidney saw her chance to turn the tables on him.

"More?" she asked. "Like the more between you and

Janie than some marketing consultancy?" She sat down at the breakfast bar with her glass of red liquid.

"What are you talking about?" He sat back and tried to feign indignation.

"Don't play stupid," she demanded. "I'm talking about your affair with Janie."

"What makes you think I'm having an affair with her?" He was trying to modulate his voice to sound calm, but his wide eyes and set jaw betrayed him.

"Matt," she said, pausing and tipping her head to one side. "I saw you two kissing on the street in New York."

Matt looked surprised, but he didn't miss a beat. "A kiss is not an affair," he said.

"No, but I also know that you never went to New Jersey over Christmas. You spent it here with her. Here in our bed, I suppose."

"Who told you that?" Matt wasn't going to confess easily, she realized. But he knew better than to deny the affair.

"No one had to. Remember when your brother said 'it's been too long' at the visitation? If you'd been there at Christmas, it wouldn't have 'been too long.'"

"I think you're changing the subject," he said. "The subject is this little publicity issue here." He jabbed his finger at the newspaper.

"No, Matt," she said. "I'm just trying to get you to acknowledge that I'm not the only one who has decided this marriage is over. Deciding who is winning and who is losing this argument is not going to get us anywhere. Pointing fingers and making accusations doesn't change the fact that we're not in love, we have never been in love, and this marriage is a sham."

Sidney was surprising herself. She had remained calm, and she had directed the conversation exactly as she had wanted to: first, they both stipulated to their infidelity, and then she restated the issue. Maybe she had a future in PR.

"But this"—he jabbed his finger at the photo again—"is going to ruin my reputation."

"Really?" Sidney asked. "You think this is all about you and your reputation? Isn't having an affair with one of your vendors against Microsoft policy? How long do you think it will take before the Seattle Times or the Wall Street Journal gets ahold of that story?

"You hardly need my help ruining your reputation," she concluded and walked back to her closet to unpack.

Chapter Twenty-One

To Sidney's surprise, Matt didn't get in his car and peel off as she had expected. He hung around the kitchen for a while, and then went down to his TV room in the basement. The squeak of basketball shoes on a gym floor, the roar of a noisy auditorium, and announcers' play-by-play leaked up through the floorboards of the kitchen.

At dinnertime, Matt turned off the noise and came upstairs. Sidney was eating a microwaved Lean Cuisine and drinking an expensive Bordeaux blend from their wine collection.

"Do you want to get your own attorney, or do you think we can settle this amicably?" he asked, standing with his palms flat on the granite kitchen bar.

"I think I'd feel a little more secure with my own attorney," she said.

"Which I will have to pay for, of course," he said sarcastically.

"Yes, you will," she said. "I have no money. But I would think it would be worth it to you."

"How much are you going to ask for?"

Sidney laid her fork down noisily on the counter. "Are you kidding, Matt? Do you think I've thought about that? Sheesh! I'm not in this for your Microsoft millions, if that's what you're implying."

"No, I wasn't implying anything," he said sadly. "I'm sorry."

"Well, I don't know what I'll need to live on until I find a job that pays," she said, letting him off the hook. "I'll talk with my attorney. Once I find one."

Matt slouched off to the bedroom, his shoulders and head hanging low. A few minutes later, he emerged with an overnight bag.

"I'm going to go stay at Janie's," he said. He apparently saw no gain in denying the affair any longer. And, he didn't seem to care.

"That's good," Sidney said, not getting up from her bar stool. "I'll call you Monday with an attorney's name."

Before he closed the door to the garage behind himself, Sidney called out.

"Matt?"

"What?" He turned back to look at her.

"What happened? What happened to us?"

Matt stood with one hand on the door knob and his suitcase in the other. He held her eyes for just a couple of seconds, and then looked at the floor. He shook his head, and Sidney thought he was about to say something. Maybe something heartfelt, something honest.

But then, without a word, he slipped out the door and left.

❧

The discussion hadn't reached the horrible shouting stage she had expected, Sidney thought, as she lay awake in bed late into the next morning. The discussion of his affair with Janie seemed to have taken the air out of his attack.

They had reached agreement on the necessity of a divorce, but now, she recognized, the hard work was ahead—figuring out a financial settlement, deciding what to do with T-Squared, determining if a workable future with Peter was possible.

But given that her first day alone in the house was a Sunday, she would have to put off finding a lawyer until the next day. She had only two things on her agenda for the day: calling Karla and calling Peter. After that, she planned to take a long walk around the neighborhood in the rain, get a latte at the Starbucks on the way, and then settle in with a good book and a bottle of wine for the rest of the day.

Karla was guardedly happy for Sidney; at least there had been no nasty blow-up and the big decision was made. Peter, however, was more excited. He saw the tabloid photo as the catalyst that enabled their future.

"Sidney, we're going to figure this out," he said, encouragingly. "We're going to find a way to spend more time together. I don't know how yet, but we will."

"I think the biggest question is what am I going to do to make a living," she said. "This charity, if it survives, isn't going to be able to pay me a salary, probably ever."

"I can help out," Peter said.

"No, that's not the answer," Sidney countered. "I paid my own way on the Tour for years, and that's how I want to live. I don't want to be dependent like I was on Matt again. Ever."

"I get it," Peter said. "But just know you're not alone."

"Peter, I feel less alone right now, sitting in this empty house by myself, than I ever had in my life. I love you. That's something I've never been able to say to someone before—honestly anyway. Somehow, that is keeping me company."

"Still, come to Madison when you get a chance," said Peter. "Spring has come early. It's not the tundra. And I need to see you."

Sidney returned from her walk to Starbucks and around the neighborhood two hours later, and settled down to read a novel she'd started two months before on a plane.

She nodded off and was startled out of a light sleep by her phone. How many times lately had her awakening been at the behest of a ringing cell phone? she wondered.

"This is Sidney," she said, after looking at and not recognizing the caller's phone number.

"Sidney Stapleton? This is Jan Morris of the Seattle Weekly. I'm sorry to bother you on Sunday, but I was wondering if I could set up an interview with you early this week?"

That didn't make sense, was Sidney's first thought. Seattle Weekly? Her issues had been with the St. Louis Weekly.

"What are you talking about? An interview about what?" Sidney said.

"We got a call from our sister paper in St. Louis," Jan said, matter-of-factly. "We want to ask you some questions about what they are reporting."

"What are they reporting?"

"Why don't we cover that tomorrow?" Jan said, putting her off. "Can we meet somewhere in the morning?"

"Not until I know what this is about."

"Okay," Jan said. "Have it your way. They are alleging that you have been working over the past six months as a high-end escort. They are reporting that you were called into the St. Louis Police Department for questioning, and then you assaulted a reporter who was covering the investigation."

"Investigation?" Sidney's voice rose to a pitch she wasn't proud of. "What investigation?"

"You don't remember going to the police department?"

"Well, yes, but there was no investigation. There was just some angry used car dealer who was pissed because I wouldn't sleep with him."

"Is that because you had promised to do so?" Jan asked. "My understanding is that he had already paid you for sex."

"Where are you getting all of this stuff?" Sidney asked, angrily. "From that jerk Niles? You know, there aren't three people in St. Louis who like that guy. His own photographer didn't bend over to help him after I slugged him. Oh, and yes, I slugged him. I pleaded guilty."

"Hold on, let me get this down," Jan said, and Sidney could hear rapid typing in the background.

"Wait!" Sidney said. "Are you quoting me?"

"Yes," Jan said. "Why? Weren't you telling the truth?"

"Look, if you want to get together to talk about something you'll have to call my lawyer," Sidney said.

"Fine," Jan said. "I'd really like to get to the bottom of this escort business you worked for. Who is your attorney?"

"I don't have one yet," Sidney admitted. "But I'm going to find one tomorrow. Don't you dare print anything I said."

"I'm afraid that's not up to you," Jan said.

"But I didn't know I was being quoted."

"I introduced myself," Jan continued, calmly. "You have been around long enough to know that when a reporter calls, everything is on the record unless we make an agreement otherwise."

"Okay, let's agree otherwise," Sidney said.

"Sure, we can do that going forward, but it's not retroactive."

"You're kidding, right?"

"Nope. Call me when you're ready to finish this interview."

Sidney took down the phone number and hung up, shaking violently.

❧

Before calling an attorney on Monday morning, Sidney called Milton, who came to the phone immediately. Allen had apparently talked with the Weekly under a promise of anonymity, she told him.

"Why would a self-respecting newspaper reporter take the word of someone who wouldn't put his name forward?" she asked rhetorically.

"What makes you think the reporter has any self-respect?" Milton asked, chuckling softly at his own rhetorical question. Sidney wondered if he was trying to lighten the mood and keep her from panicking.

"At least it doesn't sound like he's implicated the agency," she said.

"Yes, he was probably afraid that we'd find a way to make him pay if he did," Milton said.

"Would you?" Sidney asked, surprised at his implication.

"Hell, no, Sidney." Milton sounded offended. "You know us better than that."

"But you could sue him for libel, I guess," she said. "Maybe he was afraid of legal fees."

"Maybe, but that's not your worry. The agency is well protected. You just focus on taking care of yourself."

Milton's attorney called her back minutes after she hung up with him, intent on assuring her that it would be very difficult to prove either she or the agency was involved in prostitution. The agency's customers were loyal and wouldn't cooperate with a newspaper reporter or any police investigation. There were no online ads for clients like her that indicated that sex was part of the appearances they made. All of the checks she had received came from foreign untraceable bank accounts, including Peter's.

"What are the chances the FBI will follow up on this?" she asked.

"Very, very slim," the attorney said. "These days their focus is on human trafficking, child pornography, and juvenile prostitution, as it should be. They're not that interested in consenting adults who decide they want to pay for or get paid for sex. You'd only have to worry about local police, and as you saw in St. Louis, that's not likely to go very far either."

"So can you help me with this Seattle Weekly reporter?" Sidney asked.

"No," the attorney said. "I'm sorry, but that would establish a stronger connection between the alleged prostitution and this agency than we want to have."

"So I'm on my own?"

"You're no dummy, Sidney," he said. "You don't need an attorney to talk with the press. You may even decide it would be better to not talk to them at all. But if you do, just stick to your story and don't let them intimidate you or make you say things you didn't plan to say. Write down your key messages, just like you do when you talk to the press about your charity."

What charity? Sidney thought, sadly. There probably wasn't going to be one after all of this came out.

Next, she called Peter.

"Wow!" he exclaimed, answering the phone. "So many calls in one week. You really must love me!"

"Yes, I love you, but you may not be so fond of me once I tell you what's happened." Sidney told him about the Seattle Weekly story and her discussions with the agency.

"Oh, shit!" Peter swore loudly. "This guy in St. Louis is really a piece of work! Are you going to talk with the reporter? Maybe the story will have less legitimacy if you don't talk at all."

"I'm afraid I already opened my mouth," Sidney said. "All I can do is try to mitigate some of the damage."

"And don't worry," she added. "Your name will never come up in any of this. They have the photo of us at Margaritaville, but I'm sure as hell not identifying you."

"I'm not worried about me," he said. "You're the one out on a limb here."

"But I'm perfectly willing to go down with the ship

alone," she assured him. "I couldn't screw up my life much more than I have already. All I can do is make sure everyone else is safe."

≈

Sidney met the reporter the next day at her T-Squared office. She dressed in her subdued black suit and crew neck sweater, opting for her black flats instead of heels.

"You certainly don't look like a prostitute," Jan said, smiling.

Sidney wondered if that was supposed to make her feel better or endear her to the reporter.

"Why would I?" she asked, shaking her head.

She waited while Jan took off her raincoat and settled into the seat across from her desk with a notebook. The reporter was definitely middle-aged, not as young as Sidney had expected. She wore her hair long and tied in a ponytail, low against the back of her neck. She dressed casually in jeans and a wool sweater that looked too warm for nearly any day in Seattle.

Jan took a tape recorder and put it on the edge of the desk.

"You don't mind if I record this, do you?" Jan asked. "I'd hate to get anything wrong."

Sidney was willing to bet that the tape recorder was there to protect the newspaper against libel, not to protect those torn apart by its stories.

"Okay, let's get started," Jan said, pushing a button on the recorder, sitting back and smiling. Apparently she was looking forward to the interview far more than Sidney was.

"So, please explain to me why you were being investigated by the St. Louis police for prostitution," she started.

"Wow, you don't pull any punches, do you!" Sidney said

sarcastically. She pulled her chair forward and leaned her forearms on her desk. She had prepared for this interview all night, and she was ready.

"There are two ways we can do this, Jan," she said, looking the reporter in the eye. "You can sit there and ask me questions I won't answer and try to get me to say what you want me to say. Or I can make this much easier on you and tell you right up front what I'm going to say. What do you think of that?"

The reporter frowned. "Sure, you can start, but that doesn't mean I won't ask questions," she said.

"Well, you can ask questions, but that doesn't mean I'm going to answer them," Sidney retorted. She sat back and smiled beguilingly. She'd seen many interviews during her Tour years, and in many of them, a delightful smile by her Tour mates disoriented a difficult sports reporter. She didn't expect it to work in Jan's case, but she could at least communicate that she wasn't going to be intimidated.

"So, what do you want to say?" Jan asked, seemingly defeated.

Sidney laid out her three key messages. First, yes, she played golf with some men to raise money for her charity. That's what she was going to do with Allen, but he got upset because she wouldn't have sex with him.

Second, yes, she has had extramarital sex, and some of her partners were donors to T-Squared. But the fact that Allen was attacking her for refusing to have sex with her was proof that it wasn't a quid pro quo.

Third, her marriage was a sham, and her husband was having an affair.

The three statements were her spin on reality. Her only lie was one of omission, but she had decided the story she was spinning contained enough truth to pass, while keeping the agency and Peter out of it.

"What does your husband think?" Jan asked after she

ran through her quick list.

Sidney considered for a moment whether she should answer the question, or cut off the interview and stick to the three things she came to say.

"He and I are getting a divorce," Sidney decided to respond. "Not just because of my activities, but because of his affair. You should talk to him."

"But you are having an affair too, aren't you?" Jan asked. She pulled the supermarket tabloid out of her big bag and spread it out on Sidney's desk. She opened it to the page and pointed to the photo of Sidney and Peter. "Or is this one of your johns?"

"He is not a john, and a photo is no proof of an affair," Sidney said. "That's just a friendly lunch."

"Who's the guy?"

"None of your business."

"You know this story would come out a lot nicer to you if you were a little more cooperative."

"I doubt it, Jan," she said, looking at the reporter with what she thought would pass as sadness. "I am cooperating. I'm talking with you, aren't I? You just seem wedded to one theory here, and you don't seem to want to accept that it might not be right."

"Or you just don't want to tell me the truth."

Sidney sat back and smiled broadly again. It took every bit of acting skill she had to pull it off. She actually wanted to slug the woman, not smile at her. But she figured it would probably not help her case to punch another reporter.

"Or you just don't want to hear it," she finally said. "Our interview is over, but if you want my husband's phone number—or the number of his concubine—I'd be glad to give it to you."

Jan took both numbers, stood up, shut off the recorder, and pulled on her jacket.

"Thanks for coming over to Bellevue for this," Sidney

said with mock appreciation. She shut the door behind Jan.

"And stick it up your ass," she added for her own benefit.

She leaned against the closed door. The story was probably going to be terrible, she acknowledged. It was probably going to ruin her reputation. She could likely become a giggle topic on the Tour and on Golf Channel broadcasts, if not late-night TV.

It was time to open a new chapter of her life.

Chapter Twenty-Two

The story that came out in the Seattle Weekly wasn't kind to either her or Matt. It carried the implication—if not the outright allegation—that she was acting as a high-end prostitute for the thrill of the chase. The reality, Sidney knew, was close. But she had done it also to raise money for her charity, she told herself, not for the excitement. Didn't that mitigate the crime?

On the other hand, Sidney mused, it had been exciting. She had been the center of attention again. She'd had great dates, great sex, and even some decent golf. She recounted her dates: Greg, great; Philip, nice: Rich, great; Russ, weird; Blake, nice; Larry, no sex; John, okay; Daniel, fun. It was a pretty good success rate, she thought, adding up to a better average experience than she'd had on the one-night stands she'd suffered before she met Matt. If it hadn't been for the disaster with Allen, of course.

But the real clincher was Peter. She'd met Peter and fallen in love, and she still had that, regardless of her ruined reputation. Whatever happened between them, whatever solution they derived to accommodate their love for each other, it was still the first love of her life, and she wouldn't have missed it for all of the negative Weekly articles in the world.

For Matt, however, the accounting didn't look so positive. He had apparently made the same mistake she had, not setting any restrictions on what parts of the interview could be used before he started talking.

"Did my wife tell you I was having an affair? Why don't you talk to her about her recent activities?" he was quoted by Jan.

Responding to a question about the identity of his mistress, the article quoted him: "None of your flippin' business!" which was the same as saying "Yes, I have a mistress, and no, I'm not telling you who she is."

Unfortunately for him, Sidney had already told Jan who it was. Jan was just trying to get him to confirm it.

Now that it was public knowledge that he was having an affair, all she had to do was wait for Matt's boss to figure out that his mistress was a vendor who worked for him. Things were likely to get very ugly for him before they got better.

As the Milton Walton attorney had predicted, no one in law enforcement seemed interested in following up on the Weekly's allegation. She waited, anxiously, for the first week, anticipating a call from some FBI agent initiating an investigation. But it never came, and she eventually put it out of her mind.

Her alleged crimes, however, didn't escape everyone's notice. Three local TV reporters and a couple of golf magazines tried to talk her into doing interviews, which she declined. There was no benefit in lengthening the life of that story, however well she might come across.

After a few days, things seemed to settle down. No more calls, no more requests for interviews. The barista at the Starbucks didn't connect her face to the photos in the newspapers, and her accountant, Audrey, had missed the story altogether. She scheduled a meeting with her charity board; however angry they were over the allegations, she hoped they could discuss the future of T-Squared civilly and rationally.

A week after the article ran, Carrie knocked on Sidney's door in the middle of the morning.

"Hey, nice to see you," said Sidney, opening the door and stepping aside to let her neighbor in. "I didn't know if you'd ever speak to me again after what happened."

"Well, I don't know what happened," Carrie said, walking into the kitchen and heading directly for a stool at the breakfast bar. "I only know what I read, and I don't put a lot of confidence in that. But why don't we have a cup of coffee and talk?"

"Thanks," Sidney said, a little tentative about the purpose of Carrie's visit. Surely she wasn't being questioned by other reporters trying to corroborate Jan's story in the Weekly, was she?

She turned to the sink and filled the water reservoir of her Keurig coffee maker.

"So what do you want to know?" she said, dropping a K-cup into the machine and pushing the brew button.

"Well, first, do you need help?" Carrie asked. "Is there anything I can do?"

"Nah," Sidney said. "I'm fine. I'm enjoying having the house to myself. Matt is staying with Janie until we get through a divorce settlement."

"Okay, then," Carrie said, getting up to retrieve the milk from the refrigerator. "So I guess I want to know: did you do it?"

"Did I do what?" Sidney asked, innocently.

"Did you have sex with those guys for money?"

Sidney studied her friend's face. She didn't look curious as much as sympathetic.

"Does it mean enough to you to know the truth that you would be willing to never share what I'm going to say with anyone?" she asked. "Can you keep a secret forever?"

"I think so," said Carrie. "I just want to know."

"Why?"

"I guess I want to understand it all. Why Matt was having an affair, why you would have had sex with so many guys, why you were with that guy in Las Vegas."

"Why does it matter to you?"

"Hmmm," Carrie said, shaking her head slightly. "You've never had many close friends, have you?"

"Only a couple."

"Well, one of the things friends do is tell each other things. They're willing to let down their guard and share. And the benefit to them is that they have someone who understands them."

Sidney chuckled. "You sound like my father," she said. "And I mean that in a good way. He's a professor of psychology in Minnesota. He used to talk about things like that. Things like the importance of what he called 'being known.'"

Sidney pulled Carrie's coffee off the machine and handed it over the counter. She plunked another K-cup in the machine and turned back to face her friend.

"Yes, I did," she said flatly. "Yes, I slept with those guys. They made donations to T-Squared, and I slept with them. Well, with most of them. It was never a formal quid pro quo, but let's be honest: it was what I expected, it was what they expected."

Carrie sipped her coffee, and Sidney let her consider what she'd just told her. It probably wasn't easy to accept.

"How did it make you feel, knowing what you were doing?" Carrie finally asked.

"Well, at times it was fun, at times exciting, and at times it was scary," Sidney said. She paused and let her feelings rise up to where she could acknowledge and label them. "I think at first, it was the excitement, the novelty. But then, it was more than that; it was being on center stage. Being the center of attention because of what I had accomplished. I missed that after I left the Tour. These guys weren't paying big sums to sleep with just anyone. They were sleeping with an LPGA champion. I guess that was something I needed, that validation."

"And I guess you weren't getting that from Matt." Carrie wasn't asking a question. She was stating the obvious.

"No, you're right," Sidney said. "If I look at the two big mistakes I've made over the past two years, I'm afraid marrying Matt was probably worse than the prostitution. At least the escort business brought in enough money to help some young girls learn to play golf."

Carrie listened and nodded. She sipped her coffee and looked out across the kitchen into the soggy backyard and its swelling infestation of blackberry bushes. Sidney waited patiently for her response. She'd never been more forthcoming, and she wondered what it was about Carrie that allowed her to open up.

"Well, I guess we all need validation for who we are and what we do," Carrie finally responded. "I suppose after years of getting trophies for winning tournaments, you probably get hooked on that very public, very material reward. Most of us live on much smaller proofs of our worthiness. A thank you from the boss. A tip from a customer at a restaurant. A friend who comes over for coffee to see how you are doing."

Sidney smiled. Carrie—someone she only knew as a neighbor and casual friend—was right. Sidney had gone from no validation of her worth as a child to big trophies and effusive accolades from the sports media, and she'd never known a life in between the two extremes. It was time she learned to modulate her expectations.

"Thank you, Carrie," she said. "Thanks for your friendship and thanks for your honesty."

They clinked coffee cups in a toast to both.

❧

The T-Squared board meeting in the office of her attorney the next day coincided with the publication of several letters to the editor in the Weekly about her prostitution.

A couple of the letters argued for decriminalization of adult prostitution, but most of them either analyzed or expressed outrage at her fall from grace. One hit the nail on the head, Sidney thought: "*Sidney apparently suffered from a narcissistic need to be the center of attention, to be loved for her talents, her beauty and her fading celebrity, a consequence of our beauty- and celebrity-obsessed society.*" It was signed by a well-known liberal sociology professor from the University of Washington. It would only be a matter of time, then, before the news would reach her parents through the academic gossip network.

Sidney wasn't sure she could blame society for her narcissism, but she recognized herself in the description. She loved the attention, the adoration, the excitement of casual sex, the golf play, the flirting, and the fine dinners and hotel rooms. Who wouldn't? What she still didn't know was what was going to replace it all.

The board meeting was stiff and formal; having Matt there didn't help. The discussion was twisted, vague, and a bit silly, as no one wanted to name their respective sins—hers, alleged prostitution; his, a workplace affair.

"Sidney, I'd like to open the meeting by giving you an opportunity to explain yourself," Greg, the board chair, offered. He and Matt were co-workers, and Greg knew Matt well, but today, he was assiduously avoiding eye contact and conversation with her husband. Sidney appreciated that.

"I would like to apologize for the damage this recent spate of news stories have caused this organization, just as we were trying to get started," she said. She continued with a quick description of her "fundraising," although stopping short of calling it sex for money. She accepted dates to play golf with men for money, she admitted. She talked about the success of the two chapters that she had set up, including Betta's progress.

"Do you think you can continue to serve as a role model for young women, given your recent activities?" Greg asked. "Is it possible that parents would be willing to let you continue to coach their young daughters?"

Sidney knew this question was the reason for the meeting, and she thought she was prepared to argue that her crimes were alleged, not proven, and that her success on the Tour was more important to the parents than her extramarital behavior.

But, as she sat around the table with the four board members and her attorney, she changed her mind. Without the ability to raise money through her agency dates, she couldn't imagine how the charity could survive, and she didn't want to beat her head against a wall trying to raise enough ten- and twenty-dollar donations. Especially under the cloud of her alleged prostitution.

"I think it's time that I move on," she said. "I don't know if you can find someone to replace me who will be willing to do this for no salary, but I would be willing to continue to manage things until you do."

"That's very generous of you, Sidney," Greg said. "But I think it would be best for you and for the program if you resign today."

Sidney looked around the room. Her husband was looking at the floor, perhaps embarrassed for them both. Her lawyer nodded in agreement with Greg. Angela and Tom expressionless. Clearly the best outcome she could get, if she forced a vote, was a tie, and that would resolve nothing.

But she didn't deserve any support from her two supporters on the board. Even if they would have voted to save her, she couldn't ask them to do it.

"I'm ready to leave," she said.

"Thank you," Greg said. "I think that's best. One more thing: We'd like to ask you to hold a brief press conference, apologizing to the public and announcing your departure."

As much as she loved the stage, Sidney blanched at the idea. No one had ever pulled that kind of performance off without looking guilty at best and both guilty and disingenuous at worst.

Matt looked up to see her reaction, and she saw him fight a smile. He knew how much she loved to be on stage, and yet he expected her to decline this opportunity out of embarrassment. She wouldn't give him the satisfaction of being right.

"Sure," she said. "You schedule it and I'll be there."

She stood up, pushed her files over the table toward her attorney, and bowed slightly. Walking out of that room, she felt liberated. The charity was a bad idea from the start: there was no obvious constituency to support it, no way to legally raise enough money to keep it going. Now, there was nothing holding her to Bellevue or Seattle, nothing keeping her away from building a new life with Peter.

The only person likely to be hurt by T-Squared's demise was Betta, whose hopes had been raised and who would likely fail in her quest to get on the Tour without Sidney's support. She promised herself she'd figure out how to help the girl once T-Squared's tent was folded.

All she had to do now to bring this chapter of her life to a close was hold a press conference and work through her divorce.

Sidney walked on stage in the same suit and same high heels she'd worn to the first press conference, the one where she launched Tee to the Tour.

The audience was much bigger this time: besides the six reporters who had covered her first speech, the Associated Press, Sports Illustrated, Golf Week—even Al Jazeera America—had sent stringers to hear what they expected would be a confession to titillating misbehavior.

She unfolded her short script, and started: "I wish that today's press conference was going to be as uplifting and exciting as the one we held here on this stage just eight months ago."

Again, she heard her voice turn melodious and strong over the sound system. She looked up from her script, and smiled. She looked for Matt in the audience. She would make a point of smiling broadly at him this time, now that he would prefer she not recognize him publicly.

She couldn't find him. The reporters shifted in their seats uncomfortably at the long pause.

She looked down at her script, and shook her head. She wadded up the piece of paper and scanned the crowd.

"Once again, I'm going to skip the script and tell you what happened," she said. "This is my story."

Fifteen minutes later, she came to the end. The reporters had been scribbling madly, even while trying to record a video of her performance on their cellphones and iPads, testing their manual dexterity. She admitted that she had played golf with donors, and on occasion, slept with them. She didn't talk about working with Milton Walton. She didn't mention the affair with Peter.

She explained that the money she raised all went into the T-Squared fund, and that someone else would be running the organization soon. She bragged quickly about Betta's success and wished her a bright future. She said she and Matt were divorcing amicably.

"Now," she said, "I will beg off answering questions. I've told you everything I wanted to say, and while I have no right to ask you to respect my privacy, I would hope I've told you enough to avoid further requests for interviews. This chapter of my life is over, and I'll say goodbye now. Thanks for your support over the past few months and for whatever restraint you may grant me in writing your stories."

Walking off the stage, she heard several reporters shout questions anyway, but as planned, she disappeared around the curtain separating the stage from a storage area behind it. She slipped through the side door that led through the lobby of the hotel, and searched for the limousine she had hired to wait for her in the *porte cochere*.

As she looked around, a young woman spun through the revolving door of the hotel, and stood waiting beside her. She wore Christian Louboutin black patent heels just like Sidney's, and a soft, silk dress with a handkerchief hem under a faux-fur wrap. A well-dressed man approached, introduced himself, leaned in for a cheek kiss, and then led her away to his waiting car.

It was the young girl's smile that spoke to Sidney—a smile of anticipation, excitement, hope, and a hint of naughtiness.

"That's why I did it," Sidney said out loud. It really hadn't been primarily to raise money for young girls' golf dreams. It was because it was so much fun.

Until it wasn't.

Chapter Twenty-Three

Sidney waited at the SeaTac departure gate in a low-slung leather chair, listening for the boarding announcement.

Everything had finally settled down. Her divorce was over, and she was happy with the modest financial support Matt had agreed to provide until she remarried or otherwise didn't need it anymore. The sports press had finally found other salacious material to cover—mainly sexual harrassment and domestic misbehavior by other professional and collegiate athletes in the Pacific Northwest.

In the financial part of their divorce agreement, Sidney asked Matt to put up enough money to support Betta's coaching for two more years. It wouldn't go through T-Squared, though. It would go directly into a trust fund for Betta and her mother, and it would be overseen by Ben, the golf pro in Oakland. The future of T-Squared was still up in the air; Sidney guessed it probably wouldn't survive.

Glancing around at her fellow passengers, carrying their heavy winter coats and dressed in knee-high boots, she felt part of something—the anticipation of the holidays, the hope that this Christmas or Hanukah was going to be special. Her Christmas traditions could use a bit of sprucing up, she thought. Maybe this was a start.

First class was full when she booked her flight, but

Sidney wasn't disappointed with her business-class seat. It was the equivalent of first class on Alaska Airlines—free drinks; decent food; a big, comfy leather seat.

She accepted the flight attendant's offer of a glass of French Champagne while they waited for the rest of the plane to fill up, as travelers took extra time to stuff wrapped packages in the over-burdened overhead bins. She smiled apologetically at the older man settling in next to her as she put in her ear buds and pulled out her Kindle, clearly signaling she was not going to be very good company. He didn't seem to mind. He was snoring loudly before the plane left the gate and taxied for takeoff.

But she had trouble focusing on the novel she'd loaded for the flight. She thought about what was ahead. She and Peter would spend Christmas in Paris, just as he had suggested a year earlier. This would be the first year in eleven that he wouldn't be watching alone as other lovers strolled down icy streets. After Paris, they planned to travel through Europe for a couple of months, skiing in the Alps and learning to skate in Holland, before settling down in Provence where she would start teaching golf for money to adults and donating free lessons to young girls. She felt lucky she had found a golf club, a country, and a culture less concerned with her past sins than with her golf skills.

Now, her public audience was going to be one student at a time—not a gallery of golf fans, not a pack of sycophantic reporters, not a coterie of horny golfers waiting for their chance to sleep with a celebrity. She didn't need the stage anymore. And she hoped Ben in Oakland was right; she hoped she could be a great teacher.

Other than that, she craved the attention and adoration of only one person: Peter. Finally, she understood what her parents had. She hoped she deserved to have it, too, and even if she didn't, she hoped she still could have it. That was unconditional love, wasn't it?

The first meal of the flight interrupted her brief nap; the second meal interrupted a movie she was watching on the screen of the seatback in front of her. The third meal came as she shook herself out of a deep sleep and realized they'd traveled through the night. The day was just starting to break to the east, and land instead of ocean passed beneath them.

"No, thanks," she told the flight attendant. "I couldn't eat any more. All of this food and no exercise! I'll be lucky if someone doesn't knock me in the head, put me on a spit, and put an apple in my mouth before sitting down for Christmas dinner."

The flight attendant laughed appreciatively. At the end of transatlantic flights, it was hard to find anyone with a sense of humor left, Sidney imagined. She accepted an offer of a mimosa instead. It would help calm her nerves.

By the time they deplaned at the gate, Sidney had reached what she thought would be an appropriate level of blood alcohol for the occasion. Just slightly amused, but still perfectly in balance.

Shuffling through customs, first for the passport check and then with her luggage, Sidney realized that all of the preparation of the past few weeks had shielded her from a lot of emotions. How would she feel when she saw Peter's face in the crowd? Would she finally feel relief from having completed a journey that took her far from Matt and from the cloud that hung over her in Seattle?

When they met in Seattle and Madison over the fall, nothing was promised by either of them. Up to now, that had been fine. Marriage to Matt had turned out to be a horrible disaster, but she believed life with Peter would be different, however they chose to live it. For starters, she was in love with him, and he was in love with her. And, he understood her need for serendipity, for adventure, for success of her own making.

But, what about commitment? They hadn't talked about

it. They weren't really going backward as much as not moving forward. With the divorce and moving details to take care of, she hadn't seen him in a month. Had they drifted apart or had the absence brought them closer together?

Standing on her tip-toes, she peered over the tourists and luggage carts clogging the exit from the international terminal.

Finally, she spied him. He was dressed in a dark gray sweater and black slacks, looking sexier and more striking than any of the handsome Latin men that bustled around her. She maneuvered her luggage cart past the security barrier toward him.

A large crowd exiting from a domestic gate flooded through in front of her, blocking her way, and by the time it passed, she had lost him. He seemed to have disappeared into thin air.

Cold feet? she wondered. Had he seen her and decided to flee?

Shaking from the shoulders down, she pushed the cart toward where she'd seen him last. Searching through the final group of tourists between them, she let out an anxious breath. He was still there, searching for her, too. Their eyes connected, and he grinned and cut through the crowd, wrapping his arms around her and pushing his face through her hair.

He held her tight, nearly lifting her off her feet. His lips touched her ear, and he whispered.

"Marry me, Sidney. Marry me now."

Acknowledgements

I won't write about sex until my mother dies. - William Saroyan

I understand his reticence. If not for the advice of a few friends, I could never have attempted this book. You can't write about an athlete cum prostitute without writing about sex, but how do you write about sex without offending or embarrassing someone (including yourself)? The most useful advice came from Diane Larson, my super-reading "Iowa Editor," who told me that sex acts themselves aren't the issue—the language is. So, I tried to depict the interaction between sex partners without the cringe-inducing words for body parts and activities that might keep this book from passing as PG-13, as Diane described the result.

Thank you, Diane, for your help. And everyone else: I hope I have not offended you. If I have, now you know whom to blame!

Thanks to my excellent content editor, Mike Foley, who always gives me as much encouragement as advice, and to my copyeditor, Erin Van Bronkhorst, for helping polish my prose.

Finally, I thank you, my loyal readers. Let's keep this up, and someday maybe I will make a living at this.

As my husband, Ben Miller, says, "It's cheaper than therapy!"

About the author

Marj Charlier lives in Palm Springs, California, with her husband, Ben Miller. She worked as a business reporter for twenty years, including eleven at the Wall Street Journal. She worked in corporate finance for another twenty years before retiring to write novels, play golf, and devour all the books she's never had time to read. This is her fourth novel.